INCENDIARY
ATTRACTION

DAMAGED HEROES: BOOK FOUR

SARAH
ANDRE

Rick,
You're a great
neighbor!!
Sarah Andre

BEACH READS
11923 NE Sumner St, STE 320134
Portland, OR 97250

Edited by Anya Kagan, Touchstone Editing
Cover Design by Christa Holland, Paper and Sage

Beach Reads, First Edition, May 2021

Print ISBN: 978-1-946310-05-7
Digital ISBN: 978-1-946310-04-0

To Lark Brennan.

Thank you for being my critique partner these sixteen amazing years. Without you shoring me up and cheering me on, I doubt I would have made it this far. Isn't it odd how our career achievements, joys, and heartbreaks have mirrored each other's? I've always wondered about that. It's like we're writing soul mates.

DEAR READER

This is a story that covers white supremacy, hopefully without rose-colored glasses, and that may be a trigger for some. Like many authors I churn my helpless, hopeless, troubled psyche into a plot that in the end vanquishes the bad guys and offers hope for a happily ever after. My biggest challenge was using racial slurs, writing dialogue that disgusted me, and spinning a romance element around a deadly serious hunt for these cowards.

My fascination for this topic arrived almost a year before Proud Boys, Q, and Boogaloo were in the national discussion—it just takes me this long to formulate a story and do the required research. But as the story developed, so did the headlines in the real world of outrageous and unacceptable actions of white supremacists. As this goes to print, the insidious danger of men running around calling themselves "militia" and eyeing the overthrow of democracy is a critical and present danger for this country.

I tend to be black and white in my world views and judgments, and white supremacy is a perfect example.

Who are you, I ask the mug shots on the news and my fictional characters, to be disgruntled? You're white, male, and American. That combination is the undisputed top of the worldwide food chain. If you screw up that gargantuan advantage, you have no right to blame all the rest of us, no right to use your Second Amendment right to bully us into acquiescing further rights and freedoms.

Why did this take so long to write, edit, and publish? Because real life interrupted. Who wants to absorb this shock of groups who've thrown off the cloak of secrecy and are flaunting their horrific views, then sit down to their fictional work about the same topic for eight hours? It took a while to get right with my soul and remind myself that this fiction would end with good vanquishing evil. That I have the last word here, of offering hope, love, and peace. For those of you who are, like me, sensitive to hate speech, please forgive me in advance. To those who use it, this is not the book for you. To the rest of you, please enter my fictional world with your heart wide open and enjoy.

Please note: all characters are a figment of my imagination, and there is no such position as FBI Special Agent Associate.

FBI Special Agent Associate Jace Quinn crept through the dewy grass, breath steady, senses on high alert. His night-vision goggles depicted the green form of Case Agent Mark Hennessey leading the team toward a shingle-covered duplex some twenty yards to the right. The swish of FBI windbreakers, creak of leather holsters, and an allergic-sounding sniff from someone bringing up the rear broke the predawn stillness.

At the end of the thick boxwood hedge, Hennessey dropped to a crouch, and Jace and the six other multi-agency personnel swiftly followed.

"You two," the case agent murmured, pointing to Gibbs and Fontana, "go 'round back. Wait for the all-clear." They eased away.

Jace press-checked his Glock 26 for the umpteenth time. He was so damn ready for this takedown. The intensive four-month investigation, mired in dead ends and mounting frustration, had finally yielded a suspect: Thomas Bradley. This morning's arrest warrant would hopefully uncover evidence Bradley was the mastermind behind the Mosque Mohammed bombings that had killed two hundred and forty-five Muslims last June. The success of this dedicated task force was about to explode across international headlines. Today was for the history books.

"On my signal." Hennessey's harsh whisper floated back to the team. As one, they resumed their stooped positions and threaded their way to the edge of the quaint, whitewashed porch. "Go, go, go!"

Hennessey dove to the left of the door, Jace plastered himself opposite, and the four men barreled forward with the battering ram. The boom of impact and the door slamming into the foyer wall exploded the morning silence. Hennessey lunged inside, tossing a couple of flash-bang grenades, and Jace hurtled into the first room on the right. A dining room. "Clear!"

Bootsteps thundered upstairs. Another door was breached, presumably by Rogers and Gonzales, who were assigned the basement. Calls of "clear" echoed rapidly as rooms were systematically secured.

Jace sidestepped into the hall. An overpowering stench cut through the sulfur smoke, one he instantly recognized from his SEAL days. A decaying body. He breathed through his mouth as he cleared the rest of the ground floor—a rote procedure now. No one was here. No one could live with this overwhelming stink. He met Hennessey in the kitchen, who nodded toward the back door. Jace let in Gibbs and Fontana.

"Basement's secured," Gonzales yelled from below. "Looks like he was busy making pipe bombs."

"Upstairs is clear," Peters called in a strangled voice. "Body in the master."

The four men in the kitchen traded despondent looks as they lowered their weapons. "Let's go," Hennessey muttered, and led the way upward. The stench grew with each step, burning Jace's eyes, and he spastically swallowed sour saliva. He had to avoid the gruesome sight at all costs. No one but his SEAL Team Three partner, Dirk, had discovered his weenie secret. And Dirk had died in the May blast that started this horrific chain of bombings.

Peters and Morgan loitered green-faced in the hallway. "Too decomposed to recognize if it's the suspect," Peters said.

"And I think the cat's been hungry," Morgan added, then brushed by them with a breathy "Oh, shit" as he tore down the stairs and out the door.

Hennessey stopped in the threshold. "Aw, shit." Jace stared at the case agent's back, so it looked like he was peering over his shoulder. Gibbs crowded in, then muttered an obscenity that was interrupted by a gurgling retch as he too scrambled downstairs. "Call for the ME and forensics when you're done," Hennessey yelled after him.

"I'll do it." Jace half turned, relief flooding through him when Fontana, still in the stairwell, raised his walkie-talkie.

"On it." He pivoted and descended into fresh air.

Jace clenched his jaw. Between the ungodly odor and his growing panic, his breathing grew erratic and dots swarmed his vision. How in the hell was he going to get out of dealing with whatever horror lay inside that room? And yet here was a chance to impress the case agent. Everyone but Peters had wussed out...

With a sigh, Hennessey cautiously stepped into the bedroom. "Scat." A black cat burst through the doorway, its unholy, almost-human screech blending with Peters' panicked yelp as the cat shot between his legs and down the hall, disappearing into the last room on the right. Heart thundering, Jace exhaled an obscenity and braced a hand against the wall. His breathing mimicked a hyperventilating teenage girl at a boy band concert. What made him think he could do this? He had to get gone. Now.

"I'll go assist Rogers and Gonzales with pipe bomb inventory." Jace stepped toward the stairwell and blessed escape just as Mark's cell phone rang. He was halfway down when Mark shrieked an obscenity.

"*What?* When?"

Jace swung around, frowning up at the commander who now paced the hallway, eyes wide and dazed. "Is she okay? ... And the baby?"

Jace stilled. The whole department knew of Mark and Julie's decade-long struggle to get pregnant. Appropriately, she was due near Thanksgiving, but it was only October fifth.

"I'm on my way."

Jace dug in his pocket and retrieved the van key, which Hennessey snatched like a relay baton as he raced down the stairs. "Hope everything's okay, sir," Jace called to his retreating back.

"Car accident," the case agent said. "Peters, take over." He blew out the door.

Peters looked like he'd just been sentenced to hang. "I'm gonna need your help, Quinn."

Jace swallowed the primal scream. If he laid eyes on the decomposed corpse, his body's response would mark the end of his career. "You don't need anyone else's DNA in there," he said in a surprisingly steady voice. "In fact, you should remain where you are until forensics can take over."

"Guess you're right." Peters' worried expression cleared.

Jace had ten years of combat experience and decision-making on him, despite Jace's lowly special agent associate rank. All because he'd chosen to serve his country while Peters got a college degree. How was that even fair?

"I'll go help Rogers and Gonzales," Jace repeated, his equilibrium finally returning as the crisis died away. "Just take copious notes for Hennessey on any ME or forensic findings. Thomas Bradley was our only lead, so we better hope there's a written confession lying around that points to him as the sole bomber."

Peters nodded. "Will do."

Jace jerked his head down the hall. "And find that cat. Take it to PAWS on North Clybourn."

"There's gotta be a pound closer."

"It's a no-kill shelter. Go there." Something good had to come of this op.

Jace headed for the basement, steps as heavy as his heart. Joining this MOSQMO task force last June had been a professional lottery win. How had it morphed into such an albatross for his career? He shouldn't have been surprised that their primary suspect ended up as decomposed cat food and their fearless leader was winging his way to the ER. Nothing had gone right in months, and Jace couldn't bury the niggling sense that this house and this suspect had been yet another waste of time.

2

Three bridesmaids click-clacked past Jace and Kevin, ogling them with all the subtlety of Logan Square prostitutes. "Hello, ladies," Kevin drawled, eyeing them right back. "Kevin Quinn, table four."

Their giggles echoed throughout the near-empty hallway. Their hips swayed even more provocatively. The petite blond had to plant her feet and open the heavy ballroom door with both hands. A burst of amplified eighties dance music that had already been annoying decades ago filled the air. Before she slipped inside, the curvy redhead glanced over her shoulder and winked at Jace.

Kevin raised a palm. "Score."

"Seriously?"

"What?" Kevin looked over incredulously. "You don't recognize when you're being waved in for a landing? It's a law of nature that bridesmaids want to hook up."

"They look like they're still in college."

"Hey, if they're legal and they're game, it's a night of uncomplicated sex."

Jace scoffed. "Uncomplicated? The entire female species—*especially* bridesmaids—are at their most desperate during weddings. All those romantic expectations and rosy-ass glasses?" He scrunched his fingers. "They've got their claws out tonight, Kev." He dropped his hands, not bothering to hide his disgust. "Take it from me: of all the times you need to run from women, it's at weddings."

A broad grin lit Kevin's face as he gazed over Jace's shoulder. "Good evening," he purred.

Neck prickling, Jace spun around. *Oh, crap.*

An attractive woman in a floral dress stood feet away, eyeing him with amused contempt. "No rosy-ass glasses," she said, then scrunched her fingers on either side of her face. "No claws. Please don't run away." Her smile twitched like she might burst into laughter.

Jace had a distinct urge to loosen his tie. "I—I, uh..." But she was already walking by, curling her short black hair behind a shapely ear.

"Nice stuttering," his younger brother murmured.

Jace ignored him, eyes still on her slim, athletic shape and no-nonsense walk. She looked to have a decade on him, and he flashed back to the days when pretty teachers used to call him out in class for some idiotic, attention-seeking stunt. Yep, here he was at forty, feeling like an eight-year-old turd again.

He prayed for her to keep going, straight through to the hotel foyer, but no such luck. She effortlessly opened the door that had almost taken out the tiny blond and disappeared into the pounding beat.

"This night is really looking up." Kevin shot his cuffs. "Those bridesmaids are like fish in a barrel. The challenge is landing the MILF."

Jace slanted him a look. Why couldn't she have caught *that* remark?

The door swung open again and Pop poked his head out, his scowl at odds with the lively music. "Boys!" He beckoned them over. "One of you needs to take Gage home. Right now." The last two words were barked from lips white with tension.

Inwardly Jace sighed as they headed toward the ball-room. Kevin and Gage, the third and fourth sons respectively out of five, had finished their tours of duty over the summer. Integrating back into society had been rough, to say the least. Kevin humped anything that moved, marital status be damned, and Gage relied on enough daily alcohol to topple an elephant.

"I'll do it," Jace said. Why not call it a night? Weddings were so not his thing. He didn't dance, didn't eat cake, and hated this music. It also meant he could avoid the bridesmaids and reliving the ass he'd made of himself in front of that woman. And he sure as shit did not need to witness Kevin trying to seduce her the rest of the night.

"No." Pop pointed at Kevin. "You go."

"Me?" Kevin huffed a martyred breath. "I want to stay."

"You're the only one who can get through to him when he's like this." Pop held the door wider, and even among the two hundred guests mingling in the vast room, Gage was easy to spot. Face beet red, with a glower that resembled Pop's, he staggered past shocked guests, his thigh brushing the leg of an old lady's walker, throwing her off balance. As she teetered, almost in slow motion, a nearby waiter dropped his tray of drinks and caught her. The sound of shattering glass started a ripple of swiveling heads, comically resembling a stadium audience doing the wave.

"And fuck that," Gage hollered to someone over his

shoulder. "It's just another Democratic hoax to keep you sheep afraid!"

"Get him out of here," Pop said through his teeth. Jace hustled behind Kevin, multitasking snaking blindly through the crowd while bringing up the rideshare app on his phone. It'd take both of them to manhandle their beer-soaked, muscular brother into a car.

Before they reached him, Trick appeared. *Please, God, don't let him spout any of that peace-loving brotherly shit.* Jace began shaking his head to preempt him, but as usual, Trick only had eyes for the downtrodden and wounded.

"Hey, man." Trick planted a palm on Gage's shoulder. "You gotta let that toxic stuff go and open up your heart to all the love in this roo—"

"Shut the *fuck* up." Gage shook out of the grasp as Jace nodded apologetically to everyone near enough to make eye contact.

Kevin immediately gripped Gage's bicep, with much more authority. "Let's call it a night, bro."

"I'm not goin' anywhere! This is my favorite cousin's wedding—"

As Gage ranted, Jace motioned Trick away from his other side, but Trick shook his head. "I've got it under control."

Actually, he didn't. At all. Jace bit back the urge to point that out because time was now of the essence. Pop still stood by the door, his apoplectic expression disturbing the guests at that end of the room as much as this scene did these people. There was enough friction without engaging the brother who was closest in age, most competitive, and supremely annoying.

"Fine. Fuck it." Jace wrenched the beer bottle out of Gage's grip. "Get him the hell out of here before Pop bursts a blood vessel. I've ordered a ride." He glanced at his screen. "A blue Sonata will be out front in four minutes and forty-six seconds."

The three brothers plowed toward the door. Jace turned away, apologized to anyone within hearing distance, and wandered to the bar to trade Gage's beer for a well-deserved cold one.

The DJ quickly redirected the audience by booming Gloria Estefan music. Across the ballroom a conga line started, rapidly sucking in guests like a tornado.

"That'll make tomorrow's dinner interesting."

Jace half turned to acknowledge Sean's fatalistic remark. His nerdy youngest brother—and, until recently, the one he hadn't understood at all—asked the bartender for another bottled water.

"If you invite Gretch, it'll preempt Pop's inevitable lecture."

Sean snorted. "Subject her to a second night with our happy family?"

Jace tucked a couple of bills in the tip jar as the beer and water were placed in front of them. Uncle Pat and Uncle John walked over.

"Sorry about the scene," Jace told Uncle John, the father of the bride, who sure didn't look happy.

Uncle Pat pointed at the Grey Goose behind the bartender, then turned to Jace. "So what's new with the investigation? Papers are calling the mosque bombing a copycat of Oklahoma City now. What was the building called? Edward R. Murrow?"

"Alfred P. Murrah," Sean said. Always the brother with the answers, but in this case the expressionless tone hid fathoms of disdain, and Jace smirked.

"They arrested Timothy McVeigh an *hour* afterward," Uncle Pat continued, without a flicker of acknowledgement that his nephew had spoken. "You guys've had, what—five months? What's the deal?" The last three words slurred into one.

Jace took a long pull of beer. It'd been four months and three days...and this would've been the perfect time for know-it-all Sean to butt in with his precise answers. Jace swallowed and wiped his mouth with the back of his hand. "McVeigh being arrested for not having a license plate was pure dumb luck for the case." He'd already been an hour into his getaway, the stupid shit.

Uncle Pat accepted his new drink, ignoring the tip jar. "And it only took seventy-two hours to identify all the nine-eleven hijackers."

"Maybe if you brought in a profiler," Uncle John suggested.

Jace's shoulders tensed inside the too-warm sport coat. The nine-eleven hijackers hadn't bothered to hide their identities—they'd had no plans to return. And the MOSQMO task force *had* consulted FBI profilers, right from the beginning. But suggestions like searching for an alt-right white male with a blue-collar job and an undistinguished, short-term military background hadn't narrowed the field much in a city this size.

"Have you guys found another case agent?" Sean asked as Pop joined them, his bearing a lot calmer.

"Not yet." Jace was sorry to see Mark Hennessey go—he'd been a decent friend and mentor. But maybe the new guy would interpret their collective leads a different way and finally start them down a successful track. "The SAC is still interviewing team members and some outside folks."

Uncle Pat tugged his drooping earlobe. "I guess as special agent assistant, you're not eligible for the promotion."

"Special agent associate," Jace said through his teeth.

Blood thumped hotly in his face, causing his eye to twitch. "And no."

"Maybe get the case agent from the Oklahoma City bombing to consult," Uncle John said. "Although he's probably long retired by now. Wonder if he's dead?"

"No." Sean left it there, and the older generation nodded like collective bobbleheads.

Screw this. Jace thunked his beer on the bar. There was only so much unsolicited advice he could stomach from these old fogies, when they had no idea of the long hours and hard work that were leading nowhere. Everyone else in Chicago was talking about the Cubs GM firing the coach. He eyed Pop. "What's your take on the Flannigan scandal?"

His uncles and Pop spoke up at once. Sean's expression morphed into instant boredom, his gaze tracking to Gretch in the conga line, twenty feet away and closing. Hands down, the lucky shit had snagged the sexiest woman in Chicago. She shimmied and waved, while at the head of the line, Caitlyn, the bride, eyed their group like a cat spying a cluster of mice.

Jace quickly hoisted his bottle again like its presence gave him an excuse to sit out. There was no way he was joining that. Humiliation-wise, conga lines were in a class by themselves.

He took a slow pull of beer. The worst part of weddings was yet to come, though. Being forced to participate in yet another damn garter snap. Sure as shit if he wasn't sheltering in place in the men's room this go-round.

Too much about weddings was irritating. The happily-ever-after vibe. Those desperate single women. He winced as the exchange with the pretty woman zipped back, and he instinctively scanned the room for her. She was approaching the end of the line, already snapping her fingers and swaying to the beat. A delighted smile lit her face, aimed at nobody. Everything about her bearing right now was the antithesis of how he felt.

Jace turned from the approaching revelry and raucous laughter. The noise made it hard to hear any comments about the fired coach, but he adopted a rapt expression and nodded intently.

Caitlyn was upon them, nabbing Uncle John, who readily acquiesced, given he was hosting this shindig. A passing bridesmaid tried to snake her arm through Sean's, but—no surprise—his uncanny peripheral vision and black-belt skills saved him once again. Pivoting smoothly just out of reach, he beelined for the exit without a backward glance.

The same woman crooked a finger at Jace, but he held up his beer, shaking his head in mock regret. More revelers passed, with more calls to join in, more head shaking. Uncle Pat finally clunked down his empty glass and staggered into the hoopla like he was smashing through an offensive line. The woman behind him winced and limped.

Jace glanced bleakly around the ballroom. Faking a jubilant mood while avoiding the bridesmaids' come-ons and his uncles' criticisms was suddenly too much. What were the chances anyone would notice if he took off? Mom might, but it was worth her wrath.

"Uncle Jace!" He started at the pipsqueak squeal. Amy's steps were clumsy in the stiff blue dress. She let go of one of her father's coattails and jerked a thumb. "Get behind me." In front of her, Trick's lip curled in amusement; he was clearly and correctly interpreting Jace's preference to crawl through shards of glass.

Jace managed another smile and reluctant head shake. "I don't dance, honey."

"Come on, Uncle Jace!" She rolled her eyes toward the

woman holding on to her shoulders, and his gaze followed, heartbeat skipping. *Her.* Still smiling like this was great entertainment.

"Yeah, come on," the woman mocked, arching an eyebrow in challenge. The deep laugh lines around her eyes somehow heightened her attractiveness. Like she'd been there, done that in life and was unapologetically comfortable in her own skin. And here he was acting like a standoffish baby.

"Uncle Ja-ace..."

Well, shit. A conga line wasn't really dancing.

Groaning, he put down the beer and loosened his tie. Amy brightened immediately. Caving for a kid. Jeez. He side-eyed the woman as he stepped toward them, and she released Amy, affably waving him in front of her. "I'll try not to kick your heel."

"If it gets me outta this, kick away."

She laughed, the sound deep and musical. Despite himself, Jace grinned at her infectious joy.

He clasped his niece's narrow shoulder blades as the woman clamped on to his traps. If she was imitating claws, he deserved it. "Party on, Garth," she hollered, then sang along to Gloria Estefan.

He bounced off-rhythm a couple of times until he caught the beat and suddenly was sambaing and shimmying like everyone else. Guess this wasn't so bad.

The photographer nimbly skirted tables, capturing shots of the dancing goofballs. When he got to Jace and Amy, Jace stuck out his tongue while flashing rabbit ears behind his niece's head. No way would that make the bride's album. The photographer then gestured for Jace and the woman to squish together, so Jace hammed it up like a teen girl's selfie, posing cheek to cheek and puckering his lips. If Caitlyn managed to toss out every one of the photos featuring Jace, his mission would be accomplished. Weddings... What was the point?

The bride thankfully broke up the line with a final twirl, followed by wild applause from the participants. The woman's grip disappeared, and a shrill whistle blasting near his eardrum made him wince. He glanced over as the woman took her fingers out of her mouth. *Ah ha.* The tomboy. The life of a Super Bowl party, or the loudest shouter at an umpire in Wrigley Field. The type who wanted to be a pal instead of a manipulative lover. His shoulders relaxed.

"Whew, that was fun!" Her rosy face glistened. She blew upward, and her bangs feathered back in a straggly mess, which was still a great look on her. She was unself-conscious and authentic—such a refreshing combination at a wedding.

"It was fun," he agreed, as Amy bounced into his arms. "I'm Jace, cousin of the bride. And this is Amy, my rug rat niece."

"I'm Heidi." She shook firmly. "My plus-one is a friend of the groom's father. You're a very good dancer, Amy."

Amy squirmed in his left arm. "I'm a better soccer player."

"You're a champ," Jace assured her, then turned back to Heidi. Wedding pleasantries—he could do this. "So, what do you do?"

"Senior special agent with the ATF."

Another check in her favor. He grinned. "No kidding? I'm FBI." He left it there, loath to admit he was in an associate experimental program for returning vets without college degrees. He'd had a distinguished career as a Navy SEAL; he was more than qualified for special agent status, but trust the FBI to get stuck on policy and procedure. With any luck he'd finish the college credits needed by the end of the year, and this humiliating title would be in the rearview.

"Chicago office?" Heidi asked.

"Yep." The fiasco at the bar was still too fresh to mention being on the MOSQMO task force.

She brightened. "Perhaps I'll see you around. I've been assigned there starting Monday."

He opened his mouth to ask in what capacity when a middle-aged man called her name. "There's Dave," she said, her smile widening as he threaded his way closer. "He always finds a reason to leave when the dancing starts."

"Smart man."

Trick approached from the other side, holding his youngest's hand. "They're about to cut the cake, and Amy and Tina want to be in the front row."

"It was great meeting you, Heidi," Jace said, nodding to her date as he put Amy down. "Maybe I'll run into you in the hallowed halls."

They shared a final grin, and he followed Trick back to the family table, his steps lighter. Hopefully he'd altered her initial opinion of him. The Chicago field office was mammoth, but he'd keep a sharp eye out for her. Maybe ask her to coffee.

"She's not your usual style," Trick remarked.

Jace shrugged. "She's not usual." Her wolf whistle, which had almost blown out his eardrums, was the deciding vote in her favor. He was comfortable around women who were one of the guys. "You get Gage sorted?"

"Poured him into the car. Kevin went with."

Amy and Tina scrambled into the swarm gathering around a five-tiered princess cake on a blue satin tablecloth. "God save me from any of this," Jace muttered, sinking into his seat.

"Not your cup of tea?" Zamira's grin turned into a softer smile as Trick grasped her hand.

"All this pageantry?" Jace flicked a glance from the groom grasping the ribboned knife with Caitlyn to the photographer capturing the official end of this buffoon's masculinity for all eternity. "I want a wife, not a bride." His wave encompassed the ballroom. "When I get married, I'm skipping this whole deal."

"*When*?" Trick mocked. "How about you score a second date." He ducked as a blue napkin sailed past his head.

Zamira laughed. "I bet when you fall, Jace Quinn, you'll fall the hardest of all."

"I don't know about that." Trick shifted closer, causing her to blush.

Jace clamped his lips to stave off the sneer. This. This was the happily-ever-after vibe he was talking about. It permeated the room. He slumped back, catching sight of Heidi at the far end of the room. Both she and her date were turned away from each other, chatting with the guests on their other sides. Amicably. Comfortably. That was the kind of date he'd have wanted. But trying to find one other single woman that didn't hear a gonging marital clock? It was easier going stag.

Heidi threw back her head as she laughed. Even this far away, that throaty, infectious sound reached Jace. He grinned and watched her unabashedly. When she lit up like that, she was really attractive. For an older woman. Well, older than him but not...*old* old. If only he was sitting at her table, they could've talked shop and ignored all this. Jace swigged the water in front of him while everyone else applauded the cutting of the cake like it was some Olympic feat.

"Next up is the bouquet toss," the DJ announced gleefully. He tap-tapped on his laptop keyboard, and Pat

Benatar's "Hit Me with Your Best Shot" filled the air. Single women chattered excitedly as they scurried to the dance floor.

Jace scraped back his chair. "I'm gonna get some air."

"Jason Robert," Mom called from the next table, "you sit back down."

"Mom—"

"Sit."

Of course, Sean was still nowhere to be found. Zamira shook her head when Trick murmured something in her ear and stayed in her seat. Jace huffed out a breath and anchored himself sideways in the silk-draped folding chair. There were a lot of unmarried women out there. Gretch, taller than all the clustering women, examined her nails at the back of the group. Heidi halted beside her with a mischievous smile and a quip that made Gretch laugh.

Caitlyn made a couple of practice tosses then let the bouquet fly. It sailed over the crowd, heading straight for Gretch, who sidestepped gracefully away at the last second.

As if on instinct, Heidi lunged into the space and snatched the bouquet from a splattering death on the parquet floor. The surprised dismay on her face was priceless. Caitlyn shrugged to the crestfallen bridesmaids in the front and stepped off the stage.

"Way to go, Heidi," Jace hollered between cupped hands, then let out his own wolf whistle. At her sideways glance, he openly snickered and clapped along with the cheers. "ATF saves the day!"

She acknowledged the applause good-naturedly and threaded her way back to her seat. Next up: the removal of the garter to striptease music, and enough erotic antics by the bride and groom that even Jace began focusing on anything but the couple. Poor Heidi. He glanced over his shoulder, where she sipped her wine as if unaware of what happened next. Her date was busy typing on his cell phone.

"Where are my bachelors?" the DJ called, and Jace rose without Mom's prompt, inspired by Gretch's example of pretending to play along. He wouldn't let instinct overtake him like Heidi had.

Bracing himself to stand perfectly still, he plastered on a wide smile. The frilly blue garter whizzed center mass, passing a dozen men who all remained motionless too. Jace gritted his teeth as it dropped in altitude, arcing toward him. Not to be a poor sport, he didn't slide away like Gretch. Let it land on the floor.

A cheer went up, and he smirked at the sucker behind him. The guy was jeering right back. Everyone was. Jace frowned and eyed his left shoulder. The damn lace was perched on his sport coat. "Oh, *shit*." He snatched it off like it burned.

"What are the odds?" Trick laughed long and hard as he clapped Jace's other shoulder. "The oldest bachelor in here." The remark stung, but Jace caught those same three bridesmaids observing him with open disappointment, which helped ease the mortification.

"I need the lucky couple up front," the DJ hollered, his eyes on his computer screen. Jace spun around and held out a hand as Heidi stepped toward him. Her blush made her seem ten years younger, and when she smiled up at him, there was a quiver to her lips. Suddenly this whole ridiculous situation was a vivid throwback to those geeky school dances.

"That garter just magically planted itself on you," she said, eyes twinkling. "Reminded me of a heat-seeking missile." They shared a chuckle as he led her to the silk-covered ladder back smack in the center of the dance floor. He ignored the whistles, whooping, and raunchy music as he knelt in front of her.

"Let's get this over with," he said kindly.

"Aw hell, the hottest guy in the room is about to feel me up in front of two hundred pairs of eyes. Take your time." Wiggling her eyebrows, she scrunched up the hem of her dress a few inches.

His pants tightened with an instant chubby, and in his horror he fumbled with the garter, preemptively snapping it. It sailed a few feet away, and he lunged right, snatching it out of midair. More cheers and catcalls.

"No, it goes over the lady's foot, Jace!"

"Hey, that's not a toy."

"They didn't teach this in SEAL training, Quinn?"

On the plus side, the humiliation washed the blood right back out of his dick. On the minus—sweat blanketed his torso.

Heidi smiled encouragingly. "Garter virgin?"

"Slippery little thing," he joked back. "Maybe it *is* magic." At her chuckle, he wiped his damp upper lip and bent over her foot. Thank God she wasn't wearing anything resembling a high heel. Imagine the horror of tangling up around that spike. He slid the scratchy lace around her shoe and up her shapely nyloned calf, careful to stretch the fabric wide enough to avoid accidentally caressing her.

"Ladies and gentlemen," the DJ crowed, "this is the fastest I've ever seen this done."

"What's your hurry, Jace?" a drunken voice bellowed. *Fucking Uncle Pat!*

"They want a show," she said above the cheers and catcalls, those dark eyes merry with humor. "Go ahead and make a spectacle of us."

What the hell. His humiliation couldn't get any worse, and she was clearly along for the ride. Jace slowed down, trailing his fingers in millimeters along silky pantyhose and smooth skin. The cheers grew deafening. He inched up the athletic curve of her upper calf and leaned in, his left cheek all but in her lap. She threaded fingers through his short hair, nails gently scratching his scalp. The chubby was back and growing, but her throaty laughter urged him on. He kissed each kneecap and teased the lace higher, higher than where her hem lay mid-thigh, so his fingers disappeared up her dress. Her hands finally stayed his movements, and he sat on his haunches, bathing in her red, grinning face and returning a triumphant smile. The hooting and clapping were thunderous.

"Someone give this couple a room key!" The DJ spun the well-loved "Celebrate" song, and the noise turned to squeals of delight and scooting chairs.

Jace helped Heidi stand and navigate around the dancing bodies until they were off the floor. Then she turned and held out her hand, which he shook, even though he'd just been inches away from her crotch.

"If we happen to run into each other next week," she said with a short laugh, "let's not mention this. If your office is anything like D.C., the gossip will hound us past retirement."

Her face was still flushed, almost glowing, and he couldn't look away. Interesting. He had never been attracted to a middle-aged woman, but her uplifting energy was incredibly appealing. So was that self-confidence that took no one's opinions into consideration. She'd been a champ up there. He gently squeezed the hand he still gripped. "I will definitely search you out. Maybe we can have lunch? Talk shop?"

"Oh, great! I'll look forward to it."

She walked back to her table. Her date, seeming not at all perturbed about the erotic display, smiled at her approach then gestured to a passing waiter. Who was Dave to her? There'd been no affectionate gestures in all the glances Jace had snuck their way.

Jace sat to laughter from his brothers—Sean having miraculously reappeared, of course. Mom beamed proudly from the next table. Jace pushed the slice of white cake aside and dabbed his damp forehead with the napkin tucked underneath. His gaze strayed back to Heidi, laughing with her date. Nope, they definitely didn't act like they were involved. He'd find her in that mammoth field office first thing Monday morning and ask her out. God, when was the last time a woman had intrigued him like this?

She was an enigma—rare and exciting. A confident woman in a similarly grueling career, who could whistle like a man, shimmy with sexy abandonment in a conga line, and embrace the attention of that erotic show with self-assured poise. Monday couldn't come fast enough.

3

P ulse-pounding euphoria, sheer panic and way too
much caffeine... Not at all how Heidi wanted to
start this well-won promotion. Despite her confident smile, her stomach knotted painfully as even more
task force members streamed into the crowded FBI
conference room. Curious gazes darted her way as
personnel grabbed seats and greeted each other.

Heidi inhaled to steady her nerves. Heading this
MOSQMO operation would be the new pinnacle of her
career, and damn it, she had the experience and the drive
to lead it. What rubbed her nerves raw was the additional
clandestine task SAC Webb had assigned. Evidently, one
of these smiling faces was a traitor. Someone in this room
had leaked information to the bombing suspect, Thomas
Bradley. Her secondary role was to uncover who here had
betrayed their badge and this task force.

Could she lead these associates, support and
encourage them, all while digging into their backgrounds? Hell yes. In fact, had it not been for her last op,
this counterintelligence assignment would be a welcome
challenge. But memory balloons of her prior op's failure

kept bobbing against the fragile barrier of her confidence.

To maintain her unflappable poise, she instinctively began interpreting body language—gathering data these associates had no clue they emitted. Like that CPD officer in the corner. One foot was turned toward the exit as he gazed sullenly out the window. Two nonverbal signals of wanting to escape. Why would he want to be anywhere but here?

Could be he was a loner and crowds made him uncomfortable. But then why become a cop? Could be his withdrawal was directed at her... She'd gotten that instant dismissal from male subordinates before, but she'd give him the benefit of the doubt that a simpler explanation—say, an argument with his wife this morning—had put him in this displaced mindset.

She continued her slow scan of the room. Most agents and analysts talked amongst themselves. Fourteen had settled in their seats and immediately become absorbed in their cell phones. Others glanced her way now and again. Most expressions held frank interest.

Heidi scanned past the final two empty chairs to the freckle-faced redhead—how was he not in high school? —chewing gum like it was a competitive race. His gaze flitted about, never resting on anything or anyone for long. Nervous? New? Impressionable? Clear potential, given his eagerness, but he'd need guidance and mentoring.

One of the eight women looked familiar, but Heidi couldn't place her. She, along with five other women, sat forward, hands visible, expressions alert. Body language for open. Friendly. These were the type of associates who put in a hundred and ten percent. The other two jotted on a notepad they passed back and forth, smirking like junior high schoolers.

Heidi registered all the impressions, the foot tapping, fingers drumming, flitting eye contact, hands hovering around the neck. Interpreting nonverbal cues had been a survival reflex, rooted in her chaotic childhood. She'd honed the skill into her greatest professional asset. She got confessions. She called out liars. Her male counterparts assumed it was because she had that mysterious thing called women's intuition. Why correct them?

"Let's get started." Beside her, Assistant Special Agent in Charge Felix Garcia rapped on the table. Instantly the room fell silent, postures straightened, and all eyes riveted to him. "As you all know," he continued, "Case Agent Hennessey is on emergency paternity leave after his wife's car accident. Happily, Julie and their new baby girl are in stable condition at Evanston Hospital. I'm pleased to introduce Mark's replacement, Senior Special Agent Heidi Hall"—he gestured to her like she was a game show prize, and she half waved, half saluted the task force—"from the Bureau of Alcohol, Tobacco, Firearms and Explosives."

An extensive list of her credentials followed—certified arson investigator, certified explosive specialist, blah, blah, blah... Heidi ignored the rising warmth in her cheeks. As hard as she'd worked achieving every one of those skills and commendations, listing them like this sounded like bragging, even if she wasn't the one speaking.

The door behind her opened, fanning cool air along the back of her neck. All eyes swiveled to the late arrival. Most faces lit up. The teen waved in greeting. A popular member had arrived.

"—recognized as a leading authority on hate groups and has worked on more than thirty major investigations around the country," concluded ASAC Garcia, smiling at her. "It's great to have you on the team, Case Agent Hall. We welcome your expertise and fresh perspective."

"Thank you, sir."

Garcia gestured for her to take the floor. She folded her hands on the stack of case files in front of her and faced the team. The late arrival grabbed a seat next to the teen and looked at her expectantly. The steaming mug traveling toward his lips froze the precise second her heart did.

Those crystal-blue eyes, that rugged outdoorsy face... Holy hell. It was the hottie she'd enticed up her dress last Saturday. What was his name? Jace Quinn. *Oh, crap!* Her heart scrambled to pump blood back into her head, which effectively lit her cheeks on fire.

Of course she'd expected to run into him sometime during her assignment. Even looked forward to that coffee invitation and the mild flirtation that would follow. But to have him on her *team*? Be his supervisor after her two-glasses-of-wine, midlife crisis display? This was a disaster.

The teen fidgeted. Several associates frowned. Oh shit, she had the floor! "Good morning," she managed to wheeze, sweeping her attention to the members on the other side of the room. "I've, um, begun reading your interview summaries and case evidence collected. I commend you all on the—uh—hard work that has gone into this investigation."

She couldn't seem to catch her breath. How had she not run into Jace's employee file among the stacks she'd read late into last night? She should have finished them all instead of snatching a few hours of sleep. How many times did she have to relearn her lesson not to leave an assignment half-assed?

Enough. She was stammering and blushing and making a fool of herself. Calling on twenty-three years of mastering nightmare scenarios, Heidi drew a breath and plowed onward. "As ASAC Garcia mentioned, my expertise is hate groups, specifically the white supremacy groups that have exploded across the American landscape recently. I know together we'll discover which group or groups are responsible for the mosque bombing."

She peeped in Jace's direction again. He gazed back expressionless, but his jaw was locked tight, the slight flare to his nostrils unmistakable. Nonverbal cues for tense or upset. Or mirroring her shock. This wouldn't do at all. It wasn't that she didn't trust *him* not to behave professionally with her... She didn't trust herself. The pull of his sexual magnetism drew her like a love bug hitting a windshield.

No. Having him on her team was too much of a risk. As soon as this meeting was over, she'd find some menial task to keep him out of sight and way out of mind. *Too bad, Jace Quinn, no hard feelings.*

She wrenched her thoughts back to her presentation. "I agree with this task force that we're looking for more than a solo perpetrator. Thomas Bradley had help, and here's why. Your evidence suggests the truck was loaded with five thousand pounds of ammonium nitrate mixed with the common racing fuel, nitromethane, and an electronic detonating device.

"Let's start with the ammonium nitrate. There are only two ways to gather that volume of fertilizer." She held up an index finger. "One: buying in nationally allotted twenty-five-pound increments from a farming supply company over a slow enough duration to stay under the radar. Or two: a large amount was stolen from a manufacturing plant." She gestured to the group. "Since your research indicates there haven't been any reported plant thefts nationwide, it's indicative of the first supposition—small acquisitions of fertilizer were purchased from a Walmart, then a Home Depot, etcetera.

"As you know, purchasing fertilizer requires a special license, and Bradley didn't have one. Therefore we can presume we're pursuing an established group with enough members to farm out all those shopping needs across many towns and multiple states. Does that make sense?"

The team nodded eagerly, many leaning forward in their chairs. Not Jace. Not the cop in the corner. Both wore hard expressions. Both had crossed their arms the second she'd begun speaking.

Heidi ignored the way Jace's biceps popped. Brutally refused the temptation from her weaker side, a.k.a. the Flirt, to keep sneaking glances. She had no business showing him any special treatment. Someone in this room had betrayed the FBI. She hoped to hell it wasn't Jace, but right now he was as much a suspect as everyone else in here.

"I'm confident we're looking for something along similar lines as the Oklahoma City bombing in ninety-five," she went on. "Why? Because the same ANFO ingredients—ammonium nitrate and fuel—used, the truck size, and the detonation being timed for when the Murrah building would be fully occupied is the same MO as Mosque Mohammed.

"It's pretty obvious our perps studied the minutiae around Oklahoma City, and we'd benefit from a refresher analysis too. Point of fact: Timothy McVeigh and Terry Nichols were not the lone wolves the media made them out to be. They'd spent a great deal of time in Elohim City, Oklahoma, a town founded by the white supremacist group Aryan Republican Army.

"In the Oklahoma case, the ammonium nitrate was purchased throughout Kentucky over a several-year period. Granted, there was no national tracking like there is now, but I'm confident that to acquire just under five thousand pounds, the ARA gave them a hand.

"Given these similarities, I'd hazard a guess our bombers utilized great care planning this over a long time, rather than rushing for a specific target date. In fact, Mosque Mohammed may not have been the intended target, but rather the right place at the right time—unfortunately for the two hundred and forty-five men, women, and children who lost their lives."

"Are you saying this wasn't directed at Muslims?" the teen asked.

Heidi spread her hands. "My experience in studying white supremacist groups is they tend to harbor hate for anyone who isn't a white Christian. Yes, they splinter into specific factions—the most famous anti-Black group being the KKK, the most famous anti-Semitic being the Nazis. But most groups are simply pro-white male, period. If you were born anything else, you're not pure.

"The crusades and war crimes between Christians and Muslims have filled history books," she went on, "but modern anti-Muslim hate groups are relatively new. One of the largest is 'ACT for America,' or ACT for short. Interestingly enough, founded by a woman. An example of their views is that any Muslim woman wearing a hijab must be considered an extremist. Period."

"We looked into ACT," the teen blurted with the eagerness of a schoolboy, which drew side-eyes from many. He hadn't integrated well, she'd bet money on that. "No evidence pointed to them."

"Exactly." Heidi smiled at him. "At almost a million members, ACT is too big. Had they been responsible for that much death, you'd still be hearing their celebration. Most terrorist groups proudly take credit, for both bragging rights and recruitment purposes, but there hasn't been a peep in four months. You have to ask yourselves why."

A few nods. A lot of brows knotted in frustration.

"Let me familiarize you with smaller, stealthier white supremacy groups like the Race, Patriot Front, and Atomwaffen. Most of these groups are ex-military, millennials, and self-proclaimed extremists. They boast about how much more radicalized and prone to violence they are than old-school anarchists."

Around her, the team's solemn expressions reflected variations of determination and dismay. She spread out the top four files in her stack. "I'd like to follow up with the unit heads later today to see if we can probe a bit deeper than what you've uncovered. Maybe something will point to one of these groups. Shall we start with the evidence response team at ten?"

"That would be me, ma'am." The teen raised his hand. "Special Agent Josh Peters."

"Hi, Josh." Seriously. That poor boy had to be carded everywhere he went. Heidi typed the appointment into her calendar app. "Witness interviews at one?"

The cop in the corner slowly raised his hand. "Me." His breath came out like a sigh, his eyelids lowered to a squint. "Sergeant Bill Fontana, Chicago PD."

Heidi ignored the passive-aggressive cues. She'd encountered guys like him in every step of her career. Had fought the boys' club atmosphere and superior male attitude in every office she'd worked. The only thing they respected was straightforward competence and no hint of femininity. "Thank you, sergeant. CI leads?" Blank faces looked back. Maybe they called it something else in the FBI. "Confidential informants? Asset leads?"

Jace slowly raised his hand. The dread on his face was as palpable as when he'd knelt in front of her clutching that baby-blue garter.

"I guess that falls to me," he said. "I assisted Case Agent Hennessey. I'm Jace Quinn."

The anxiety clogging her throat loosened a notch. He was keeping their prior encounter secret. For now. "Yes, Jace. And that's special agent?"

His hard mouth curled down. "No, ma'am. Special agent associate."

Associate? What the hell was that? She glanced up, frowning between him and Josh. Jace had to have fifteen years on this kid. How was it possible he ranked lower? Jace glared at the tabletop. The tips of his ears were red. Okay. A conversation for another time. "Four o'clock?" Heidi said briskly.

"Sure." The word came out sullen, and Jace cleared his throat roughly.

Three people were now glancing between them with knitted brows. She dared not look right to read whatever was on Garcia's face.

"Explosives evidence?" One of those open, ambitious women raised her hand—the one who looked familiar. She had a TEDAC insignia on her navy polo. Heidi brightened as the memory fell into place. "Oh, sure. You worked with me on the McMorran investigation." The fellow ATF agent was a brilliant specialist with the Terrorist Explosive Device Analytical Center in Huntsville, Alabama.

"Yes, ma'am. Special Agent Alma Reyes. I also provided remote backup support for your Wastewater team."

Heidi barely held back a wince. Wastewater. Her latest professional triumph and greatest personal failure. She swallowed hard. On the one hand, Alma's intelligence would be an asset, and as a fellow female, fellow ATF agent, she was someone to tap for deeper personal information on these team members. On the other hand, if Alma had somehow acquired inside knowledge about Evan's death, she could easily turn into a lethal adversary. It didn't take much to demolish a female agent's reputation. There was only one way to find out whether Alma would end up being a friend or foe. Heidi pasted on a bright smile. "Great to have you back on my team, Alma. How about a working dinner at six?"

"Sure, that'd be great."

Instantly three of the men around the table sat back and folded their arms, lips forming straight lines. No doubt they smelled favoritism or some kind of sister-hood-of-the-ATF-pants thing. Too bad. She didn't play that way. She rewarded smarts, loyalty, and ingenuity. They'd learn fast enough that she didn't tolerate entitlement or pouting.

———

HEIDI OPENED the file on Thomas Bradley. Best to dive right in. "Okay, people. Have we received an autopsy on the suspect? Forensics from the scene?"

"Nothing from forensics yet, ma'am, but we expect the autopsy later this morning," said the young, perky woman sitting beside Alma. "I'm Kelly Morgan, communications analyst, ma'am."

"Looks like a straightforward suicide," Bill Fontana added. The chest puffing made his CPD badge glint in the sunlight streaming in from the window. "Gun was found in his hand, no evidence of a struggle."

"Suicide note?"

He squinted again. This guy was racking up the nonverbal cues. "Nothing so far."

"Have we found anything linking Bradley to any WS groups? Or any additional suspects?"

Expressions grew bleak. Kelly tentatively raised her

hand again. "So far we haven't, but we're still looking into his social media presence."

"Have you identified any similarities from other bombings with the ANFO remnants recovered from the mosque?"

"No, ma'am."

"We collected fifteen pipe bombs, though," Alma said. "We're still analyzing them to identify a signature we can link with other crimes."

Heidi drummed the stack of case files. Something didn't sound right. "Question: if Bradley's weapon of choice was pipe bombs, why did we home our investigation in on him in the first place?" That was the equivalent of using Roman candle fireworks versus an M-80.

"Rental surveillance," the agent on the other side of Alma said, dipping his chin. "Special Agent Manny Gonzales." He tapped his iPad a few times and continued. "Bradley rented the sixteen-foot Penske truck at the Home Depot on South Clinton last June the second. He prepaid for one day under the name of Robert Smith."

"And it took until last week to identify him?" All activity ceased. Heidi took in the frozen expressions. She reviewed the shape of the question and her tone. It hadn't been accusatory or critical. The collective sensitivity of this team, the sunken morale at the lack of success or slow progress, was a handicap.

Manny cleared his throat. "We identified him almost immediately, ma'am. It's taken this long to be able to track his whereabouts. We were close several times, but he slipped through our grasp."

Heidi nodded. It was this reoccurrence that had finally caught the attention and suspicion of SAC Webb. Someone in here kept alerting Bradley. She took another long look at the agents and analysts staring back at her. Whoever the leak was, they had great control over their limbic system. All humans learned how to control their face to lie or hide emotions early in life, so trying to interpret expressions was an exercise in futility. But the limbic system, that primitive part of the brain dealing with survival, gave off signals left and right. Fidgeting, rapid blinking, avoiding eye contact, folding arms, crossing legs... These were nervous or closed signals most people had no clue they were emitting. She finished the visual sweep of the room. Not one associate had moved.

"Well then," she said briskly, "our task is to find out everything about Bradley's movements and known associates. Volunteers?" Twelve hands shot up, among them Jace, Josh, Bill, and Alma. She took down every name. The leak would be in this dozen. He or she would want to drive away any investigation into Bradley's background that could implicate him or her.

From that list, Heidi assigned five associates: one each from ATF, CPD, and FBI, and two analysts. "Until further notice, I'd like the task force heads to meet here every morning at eight for updates and brainstorming. To all of you, you'll find I'm a hands-on, in-your-face leader. I'll ride your ass until it's chapped raw, but I'll also go to my grave sticking up for you to the higher-ups. Trust your instincts. Start thinking outside the box."

Garcia stood, stuffing his reading glasses into his breast pocket. "Allow me to speak for the team, Case Agent Hall—it's good to have you on board."

As he left, Heidi began shoving her case files in her briefcase. The room erupted in murmuring voices and scraping chairs. Jace was the only one who remained seated, bowed over his phone, texting or jotting notes. How remarkable that he wore the same navy polo as most of the FBI agents striding out, yet his muscular physique molded the fabric in such mouth-watering ways. *Enough.*

Jerking her attention to the associates filing past, Heidi noted who stopped and shook her hand, introduced themselves, and welcomed her. Josh, unsurprisingly, had a damp palm, weak grip, and ingratiating greeting. Sergeant Bill lumbered past without eye contact.

Once the room emptied of everyone except Jace, she allowed herself a long moment to absorb his stunning good looks. The broad physique, chiseled jaw, and his powerful self-assurance. Their sizzling interaction last Saturday had awoken a dark, dormant lust in her, which had smoldered long after the wedding was through. Even Dave had laughingly noticed.

But now Jace was a career-ending danger to her. He'd witnessed her other side: the single, middle-aged desperada she'd named the Flirt, who'd have gladly lost herself to an impulsive one-night stand. Being attracted to him, accepting that hypothetical casual coffee date, was no longer an option—full stop. How on earth would she grind that message into the Flirt, who was currently fantasizing outrageously creative things to do with him stretched out on this conference table?

"Thank you for pretending you didn't know me, Jace. For introducing yourself."

His thumbs stopped moving. He flicked a glance of such dark, sensual heat that her insides began dancing the cha-cha. Holy hell, this was not good. He was so off her team.

"You'd made it sound like you were only here in Chicago to consult," he said mildly.

"I don't believe I framed it that way at all." She used her iciest none-of-your-business tone, and his seductive expression withered. She went on, "After an in-depth discussion with SAC Webb last week, I was offered this position. Will there be any issue between us?"

"No." He spread his palms in supplication. "No, *ma'am*." His smile was brittle. His eyes burned with the knowledge of how her thighs had trembled under his touch.

"Good. See you at four." Heidi snatched up the brief-case. Seven whole hours to lock the Flirt back where she belonged—far away from Jace.

4

The CCTV surveillance of the June second mosque attack was worthless. The south- and east-facing cameras had only captured rush-hour traffic, a few pedestrians, and a jam-packed parking lot on that last day of Ramadan, the Muslim holy month of fasting. Unfortunately, the blast had occurred on the west side of the structure. Had it happened during any of the other twenty-three hours, clear images of the suspects parking and leaving the truck would've been obtainable, but the bomb had detonated at sunset. Each grainy image before the explosion was barely detectable above the glare coating the lens.

Heidi collapsed back in her chair and rolled her stiff shoulders. Hunching over reams of photographs, videos, witness interviews, and lab results from the three tons of collected evidence was excruciating. Give her an outdoor assignment any day. Even working a scene in crappy weather was way better than this. Chasing down a suspect, handcuffing him, and reading him his rights ranked among her best days. They were a long way from that with this case.

She clicked on the north-facing surveillance. Seven minutes and forty-two seconds before the blast, a plain white box truck crept down Wabash, then turned left off camera. Security footage from businesses along Wabash had captured multiple images of that vehicle, with glimpses of two men with ball caps pulled low over their brows, wearing long-sleeve shirts and dark winter gloves. In June. The Illinois commercial license plate had been stolen off an abandoned van, one of many littering the front yard of a farm way out in Bellevue.

Whoever was behind this heinous bombing had been a mastermind at planning, working around surveillance, and covering their tracks. That actually narrowed the field of suspected groups. White supremacists continuously needed to grow their movement, so most weren't stingy about whom they recruited, resulting in many foot soldiers who weren't the sharpest tools in the shed. But this type of precision and secrecy was looking like the work of the Race or Atomwaffen Division, two newer, sleeker groups known to be a whole lot more militant and dangerous.

Heidi closed the video file and checked the time—almost four. Sliding off her reading glasses, she rubbed her strained eyes. CI reports next. Jace Quinn again.

She finger-combed her hair then huffed out an exasperated groan. Seriously? This odd magnetic pull was truly unwelcome. She couldn't afford to be distracted or have even a hint of this attraction get out to her new team. Hell, she'd learned that lesson during her rookie year. A brief affair with a fellow ATF agent had resulted in a bunch of attaboy winks for him, and a "reputation" and stern lecture for her. Work liaisons. Never again.

She would remain rigidly professional with Jace until she could assign a task that guaranteed little face time. The giddy, girlish Flirt began to drain away. She was making the right call never letting Jace encounter *her* again. What a disaster! And hopefully, unlike the other two unit heads, he would walk in here with something—some tiny, overlooked detail from his confidential informants that could jump-start a new lead.

A soft rap on the office door. "Case Agent Hall?"

"Come in, Jace. Have a seat."

He claimed the seat across from her, one hand gripping an iPad, the other a mug that sported the Navy SEAL trident and a motto, the font too small for her to read. The freshly brewed coffee smelled dark and delicious.

She eyed the trident. Start on a new footing. "Which team did you serve with?"

"SEAL Team Three."

Odd-numbered teams were stationed on the West Coast. "I love Coronado," she said. "When did you get out?" She put on her reading glasses again and squinted at the mug. *Lions mustn't concern themselves with the opinions of lambs.* Hmm.

"Just under two years ago."

She lowered the specs. "May I ask why?"

Jace gave a one-shouldered shrug. "Figured it was time." He drummed the side of his thumb on the tabletop, signaling anxiety or a downright lie. "Figured my career could go a whole lot farther in one of the alphabet organizations." His thumb sped up.

Screw it. Their relationship was fractious enough. She wasn't calling him on how his words differed from his limbic brain. Besides, she'd glanced through his personnel file on her lunch break, and he'd been honorably discharged. Let him keep the real reason for leaving the SEALs a secret.

"You've made quite a name for yourself here," she remarked. "The capture of a Syrian terrorist last spring.

The return of the stolen painting from the Isabella
Gardner Museum. And you apprehended one of the top
mob bosses, didn't you?"

A corner of his mouth pulled down. "His arrogance
made him easy to find. I don't know how the dumb fu—
uh, idiot came to head a syndicate." Abruptly he registered open-mouthed shock, like she'd slapped him.
"Wait," he sputtered. "You read my file?"

"It's in my interest to know the background of every
member on this task force."

"On your first *day*?"

She knew that bewildered look well. It signaled the
moment each team member clued in to how controlling
she was, how workdays didn't end, how she couldn't let
go of any lead until it was fleshed out. This initial
surprise and maybe even respect would eventually turn
to annoyance and eye rolls. Not that she cared. As long as
the job got done.

"I'm thorough," she responded. And in this case, how
else could she begin homing in on the snitch? Heidi eyed
him across the desk. The contours of his solemn face
were classically handsome. Draw a cartoon of a super-
hero, and the only thing missing was the cape.

Could he be the leak? It seemed inconceivable. But
the other thing she'd uncovered, the not-so-surprising
flaw from such an alpha ego...

Was it too early in this fragile alliance to bring it up?
Jace began fidgeting with the mug handle, like he knew
what was coming. Why not clear the air, then? Give him
a chance to resign from the task force. "Despite your
excellent record, Jace, I understand you had an issue
working under Special Agent Margo Hathaway last
spring."

Without twitching a muscle, he suddenly radiated
predatory alertness. His luscious mouth formed the

shape of a syllable, rejected it for another, then pressed tight. She waited him out.

"And?" he said.

"And I'm leading a case that's all but dead in the water." Heidi spread her hands. "I need to know right now if you have a problem following orders from a woman, Special Agent Associate Quinn."

A cold glint electrified those blue eyes. Clearly he hated that title. "Agent Hathaway received the OPR, not me. She was the one sleeping with the enemy. She also endangered my brother's life."

Heidi acknowledged those facts with a dip of her chin. Yes, the records indicated Jace had been cleared of wrongdoing, but her interpretation came from reading between the lines. "Your inability to take direction from Margo long preceded that Office of Professional Responsibility investigation. I repeat, do you have a problem following orders from a woman?"

His hesitation and the rigid set of his shoulders spoke volumes. "No. Ma'am."

"Good to know." She had to leave it there. If there was a pattern of misogyny, it would repeat under her command, and despite her hot fantasies, she'd jettison him off the team. In fact, his ousting would be a relief. Her own career would be safer for it.

She dismissed the topic with a fluttered wave. "I'm asking each member this. What's your view of this team and the investigation?"

The thumb-rapping resumed. "We've had a string of bad luck."

That made three members so far who didn't suspect sabotage. "What's your take on morale?"

"Free-falling." He sipped coffee, brow furrowed in thought. "The more time goes by without results, the more pressure we're under by the governor, the mayor, the citizens... And tension between Muslims and Christians keeps escalating. The Muslim community is accusing us of stonewalling the investigation because we aren't interested."

Heidi nodded. She'd passed dozens of peaceful Muslim protesters outside headquarters this morning, their posters reading:

Pretend the bomb was planted in a Baptist Church.

What if 245 Christians had been killed?

"And don't get me started on the insults from social media's cancel culture," Jace said, thumping the mug back on the table. "That's a freaking dumpster fire. Outside these walls, most of our team won't admit to being on the MOSQMO task force anymore."

He wasn't the first to tell her that, either. All this fury directed at personnel who'd labored almost around the clock for months. Her rose-colored glasses at being chosen to head this prestigious investigation had definitely slipped. In actuality, she was commanding a crippled team who'd lost confidence in their own skills. "Thank you for your honesty, Jace." She tapped her iPad back to life. "Let's see what your confidential informants have told you. Maybe fresh eyes can spot something."

His tight good-luck-with-that expression came as no surprise. She'd seen it at the wedding reception, when he'd rallied from embarrassed to smoldering because of the jeers. This guy didn't like to be bested, period. Well, neither did she.

Jace tapped an icon on his device. "Between CPD and FBI, a total of twenty-three informants were contacted. Twenty-one went nowhere." He scrolled down a page. "The most promising intel comes from the wife of a Leavenworth inmate who's doing ten for blowing up a convenience store. She waitresses at Devil's Den, the main hangout for Hells Angels. She told her handler ten days before the MOSQMO incident she'd overheard two members talk about a bomb. We've tried to track down these dudes, but it's like they vanished."

"And you issued a nationwide BOLO alert?"

"Yes, ma'am."

She let a beat go by. "You can call me Heidi, Jace." She took the proffered iPad and slid on her peepers.

June 19, Devil's Den Bar, South Western Avenue.

CI served two known Hells Angels gang members at six p.m. yesterday. Asset identified gang members as John "Big John" Stone and Marvin "Hatchett" Endicott. Asset overheard Big John say a "bomb" and "goddamn takedown" to occur in the "near future." Serving another round approximately fifteen minutes later, asset overheard Big John say, "The massive damage will earn us the Filthy Few." (A Nazi insignia patch believed to indicate the wearer has committed murder for their club.)

"Hmm. Big John has a big mouth." Heidi frowned. This certainly sounded like a lead, but Muslims as the intended target? That was highly unusual. "Historically, Hells Angels target the Outlaws," she said. "Was there any other explosion in the days or weeks surrounding the MOSQMO incident that we could attribute to this?"

"Nothing in the CPD database."

"Did you search nationally?"

"I didn't. I'm not sure if Mark did." Jace jotted a note on his cell phone. "I'll get back to you on that."

Heidi reread the report. She'd worked a biker gang investigation early in her career, and her takeaway was how tight the members were. How willing they were to die for each other—very similar to the brotherhood established in the military. Also, a common trait for white supremacy groups.

The Angels definitely had the precision and discipline to carry this off, but it flew in the face of the theory she'd put forth this morning. Such a coup would rarely stay under wraps in a group this size. Especially afterward, when the lure of bragging rights would be strongest. "Was there any chatter besides this lone man?"

"No, but they have the manpower to collect the required fertilizer without raising red flags. They could have stored it in any of their chapter houses in the surrounding states for as long as they wanted." Jace spread a hand. "The VIN and license plate from the stolen van in Bellevue is registered only a few blocks from an Angels chapter house."

Heidi nodded to acknowledge his points. Even better, Jace was thinking along broad, flexible lines. "Promising lead if we can bring those two in for an interview. What else do you have?"

He flipped the iPad around and tapped a few times until a fresh report popped onscreen. "This informant is a low-level street thug with Gangster Disciples, and his reliability can be spotty." He slid the device back to her. "He says he was pressured to steal nitromethane back in March. He didn't like the guy's attitude and passed."

A street gang member? This was even further out in left field. "Was the buyer from a gang?"

"No one he recognized. We brought him in to look at mug shots, but he only described the guy as white, late twenties, with a crew cut." Jace pointed to a sentence at the bottom. "Denny said the guy spoke like he was educated. Wore a t-shirt that was partially visible. 'Something, something pace, join the something.'"

Heidi started. "The Race?"

"What?"

"*Pick up the Pace. Join the Race.* It's the slogan for one of the groups I mentioned earlier," she said. "They're a neo-Nazi movement that cropped up a couple of years ago, but they've grown so fast they have branches in Canada and Europe now." She mentally ticked off the mosque evidence she'd studied this past week, and elation surged through her. This was a solid lead—on her first day. "They call out other supremacist groups who are satisfied with protesting or being keyboard warriors. The Race is much more militant. And sneaky. They go out of their way to infiltrate peaceful protests and incite crowds, initiate looting, and target hostilities against police. They use Twitter hashtags to keep their warriors instantly mobile, like flash mobs. Look at any of the recent riots, even the early Black Lives Matter movement, for example, and members of the Race and their sister group, Atomwaffen Division, were arrested."

Jace scoffed. "White supremacists supporting Black Lives Matter?"

"They don't care what the cause is. They even helped Antifa in Portland."

"No way."

"It's the age-old strategy of losing the battle to win the war. Their aim is to instigate riots, destabilize society, cause widespread anarchy to get citizens to lose faith in law enforcement and the government. Then, in the subsequent power vacuum, the Race will seize control and begin racial cleansing to 'save the European race.'" Heidi used finger quotes.

He folded his arms, skepticism knotting his brow. "'Pick up the pace, join the Race'? That's a stupid slogan."

"It's actually what sets them apart. These groups are known as accelerationists—they'll do anything to speed up the process of destabilization. It's a theory in a manifesto Brenton Tarrant wrote before he massacred all those Muslims in New Zealand mosques back in twenty-nineteen. Perpetrate violence to accelerate the end of civilization as we know it. The Race considers terrorists like him and McVeigh saints."

The skepticism on Jace's face morphed to thoughtfulness. "There were some fractious protests against Muslims in the latter part of May, after a Syrian nationalist set off bombs around the city," he said. "No rioting or looting, but the mood was a lot nastier than that Muslim crowd out there on the sidewalk today."

Another lead! Heidi picked up the console phone and pressed the video-tech button. "This is Heidi Hall of the MOSQMO task force. I need all CCTV video of any anti-Muslim protests the two weeks before June second. We'll be right down." She hung up and gathered her iPad. "If the Race is true to form," she said, rising, "we might be able to identify some of the infiltrators."

Jace stood as well. "Besides that t-shirt slogan, how will we recognize them?"

"It'll be hard," she admitted. "The key to their fledgling organization is operating only in two- or three-member cells."

They crossed her new office, still littered with Mark Hennessey's personal touches. She reached for the doorknob, but Jace got there first and held the door for her.

"Thank you, Jace." They shared a more relaxed smile —the kind from the wedding, which she was okay with, because this giddiness had nothing to do with a hottie molded into his shirt. It was the remarkable progress that charged her now. The lead was solid; the chase was on.

Once in the elevator, she continued. "Each Race cell has either minor or no interaction with other cells. That strategy keeps the overall movement safe, because a bunch of lone wolf packs creating havoc make it almost impossible for law enforcement to identify, infiltrate, or catch the overall leader."

"The proverbial needle in a haystack."

"Exactly. When they do communicate, it's through encrypted hate forums and apps we haven't been able to hack." The elevator dinged open, and they followed the signs to the audio-video forensic lab. Jace greeted associates every few steps—all male, clean-cut, with almost identical expressions of pride at who they were and what they did. He was obviously well known, well liked, and fit right in with this crowd.

An idea blazed in clear detail, the perfect answer to both their prayers. It was impulsive, potentially reckless, but Jace would be out of her hair, and she'd be handing him what he probably enjoyed best—an assignment with action and the potential for glory.

"How do you know so much about these groups?" he asked, and it took her a moment to compose herself enough to answer.

"I went through an immersion course at the ATF National Academy a few years ago and have sought out white supremacy cases ever since."

"Should we be looking at Atomwaffen Division too?"

Heidi shook her head. "They're larger and haven't adopted the lone wolf strategy. I think the tactic of individual cells may be the reason your task force has had such a hard time tracking down leads. The Race is militantly secretive. Not so much with Atomwaffen. The victory of two hundred and forty-five Muslim deaths would've been blared across the white supremacy forums. Not to be crude, but it would've helped them enormously with recruiting. I'll assign someone to look into them, but my hunch is on the Race."

They reached the A/V double doors, and he turned to her, a flare of determination lighting his eyes. "Assign me to head the Race inquiry, then."

The demand, hardly couched as a request, was not lost on her. She'd let it slide this once; she was too elated. And besides, this confirmed her prediction that he was driven and ambitious, and she couldn't fault those traits.

"I have a better idea, Jace. If I'm right and there's evidence that the Race was present at these earlier anti-Muslim protests, I'd like you to join them."

"Join them?"

"Infiltrate," she said. "Go undercover."

5

J ace gaped at Heidi. Undercover? Intoxicating triumph rocketed through him. Then stalled into free fall. "I'd love to, but the FBI has their own undercover department." He scowled, punching in the cypher-lock code and yanking open the lab door. "Their training is pretty extensive and requires five years of street experience first." He followed Heidi inside. "I barely have two."

"Don't worry about the regs," she said over her shoulder.

Jeez. Either she had a tremendous ego, or ATF agents ran roughshod over their departmental policies. She was in for quite a surprise working here. "The SAC will never approve me, Heidi."

"Leave him to me." She waved at the tech deep in the bowels of the lab then turned back, scanning him coolly, the complete opposite of the laughing, spirited woman from last Saturday. "You have infiltration experience as a SEAL, and more importantly, you fit the profile of a Race member perfectly. You're a white, educated male with ex-military experience and a deeply held belief that you're at the top of the race and gender heap."

Any remaining euphoria disintegrated. "Ouch." How had he ever mistaken the attraction as mutual? She couldn't stand him.

"Are you telling me I'm mistaken?"

"You hardly know me," he sputtered.

"Right. So let's assemble the facts I have gathered. There's this witty example"—she nodded at the slogan on his mug—"and the Jace I first met in the hotel foyer was quite the misogynist."

A flush burned up his neck. He was never going to live that down. "I was joking."

"You most certainly were not. Don't forget I've spent my career in this boys' club with all their 'jokes'"—she made air quotes with her free hand—"about the fairer sex."

Here we go. "Don't tell me. You've had to work 'a hundred and ten percent' to prove yourself equal."

The light in her eyes went flat. She opened her mouth, but the tech, Adam, had arrived. Shoulders hiked up around her ears, she spun around and greeted him in a tone sharp enough that the poor geek's eyes widened in panic.

Jace mentally kicked himself. She'd just tried to give him the best assignment of his FBI career. Why bait her like this? *She started it,* an inner voice argued. *All that gender inequality bullshit.* The topic was guaranteed to spike his blood pressure. He was so sick of the whining and the fury, and how every little thing was a trigger for women or minorities these days. It was a goddamn insult that anyone would attribute his achievements to white privilege or male cronyism. His success was due to his single-minded focus. Win at all costs. Be superior to everyone—white men included. If everyone else gave a hundred percent and Heidi gave a hundred and ten, then sure as shit he gave a hundred and fifty. The pride and satisfaction in who he'd become didn't make him an alt-right asshole. *"You fit the profile of a Race member perfectly."* Shit. He'd spent his career protecting the country from all flavors of terrorist, and now he was being compared to a domestic one? He swallowed back the fury with effort. He looked forward to proving her dead wrong.

Adam showed them to an elongated desk with surveillance footage paused on three monitors. "These are compiled from security cameras of local businesses and cell phone footage after the FBI requested help last June. I've lined them up sequentially." He pointed to the monitor on the left. "This protest is Wednesday in Cragin Park. The center monitor is the Thursday protest outside of the Al-Sadiq mosque, and this is the east side of Mosque Mohammed, right before the blast went off on Friday. Lucky for those protestors, the mosque was built like a fortress, so they didn't get injured."

"I went through some of that footage." Heidi took a seat at the middle console. "But I was only searching for passengers in a white truck. What we're looking for now is any t-shirt, ball cap, or tattoo with the slogan 'Pick up the pace, join the Race' or their insignia. It's a triple sig-rune." She grabbed a pad by the monitor and sketched three lightning bolts, similar to the Nazi SS symbol. "Sig, or the German word *sieg*, means victory."

Jace hauled out the chair to her right, choosing the protest outside Mosque Mohammed. This had been the largest of all the demonstrations held after that Syrian nationalist set off pipe bombs in late May, one of which had killed his best friend. Jace pressed the play button and dug in, determined to be the first to spot something.

The surveillance cameras were too high, rendering facial features and hand-scrawled signs grainy. Soon the tedious pausing, rewinding, and focusing on the minutiae of each protestor triggered a headache.

"Here's something." Adam's voice cracked like a teen's.

Jace and Heidi tilted left, peering at his screen, and this close, Jace caught the scent of her hair, fresh and citrusy.

Adam pointed out a man in the Cragin Park protest. "You can kinda see the bottom of those three sig-things under his sleeve." Sure enough, jagged S's pointed from beneath the white t-shirt.

Adam panned in on the protestor's face underneath the shadow of a plain blue ball cap. Except for a lean jaw and mirrored shades, there wasn't much to distinguish him. He held up a hand-drawn poster:

"What's eighty-eight?" Jace asked.

"The eighth letter of the alphabet," Heidi answered, "so HH. Heil Hitler."

He rolled his eyes. "These guys aren't very original, are they?"

"Be on the lookout for 'fourteen' or 'fourteen words,' too. It's the neo-Nazi slogan for the fourteen words: 'We must secure the existence of our people and a future for white children.' You'll often see the number codes together." She pointed to another protester a few people away from the first guy, whose poster, unfortunately, obscured his face. Above and below his swastika was: 1488. "The numbers by themselves could indicate any white supremacy group, though. We're looking for... There!"

A poster way in the background said: "14 Wordsss." The three S's were the sig-rune symbol. "That's definitely the Race. So, between the tattoo peeking out of this guy's sleeve and that poster, we have at least two confirmed sightings at the park protest. In fact, that probably makes up one cell right there."

Jace returned to his seat, fresh determination tamping down the headache. He was going to find evidence of the motherfuckers on the east side of Mosque Mohammed too, although identifying two or three members in this teeming mass of people really was looking for a needle in a haystack. Pause, rewind, play. Pause...play. Pause, rewind, play. He lost track of time, searching for sig-rune symbols or the Race slogan on tattoos, posters, ball caps, or t-shirts.

When Adam declared he was going home, Jace startled in his chair. He glanced at his watch. Five forty-five.

Heidi arched her spine, moaning when a vertebra popped. "I need to get to my next appointment too," she said in a tired voice.

Oh yeah, she was having dinner with Alma to catch up on everything they'd uncovered about the explosives. Jace scraped his chair back and stood, stretching stiff muscles. They hadn't found any type of signature tying the bomber to any previous explosions, but then Heidi had whipped up all this fresh evidence in a few hours. Maybe she'd see a different perspective with Alma too.

Jace followed them to the door. He had to give Heidi kudos for working this hard. By the time she got home this evening, she'd have clocked more than twelve hours on her first day. Thankfully, all he had planned was a long run, a couple of beers, and watching the Cubs game.

In the hallway Heidi thanked Adam once again, and as soon as the lanky man was out of earshot, she turned to Jace. "I'll text you some of the public chat rooms the Race has been known to hang out in. I want you to start reading their thoughts, understanding the lingo, and memorizing their dogma. Google everything known about them. We'll meet in the cafeteria for breakfast at eight, and I want you to wow me with something I don't know."

He frowned, both at the homework assignment that killed his plans and how, in the span of seconds, she appeared so perky and energetic again. "That's pretty open-ended," he said. "I don't know what you don't know."

"That's my point. Analyze the group to the point of mastery. It'll save your life when you go undercover."

"Yeah, about that." This was her first day. The first time she'd been in the Chicago field office. Maybe where she was from, they didn't have these kill-or-be-killed interoffice politics. "Even if you can get the higher-ups to ignore my lack of undercover experience and my associate status, there are a lot of street agents who'll be offended at being passed over. They'll generate a lot of flak."

"As if you care what people think about you." She smiled. "Oh, wait. You do."

His ears burned at the nod to his awkward garter performance. "It's more about the minefield you're marching into," he said stiffly. "It's a friendly warning about the optics of choosing someone as inappropriate as me. That won't fly around here."

That confident smile never wavered, and honestly, it was a great look on her. "Just absorb the material and be ready to impress me. Oh, and, until further notice, your role is top secret. Tell the task force you've been reassigned, and once you're undercover, there's no visiting this building or socializing with *any* agents unless I approve it. Are we clear?"

"Yes, ma'am." Not sharing the news with his team was an odd request, but if she could pull this off with the desk jockeys upstairs, it wasn't worth ruining this opportunity by questioning her. "I am finishing a degree through night school, though—"

"I highly suggest a leave of absence, Jace," Heidi interrupted curtly. "Undercover work is not a nine-to-five job, and most of these cell members work all day and meet in the evenings. I need your full availability. Is that something I can count on?"

Graduating in December was the only pathway to special agent. He had less than two months to go and wanted the promotion so damn bad. But undercover work... Who turned their back on an assignment like this? Besides, what were the odds she'd get the red-tape approval? He knew the way things worked around here. Nobody drew outside the lines in this building. "Sure," he said. "If upper management approves my role, I'll take a leave of absence."

She walked away with that no-nonsense stride. No self-conscious hair patting or glancing back to see if he was watching, which, for some reason, made him watch her until she rounded the corner. He turned in the other direction and took the stairs two at a time. Heidi didn't fall neatly into any of his female groupings. She'd come on to him at the wedding then frozen him out this morning. She'd schooled the whole task force on the kind of white supremacists they should direct their attention to, but not once had she sounded like a condescending know-it-all. This afternoon she'd made him feel two inches tall, regurgitating the fiasco with Margo, then rewarded him with the undercover role like he'd impressed her. If he couldn't sort her into one of his neat categories, then he didn't know where he stood. And that was unacceptable.

Back in the cubicle maze known as the bull pen, Jace sidled up to Josh's workspace, biting his tongue to not blurt out the secret assignment. "Whatcha working on?" he asked from behind, and Josh slammed his iPad cover shut and spun in his seat.

"Oh, it's you," he said shortly. "Checking personal emails. I've already signed out."

Jace frowned at the defensive tone. He didn't care. Matter of fact, he was about to check his own email.

"So?" Josh asked with a smirk. "How'd it go with the ballbuster?"

Jace dumped his stuff on his own desk. "Good." She definitely didn't fit into that category either, and hackles rose at the derogatory nickname. Although this was Josh, who usually thought the same way Jace did about pushy women staking claims in men's professions. It'd look weird to suddenly jump to her defense. He glanced over. "You sure were licking her shoes in the briefing."

"That was this morning." Josh folded his arms, his foot tap-tapping. "In the one-on-one, she all but said I needed to up my game if I wanted to continue on the team." He screwed up his mouth and spoke in falsetto. "Think outside the box. I need you to wow me."

"She's probably giving everyone that pep talk."

"Fucking hypocritical, given she slept her way to senior special agent."

Jace's hand stalled on the mug he was about to wash. "You don't know that."

"Dude, it's already common knowledge. Someone drew a pretty graphic cartoon in the men's room."

The vision of Heidi's hiked-up skirt on Saturday and the erotic come-on in her eyes kept Jace quiet. She definitely possessed the sexual boldness to climb the ATF ladder, so why did his mind rebel? Why this powerful urge to confront Josh? Jace rubbed at the torqued feeling in his chest. "She impressed me in my meeting with her just now. And Garcia was listing a buttload of awards and commendations when I walked in this morning."

"More proof she gets around."

Jace set his jaw. Forget washing the mug. Time to split before he said something he'd regret. His phone dinged with an incoming text, and he muttered, "Goodnight," as he dug out the device and stalked off.

Kevin: *Need help getting Gage out of Harold's Brewhouse.*

Jace muttered an expletive. Goddamn it. Another rescue of a brother who violently refused rescuing. *On my way.*

He got in the elevator and descended to the parking level before the full consequences of Josh's comments finally registered. Shit. The elevator dinged and the doors rolled open.

Exhaling another obscenity, Jace poked the button for his floor again. Sure, he didn't know much about Heidi and couldn't fit her in a category, but sleeping her way up the ladder absolutely didn't fit. And besides the fact that no one deserved an obscene drawing on a bathroom wall, Heidi had handed him a prime assignment. He owed it to her to clean off that graphic cartoon.

6

Heidi texted Alma that she'd be half an hour late and knocked on ASAC Garcia's door. "Agent Hall," he said in surprise. "Have a seat. How was your first day?"

She perched on the edge of the chair, energized to be bringing in such a solid lead, and caught him up on the Race. "I'll assign agents tomorrow to search for local cells in and around Chicago and pursue any connection between the Race and Thomas Bradley."

"This is all very impressive."

The ropelike tension in her shoulders eased. "Thank you, sir." If only the entire investigation could go this quickly and smoothly. "I'm confident enough in this lead that I'm going to set up a top-secret infiltration of the Race."

"Top secret?"

"If there's a leak on the task force, I don't want anyone knowing we're going undercover."

Garcia nodded. "Of course. Do you need recommendations for an operative?"

"No, sir. I've selected Jace Quinn." She said the words

rapidly, her posture ramrod straight. Jace's warning of administrative bureaucracy was charming—as if she hadn't been toiling away at a sister organization while he was still in high school. This choice would be a fight all the way up the ladder. One she'd win.

"Jace?" Garcia stroked his chin, dismay plastering his face. "He has no undercover training."

"He's spent a career infiltrating behind enemy lines. And physically he can blend right in to an action-oriented group that prides themselves on their strict paramilitary training."

"But Jace is on MOSQMO, so he's compromised until we find out who's engaged in the counterintelligence—"

Heidi flipped a dismissive wave. "I'm confident he's not the leak." Ninety-nine percent confident, but the miniscule risk was worth it to get him out of her nine-to-five presence. She'd never be able to complete her assignment if she had to keep battling the Flirt's incendiary attraction to him.

"And he already brings a thorough knowledge of the investigation," she continued. "What do you say?" She tacked on the question to soften the image of bullheaded resolve. It was the correct impression—she didn't give an inch—but she was new enough here to at least try to create a gentler first impression. Which in itself was annoying. She doubted Mark Hennessey had ever come in here with a demand followed by "What do you say?" The irony of choosing a career dominated by authoritarian males when her biggest triggers were being bossed around, manipulated, or treated like a fluff head was never lost on her.

"I agree with your points, Heidi," Garcia said, "but we already have experienced UCA operatives trained to think fast on their feet—"

"Jace had to think fast behind enemy lines." She

crossed her arms and gave him a frank look. "And you and SAC Webb assured me several times that I'd have carte blanche here." She'd made it an ultimatum during her interview. Without complete autonomy, this investigation would end up like Wastewater.

"Yes," Garcia said, exasperation building on his face, "but—"

"I warned you both that if I got wrapped up in admin red tape, this investigation would stall, and here's the perfect point. If you tie my hands and we wait for someone to be assigned, transferred, and brought up to speed, we'll lose precious days. We need to act now, sir. Jace is ready to go."

Garcia swiveled in his chair and gazed out the window. Long moments passed. Footsteps and murmuring voices from beyond the closed door filled the tense silence. Heidi remained motionless, hands fisted in her lap.

He swung back, lips forming a resolute line. "I got this promotion after Jace wrapped up all those impossible cases last spring," he said quietly. "In a way, I owe him big. I'll authorize it."

Tension drained from her shoulders. She loosened her fingers. "Thank you, sir."

"And you'll be his handler."

What? Her breath caught. "I—I'm heading the main investigation."

"You can't do both?"

"Well, yes," she sputtered automatically, "of course I ca—"

"Let's run with it, then."

While her flustered brain protested, her mouth said, "Yes, sir."

Another exasperated expression flashed, like her answer was not the one he'd expected. Cognition sparked. She'd thrown down an ultimatum, and in acquiescing, he'd also made sure to punish her. She should have folded, as any sane case agent would, and told him she wasn't up for the tremendous dump of additional work, but once again she was completely overextending herself in the name of proving she was as good as a man.

"If there's so much as a glimpse that he's not up for the role," Garcia warned her, "or it's taking too much of a toll on him, you pull him out."

She swallowed hard, the reality of her future settling in her stomach like a lead weight. On the one hand, she'd gotten what she wanted, but on the other... This assignment was supposed to get Jace out of her hair! "Yes, sir."

"You'll also need a tech to install and monitor all the surveillance, and at least one analyst to help compile all that data."

Heidi sank back in her chair. "They can have no previous relation to MOSQMO."

"Understood. I'll email you recommendations of employees I find trustworthy." Garcia waited a beat. It was obvious neither of them was happy with this new decision. "Jace will need an experienced undercover operative to train him on the basics and help launch him into the assignment. I know just the man. He recently ended a massive Group One assignment—"

"I'm sorry, sir?"

"An undercover operation here is known as a UCO," Garcia said, "and is classified either a Group One, which lasts from one to three years, or a Group Two, less than a year. After a Group One assignment, the agent, or UCA, is required to wait a number of months before accepting another assignment." He waved a hand, like he was stating the obvious. "Cuts down on the psychological wear of being among thugs and killers without a break.

I'll see if his supervisor will loan him out. Charles Jackson. Goes by Chaz."

Heidi knew all about the psychological breakdown of being left without support. She tangled her fingers in her lap. This wasn't the time to think about all that. Overall, today had gone so much more smoothly than she'd expected. So what if she had more work now? More face time with Jace. She'd figure something out. "And you'll let SAC Webb know of our decision?"

Garcia's smile was Cheshire-like. "This was not *our* decision, Heidi. If anything goes wrong, this was your judgment call." Something in his soft tone sent a chill up her spine.

"I plan to keep Jace Quinn under tight control," she said firmly. She would relish the imminent battle of wills, because in the end, she'd win every skirmish. Glancing at the time, she rose. "I have another appointment to get to. Thank you for your trust in me, sir."

"A friendly warning about Jace," he continued, pulling out his phone and scrolling. "Things either go very right for that young man, or they go catastrophically wrong."

Catastrophic? Nothing had been listed in Jace's personnel file. "Could you elaborate?"

He was about to respond when whoever was on the other end of the line answered. "Chaz? Felix Garcia in Chicago..." Garcia flicked her a glance and a wave.

Heidi nodded and slipped out. She'd get to the bottom of that odd remark tomorrow. All things considered, today was a triumph. Sure, she was buried under more work, but snip-snip, Garcia had cut through the red tape. To have had him as her boss during Wastewater would've been a dream. No doubt a lot of errors could have turned out differently. Maybe Evan would still be alive.

7

A lma's flushed cheeks and bright eyes were a direct result of the bottle they'd shared with dinner. "The actual fuel mix was anhydrous hydrazine and nitromethane," she said, lifting her wine glass. "It's a powerful and volatile combo that goes back to the early days of drag racing when it would literally blow up the engines. But if used correctly, it's beyond powerful. This was the fuel used to power the Titan rockets into outer space."

"Isn't diesel the common choice for bomb makers?" Heidi asked.

Alma nodded. "But don't forget the MOSQMO bombers appear to have been emulating McVeigh's footsteps, and during his trial, witnesses testified he'd been searching for racing fuel."

"How have you followed up on the fuel angle?"

"My team's been interviewing the different racing organizations around the nation—NASCAR, Formula One, IndyCar, Global Rallycross... We recently requested assistance from Mexican and Canadian authorities in case that much supply slipped across the border."

"Is that what your gut tells you?"

"No. I think the supplier is somehow connected to the bombers."

It was an intelligent answer, and Heidi gave the AFT agent kudos for the depth and breadth of her branch in this investigation. "Tomorrow I want you to run through your research again. See if there's any link between the racing owners, drivers, racetrack supplies, and fuel delivery companies to a neo-Nazi group known as the Race."

"The Race?"

"I'm sending around a memo tonight to catch everyone up to speed. Once you read it, you'll be clear on the direction I'm pointing the investigation."

"Okay. Great."

Heidi pushed her barely eaten dessert to the side and leaned her forearms on the table. "I'm also asking this from the heads of all the teams: what's your view of the overall investigation?"

Alma's gaze flitted to the restaurant exit. She was clearly uncomfortable with the question. "It's been frustrating," she finally admitted. "Hennessey's a decent agent, but in my opinion too much of a pal to be an effective case agent."

Heidi lifted an eyebrow. This was the first negative comment she'd heard about him. "How so?"

"His management style is laid-back, nonconfrontational—he wants to be one of the guys, you know? Which made for a relaxed work environment, but there was no whip-master pushing to close leads."

"You've got one now," Heidi said severely, and Alma laughed, hoisting her wine glass again.

"Yes, I remember how you kept insisting we ignore McMorran's rock-solid alibi and search for evidence he was behind the convenience store bombing."

Heidi grinned at the memory. The suspect who'd used his identical twin's alibi was the first case her uncanny ability to see through lies had been noticed. Anytime she pressed McMorran about that alibi, he'd answer using eye-blocking behaviors—shielding his eyes with a hand, rubbing them with a fist, adjusting the brim of his ball cap lower. All other questions he answered without exhibiting limbic behaviors, and yet she'd been the only one to interpret that very telling body language. "Tony thought I was batshit crazy for suspecting him."

"Are you still seeing Tony?"

They were wandering into dangerous territory. Even with colleagues on her same pay grade, Heidi kept her private life private. She made sure her voice was clipped. "It was on again, off again for years, but no. We're no longer together."

"I'm surprised." Alma put her elbow on the table and her chin in her hand. "He was real hung up on you."

That had been the problem. The more serious they got, the more they fought for the alpha role. Soon the overtime Heidi worked, her prioritizing cases over all else, and her predisposition to sacrifice sleep or time spent with him led to exhaustive fights. Tony had pressured her to embrace gender norms, like coming home to cook dinner, wearing flattering dresses on evenings out, visiting a salon... Except for her compulsion to clean house, none of that was who she was or how she intended to live her life.

Heidi lifted her glass in salute. "Let's just say, same problem, different man."

"Divorced three times," Alma said, and clinked her glass. "Here's to being a hard woman to love."

"I get all the warm fuzzies I need from my teams. Not initially, of course. They have to get used to my style."

Alma swayed on her anchored elbow as she laughed.

"That was evident by this morning's histrionic grumbling after the meeting. It was priceless. You'll have your work cut out for you changing the MOSQMO attitude."

"I'm used to it." Heidi shrugged as she toyed with her spoon. "First up will be rumors that I slept my way to the top. Next come passive-aggressive attempts to undermine my orders. Slackers will double down. The ambitious types will jump the chain of command and complain to Garcia. I welcome it. I have no problem reorganizing the task force and keeping the hard workers."

"You can always count on me, Heidi."

All the limbic cues showed Alma was sincere. "I appreciate that."

Tonight's honest camaraderie and previous work history had fast-tracked them into a cozy friendship. Why not get her opinion on some of the team members who'd stood out this morning—starting with the fidgety agent who resembled a boy cutting class. "So, what's your take on Josh?"

Alma chuckled. "The first thing you need to know is his father and grandfather were special agents. I'd be surprised if that wasn't the first thing he brought up after introducing himself."

Heidi smothered her own smile. "He may have mentioned it this morning." Specifically that becoming a third-generation street agent was his only career goal. "But surely that legacy motivates him to overachieve?"

"Right? But he tries too hard. He grew up with all these stories about the good old days in the FBI and constantly tries to emulate the tough talk and swagger, and all these sleazy pick-up lines from back in the fifties." Alma's lip curled in disgust. "Talk among the female agents is that he's heading for a hashtag-MeToo beatdown."

Heidi frowned. Not if she got there first. She'd

observed a bit of old-school attitude in the evidence response interview with Josh, but she wouldn't stand for misogyny or sexual harassment, especially in someone so young and moldable. "What about Bill Fontana?"

"Aw." Alma's shoulders slumped. "The sergeant's harmless. Mostly keeps to himself. Does the work he's assigned, but rarely goes the extra mile, and is out the door by five sharp." She crossed her legs, settling into her story. "I heard he's in the middle of an ugly divorce and is retiring from CPD at the end of the year. Poor guy. Can you imagine walking off into the sunset with so little to show for yourself?"

That could explain Bill's behavior this morning, staring out the window with his foot explicitly pointing toward the exit. Heidi had only skimmed his personnel file, but, like Alma had observed, nothing remarkable stood out.

Now for the big name. "Someone told me that when things go wrong for Jace Quinn, they turn catastrophic." Her remark hit the perfect mix of relaxed and gossipy. She topped it by waving for the check.

"Jace." Alma rolled her eyes, reaching for her wine. "You mean Mr. Marvel?"

"Come again?"

"That's what the women on the team call him." She paused for a sip. "You know, as in the superhero comic books?"

"Complete with cape and tights?"

"Right?" They laughed and clinked glasses again. "No, not just the outfit," Alma said, her abrupt hand gesture almost sloshing her wine. "There's no off switch with Jace. He's always going the extra mile to save the world. Of course, this is all speculation because he doesn't get together like this"—she waved the glass again, this time between them—"outside of work. And he never dates from our very eager pool of LEOs."

Except for not dating law enforcement officers, Heidi and Jace had those characteristics in common. Alma's derogatory tone stung. "Isn't saving the world an asset?"

"I guess it's the way he goes about it. On the surface he's this great guy, crazy hot, friendly, funny...the kind of guy who'll eagerly take one for the team. But underneath?" Alma took another sip of wine. Her eyes were looking heavy-lidded, her eyeliner beginning to smear. Splitting a bottle, when Heidi had only consumed half a glass, might not have been such a great idea. "Underneath, Jace is pure cutthroat ambition. A guy who's only interested in walking away with all the glory."

Again, not a bad thing. Heidi nodded her thanks as the waiter dropped off the check and reached for her wallet. "I'm A-okay with one person on this task force nailing the bombing suspects."

"Not if they turn rogue, if you catch my meaning."

They were back to this. Heidi's fingers stilled on the credit card. As much as she didn't want the dinner to turn into a rumor-fest, here was another woman's take on the episode last spring. "You're talking about Special Agent Hathaway?"

"I am. Speaking of things that ended catastrophically." Alma arched a brow, her expression full of meaning. "I'm not saying Margo didn't deserve the suspension, but word is Jace undermined her authority on every decision. And when the investigation suffered for it and they were hauled in front of Garcia, Margo got the brunt of the punishment and Jace got an itty-bitty hand slap."

"Were you around then?"

"I was in the building, but on a different task force."

Heidi let a beat go by, processing. "From what I

understand, Jace captured a mob boss and uncovered a famous stolen painting that very same week. Solo."

"All true." Alma spread her palms. "Which started the Mr. Marvel nickname. I'm just giving you a friendly word of advice. You may think he's on your task force, he may act like a team player, but when his opinion differs from yours, you'll be hard-pressed to rein him in. And upper management has a history of siding with him."

A chill skated up Heidi's spine as she recalled Garcia's warning from only a couple of hours ago. *"This was not our decision, Heidi. If anything goes wrong, this was your judgment call."*

Her recklessness in trying to get rid of Jace had already boomeranged back in her face, but had she also set herself up for a no-win situation? Jace undermining her authority and the big bosses supporting his actions? She'd have to watch her back.

"Thanks for your honesty," she said, glancing at her watch. It was after nine, and there was still so much left to do.

"Anything I can do to help. And I'm thrilled to work with you again, Heidi. I know you can breathe life into this investigation."

I already have. "We'll have some fresh leads shortly," she said cryptically. "I better go write that memo about the Race." And think up an explanation for Jace's abrupt removal from the task force.

HALF AN HOUR LATER, Heidi let herself into her extended-stay motel room and snapped on the light. Ignoring the mental fatigue and muscles crying out for the soft mattress, she methodically flipped open the smaller suit-case, stuffed with her cleaning supplies. Other people drank after a long day or zoned out in front of the TV. She unwound by dusting and scouring.

She set to work in the bathroom, substituting the industrial smell for her top-of-the-line organic products. Moving into the bedroom, she stripped and stored the maroon bedspread in the closet and substituted the starched white sheets with her well-worn bamboo set, then smoothed out her ancient eiderdown duvet—her first purchase when she'd moved out of the foster home at eighteen.

Next, she tackled the hard surfaces and took apart the mini coffee station, scrubbing the already clean elements and reassembling the machine for her first morning cup. The comforting sense of control and familiar cleanser scents lulled her, opening her mind to uncovering the traitor on her team. Josh was the perfect age to be targeted and recruited by white supremacists, but his pride in being an agent and the generations of pressure to toe the straight and narrow made him being the traitor unlikely. Bill didn't look like he'd have the energy to pull off a double life of betrayal. And Jace—well, it seemed inconceivable that Mr. Marvel would be anything less than militantly heroic. But during her initial interview, both SAC Webb and ASAC Garcia had been convinced of a problem.

"We don't think the task force is experiencing bad luck," SAC Webb had said.

ASAC Garcia had leaned forward, arms on his knees, his voice lowered as if the walls had ears. "Every time we've gotten close to identifying who's responsible for the Mosque Mohammed bombing, persons of interest are tipped off, witnesses scatter, evidence disappears... We discounted a few coincidences, but it's apparent now that our investigation is being compromised by someone on the task force."

Hundreds of city, state, and federal law enforcement officers had swarmed to be on this JTTF. And one of them was tipping off the terrorists? "Do we have any hard evidence?" she'd asked.

"Mark Hennessey came to us a few weeks ago," Garcia continued. "Once the team had finally identified Bradley's location and was drawing up a warrant, Mark arrived in his office one morning. Enough items were out of place on his desk for him to be suspicious. He immediately checked the logged calls from the office line, and a call had indeed been placed at eight o'clock the night before. To Thomas Bradley's landline. By the time we'd gotten the warrant and developed a takedown strategy, Bradley was dead."

Heidi sank onto the bed, the sponge in her grip forgotten. Maybe Mark Hennessey had ideas or suspicions. She glanced at the sparkling clean digital clock, which flipped to ten thirty-three p.m. She'd call tomorrow. Her invigorating scouring had given her yet another second wind. Time to create a checklist of action items, like examining the cypher-lock entries and exits in the vicinity of Mark's office at eight o'clock on the night his phone had been used. Narrow down the list of the people still in the building that evening. Somehow, someway, she'd find the LEO who'd flipped for a white supremacist cause. This op was her ticket to finally getting the ASAC promotion. She was not going to let one detail slip through her fingers.

8

The file with Thomas Bradley's autopsy results was on Heidi's desk the next morning, along with a stack of photos. Bracing herself, she flipped through the gruesome shots that combined what her team had encountered at the scene with photo documentation of the autopsy. In her twenty-three years with the ATF, she'd stomached the sight of bodies burned beyond recognition or blown to bits, but this was her first up-close of a decomp. The bloated corpse had multicolored, slack skin and dark foam emanating from the nose and mouth. As weak as the motel coffee had been, it churned noisily in her gut.

She quickly slid the photos aside and reached for the autopsy report, skimming down to the cause of death. Gunshot wound to the head—9mm Parabellum still lodged in the right cerebral cortex. The ruling was listed as "undetermined." Meaning the ME had concluded there was insufficient evidence to rule the death a suicide. Huh.

Frowning, Heidi read the summary paragraph above

it. No defensive wounds, no overt sign of murder. Body had been in the second stage of decomposition, known as bloat. Given the mild indoor environmental factors, it was determined Bradley had likely been deceased for three to five days. The fingerprints on the Luger found near his right hand were definitely his. The problem? Bradley had been left-handed.

She dropped the pages on top of the photos and slumped back. Forensics was still processing the items collected at the scene, but no one had mentioned a break-in or damage inside the home. Had Bradley opened the door to someone he considered a friend? Someone from a Race cell? Or had the mole using Mark Hennessey's office phone not called to warn him, but to set up a meeting and kill him? And how on earth would she delve deeply enough into each of her team members' backgrounds to find an association with Bradley?

Maybe the previous case agent suspected someone? She studied the silver-framed wedding picture still perched on the left side of the desk. Hennessey's short, thick black hair and tall build contrasted sharply with his wife's long blond hair and petite stature. Both were good-looking, fit, and captured mid-laugh. Heidi examined the photograph with the same dispassion as the autopsy photos. Fairytales of true love, vows of commitment, even smiling that broadly, were completely alien to her. Seeing photographic evidence of "bliss" triggered the same disengaged feelings she'd had at last week's wedding. Sure, the dancing had been fun, and the garter thingama-jiggie a hoot, but all that goopy bride and groom stuff... So not her thing.

She glanced at her watch. It was awfully early to wake the new parents, but maybe they'd never gone to sleep. Pulling up the interoffice directory, she dialed Mark

Hennessey's personal cell phone. He'd gone on paternity leave two days after reporting the office breach, but surely in the four months of heading this team, he'd formed some suspicions on who wasn't being a productive team player.

He answered in a groggy growl.

"Good morning," she said crisply. "I'm Senior Special Agent Heidi Hall, the new case leader for MOSQMO."

"Oh yeah." He groan-sighed, not like he was tired, but like he'd reluctantly pulled himself from a supine position to sitting. "Sorry I can't be there to help transition you."

"No worries. How's the wife and daughter?"

"They say the baby will be in NICU for another four to six weeks, but I'm bringing Julie home this afternoon."

"I'm so glad to hear that," she said. "I'll pass on the good news to the team."

"I'm assuming you're completely buried under the documentation we've generated. What can I clear up for you?" A man who didn't pull punches. She warmed to him.

"I'm staying afloat. Actually, it's the counterintelligence leak I'm calling about."

"Yeah." Mark blew out a breath. "That came as quite a shock."

"Anyone on the team you'd advise me to focus on?" She grabbed a pen from his dusty red OSU coffee mug, jammed with ballpoints, peepers, and a bottle opener.

"Believe me, I've been racking my brain this past week and don't even have a hunch." The sound of heavy footfalls on wood stairs came over the line. "You won't find a more dedicated team than MOSQMO."

"Webb and Garcia said you traced the call to Bradley on October third. Did you dust for prints on the console or the cypher lock on your door?"

"I'd already touched both again before I figured out my stuff had been messed with."

She flicked the pen in a seesaw blur. "Did everyone on the team know the code to get into your office?"

"No. The Bureau is rigid about adhering to security policies." The sounds of running water, drawers shutting, and the clink of a mug mingled with his words.

Straightening his wedding picture frame to align with the corner of the desk, she asked, "What about cross-referencing your team's names with all employees still in the building that night?" The only way out of the main reception area was waving a badge ID at the electronic scanner. All entering and exiting personnel were tracked.

There was a slight pause. She tuned in to the gurgle of a coffee machine on his end. "No," he said in a bemused tone. "I didn't check that."

"Security footage from the hallway?"

"Garcia requested that, I believe. Honestly, this happened so close to the takedown, I was focused on those logistics. Sure, I was alarmed the call had been to Bradley, but it was only when I encountered the body that I realized we had a serious problem."

Heidi filled him in on the ME's findings. "So on top of the mosque bombing, the task force is about to open a possible murder inquiry."

"Assign Bill Fontana to head it. And call Superintendent Navarro over at PD. Tell him I said to assign one or two of the crew who worked the Syrian bombings."

Ignoring the surge of irritation, Heidi thanked him for the advice and ended the call. Mark meant no offence ordering her around. Men in leadership roles took control like they breathed air. And he had been running this investigation. That his authoritarian behavior ticked her off after a lifetime of living and working among dominating males was her problem. The bottom line: Bill

Fontana leading the murder inquiry was the best option. He was CPD, this would require the cooperation of his own department, and he'd know the personnel and how to work the system to get things done.

She texted Bill to report to her office as soon as he arrived, and in less than a minute, there was a strong knock on the door. "I didn't expect you to be in yet," she said, stepping back and waving him in.

"I don't sleep past four anymore. Might as well put on the old uniform and get to it." He trudged past like the weight of the world squashed him. He'd behaved in a similar manner during the witness interviews update yesterday, which she'd chalked up as rejection of her command. In light of last night's divorce gossip, Heidi reconsidered the body language. This guy didn't just not want to work for her; he didn't want to be in the building. This new responsibility might be too taxing.

Heidi motioned to the chair across her desk and reclaimed her seat. "We didn't have a chance to chat more in depth yesterday. How long have you been with CPD?"

"Twenty-one years." His utility belt creaked, and a knee cracked as he lowered himself heavily to the chair. "I'm retiring next spring."

"Oh? Any post-career plans?"

"I have my eye on working in-house security or private contracting. Surveillance consults, maybe."

Heidi plastered on an interested smile and nodded. He'd have to show a lot more energy to go in that direction, but it wasn't her place to say. "Now that witness interviews are wrapping up, Bill, I'd like you to head a new investigation."

His eyes widened and he leaned forward. Language for open, engaged. "We have a fresh lead?"

She slid the autopsy file across the desk. "The ME couldn't confirm suicide or rule out homicide."

"What?" As he scanned the report, his lips parted.

"Which means we need to open a murder inquiry," she went on. "I'd like you to liaison with your department and forensics, revisit the home if you have to. Narrow the timeline of his death by searching out who saw or spoke to him last. Pull all cell records, texts, and any GPS signals. Find out what happened. Yesterday I assigned Josh Peters to work the white supremacy angle, so liaise with him if you uncover anything pertaining to hate groups."

While she talked, his eyes never strayed from the report. Now in the silence he remained in that frozen position, like he was dumbstruck or awed. It seemed such an odd reaction that she studied him for limbic cues. He lifted his gaze. "I appreciate your assigning this to me." Color bloomed in his face, and the relief there sent a wave of sympathy through her. "Count on me, ma'am. I'll figure out what happened."

She nodded in dismissal, and he departed with a miraculous change in spirit. Good. One more convert. In twenty-four hours, Alma, Jace, and Bill seemed solidly behind her leadership and directional changes. Josh was a holdout and would take more strong-arming. During yesterday's interview, his utterances had been riddled with misogynistic passive-aggression, like interrupting her before she'd finished her question or reacting to her directives with "That's not how Mark worked the case," or "Mark did it this way."

Given Heidi had been a rookie agent before this kid was even a twinkle in his mother's eye, his attitude had been beyond a slap in the face. But Josh was young, he was moldable, and before this case wrapped up, she'd knock those generations of old-school FBI arrogance right out of him.

One more glance at her watch confirmed it was time

for the mandatory daily meeting. Heidi grabbed the thumb drive with her PowerPoint presentation on the Race, her smile confident and determined. The days of broad leads that went nowhere were over. This joint terror task force was about to careen around a corner on two wheels. *Buckle up.*

9

Three Weeks Later

The double sig-rune temporary tattoo on Jace's bicep was almost complete, with room to ink in a third lightning bolt once he became a member of the Race. "You can shower and moisturize, but don't exfoliate," the tattoo artist said in a monotone, which went with her perpetually bored expression and faraway eyes. "This should begin to fade in about two weeks, so come back for a touch-up if you need it."

Jace nodded, not trusting himself to speak because he was so fixated on all the rings that pierced her nostrils, lips, and eyebrows. Even more dramatic were the full sleeve and neck tattoos and saucer-like objects enlarging her earlobes. He could stare at her all day, which was undoubtedly rude, but maybe people who went to these extremes wanted the attention.

On the other hand, he was inking himself with clear symbols that he was a hate-filled white supremacist, and she hadn't displayed the faintest hint of judgment.

He glanced in the parlor's mirror at his other arm, where *Ex Gladio Libertas* was boldly stenciled above a swastika. He'd have to make sure not to wear short sleeves around Mom for the duration of this UCO.

"What does that mean, anyway?" the artist asked, following his gaze.

"'From the sword, liberty.'" It was the Race's motto, adopted from the Northwest Volunteer Army after their leader had died unexpectedly. Jace reached for his shirt. In the last three weeks he'd memorized every article, podcast, and archived chat-room discussion from or about the Race. In the meantime, Heidi had pulled off a miracle by cutting through the FBI red tape and getting him cleared to go undercover. The only condition was that an experienced UCA had been flown in to train him and monitor the op alongside Heidi. Chaz Jackson, borrowed from New York City's drug squad, had been relentless in his advice and ruthless in his role-playing drills these last weeks. His varied exercises were designed to make sure Jace stayed in character during even the most stressful moments, while constantly building a solid case for the prosecution without engaging in entrapment.

Jace slid his arms gingerly through the shirt sleeves, then his coat, and headed out into the brisk November day. He looked up the address of his temporary digs—an FBI house, which the bureau simply referred to as a bu-house, on West Leland Avenue in Mayfair. It was a simple blue-collar neighborhood near the Brown Line, and perfect for his construction supervisor cover story. Fifteen minutes later, he was knocking on the door.

Heidi answered, phone to her ear. She waved him impatiently into the living room, where his bu-phone and all the documentation he'd need under his new alias was scattered on the cocktail table: Jason McGowan's driver's license, ATM and credit cards, Construction Labors Local 4 union card, and filler items like a partially punched buy-nine-get-one-free sub card.

Jace traded them out with the identification in his wallet. Just to get to this point had been the typical red-tape snarl-fest that drove him batshit crazy, but it was worth it. Besides the insane preparation and research, he'd assisted Heidi with the extensive FBI paperwork of goals, objectives, and targets, helped Chaz fabricate an authentic background for Jason McGowan from birth until now, coordinated every detail of the op with Assistant U.S. Attorney Heather Rhines, and obtained Title III approval to wire this house for audio and video. A flick of the switch by the front door activated everything.

"I said I'd take care of it when I returned," Heidi said in a low, harsh tone as she walked to the window. Jace frowned at her rigid back. During their infrequent inter-actions these last weeks, she'd always been unflappable, easygoing. She relied on humor to mitigate tensions between him and Chaz. This tone sounded more like a personal call. But that in and of itself was even stranger.

He wandered into the bedroom, but his footsteps stalled on the other side of the doorway as he actively eavesdropped.

"Why would I email? I made my thoughts about us clear months ago."

Was this Dave from the wedding? She'd been very stingy with personal information, another trait so different from other women he'd worked alongside or dated. Was she married? Divorced? Did she have kids? She changed the subject whenever he steered any conver-sation toward the personal. And for some reason, that reticence made him want to solve the mystery of who she was underneath the "senior special agent" and "case leader" titles.

"I refuse to discuss it now. I'll call you when I get back to my motel tonight."

In the ensuing silence, Jace moved to the bedside table, thrusting his real ID and credit cards deep inside the drawer.

"Let's see," she said, and he spun around with a gulping inhale. Jeez, she could creep up on people as silently as Sean.

"What?" he sputtered.

She motioned to his chest. "Your tats."

Had her mouth not continued to press in that irritated line, he'd have joked about #MeToo and undressing for his superior in a bedroom. It wasn't worth pushing his luck. Nimbly unbuttoning his shirt, he let the fabric slide to his elbows. He turned right, then left, studying her flushed face—another oddity, but that was probably from the phone call.

She folded her arms, a faint smile replacing the bitter lemon look. "The artist did nice work." Her eyes traveled along his torso, lingering on his abs. A hint of the sex-hungry woman from the wedding shadowed her face, and his cock began to salute. "How come you never got inked with the SEAL trident?"

"How do you know I haven't?" He hadn't intended for his voice to drop an octave. Luckily, she was heading for the door.

"Get dressed, frogman," she said airily. "Chaz is bringing lunch, and we're going over the meet-and-greet one more time."

Jace fumbled a button, then forced out an antagonized breath. What was his goddamn problem? Why was undressing for her in his bedroom so hard to shake off?

She was his immediate superior. Had to be a decade older. And, based on that pissed-off conversation he'd walked in on, most likely had a significant other. This adolescent groping for buttons and the changing voice—what the fuck? He was about to submerge into the ugly world of white supremacy. He'd better get his head in the game.

Jace jammed the hem of his shirt into his pants and ran a hand through his hair. Weeks ago, Chaz had judged him to be too much of a military poster boy. While the Race actively sought men experienced in weaponry and tactical combat, they were also highly paranoid about being infiltrated by the government. Chaz had advised the clerks providing Jason McGowan's backstopping documentation to shorten his time in the SEALs by having him wash out of BUD/S training during Hell Week. That had led to an unchecked ego tirade on Jace's part that embarrassed him still. He shook off the memory, grimacing at his longer hair in the mirror on his way out. Just one of many sacrifices required for going undercover. He hoped this was all worth putting his degree on the back burner and delaying the coveted special agent promotion.

Heidi sat with her back to him on one of the two barstools, texting furiously. At the commanding double knock, he strode to the front door. "'Sup," Chaz said, sweeping in with fragrant bags of Chinese. "You ready for this evening?"

"As I'll ever be." Jace followed him into the compact kitchenette. "I confirmed with Man-o-War this morning. We're meeting at eight, the bench in Howell Park." The vetting process to get to tonight's face-to-face was a result of weeks of encrypted chats back and forth with this local Race member, which had then rolled into an hour-long phone call last week, where the man had finally extended this invitation.

Chaz lined up the little white boxes precisely on the counter. Crispy duck and orange filled the air, and Jace's stomach growled. "Be prepared to be tested almost immediately." Chaz upended the bag, and chopsticks clattered about. "Anticipate trick questions. The license for C-4 explosives we've backdated for your construction firm is your carrot into this group, but enough reporters and law enforcement have infiltrated these groups that you should expect a lot of traps." He paused dramatically, his stare as fierce as a drill sergeant's. "The entire op rests on how convincing you are tonight. You don't get a take two."

Jace nodded. "You've mentioned that a few times."

"You really think this danger is something you should joke about?"

"Enough," Heidi said in a tired voice, and Jace didn't bother to look over. He was being immature and obnoxious. Yeah, Chaz annoyed the hell out of him, but truth be told, Jace *was* anxious. He embraced this chance to finally prove himself. Still his upper lip was beginning to perspire. He turned to grab paper plates and paper towels for napkins, while surreptitiously wiping his mouth on his sleeve.

"Let's pretend I'm Man-o-War," Chaz said in a conciliatory tone. "Why do you think you'll be a good fit for the Race as opposed to any other white supremacist group?"

The last three words were all but spat out, and Jace's skin prickled at the loathing in his voice. Chaz's tense expression spoke of lifelong racial injustice, and yet here he was, deep in a white supremacy op.

And here was Jace, having to say the n-word again to a Black man. He steeled himself against the fluttering in his stomach.

"I despise armchair warriors," he answered flatly. "Most groups are all talk and no action. I want a hand in saving the white race from niggers and wetbacks and towelheads, and I want brothers who have an actual plan."

"Too philosophical," Chaz barked. "They'll see through you in an instant. You're pussyfooting through the slurs. Put more *emotion* into it." He stabbed the box of rice with his chopsticks. "*Nigger. Wetback. Towelhead.* Do it again."

Everything in his tight expression backed up the judgments he hadn't held back on earlier this week: Jace wasn't ready, the op had been pulled together too fast, an experienced UCA should've been chosen...

Jace huffed out an exasperated breath. At himself. His ego wasn't so inflated that he couldn't see the truth behind those concerns. His prior experiences had been nothing like this. SEALs were over-prepared for *every* scenario. They expected missions to go FUBAR and rehearsed backup scenarios from Plan B to Z. Undercover ops? They were one hundred percent fly-by-the-seat-of-your-pants. Sink or swim. Survive by your wits and your acting ability. The potential for fucking this up was huge. The likely result: death.

His lip was so damp that he didn't bother to hide the sleeve swipe this time. He had to nail this interview. In a forceful voice, he said, "There *will* be an imminent race war. It's only a matter of time before whites take back our country. We need to get beyond the goddamn narrative and accelerate the destruction of this Zionistic government. The Race is the only group with a plan, and I want in."

"Pretty good," Heidi said quietly. "But you avoided the slurs."

"If nigger is too much for you, it's just as derogatory to

use Negro. Prolonging the vowels makes it especially offensive for my race," Chaz said. "Nee-grow."

The matter-of-fact tone Chaz used while teaching how to denigrate people was too much. Jace couldn't even bring himself to look over, much less acknowledge it.

Once again Heidi read him right. "Jace, you need to embrace the labels. Emote more fear-laced hate. These men honestly believe their Caucasian way of life is in threat of extinction. This is their fight for *survival*."

"Yeah, but some of this conspiracy shit is just so out there," he said. "Even you've said there's ridiculing of one group versus another for their beliefs. How do I know how crazy I need to sound?"

"Easy," she answered. "No matter how revolting Man-o-War's world-view is tonight, you spew it right back. Under no circumstance do you correct him or back away from using racial slurs."

"Yep, yep. Got it with the racial slurs already."

Chaz's face shut down and Jace turned away, gut churning with...frustration? Guilt? Disgust? How did undercover agents survive turning into the very thing they hated?

It was one thing to hear others use slurs. Jace had been exposed to "naughty" words on the playground by older, cooler boys, but he'd only ever played along without uttering slanderous terms, because provoking his father's wrath was to be strictly avoided. Nothing sent Pop around the bend quite like overhearing one of his sons verbally disrespecting another race or religion. Somewhere in the years of growing up under his father's roof, it became a principle Jace had adopted too.

Now, in this brightly lit kitchen, he was being forced again and again by a Black man and female supervisor to practice sounding more *authentically* bigoted. His skin crawled with self-loathing. How would he survive this op? Or fool Man-o-War? At the moment, he didn't have the slightest idea. When the time came to spew racial hatred tonight, he'd have to figure something out on the fly.

Reaching for a paper plate, even though his stomach was now a knotted ball, he said, "I plan to bring up how pumped I am that so many Muslims lost their lives in June and ask if one of their cells had a hand in it."

"Oh, hell no!" Chaz bellowed. "Don't ask *any* questions. Don't mention the bombing. This initial meet is all about you wanting in the organization with just the basic info you've found on them. I doubt he's going to welcome you aboard without the leader speaking to you, so just play it cool. Let the interview end without trying to close the deal."

Jace gave a short jerk of his head. If the opportunity arose, it would be stupid to not take it, but he wouldn't argue further. Chaz's fuse looked shorter than a pinhead, not that Jace could blame him.

Heidi slid a booklet over the counter. "Here are guidelines for the progress reports we expect. I highly advise you to write them up immediately after every point of contact. The second you let one night slip, the documentation will bury you."

He groaned inwardly.

"Post racist shit on your Jason McGowan's social pages all day," Chaz ordered him. "Be on there every free moment and tag the Race on everything. Like and comment on even the most degrading posts. The more you're offended, the more you get behind that particular opinion."

Perspiration recoated Jace's upper lip. "Got it."

"We'll be monitoring the regular chat rooms, but they

have a private one that hopefully you'll be invited to soon." Chaz tapped the booklet with a chopstick. "It'll tell you in here, but let me reiterate—copy and paste every conversation you post for our files, too. And if they have any active plans to rob, bomb, or kill, we want you at the head of the volunteer line."

"Got it."

"Wear the wire every time you go out of this house," Heidi said.

"Yep."

She laid a hand on his forearm, like he was answering too fast or too flippantly. Worry lines etched her brow. "Our van will say One-Stop Cleaners. We'll be on the south side of the park. I can't conceive of this op going haywire at such an early stage, but if you're in imminent danger, your emergency word is *Orlando*. Your emergency signal is to take off your coat and throw it on the ground. We'll come running."

"Got it."

"Never, *ever* get in the subject's car," Chaz said. "You automatically lose control of the situation. Make up any excuse to drive. If they push it, then you need to ask yourself why. It can't be a good reason."

"Got it. When do we press about the mosque bombing?"

"When you've gained their trust," Chaz barked.

"Yes, but what's the typical ETA?" Jace spread his hands. "Are we talking weeks? Months?"

Heidi shrugged apologetically.

Chaz snorted. "You're in this for the long haul, Quinn. I've had ops go on for a couple–three years. Those cushy fifty-hour workweeks are over. From tonight on, you're Jason McGowan, construction supervisor living in Mayfair. You live and breathe white supremacy dogma and collect evidence until we have a prosecutorial case that Heather thinks is airtight, you dig?"

Jace swiped his upper lip. "Yep." Getting the op underway would be a hell of a lot better than this tedious training and documentation. He was born for action. He looked forward to proving himself to these two.

10

S hit, she'd forgotten to warn Jace about his body language. Heidi grimaced, squinting through her binoculars at the virgin undercover agent striding alongside the white supremacist. They were an hour into the meet-and-greet, and verbally it was going smoothly, but Jace's crossed arms, stony face, and lack of eye contact were highly problematic. Even without her honed sense of deciphering body language, Jace's blatant signals of rejecting Man-o-War's racist rants were a dead giveaway. He'd seemed so perfect for this op...

"Ya feel me?" Man-o-War said for the umpteenth time, almost bouncing with twitchy energy. The tall, thin man was unfortunately unidentifiable because the collar of his green peacoat was turned up and his knit cap was pulled low.

"I do, man. Something's gotta be done."

"We're sinking here," Chaz said under his breath, followed by the whirring of his Nikon.

"Cut him some slack." Heidi swallowed the cold lump of fear. "He can do this."

"The only reason this op hasn't gone belly up is

because Man-o-War is on such a tirade he's lost focus of the interview."

"Well, we just got evidence for the Chi-Town Firearms robbery we can hand over to the CPD, thanks to Jace. That's not bad for a night's work."

Chaz grunted an acknowledgment. The camera whirred another dozen photos in a split second. Heidi's phone dinged, and she lowered the binoculars. The text was from an analyst working overtime with the FBI's NGI system to identify the probe photos they'd sent over of Man-o-War.

Attaching 2 potentials

The download showed two mug shots of men with similar features along with their rap sheets. Heidi showed the photos to Chaz. "I wish Man-o-War wasn't so bundled up."

Chaz pointed to the second photo. A bearded man with dirty-blond hair shaved on the sides and sprouting on top glared at them. Behind him was the standard height chart. "I'd say he's closer to six-four than six-two."

"Travis Wayne Trenton," Heidi read off.

"Why are all the fucktards named Wayne?"

"Thirty-two years old. Three arrests dating back eight years. Convicted of possession of a controlled substance with thirty days' jail time and thirty-six months' probation, third-degree assault with charges dropped, and robbery with a firearm, a thousand-dollar fine, two years' jail, three years' probation."

"Now why is a nice white boy like you screwing up your privileged life?" Chaz murmured into the lens, resuming the photographic documentation. Through their headsets, Man-o-War was giving a detailed example of how to blow up the commuter track at the 111th Street-Pullman station.

"Good," Heidi said, "we've segued into bombing." *Come on, Jace, dangle the carrot. Don't let me down.*

"Hundred and eleventh would be a great choice," Jace agreed. "Neighborhood's so vandalized that any security cameras probably don't work."

"The Race has friends who work in a couple of surveillance shops around town." Man-o-War spat on the sand-packed path. "We can get a heads-up anytime on camera placements, angles, and which ones are needing repair. Hundred and eleventh is basically dark, and the cops could give a shit patrolling those neighborhoods. Let the gangs kill each other off."

"Yo, I got access to C-4," Jace said, and Heidi sent up a prayer of thanks. When she opened her eyes, another prayer was met. Jace was finally animated, arms swinging at his side, head turning in active engagement. "Your example, it'd only take a small amount, say five kilograms."

Man-o-War halted, a long breath vaporizing in the chilly night air. "Does it come in a stick or something?"

"More like modeling clay." Jace pantomimed a small brick with his hands. "All you'd do is insert a blasting cap, mold it to the side of the track, and blam!"

The twitchy energy increased tenfold as Man-o-War performed a stilted dance, arms jerking upward in celebration then swinging into an umpire's you're-out motion. "Damn, that'd show them." He whooped into the night sky.

"You just tell me what you need...who to speak to. I want in, Man-o-War. I wanna be a part of the team."

"Yeah, yeah." Man-o-War bounced on the balls of his feet. He had to be hopped up on something. "I can tell you're one of us. We can probably drop our onscreen names. I'm Travis."

"Bingo, motherfucker." Chaz lowered the camera. "What a gullible idiot."

"Jason." Jace stuck out his hand, and they shook. "What happens next?"

"I report in to Calvin; he's the head of us."

"Yeah, I know. The guy in Russia."

"Well, he's seeking asylum there for the moment, but he's actively involved with all of us and plans to take over a huge territory in the Northwest. A white ethnostate." Travis paused, his expression just short of rapturous. "Anyway, he'll call you if he thinks you're a good fit, and man, I'm giving you a glowing rec. Then he assigns you to a cell, probably not mine. Each team keeps to themselves. We don't interact unless it's something big—"

"Like when those Ramadan motherfuckers got blown up," Jace finished.

Heidi gasped. Chaz held the camera suspended halfway to his face. "Too soon, man," he growled. "You blew it."

A beat or two passed. An eternity that stretched forever.

"Well." Travis chuckled nervously. "I don't know about that. But something like that. Something big."

"Cool."

Heidi exhaled and pulled the nail she'd been biting out of her mouth, then looked at it as if it didn't belong to her. She hadn't bitten her nails since sixth grade. What the hell was this?

The two men shook again, reassured each other of their outstanding impression of the other, and went in separate directions. Travis immediately dug out his cell phone and made a call. Jace hummed tunelessly as he headed out of the park, steps brisk, hands in the pockets of his jeans. "I'm clear," he muttered, following Chaz's adamant training of signaling the van crew the moment he felt safe enough for them to stand down.

"It was a good first meet, I gotta give him that," Heidi said, packing away the binoculars.

"He did okay." Chaz tucked the camera in the Styrofoam mold and shifted the van into gear. "He's gotta learn to control that ego of his. Might work for a SEAL, but it'll bring down an undercover agent in a New York minute."

"Do you mind dropping me off at his house?" Good. Her voice sounded casual. "Even though this was a preliminary meet, I might as well begin the hot washes."

He didn't answer. The intermittent glow of streetlights illuminated his knowing grin.

"I'm his handler," she snapped.

"I know."

"Then stop inferring anything sexual. I'm a supervisor doing her duty to make sure a subordinate remains psychologically fit. His house provides the most privacy. That's all."

The mocking half-smile remained. It took a long moment for him to answer. "If only you could convince yourself of that too, Case Agent Hall."

JACE CROSSED the street and began the long process of what Chaz called dry-washing—zigzagging his way home through random streets, doubling back, stalling in shadows, all to make sure he wasn't being followed.

Within blocks, the dynamic stress of the last hour converted to a giddy endorphin rush. Modesty aside, the op had gone exceptionally well. Sure, he wanted to wash his mouth out with soap, but he'd left enough of an impression that the leader in Russia, who went by at least five aliases, would be in touch.

This was the first real break for MOSQMO in months, and—

His footsteps slowed. The first big break, and no one to tell. His euphoria faded. Just like his clandestine SEAL missions, tonight's accomplishment would end up a measly footnote in a confidential filing cabinet.

He grasped his cell phone but couldn't bring himself to pull it out of his pocket. Calling Heidi to get her take on the night would totally come off as insecure. Like he was fishing for compliments. But a part of him was. Acting wasn't in his wheelhouse. Becoming a radicalized racist after only three weeks of training deserved some kind of acknowledgement.

And Chaz sure wasn't the type to offer up praise or constructive criticism—it was trial by fire with that guy, just like Pop's strategy of raising five boys. Substitute Chaz's name with Heidi's, and the answers were immediate and emphatic: Jace couldn't give a flying fuck what the experienced UCA thought of this initial performance. Which left the uncomfortable final question—why should Heidi's opinion mean anything different?

He withdrew his hand and ascended the El platform. Skip calling Heidi. Time to revert to Jace Quinn, FBI special agent associate, and provide the extensive documentation and legal backup for the assistant U.S. attorney. He was just fine celebrating tonight's success with Chinese leftovers and a beer.

Thirty-five minutes later, he strolled up his driveway, spying a shadowed figure in the darkened doorway. Before he could reach for his Glock, a voice called out, "It's me."

Heidi's silky tone ushered back memories of the free-spirited woman he'd first met, and his heart beat an extra couple of thuds.

"What are you doing here?" he asked as he

approached. The nighttime had softened her face. Her wide eyes looked luminous, and the way she huddled in the threshold for warmth resembled a timid teen waiting for her crush. He, of all people, knew how deceptive the illusion was.

"After each encounter, the operative and handler talk about how it all went down," she said, her words misting and dissipating. "It's called a ho—"

"Hot wash." He unlocked the door, flicked on the living room light, and stood aside to let her pass. "SEALs require it too." He shot the bolt and nodded to the false light switch. "Do we record it?"

"No. You talk, I take notes. No pulling rank, no judgment." Her rosy cheeks glowed with impish health, and she smelled of fresh night air. She handed him her coat, adding, "Consider this a time to be brutally honest about yourself, Chaz, me. I have a feeling you'll thrive at hot washes." Her chocolate-brown eyes sparkled with feisty humor, like when she'd beckoned him up her smooth calf.

A thrum of raw desire pulsed through his veins. After weeks of surviving her battleax-supervisor persona, here she was again, this funny, vibrant woman. Did she know she gave off such a sexy vibe? Would this take-charge energy extend into the bedroom? Not the kind of woman he usually chose to have sex with, but the thought of a mutual struggle for dominance between the sheets was suddenly crazy hot. Did she want him to make a move? He was never any good at reading women's signals.

"Is everything all right?" Her brows knitted, forming a wrinkle above the bridge of her nose, and he blinked to attention. Jeez, he was still standing here like a glorified coatrack.

Roughly clearing his throat, he motioned to the sofa. "Have a seat. Can I get you something to drink?"

"Water is fine, thanks."

Folding her coat over the nearest chair, he escaped to the kitchen and forcefully pulled himself together. Enough with the fantasies. What a massive complication it'd be to bed his boss. His track record with women was love 'em and leave 'em, but there was no leaving this woman. He'd see her almost daily until this op was complete. Nope. The fallout wasn't worth it. He'd have to keep this smoldering attraction locked down. Problem solved.

Jace returned with an ice water for her and a beer for himself. Heidi was tucked into a corner of the sofa, so he grabbed the wing-back chair on the far side of the room, ignoring the surprise flashing across her face. He hoisted his bottle in a salute. "Here's to the initial meet."

"Yes." She sipped her water and placed the glass on the coaster, then swiped her iPad awake. "I know you've still got documentation ahead of you and this was a minor encounter, so I'll limit this to a couple of questions."

"Shoot."

"How do you think tonight went?"

"Outstanding." Jace stretched his legs and crossed his ankles. "I hooked Travis. I know Calvin Sheer will contact me from Russia, and I'm as good as in. How do *you* think it went?"

She gazed at his jiggling foot for a beat, then blinked back up at him. "This is your hot wash. It's your opinion that matters." A trace of that no-nonsense curtness was back. "How could this evening have gone better?"

He swigged beer to stall for time. Honestly, he couldn't have improved anything, but if he said as much, he'd come off looking arrogant. And why did she keep fixating on his foot? He sat up, planting his boots firmly on the rug. "It would've gone better if I'd figured out a way to get Travis to implicate the Race for Mosque Mohammed." He slumped back, frowning. Undercover work was like anticipating two sentences beyond the present moment. How would Chaz, with all his bravado and experience, have scripted the scene?

"So you were hoping to wrap up this case in one night?"

He laughed, but it sounded false even to him. Heidi had a way of reading him that was disconcerting. And he didn't appreciate the hidden rebuke that came with that mild tone. "No," he countered. "I'm not an imbecile. I get the complexity of this case. I know it'll take months to crack. You asked me what could have gone better, and that's my answer."

"Are you anxious about something, Jace?"

"Me? No." Why the hell would she ask that? Oh, right. She was peering at his knee now, which happened to have taken over the jiggling. He anchored it too. "Burning off adrenalin."

The worry wrinkle above her brow didn't smooth away. She closed the cover of her iPad. "Why don't we finish here tonight? And even though I just told you this isn't the place for supervisory feedback, let me add that I think you did a fantastic job. I'm really pleased."

Instantly his muscles drained of tension. His hyperactive limbs stilled. How strange—he hadn't been aware he was even remotely uptight. "Thanks."

"Is there anything you'd like to ask or tell me?" She grinned, her upturned palm sweeping in a welcome gesture. "Anything goes in confidential hot washes."

There was only one question front and center in his brain. It had been there for weeks. Why not? "Who's Dave?"

"Dave?"

"From the wedding."

The flash of startled recollection, like she'd forgotten all about him until this moment, was a good beginning. "Oh, uh." A long moment passed as indecipherable expressions warred across her face. Finally, she braced her shoulders and lifted her chin. "He's my foster brother. There were nine of us, but we were oldest."

Jace gaped. She grew up in foster care? She went to weddings with her *brother*? The follow-up questions tumbling through his mind were mostly inappropriate to ask. In the end he blurted, "He couldn't find a date for himself?"

She shrugged. "Dave is a highly sensitive individual and tends to be overly anxious where women are concerned. I happened to be flying to Chicago for the case agent interview, so it seemed easiest to go as his plus-one."

"Huh." Having grown up with four brothers, none of whom could even remotely be described as being overly anxious with women, it was hard to formulate an opinion on the gesture. Was it generous? Enabling? But the foster care bombshell... Was it rude to ask for more details? "How long were you in the foster system?"

"I'm not comfortable discussing that," she said, the snappish supervisor tone solidly back. She stood and tapped her cell phone screen. A few seconds later, a half-smile appeared. "Good. My rideshare is only a couple blocks away."

Jace managed to get to her coat before she did and held it out for her. The easy rapport was ruined. He should have kept his mouth shut. "Let me walk you to the curb," he said, escorting her to the door.

Heidi chuckled. "I'm a fully trained agent armed with a gun, Jace."

Wordlessly he opened the door and followed her into the frigid night. He'd caught on to her prickly response whenever he or Chaz conformed to traditional male gestures, like holding doors or escorting her in the dark. Her chin would jut out; her responses became terse and dismissive. Well, tough shit. He'd been brought up this way, and in these brief moments, she'd have to survive being treated as the more vulnerable sex in need of protection.

The headlights of the rideshare blinded them as it pulled to the curb, and Jace snatched the door handle a second before she could. "Have a good night, Heidi."

"Thank you," she said curtly, sliding inside.

He watched the taillights until the car turned out of sight, his mind churning with the startling information he'd gathered. A ballbuster of a boss, who rarely let her sexy, feminine side loose, had been raised in foster care and was either generous or protective enough to attend a wedding to shield her brother's odd insecurity about women. Personalities didn't get more complex than that. He stepped back inside with a sigh and flicked off the outdoor lights. He might not be able to sleep with her, but before the op was through, he'd figure out which box she belonged in and get her out of his head.

11

"We're an equal-opportunity hate group. If you're not white, you don't belong on our land," the Race leader said.

"Amen." Jace rolled his eyes. Although this phone conversation was a testament that he'd made enough of an impression, Calvin Sheer was a condescending ass. "I understand you've bought parcels out in Oregon."

"Over thirty acres. It was a steal because the area is too remote to ever install utilities. Which is perfect for us. This will be our training facility." He paused for a bronchial cough. "Sorry. Anyway, it's a requirement for every one of our soldiers to go through paramilitary exercises as soon as possible. Is that something you could commit to?"

"Hell yeah, with enough notice to arrange my schedule and get a replacement manager. I'm not sure how much Travis told you, but I'm a supervisor with Whitehead Construction."

"He did indeed tell me that, as well as about your access to C-4." Sheer's voice echoed slightly, like he was speaking in a tunnel. "And your military experience at SEAL boot camp."

"I washed out." Jace cringed as he laughed at his lie. "Those guys are a cut above. But I learned a lot and am willing to use it to 'pick up the pace,' as your posters say. When do I join a crew?"

"Our micro-teams are formed by me and based on what motivates you most. Me? I want to annihilate every Jew off the fucking planet, heil Hitler, but if you're inspired to kill niggers, then I'll stick you with like-minded people."

Jace gripped the phone tighter. This was it. "Muslims." He let the word seep through clenched teeth. "They're all a bunch of fucking jihadists and should never have been allowed to set foot in America."

"Ah, still marked by nine-eleven, I see." Sheer had an oddly formal way of speaking, although the extensive research into the recluse indicated he was mid-forties, with a tristate East Coast background. Not a trace of a New York accent, though.

"Nine-eleven is why I signed up to be a Navy SEAL right outta high school," Jace said. That much was true. His career among the most elite of forces was still his single greatest achievement. "Put me with a cell that can replicate the success of that mosque bombing last June, and I'll make you proud."

A pause stretched over the line. Air stagnated in his lungs. Chaz's rebuke of pushing the conversation too early swept over him. He'd thrown down the ace too soon. He'd blown it. Jace's stomach flipped like an Olympian on a balance beam. More people would die because he couldn't take the Race down. How would he ever live with this failure?

"That's actually convenient," Sheer finally said, and Jace expelled a silent breath. "We lost the lead member of a particularly important cell last month. You sound like you'd be a perfect fit."

Thomas Bradley, the decomposed corpse. "Hook me up."

"We've checked into you, and you definitely qualify for entry into the Race. But we do have an initiation of sorts."

"Sure, Calvin, what's that?"

"We demand one act of racial violence to prove your loyalty beyond a shadow of a doubt."

Hair prickled up Jace's neck. Racial violence? Maybe given all the UCOs over the years, the FBI could set up an illusion and stay within the law. Besides, it wasn't his problem—whatever Sheer suggested, Heidi would have to orchestrate. "Sounds fair," he said evenly. "You want me to think one up, or do you dictate what it is?"

"I want you to rape a Muslim woman."

Jace's heart stalled. No way. End of mission. Even the illusion of assault was too much. He regained enough composure to utter, "Maybe you didn't hear me. I loathe Muslims. No fucking way I'm sticking my dick in one."

"You will if you want in."

Jace wiped his upper lip, mind ticking through a thousand scenarios on how the task force could pull this off. Maybe dummy up some pictures as proof? Maybe there was a Middle Eastern female agent who'd agree to staging a roughed-up attack? Jace swallowed convulsively, the panicked, trapped-rat feeling gnawing at his chest both new and abhorrent. "I don't know if I could get it up enough to finish," he admitted.

"It's all about showing us how committed you are, Jason."

The sound of the receiver being covered and Sheer hacking up a lung gave Jace precious time to get his act together. Shit, this was hard, living the life of someone he despised. Not having a team around to draw bravado from or shoot the shit with to decompress from wandering down this darkly evil path.

"Sorry." Sheer's voice sounded strangled. "Caught one of my kids' upper respiratory infection."

Goosebumps remained at attention. That this monster had a wife and kids and a loving side was beyond imagination. "I'm in," Jace said, suddenly anxious to get off the phone and contact Heidi and Chaz so they could start brainstorming what the fuck they were going to do. "I'll provide some kind of evidence when the deed is done."

"I'll do you one better," Sheer said in an amused tone. "The head of your cell will be Nate. I'm going to give him the heads-up that he's got a new member on board. He'll text you a designated meeting place within twenty-four hours and point out the woman you're to target. He'll also stick around while you do the dirty deed, so we have eyes-on proof you're ready for our way of life."

Heart now thumping off-rhythm, Jace managed to change the profanity-laced refusal to a strangled sound. "I *know* I can't perform if some strange fucker is watching me."

Sheer laughed, which brought up more respiratory gunk. "This isn't some homo experience, Jason. His primary goal is to gauge the extent of your hatred for Muslims. Maybe he'll have a go at her after you're through, but who cares, am I right? Don't disappoint me. Get it done."

———

HEIDI IGNORED Jace's agitated pacing and Chaz's I-told-you-so glare. She was in way over her head. It was taking all her energy to hide her panic from these alpha know-it-alls. Setting her cell phone back down on Jace's White-head Construction office desk, she said calmly, "I've emailed Janus for recommendations." The FBI department responsible for all the backstopping authentication for these undercover operatives had a global pulse on agents. Janus knew who was available, who had prior op experience, and who could pass for a Muslim woman for an evening. "We don't have the luxury of developing a full persona for her, so I've asked them to set her up with one of their pre-made shelf IDs. Add a round trip to Chicago, and this nightmare initiation will be behind us."

"So what if Janus finds the perfect Muslim?" Chaz said, spreading his hands. "How are we going to fool this Nate standing two feet away?"

Heidi waved away his scorn with a flip of her wrist. "That's secondary to making sure the woman is a trained operative." She swallowed past the lump in her throat, thinking fast. There had to be a solution! "Hollywood does it all the time; we just have to seek advice on how to stage the optics. Like maybe Jace turns his back on Nate and presses her up against a wall."

Chaz shook his head. "A victim can still flail left or right. She'll topple right out of his arms."

Heidi bolted up from behind the desk, her brain firing scenarios to drop-kick this constant barrage of pessimism. It hadn't escaped her that those two finally saw eye to eye on a subject—criticizing her leadership skills. Neither had offered any solutions of their own. "Maybe if Jace anchors the woman to the wall with his shoulders?" she said on an exasperated breath. "Maybe..." *Got it!* She stabbed a finger at Jace. "Hoist me up and wedge me in that corner."

Jace's jaw dropped.

Chaz sputtered, "What?"

Heidi marched to the corner by the door and backed

into the wall, waving him over. If this was what it took to gain their damn confidence...

Jace hesitantly obeyed, stopping before her. She lifted her arms. "I'll struggle for real. Let's see if this works." It *had* to work.

He turned and glanced at Chaz, who was observing wide-eyed, like he was watching a ten-car pileup.

"Let's get this over with," she snapped, her face in flames.

Jace half squatted and clasped the curved area where her buttocks ended and her hamstrings began. The tips of his ears reddened. "Sorry in advance," he muttered. In one fluid motion, he hoisted her to his waist.

This lewd position awoke the Flirt, the hungry side who'd fantasized about the forceful press of his groin more often than she cared to admit. Heidi shoved her into the recesses where she belonged. Her entire career was at stake here. The Flirt was not welcome.

Heidi gripped his taut, coiled, rock-hard shoulder muscles and leaned in, smelling male soap and crisp fabric softener. Their combined body heat was causing a combustible flashover inside her. "All right," she said crisply, "pin me against the wall."

He slowly pressed her into the corner, until her back protested the uncomfortable forward bend. She swallowed the instinctive directives like "that's enough" or "stop right there." This had to look authentic, and she had to pre-gauge what the female agent would experience. Already her lungs felt squeezed, and panic buttons pinged terror messages in her brain.

"We need to stop meeting like this." Although Jace's words were uttered through grinning lips, tension lined his jaw. His irises were a mesmerizing blue, many shades darker than normal.

She tore her gaze away, focusing on Chaz, watching

with a skeptical tilt of one eyebrow. "You be Nate, standing there watching," she ordered him, cursing the breathiness of her voice. It wasn't the Flirt—she wasn't getting enough air! "I'm going to fight like this is real. Let's see if the illusion works."

Chaz sauntered closer and folded his arms. "Knock yourselves out."

"Here we go." She veered violently to the left. Jace shifted his considerable upper body mass to easily restrain her, fake thrusting. More of her panicked, like her body didn't know this was pretend. She genuinely struggled, swerved, pushed. His pelvis hammered into hers. Hair flopping in her sweaty face, she violently shoved those broad shoulders with all her might, but she was locked in. The constriction of his weight on her chest compressed her lungs. The scenario had hardly begun and she was out of fight. "Enough."

Thankfully, Jace immediately eased away. She sucked in fresh air.

"See?" she gasped. "Between the struggling and screaming, and all the flowing fabric from the whatever it's called— caftan? —there's no way Nate will be able to tell what's going on."

"I agree," Chaz said with grudging respect.

Jace gently lowered her to her feet. His face was flushed, but he wasn't the slightest bit out of breath, which was impressive. She ignored the protrusion in his pants. She hadn't even remotely experienced that kind of a response. She'd proven her point but ended up shaken and slightly sick.

He turned away from both of them, tucking in a corner of his shirt. "How are we going to stop Nate from having a go?"

"We'll have CPD on standby." That part was easily solved. "The second you're 'done'"—she used air quotes

—"the lights and sirens come on. It would make sense that a witness would've overheard the struggle and called the police." She winced and bent backward to ease her cramping lat muscles, then walked back behind Jace's desk on wobbly legs and sank gracelessly into his chair.

"We'll instruct CPD to make sure you and Nate get a head start running away." She nodded to herself. This could work. "Maybe the Muslim agent can bite down on a fake blood capsule to add a hint of violence."

"It's crazy enough to succeed, but you're gonna have to control every aspect of this scene, Case Agent Hall." Chaz's clipped words dripped with warning. The formality of her title instead of her name was not lost on anyone. He was completely distancing himself from this.

"We'll write out each step in the sequence. Rehearse it again if we have to." Not with her, though. The Muslim UCA could take it from here. "As soon as Jace knows where the meet will be, we'll scour the locale for the perfect angle to limit Nate's view."

Jace tapped his temple. "I see it. This can work."

Chaz rolled his eyes.

"What? That's how we train in the SEALs. We visualized every aspect of the mission."

Instead of engaging, Chaz said, "I'm going to hit the head."

"Down the hall to your right."

When the door closed behind him, Jace sat on the other side of the desk. He leaned his forearms onto his knees, once again offering her a glorious view of the wide expanse of shoulders and rolling curves of his biceps. How was she ever going to master this incendiary attraction?

"Are you okay?" he asked quietly, his gaze intense.

She huffed a laugh. "Except for feeling like I went

through a spin cycle, I'm hunky-dory. How are you holding up?"

Those shoulders squeezed into a shrug. "I have to get past the revulsion of what I'm doing."

"Keep your mind on the long-term objective. Once you're in with a cell, you can dig for irrefutable proof they were responsible for the bombing."

"Taking down a three-man cell of this beast isn't going to do much."

"That's the beauty of Sheer's setup, isn't it?" Heidi said. "Losing one cell is a small sacrifice. A blip in his overall goal to keep destabilizing society. It's essential we collect irrefutable audio and video evidence that will implicate *him*. If we can show he was behind the order to bomb Mosque Mohammed, we can take down the entire Race operation."

Chaz returned and sprawled in the chair beside Jace with a grunt. Ignoring him, Jace cocked his head. "How would we extradite Sheer from Russia?"

"We'll have to find a way to lure him back here."

Jace snorted. "You sure have lofty goals for someone without a plan. This flying by the seat of my pants is a real stretch for me."

"Don't think of it like that," Chaz said quietly. "Being undercover is like being both the actor and the screen-writer. You don't know the next sentence out of the perp's mouth, so you need to keep creating the script. You also don't know what he may misinterpret or what triggers him to reach for his weapon. Start relying on your intu-ition. Learn to read the situation and then react. You're going to need it to survive."

Jace looked away. Inwardly, Heidi sighed. The dynamic between these two was still tense and distrust-ful. Someone with an elite military background probably wouldn't find Chaz's actor analogy comforting.

She tapped the thick black notebook on the desk. "Jace, this is a Grade Two op with reams of readymade scenarios and scripts. There are suggestions in here on how we can get them to admit their crimes while meeting the legal threshold Heather needs. We have warrants for state-of-the-art video and audio surveillance, and a budget that is surprisingly generous. You are supported."

"But we don't have the entire task force at our disposal anymore," he countered, "because for some reason this is top secret."

Chaz studied her right alongside Jace, but neither was getting enlightened that there was a traitor on the team. A traitor that had so far left no clues.

She leaned her forearms on the desk, anchoring herself in a dominant position. "Just know they're working their end, and this op is the most important part of the investigation. You still need to up your game at selling your hatred."

Jace grimaced but nodded. He flipped his buzzing phone over and glanced at the screen. "It's that Nate guy," he said, and blew through pursed lips. "The meet is on for four o'clock tomorrow."

Chaz slapped his knees. "Showtime."

12

"How's everything proceeding?" SAC Webb leaned back in his chair, his smile expansive. He looked like the epitome of an FBI agent: clean-shaven, neatly trimmed silver hair, and attired in a sharp navy pinstripe suit. Beside him, ASAC Garcia was the younger, darkly attractive Hispanic version.

Heidi raked a hand through the bob she'd only had time to damp-comb after massively oversleeping. Her eyes stung from staring at her computer screen into the wee hours. Her muscles felt fatigued and at the same time stretched tight—how long since she'd worked out? She filed the thought away and filled them in on Jace's remarkable progress and the meet that had been set up for this afternoon.

As the men traded pleased looks, Heidi took the opportunity to suck down more coffee, mindless of the lukewarm temperature. Her mouth needed the moisture, and her cells screamed for caffeine. "On the task force front," she went on, "we've discovered chemical markers on the ANFO evidence that trace back to several fertilizer manufacturing plants in the upper Midwest. We're gathering warrants to collect samples, which should narrow the field. Since the amount is so substantial and yet none of the plants reported a theft, our hunch is that one or more employees are affiliated with the Race. We've ruled out Thomas Bradley—he had no license to acquire the fertilizer—so we believe our unsub may be a plant supervisor or someone in an oversight position. They'd be the sole person to know their factory is short five thousand pounds."

"Makes sense." Webb nodded again. "Good work, Heidi. Now where do we stand on finding the leak?"

She clutched the mug in both hands. "Nothing so far, sir. I've found each member of my task force to be extremely dedicated to their particular job. No one's slacking off; everyone cooperates and seems highly driven. I pride myself on reading body language and am getting no overt signals. I'm still poring through everyone's personnel files, but I haven't found any connection to the Race or white supremacy."

"Have we had any kind of reoccurrence?" Garcia asked.

Heidi shook her head. "No media leaks, either. Could be the person wised up or is lying low... Or maybe they're suspicious that we've been tipped off." Could even be that the leak was Mark Hennessey, covering his tracks by throwing shade on someone on the team.

She sucked in a breath. Where had that notion come from? It was far out in left field, but worth checking out. His was the only file she hadn't scoured.

"Very well." Webb leaned forward to tap his computer awake. "Keep us apprised."

Reading the obvious dismissal, Heidi excused herself and trekked to the other side of the block-long building, frustration making her footsteps an angry click-click. Until she found the traitor, anything the team uncovered was at risk to be leaked to the Race. And compartmental-izing the tasks to a handful of agents and analysts just to narrow the search field slowed the investigation's forward momentum to a crawl. None of this was acceptable, and neither was the creepy spied-upon feeling that every decision she made was being leaked. Who was it?

Once in her office, she filled out the internal paper-work to acquire Mark's personnel file.

"Case Agent Hall?" The timid voice was paired with a timid knock, and she glanced up with an automatic smile. A familiar analyst stood there—Katie? Kelly? When they were first introduced, Heidi had thought the petite, pixie-faced woman looked like she was twelve. "You were due at our breakout meeting twenty minutes ago, ma'am."

"Oh gosh," Heidi said, jumping up. "I'll be right there. Tell them... Well, never mind. I'll tell them."

The young woman slipped away as Heidi hurriedly collected the appropriate files, kicking herself for forget-ting about the meeting. This was more of the same brain fog that had plagued her all morning. She'd thrown out her toothbrush instead of the floss, stuck the cereal box in the mini refrigerator, and now this. God knew what else she hadn't yet caught.

"Sorry, sorry," she exclaimed, racing into the meeting room. Alma Reyes, Manny Gonzales, Josh Peters, Bill Fontana, the pixie analyst, and another woman kicked back around a table littered with laptops, coffee mugs, and colored file folders.

Heidi claimed a seat, dumped her files beside her, and flipped open her laptop. "Bill, where are we with the Bradley murder inquiry?" As he opened his file, she sped to the sideboard that held a single-serve coffee machine and accoutrements, and helped herself to more caffeine, even though her hands were shaking.

"Thomas Bradley was last seen on October third," Bill said in an authoritative voice. "Surveillance video from a Shell station a block from his house shows him filling up and then buying cigs and a lottery ticket. Drove off at a quarter to six that evening. Bradley was an independent plumber subcontracting for a residential job out in Arlington Heights. The contractor he worked for says Bradley never showed up after that day."

Great. At least they'd established he'd been dead three days, not five. "So who came to his house the night of the third?"

"We've reinterviewed the neighbors," Bill said, shaking his head, "and combed through all the residential surveillance on the street without success. Besides Bradley's F-150 in the driveway, all other cars drove on by. No one recalls anyone showing up at his home. And forensics show neither the front nor back door was tampered with, so if Bradley was shot, he let the perp in."

"If?" Heidi snapped. "It's unlikely he'd have grabbed his Luger with his non-dominant hand and finished himself off just to confuse the cops."

"My grandfather had a case like that—" Josh began, and Heidi immediately held up a hand. Josh and his generations of FBI case histories... At least he was enthusiastically toeing the line these days.

"Come on, people. No way would he off himself knowing his cat would starve and he would decompose." She tried not to frown at Bill. This was not the progress she'd expected. "Keep on it, Bill. Josh, wow me. What have we found to connect Bradley to the Race?"

"Bradley had two convictions that led to twelve years of jail time," Josh began, swiping his iPad screen. "Got out four years ago. He did his time at Marion Penitentiary in Illinois. Three years for assault and nine for blowing up his girlfriend's car with a pipe bomb. Authorities found a strand of his hair on the duct tape around the device, and there were similar pipes, black powder, and switches found in his basement."

Bill, face fully flushed, glared formidably at Josh. No surprise. Not only had Josh wandered into the cop's area of investigation, but Bradley's experience with pipe bombs was already well known.

"Connection to the Race," Heidi cut in.

"Yeah, okay, I was just giving you the background. I went to the prison and interviewed his cellmate. Bradley was a top lieutenant in the Aryan Brotherhood, a nationally known gang on the inside. His body was covered in Nazi tats, even two lightning bolts on either side of his tongue." Amid the disgusted gasps, Josh stuck out his tongue, pointing to either side of the flat surface. "Cellmate says he couldn't recall a triple sieg-rune, though."

"He could have joined the Race after he was released," Alma remarked with a shrug. "Didn't it only form a few years ago?"

"ME says the body was too decomposed to identify the symbol, but I double-checked the forensic photos anyway. All of them." He stuck his tongue out again, this time making a gagging sound. Of all the team members, he seemed to be the jokester, definitely the most immature. "Didn't eat for a week," he continued gleefully. "End result: no identifiable triple sieg-rune."

"Thank you." Heidi suppressed a shudder at the memory of those grisly autopsy photos. "How about his online communication?" she asked. "Anything there link him to the Race?"

The Katie-Kelly analyst raised her hand. "I looked through his Facebook and Twitter handles; both went back over a decade. It appears he was a member of the National Socialist Liberation Front until that leader passed away, then all his hashtags refer to both Atom-waffen Division and the Race."

"Excellent work, Kelly." Alma high-fived her.

Heidi silently thanked Alma for the correct name, then smiled at Kelly. "The Race adopted a lot of the NSLF playbook when it went defunct. Sounds like a strong connection. Was there any direct communication with Calvin Sheer in those Race posts?"

"On social media it was more like Sheer would affirm something Bradley posted. Or he'd share, retweet, that kind of thing. If they interacted in terms of planning something, it wasn't over such a public forum. But in the alt-right chat group Gab, Bradley mainly railed against multiculturalism and political correctness." She giggled behind her hand. "It's so weird how he and his friends post such ignorant conspiracies but use this highbrow vocabulary. The posts are peppered with words I had to look up, like 'miscegenation.'" She giggled again as she stumbled over the word, then sobered with an apologetic look at Heidi. "It means interracial breeding. Needless to say, they're against it. And they ignore the previous two hundred and fifty years of history and blame the Boomer generation for handing the nation over to immigrants."

Heidi nodded impatiently. They could go down this rabbit hole for hours. "Phone calls? Texts that establish a clear link to Sheer or the Race?"

"That would be me, ma'am, Christine Dankowski." Heidi nodded for the second analyst to proceed, and Christine passed around a one-page list of numbers. "As most of you know, we found a suitcase with twenty-six unopened burners in Bradley's house. We believe he used a burner for a one-time call or a texted conversation and then threw the phone out."

"One phone for one conversation?" Bill rolled his

eyes. "Sounds impractical and expensive, if you ask me." His cop belt creaked as he shifted in the chair.

"You can pick up a burner these days for less than thirty bucks. That's actually incredibly cheap for untraceable privacy." Christine steepled her fingers together— body language for high confidence. Good for her. "Although I doubt many Race members get to a high enough level in the organization to be able to justify that."

She nodded to the copies in front of each of them. "We took the box of unopened phones and were able to search each one's IMEI, their international mobile equipment identity. It's like a car's VIN. In front of you is a list of stores where those phones were purchased. If we get warrants to pull the store receipts, we can cross-check these IMEIs to identify the other phones he bought, used, and threw out. Once we isolate that lot, we'll be able to pull his text and phone data."

Heidi gaped at the brilliant woman. "Excellent work," she said. "Way to think outside the box." The potential leads this could generate made her lightheaded.

Christine's smile held a hint of arrogance, as if receiving praise was second nature, which it probably was. "If we had a way to identify any other Race members," she went on, "we could look up their cell numbers and also target any connection to Bradley that way. *Their* text conversations with him might be accessible."

As one, the team swiveled to look at Heidi, hope on some faces, speculation on others. Heidi didn't have Nate's last name—yet, but she'd kept Travis Trenton's name on the lowdown for two reasons. One, obviously, because there was still a leak somewhere. Two, to make sure Jace could infiltrate successfully enough to get to a terrorism-planning stage.

She made eye contact with her core team in the growing silence, gauging their expressions and body language. In the weeks she'd led them, they'd worked their tails off and problem-solved in ways that were impressive. The instinct to trust these five was strong. If she divulged Travis's name, Christine's data analysis could progress at lightning speed. And if his name was subsequently divulged to the Race, then that narrowed the traitor to these six team members.

The risk was huge, though. If word got back that Travis was under federal investigation, the Race might put two and two together and finger Jace as an undercover agent. She would be putting his safety and his op in grave jeopardy. Was it worth the cost to investigate communication between Travis and Bradley? What should she do? If only she were thinking clearer today.

Heidi inhaled, sending up a quick prayer. "We've identified another name I want checked out, but hear this: whatever information we gather stays within this inner circle. No exceptions. Got it?" She met the puzzled eyebrows with a hard stare and one by one received a nod. Tossing aside her last reservation, she named Travis Wayne Trenton. "Alma, search for any information linking him to previous IED histories or component purchases. Bill, pull records for any arrests or complaints against him. Christine, his phone number should uncover the communication you seek, but we could also be looking at another member using burner phones. Check it out. Kelly, compile the social media interaction, and Josh, you help look for interaction between Travis and Calvin Sheer."

She paused, waiting for any gut instinct that this was the wrong call, but came up blank. "Remember. No sharing to anyone outside this room." One way or another, she'd find this traitor and bring them to justice.

13

Jace glanced at his watch, his breath vaporizing in the bitterly cold air. Four minutes to four. He stamped in place, studying the postwar industrial buildings lining the block on the near-west side, then spun a slow three-sixty, seeking out anyone that looked like they were on their way to meet him. Only two women were visible, both bundled in hats and scarves, heads down as they scurried toward their destinations. Several cars drove past, but no one slowed. A block away, a navy One-Stop Cleaners van looked empty but housed Chaz and Heidi in the back. It was probably toasty warm in there.

Jace blew on his hands. His mind should be on this third and hopefully final meet before he was welcomed into the Race. Or he could be rehearsing some of the tedious dialogue examples from Heidi's black notebook, designed to elicit solid prosecutorial evidence. Instead, he replayed every moment of the staged assault one more time.

The surge of primal satisfaction he'd experienced yesterday at effortlessly overpowering Heidi had disturbed him the second she slipped from his arms. Today the memory of that response was downright revolting. He didn't get off on S&M, or anything remotely sexually violent, so why had physically dominating her awoken such a beast? Like he was the supreme king of the jungle. A conquering warrior. A club-carrying caveman.

A recent genomic test had unsurprisingly informed him of his ninety percent Northern European ancestry but also noted he had more Neanderthal DNA than ninety-seven-point-six percent of the tested population. At the time he'd laughed off the implication, but pushing his groin into hers midair had triggered something ancient and primitive, and he very much craved a do-over. For real, this time. With her. Without clothes. And definitely no sexual assault aspect.

The only problem was that she clearly didn't share that desire. Jace turned his back on a blast of north wind, squinting in agony and bone-numbing cold. Everything about them hooking up was wrong, but the less Heidi showed interest in him, the more he wanted her. How fucked was that?

"Yo!"

Jace spun around at the greeting. A man turning the corner from Roosevelt waved as he jogged toward Jace, who raised a hand back. "Here we go," he muttered for the agents' benefit. The mic had been attached to his inside jacket collar this morning. The top button hid a microscopic state-of-the-art camera. Both had been extensively tested, but based on the multiple layers this guy had on, facial recognition would be a no-go. Brittle blue eyes, a hawkish nose, red from the cold, and the upper part of a thick brown beard were his only visible features.

"Hi," Jace said as the man strode up. "Jason McGowan."

"Nate Smith." They shook hands, exhales misting. "Nothing like February weather in November, huh?"

Jace gestured around the dismal block in the middle of nowhere. "Interesting place to meet."

"You'll understand soon enough." Nate beckoned him to follow, and they headed southbound. "You sure impressed Sheer," he said with a grin. "I haven't heard him this excited by a new soldier in a long time."

"We had a good talk," Jace answered noncommittally.

"He researched your background pretty thoroughly and sent me the highlights. We really think you'll be a good fit."

"Outstanding." Thank God for the Janus department's backstopping magic. In the era of Google, it took great skill to construct a lifetime background and predated social security number that could hold up under technical scrutiny. Backdating a fabricated bank account with deposit and withdrawal activity for twenty years, creating a full school curriculum with student activity, providing personal and employment references from actual people who would vouch for him in case of inquiry...

The department preferred several months to build such a viable background. Heidi or Garcia persuading them to accomplish it in a few weeks was a freaking miracle. Jason McGowan's persona and timeline as a budding white supremacist was watertight. Now he had to live up to it.

"Here we are," Nate said, slowing. They stood in front of a chain-link fence surrounding a decrepit basketball court. Litter scattered in the wind, and a can clanked as it hit the pole. Jace threw him a questioning glance, but Nate had turned away to study the squat yellow brick building across the street that resembled a detention center. A white sign with blue lettering above the double glass doors read Better Days Supervision.

"What is that?" Jace asked, frowning.

"Where you go when you've lost custody of your kids."

A chill pricked up Jace's spine. Trick had been assigned to one of these for a few weeks last spring. The humiliation and helplessness Jace had witnessed still haunted him. "Why are we here?" he asked quietly.

"There." Nate jerked his head. A woman in a pink hijab and silver down jacket was pushing through the exit. "Right on time."

Recognition slammed into Jace with a sickening thud. What were the goddamn odds? "Fucking Muslim," he managed, instead of erupting with the name of Trick's beloved. Yep, his brother had definitely gone to this place to see Amy and Tina.

"Her name's Zamira Bey," Nate said with hostility. "She made security escort me out on my first visit—right in front of my kids, man." He spat on the ground. "The next time, she had some lib with her who assaulted me." He shook his head, the visible portion of his cheeks stained with color. "I lost visitation rights for months because of that bitch."

Jace gaped at him, trying to channel the racist phrases he'd practiced, but this was Zamira, the shy, compassionate, *perfect* addition to many Quinn family dinners. *She's dating my brother* kept wanting to burst out. This was crazy. Twilight Zone stuff. Nate glanced over, eyebrows knotted fiercely because it was well past time to have responded.

"They come over here and carry out jihad on our soil," Jace sputtered, watching her Accord turn right and disappear down South Racine. "That's so wrong."

"She's your target." Nate motioned down the street as if the car were still visible.

Jace spun toward him, shaking his head fiercely. "Sheer said *a* Muslim. I have one picked out."

"Fuck that." Nate jerked a thumb at his own chest. "I'm the head of this cell, McGowan. I don't care what Sheer told you. He's thousands of miles from us. You're *my* foot soldier. You do what I say, and I say that bitch needs to suffer."

Jace exhaled harshly, his gaze straying to the depressing neighborhood over the other man's shoulder, and the van way in the distance. Hopefully, the team was already brainstorming a way out of this. He'd quit this assignment—hell, quit the FBI—before he pulled Zamira into this sick shit.

"Dude," he said, looking back at Nate, "I just want to blow stuff up. And I'm good at it. I want to target towelheads in general. Send a message to a whole lot of 'em, not some chick who screwed you over." He spread his hands. "This is your vendetta, you feel me?"

"You wanted action? Well, here it is." Nate slapped a piece of paper at Jace's chest. "That's the time and place. Do it or join a group that thinks ranting online is going to change the world."

14

The second Trick and Zamira got off the elevator, Trick smothered a laugh. "Nice scruff, hippie." He peered at Jace's longer hair and his whiskered jaw. "Way to turn your back on that clean-cut SEAL look. Has Mom seen you yet?"

"It's for an assignment," Jace said in a tight voice. "The conference room is this way." He gestured to the right and began leading them down the hall. "Thanks for coming, Zamira."

"Am I in some sort of trouble?"

The distress in her voice made him pause. He'd been so anxious to show Heidi he could control all facets of the altered plans that he hadn't thought to reassure Zamira over the phone after he'd ordered her here on the double. "No, of course not. But you didn't tell anyone where you were going, right?"

"We're covered." Trick ushered Zamira into the FBI conference room. "Mom's looking after the girls, and Zamira's parents think we're out to dinner. What's going on?"

"My boss will explain shortly. Did Pop convince Gage to enter rehab?"

"Nope, and tensions are high at the Quinn house. You missed an epic argument at Sunday dinner."

It was rare for any of the brothers to skip the weekly dinner, but the mountain of UCO documentation burying Jace and the backtracking he'd have to do to make sure he wasn't followed wasn't worth it.

Heidi and Chaz walked in, interrupting Jace's answer, and Trick did a double take. "Weren't you at our cousin's wedding last month? You caught the bouquet?"

Heidi's saucy grin answered him, and Jace hurriedly introduced everyone. Zamira and Heidi traded quips about Jace's performance with the garter.

"We should probably get to it," he snapped. It wasn't that he didn't have a sense of humor about the ass he'd made of himself. It was the smirk on Chaz's face.

"Yes, we should start." Heidi pointed to the designated seats, ending up at the head of the table with Trick and Zamira on her right and Jace and Chaz on her left. After thanking the couple for coming, she zeroed in on Zamira. "We'd like to talk about one of your clients. He could be using an alias. Nate Smith?"

Zamira paused, curiosity and confusion etched in her polite smile. "I'm not working with anyone by that name, but just so you know, I can't discuss my clients."

Jace leaned forward abruptly. "This man means you harm, Zamira—"

"Me?"

"Jace." Heidi cut him a look.

He ignored the interruption. They faced a DEFCON One situation; it was time to cut to the chase. "We came across some information today and need to get a handle on who he is."

"Harm *me*?"

At the apprehension on her face, Trick reached for her hand. As much as his temperament and life goals were exactly opposite Jace's, the deadly look that washed over his features now was totally relatable. "What information?"

"I'm sorry," Heidi said, still glaring at Jace. "That's classified. He was too bundled up to identify him through facial-recognition software, but he mentioned he'd been escorted from your office by security and that another client of yours had attacked him. Do you know who we're describing?"

Zamira scanned their faces, slack-jawed.

"It seems like you recognize him," Heidi promptly gently.

"Yes, but I can't—"

"Zamira," Jace said between his teeth, "screw your confidentiality clause. We need a name."

She fiddled with the hem of her hijab for a long moment. Finally, she sighed. "Nate Henderson."

Chaz, who'd viewed the entire exchange with corpse-like stillness, immediately excused himself and slipped from the room. Even before the door closed, Zamira continued, "But I haven't worked with him since last May, when it happened. As a matter of fact, he was only my client that one time. He immediately requested someone else." She turned to Trick. "You're the one who attacked him, don't you remember?"

"Oh," he said, with a startled frown. "Is he the asshole who ripped off your hijab?" At her nod, he turned to Heidi. "It was a completely unprovoked attack. All I did was hold him against a wall until he apologized. Why is he threatening her now?"

Heidi redirected her attention to Zamira. "We were hoping you could help us figure that out."

A longer silence passed. Reluctance and dread skimmed across her face.

"I know this is distressing," Heidi continued, her tone and expression gentle—another side of her Jace had never seen before—"and telling us about Henderson's case is against policy, but we need as much information as quickly as possible, and you're a better source than whatever Chaz pulls off our database."

Zamira's shoulders slumped. Her face grew steadily pinker. "Mr. Henderson can only visit his children under the direct supervision of a court-ordered provider. He's been a client at our center twice a week since mid-May." She took a deep breath and hesitated, like the next part was too difficult to say.

"Go on," Heidi said. "You're doing fine, Zamira."

"His final custody hearing is next Monday. Ann—she's his provider now—doesn't think he's made a lot of progress, and evidently he's skipped too many anger-management sessions at our sister facility, which was also a condition of the judge's order. So jointly, we're recommending the judge not grant him partial custody." She gestured with the hand that wasn't clamped to Trick's. "While he doesn't know that's our recommendation, his lawyer must have shown him the list of who'll be testifying. My name is right below Ann's. She's asked me to relate the details of that attack as one of the many reasons we don't think he can hold it together alone with his kids. If Mr. Henderson saw my name, he may have put two and two together."

"Is he targeting Ann too?" Trick asked.

"Not that we know of," Heidi answered, then looked back at Zamira. "Is she Caucasian?"

"Yes."

"Then it's unlikely."

Trick shook his head. "Sorry. I'm not following any of this."

"It's his MO," Jace said, recalling Nate's icy glare as he'd tracked Zamira scurrying to her car. "He doesn't acknowledge his ineptitude with the program or noncompliance with the judge's orders. Nothing's his fault, so he's going to look for someone else to blame—in this case, a Muslim. It all started that first day, being assigned to Zamira. I've been studying men with similar characteristics. An us-versus-them fixation is common. Everything they consider wrong with their life or in the world is due to someone else. Usually someone from a minority group."

"I'm well aware of people like that," Zamira said gravely, "and you definitely described him, but I thought his vendetta against me ended last May." At the sudden glistening in her eyes, Trick brought her hand to his lips, murmuring something indecipherable. His usual laid-back yogi countenance was long gone.

Jace's own surge of protectiveness caught him by surprise. It wasn't just about keeping Zamira safe from Nate's revenge. Last spring, Trick's life had spiraled into the lowest circle of hell, and Zamira had become his undisputed lifeline. Together they were finally getting his life sorted out and striving to be a couple, despite judging glances and overt whispers. If anything happened to her now, there would be no end to his brother's pain. Surely Nate could be arrested on some other charge to get him off the streets.

"We've coordinated with CPD for around-the-clock protection for you until further notice." Heidi's smile looked wan and exhausted. "However, we strongly recommend that besides going to and from work, you stay inside your house until the court date."

"Why would he stop targeting her after the judge's

ruling?" Trick asked. And that was the million-dollar question. Nate was about to lose custody, which would further ramp up his need for vengeance.

As Heidi reassured them the task force was doing all they could, Jace scraped a palm over his bristled jaw. If only he'd infiltrated the cell earlier and wormed out information on the bombing by now. He shared a meaningful look with Heidi as the meeting concluded. After Monday's ruling, a new fuse would be lit. They might as well chuck that notebook of controlled scenarios out the window. They were punting blind now.

CHAZ RETURNED as Jace escorted Trick and Zamira out to the elevator. He nodded politely to the guests before closing the conference room door and handing a few sheets to Heidi. "Henderson's in the database for domestic violence on three occasions and a drunk and disorderly two years back. Nothing connecting him to white supremacy violence."

Heidi scanned the police reports and studied his driver's license photo. Brown hair, blue eyes, not unattractive per se, but no feature stood out to make his face memorable. He'd make a great spy. Or racist blending into a crowd. "The white man's fragility," she murmured.

"Don't let Quinn hear that generalization."

She tossed the pages aside with a sigh. "I just get tired of the conspiracy theories and the whining about how unfair everything is. They're the lottery winners of gender, race, and rights. They don't get to blame anyone else for failing at life."

"You're preaching to the choir, case agent."

Heidi looked over, bleary with fatigue. Chaz had a way of spitting out her title that was much more powerful than any derogatory term. "You either don't like me personally or don't like that I was made case agent."

A long period followed where they stared at each other. Chaz blinked first. "Let's just say I'm suspicious." He leaned his forearms on the table and interlaced his fingers. His smile held no humor. "I'm suspicious of anyone who can walk into the middle of a task force team and take command. I'm suspicious why the FBI higher-ups would assign this coveted case agent role to the ATF"—he waved a hand impatiently—"even with all your lovely commendations and awards. And I'm *highly* suspicious of said case agent then choosing an inexperienced associate to go undercover and not only getting the upper echelon's blessing, but getting Janus to drop everything to create an identity three times quicker than any undercover op I've ever been on."

She rolled her stiff shoulders and pushed the print-outs on Nate Henderson into her file. What would it hurt to tell someone? Chaz looked like the kind of loner agent she was. Friendly to all, but only on the surface. Career was everything. Relationships were sacrificed, even casual ones. She didn't see him going out often for beers with "the gang," and if he did, there was no way the strong, silent guy would gossip. "It's actually simple—"

Jace burst into the room and took the chair closest to the door, the one his brother had sat in. "We have to take Henderson out before the hearing."

Heidi closed her mouth and gave Chaz a "we're done here" look. His return expression was a mocking "how convenient for you." She swiveled toward Jace, bristling at losing the nonverbal exchange. "We've got nothing on Henderson," she said patiently. "We're going to have to somehow physically delay him from meeting you and convince Zamira to let you take a photo of her with her skirts and hajib mussed."

Jace's mouth dropped open at the word "photo." The astonishment was all too familiar—the dawning of a man's "holy shit, she's crazy" thought. That look happened early on in each of her assignments. The crystal-clear realization of the lengths to which she was willing to go for the end goal, and that it was several shades past their comfort level.

"When Henderson shows up," Heidi continued smoothly, "she'll already be gone, and you'll have the photographic 'evidence.'" She air-quoted the last word. "He's the one who got delayed. You performed the initiation rite in good faith."

He exhaled a short laugh. "You'll never convince Zamira to show some skin."

"I wasn't going to. The directive would be easier for her to swallow if it came from someone with whom she's familiar and comfortable."

Jace sputtered. The tips of his ears reddened—such a darling look on a brash alpha male. Heidi hazarded a glance at Chaz but got nothing from the poker king. Either she hadn't scared him off with her aggressive idea, or he could out-crazy her any day of the week. She'd bet the latter.

"Everything about Zamira is sheltered, modest, and devout," Jace said, the controlled patience in his voice at odds with his obstinate expression. "We need to come up with a different plan."

Heidi shook her head. "Nate's not an idiot. He hates her too much to be fooled by a lookalike. I want you to approach her first thing tomorrow and work with her until she sees our side."

"*Our* side?" The knitted eyebrows and thunderous frown were deeply formidable, but still sent tingles of awareness to her lower belly. *Down, Miss Flirt.* Jace swiveled to Chaz. "What's your take?" he asked between clenched teeth.

Heidi stiffened. He'd never have asked that if the case agent were male. She debated shutting down the conversation with a brutal putdown for insubordination, but hesitated. This inner team would always land in a two-against-one triangle. How would the dynamics play out here?

Chaz took his time answering, his composure still impressively unflappable. No body language to read on this guy. What had he been through in his undercover career to give him such control? "Staging an assault is the only way to get Nate off her back," he said. "Zamira trusts you, dude, so it should be you who tries to convince her."

The tension draining from Heidi left her limp, but fury remained like a sharp-edged rock in her gut. The only reason she'd won this round was because of another man's opinion.

She opened her mouth to respond, but Chaz continued without a glance her way. "Heidi can take the photo. No need for you to be in the area. We can guarantee Zamira it'll be deleted the second Nate acknowledges the assault happened. But the victim has to be Zamira. No female UCA will do."

Shit! Heidi slapped her forehead. "The undercover agent." Granted, it was a cameo role, but the woman was probably winging her way to Chicago.

As she texted the message, Chaz said a stiff goodnight and left. Getting him to trust her would have to wait another day. Too many moving parts were spiraling out of control. And right now, all her attention was focused on laying into Jace.

The second the door closed, she eyed him. "Don't go anywhere. We need to clear the air."

"Yes," he said hurriedly, "I haven't had a chance to apologize yet."

She put the phone down. "Apologize?"

"For—you know—my behavior during that practice assault." His face reddened as he glanced away. "I know you felt"—he took a quick breath—"it."

She fought a smile. Jace from the wedding was back. "You mean your penis?"

"Well...yeah." He rocked back in the chair, crossing his arms and jamming his hands under his armpits. Disregarding the thick, sculpted biceps, he looked like a little boy in trouble. "It's just...well... Something that began at the wedding kinda continued for me." He side-eyed her with such throwback angst that she had to swallow the burst of laughter. It was pretty obvious this alpha soldier didn't open himself to vulnerability often. Under no circumstances could she tease him or flippantly disregard what he'd just shared. And for sure she had to shut down any return signals revealing the mutual attraction.

Heidi exhaled slowly. When her face was firmly cemented in a cool neutral, she said, "For the good of the op, why don't you put both events out of your mind. I certainly have."

His nod was more of a head jerk, like she'd slapped him. His Adam's apple bobbed once.

"And going forward," she said, "don't you ever undermine a direct order from me again. If I want Chaz's opinion, I'll bring him into the conversation. Are we clear?"

He dropped the folded arms and slouched posture. "Yes, ma'am." Unfortunately, by the biting tone and glittering eyes, he still had some fight left in him over Zamira showing some skin. Heidi closed the laptop, gathering her thoughts.

"While I appreciate your respect for the Muslim culture, Jace—"

"Nothing's more important than the investigation," he finished. "Yes, ma'am, I'm beginning to understand the way you operate."

He made ambition sound like a bad thing. She wasn't wrong about this decision. And why should she justify it to him anyway? Heidi white-knuckled the cool metal of her laptop. "If this were a SEAL mission, would you honor Zamira's modesty or get the job done?"

A muscle twitched along that hard jaw. Silence charged the air, lifting the hair off her neck. She stared unblinking into his smoldering eyes, almost an iridescent blue now. There was something highly erotic watching him struggle to harness his anger. Seriously. If she didn't get the hell out of here, the Flirt would erupt on a sexual rampage.

"I guess I thought that as a woman you'd be more understanding of the trauma you're putting her through," he said, instead of answering the question.

"I'm fully aware of it," she said, rising. "But I'm not the kind of commander who wrings her hands about it publicly. If I stayed awake all night worrying about everyone's feelings, I'd never close cases."

She headed for the door. "Let me know when you've set up the photoshoot."

"Yes, ma'am," he said tightly.

She let the door swing shut without a backward glance.

15

"Unit four to base. Target heading west on West Belmont."

"Copy, four." Heidi tracked the red dot onscreen traveling toward her position. It'd be great if something as simple as a traffic stop delayed Nate Henderson. The dot slowed at North Central Avenue. She raised the walkie-talkie again. "Unit three, if he so much as forgets to use his blinker, I want you to light him up."

"Copy."

"Unit four to base. Target heading south on North Central."

"Copy, four. Unit two, get into position." She switched to the surveillance feed that had been installed on unit two's dashboard. The mid-sized white truck, compliments of the Bureau's seized supply, lumbered out of the parking garage halfway down North Central. Inside it, Josh waved a few slowing southbound cars past, then eased the truck farther until it blocked the north- and southbound lanes. He cut the engine. "Unit two in position. Target stopped."

Heidi wrenched the mangled fingernail from between

her teeth with a *tsk* of self-disgust. "Copy, two." The dashboard cam showed Nate Henderson hopping out of the Acura, shouting and waving his arms. Josh rolled down his window, pairing a placating wave with the practiced excuse: truck had stalled, hold on a sec, etc.

Henderson looked around frantically. Traffic behind him was backing up. Unit three, a CPD cruiser, was four cars back and patiently waiting along with the rest of the southbound travelers. "Come *on*," Henderson yelled again, actually grabbing his short hair. "I'm in a hurry!" His face was red, eyes wide and wild. He was late to a rape.

"Unit three," Heidi said, "you're up."

The cop car engaged its lights and burped the siren. An officer exited from the passenger side and leisurely strolled toward the scene, hand resting on the butt of his gun. Henderson spotted the cop and jumped back in his Acura. He nudged the car as far to the right as space allowed, then backed up, barely missing the bumper of the sedan behind him but evoking a long honk.

"What's he doing, people?" Heidi said into the walkie-talkie.

Henderson repeated the backward-forward motion, jerking his vehicle at an angle. One more attempt would put him over the curb and onto the sidewalk. The cop, still two car lengths away, paused.

"He's going onto the sidewalk," Heidi yelled. "Get those pedestrians outta there!"

The cop began running toward the Acura, shouting at Henderson to stop and gesturing for the gawking pedestrians to flee. They scattered into the street, shrieking, just as the Acura shot forward, scraping the backside of the white truck as Henderson catapulted onto the pavement. The cop halted, drew his weapon and crouched in a shooting stance. It was too late. Tires screeching, the Acura spun around the corner.

"Shit!" Heart pounding, Heidi started her rental car. She was the only boundary left between Henderson and his destination. If he went around her, he'd make the rendezvous in time to know not only was there no rape, but Zamira was long gone. Heidi frantically scanned up the street. Henderson was half a block away, honking and tailgating a slowing SUV with its left turn signal blinking. The instant the vehicle's rear bumper cleared, Henderson squealed past, now feet from careening by her.

On instinct, Heidi stomped on the gas. The crunch of metal on metal, the impact of her body jolting to a standstill, and the deployed airbag punching her face all occurred in a nanosecond. Distantly, she registered the taste of blood.

Someone pounded on her window, the sound muffled by the ringing in her ears. Heidi focused on the deflating white bag, the chemical scent pungent and nauseating. What had just happened? Oh yeah, she'd crashed into Henderson's car. It had been impulsive and reckless, but at least she'd delayed him.

She blinked and turned her blurred gaze toward the incessant hammering. The fist was attached to a shouting cop. He gestured for her to unlock the door. Swallowing bile, she pulled the door handle. The rush of fresh, frigid air instantly helped clear her head.

"We have an ambulance on the way." It was the cop who'd raced after Henderson. Like the rest of the LEOs out here today, he knew he was helping an FBI case, but didn't know the details or that she, in fact, was heading it. Her cover was officially blown with Henderson, though. Once he had a clear look at her face, she was done with any part of the op except sitting in a van. She would not compound the problem by flashing her badge at this cop.

Even if Henderson didn't see it, the cop would instantly clear her, which would raise Henderson's paranoia enough to bring down the entire investigation.

She fumbled to unhook her seatbelt. That airbag had done a number on her coordination; it took three tries before the latch clicked.

"Stay where you are," the cop said. "Are you all right?"

"Yes." Her voice sounded so feeble. "I need to check on the other guy."

"That's my job. Sit right there."

Swiping away more trickling blood, she hauled herself onto the sidewalk, ignoring the queries from several bystanders. She turned, swaying, but caught herself and studied Henderson. He stood feet away, surveying his mangled passenger-side door. His face was still mottled with fury, but his shoulders were slumped in defeat. She staggered the car length and interrupted the cop demanding his license to issue an apology. Thankfully, she sounded like a breathless airhead.

"How do you even have a driver's license, lady?" Henderson snarled.

"You must have been in my blind spot."

"Blind spot? Of all the—"

"Enough." The cop motioned for both to quiet down. "Ma'am, I'll need to see some ID."

She stumbled back to her car and her ringing cell phone. Sirens sounded in the distance. Her head was beginning to really throb. She ducked inside and felt around the floor until she clasped the phone. Chaz. "I know," she said wearily. "I compromised the op."

"And saved it, too. When the ambulance arrives, get in."

"I'm all right."

"Get in. You need to leave the scene as quickly as possible."

She spied the cop handing back Henderson's license and making his way back to her. "Got it." She tapped *end*, threw the device in her black canvas bag, and snatched the Bureau registration from the glove compartment, tucking it in the side sleeve of her bag just as the cop rounded to her side.

"Ma'am. Your license and proof of insurance, please."

The ambulance was upon them. Heidi sagged in her seat, massaging her forehead. "I'm suddenly having trouble seeing, officer."

The cop spun toward the ambulance, beckoning them, then hunkered down. "Can you give me your name?"

"Rosie," she said weakly.

"Rosie what?"

She looked over his shoulder at the ambulance tech, which prompted the officer to do the same. Reluctantly, he got to his feet and let the man pass. "Get her last name for me, will you?"

Up the street, the flashing yellow lights of a tow truck came into view. She breathed a sigh of relief as Henderson waved at it. The mission to delay him was complete. Now to figure out how to spin this shitstorm so as to placate Webb, Garcia, and the bean counters who'd have to pay for all this damage.

JACE PEERED through the concrete slabs of the parking structure, spying Nate getting out of a rideshare. He was fifty-three minutes late. Jace grinned at the other man's livid demeanor, then hurried toward the parking garage stairwell. Ascending the steps two at a time, he banged out the door onto the roof, lifting his face to the brisk wind and wan sunshine. Within minutes, the door popped open again and Nate appeared.

Jace raised his arms in an aggravated gesture. "What the fuck, man?"

Nate looked around, scowling. "Where is she?"

"Long gone, like we should be. What if she tells someone?"

"I told you I had to witness it."

"No shit." Jace cocked his head. "And then you no-showed. I had to do it before she started screaming. The deed is done."

Nate paced in a circle muttering obscenities. It was obvious he'd had a shitty morning and was spoiling for a fight, but he also knew Jace was right. "How do I know you didn't pussy out and let her go?"

Jace rolled his eyes and snatched his phone. A swipe and a tap, and he held it a foot from Nate's face. Onscreen was a clear shot that had evidently taken Heidi and Trick several attempts to stage. Zamira had shown more skin than she was comfortable with, but that made the wide-eyed horror on her face and the fake blood oozing from her gagged mouth all the more realistic. She was a champ to save the op like this, and Jace was damned if she'd have any further involvement in the investigation.

He shoved up his sleeve, revealing a trail of scratches, which were real and hurt like hell, compliments of himself. "She didn't go down without a fight."

Nate exhaled a harsh breath, mollified, which made Jace want to punch his lights out.

"Was she a virgin?"

"What do you think?"

Nate smirked. "Outstanding."

It was a term Jace often used with his former team-mates following a successful SEAL mission, and his skin prickled. He had nothing in common with this piece of shit. "Am I in or not?" he asked curtly. Nate paused, and Jace's heart stalled. "I did what you asked."

"AirDrop me a copy of that shot."

Jeez, either this guy was fixated to the point of stupid or he thought Jace would follow him off a cliff. Jaw clenched, he hit the delete key instead.

"Hey!"

"I'm not AirDropping evidence that incriminates me."

Nate thrust out his chin, his mulish expression the last straw.

"If you're looking for a henchman to dole out your personal vendettas, count me out." Jace pocketed the phone. "I'm interested in a race war. If that isn't what you're offering, I'll request another cell and you can explain it to Sheer."

"All right, all right, you're in." Nate scowled. "I'll text you the time and place. We meet tonight."

16

"Here we go again." Nate slapped the folded *Chicago Tribune* on the coffee table and unzipped his coat. "Fuckin' A-rabs stealing what's rightfully ours. Just another variation of brown niggerdom."

Jace scanned the headline. *Pakistani Restaurant Opens in Iconic Johnny's Locale.* Pakistan wasn't even an Arabic country. The level of ignorance from these good ole boys, who'd probably never even crossed the state line, was astounding, but he grunted with the right amount of disgust.

Dennis Howe, the third man in this cell, snatched up the paper. In the past ten days they'd met every evening except Sunday, and it had quickly become apparent that although Nate was the leader, Dennis was the psycho.

"Kill 'em all," Dennis muttered. "Women and babies first."

"When will the sheeples listen to us?" The rhetoric was tedious by now. There was *us, them,* the ZOG—or Zionist-Occupied Government—multiple Deep State conspiracies, and finally *sheeples*—white people being led down a treacherous path like unaware sheep. Sports, TV shows, or girlfriend problems were brought up only as they related to the furthering of hate, fear, and persecution, such as athletes taking a knee during the national anthem, sitcoms normalizing mixed marriages, etc.

Responding correctly to their rants was like traversing a field littered with IEDs. His taped responses needed to imply racism without using actual slurs, otherwise he'd hurt the prosecutor's case. Chaz had warned that juries hated hearing evidence of agents stooping to the level of the criminal, even if it was for the good of the investigation, so the hardest part of this op was the rapid-fire thinking required before Jace uttered a word. So far, he'd relied primarily on nods or rude gestures for agreements or denigration. The irony? Since every utterance would be scrutinized by future defense attorneys, Jace was left overly cautious and paranoid—behaviors that blended well with these two men.

"My family loved Johnny's," he said, then muttered an obscenity about Pakistani food, even though he'd acquired a taste for it overseas and planned to visit this new place as soon as the op was over. "That restaurant was a fixture in Chicago."

Because it was required of him, he glanced at the article when Dennis shoved the paper over. Johnny Mulroney was retiring to Florida after five decades of running his beloved steakhouse, which had made Chicago's annual top ten favorites list for years. The restaurateur of Lateef Kebobs was excited to introduce the flavors of his homeland to the good people of the city. The article was bland, the transition of ownership harmless, but it was enough to trigger tonight's underdog outrage at a "diminished" America.

Jace tossed the newspaper aside and snatched up his beer bottle, his sigh of frustration completely unrelated to theirs. Entrapment was an even bigger obstacle than parroting their rants. If he initiated a plan of action against Lateef Kabobs, it would be Nate and Dennis's get-out-of-jail-free card. Anything he suggested could be interpreted as the government entrapping citizens who would not have broken the law without this provocation.

Which left him sitting here night after night with his thumb up his ass, because these two loved to hate but had no plans. So much for the Race cells being accelerationists. Meanwhile, the expense of FBI analysts monitoring surveillance, taping, transcribing, and backing up his undercover life as an embittered schmuck kept growing.

Based on how short Heidi's temper had been the last few hot washes, the pressure on her had to be enormous. She'd mentioned she was finally seeing the same fruitless results the task force had encountered all these months. She'd become the new whipping post for the governor's demands for answers and the media's calls for transparency.

How in the hell could he provoke this disgruntled cell and get them to incriminate themselves? "I read somewhere that Muslim fertility rates are the highest in the nation." Another lie. The article was actually how Muslim-Americans were interested in higher education, which directly correlated with declining birth rates. "And try to find a doctor that doesn't have an Islamic name. Have you noticed that?"

"My mom went to one," Dennis said. "Even though I warned her not to." His lips pulled into a deep scowl. "Bastard left a scar on her nose from taking out a growth and then expected her to be happy about being disfigured."

"You shoulda sued him," Nate said, a phrase Jace could have mouthed right along with him. The victimized discourse was like watching the same damn play every night. Now Dennis would say...

"What, so some Kike lawyer can get most of our reward money?"

Jace managed to exhale instead of groan. He had to instigate some action. "It's like when they bombed our city last May, and then when that mosque blew up as payback, *they* had the audacity to sue. Even if the city and state settle, guess who ends up paying the bill? Us taxpayers." He motioned to the *Tribune*. "They take over our restaurants and the medical field. They put their people in government and on school boards—"

"Not to mention losing custody because of them," Nate growled.

Jace quickly deterred any further focus on Zamira by spouting new Muslim info he'd researched. "You know they don't celebrate birthdays?"

"Why the fuck would you want to celebrate those births?" Dennis sported perpetually bloodshot eyes, which went well with his explosive anger. He sucked down the last of his beer and got up to throw it in the trash.

"The only birthday Muslims celebrate is Mohammed's," Jace went on, crossing an ankle over his knee. "Which is right around this time of year. Between Halloween and Thanksgiving."

Nate sneered. "Can you imagine if they gain any more political power? They'll cancel Thanksgiving and make the holiday Mohammed's birthday."

It took so little to stoke their paranoid fears. Every scenario Jace brought up, carefully using "us" versus "them" language, they finished by predicting Armageddon. Such small, depressing lives.

Dennis returned with a fresh bottle, saying, "The way they're taking over, I totally see a day when there are few enough of us left to celebrate the meaning of Thanksgiving. It's all happening right under the sheeples' noses, and it's like they don't care that we're going extinct. Shit, if we weren't around to save them, they'd be fucked."

"We have to do something." Nate pounded his fist into his hand. "Towelheads, niggers, Jews...they're all a cancer. We are a dying people. The minority, can you believe it?"

Jace nodded, quoting the slogan. "We gotta pick up the pace." *Come on, guys, the Race is supposed to be action-oriented. Put a plan together!*

They sat in silence for a moment, Dennis sucking beer and glowering, Nate brooding absently at the newspaper. Suddenly Nate stroked his beard. "You know what?" He glanced up at Jace. "When's that birthday celebration?"

"This year? The day after Thanksgiving."

Jace's adrenalin pulsed to life as Nate's face lit with a malicious grin. "I say we help those motherfuckers celebrate."

"Like how?" Dennis sat forward.

"I dunno yet." The leader of the cell jumped up and began pacing. "But it's a birthday, and we should celebrate it with a big bang, know what I mean? Someplace symbolic. Like, you know, that kabob restaurant."

Blowing up a building. Jace's breath grew shallow. Maybe in planning the event they'd incriminate themselves or another cell in the Mosque Mohammed bombing.

"That'd honor Johnny," Dennis said. "I vote for the kabob place."

Jace nodded his assent. "I'm available for whatever. If you're targeting Mohammed's birthday, though, that gives us little more than a week to prepare, which is real tight." At their baffled expressions, he shucked off his newbie passive act.

Nate stroked his beard. "We'll have to scope out security along that block, see if it's in a neighborhood that has a lot of police drive-bys. We need to decide whether to blow a substantial hole or the whole thing—"

"The whole thing," Dennis interrupted. "Our goal should be obliteration."

"Then we'll need access to the architectural plans," Jace said. "Even tour the structure if possible. Maybe I can get in under the guise of bidding on any renovations they have planned."

"How much C-4 can you get us?" Nate asked.

"Enough for obliteration if it's attached to the most vulnerable point of the load-bearing wall. We pack at the top and let gravity do the rest, like those demolitions you see on TV of old buildings."

The other two nodded enthusiastically. "What else do we need besides C-4?" Dennis asked, and Jace paused a moment. The fact that they were asking questions like this, that they had little cognizance of the tremendous organization needed to pull this off, proved these two could not possibly be behind the Mosque Mohammed bombing.

"A detonator, like a blasting cap," Jace said. "It'd be wise to have an electronic timing device so we can get well clear of the neighborhood. We need to establish alibis." He gestured impatiently. "If you want to pull this off in nine days, you're going to have to bring in more people. Preferably those with bomb experience."

"Leave it to me," Nate said, almost glowing with pleasure. "I'll call Sheer tonight and arrange to meet more cells. We're doing this."

"HOT DAMN!" Heidi tore off her headphones and high-fived Chaz. "Probable cause. I'll request communication intercept warrants tomorrow morning." No judge would've granted them when suspects were only sitting around exercising their First Amendment rights, but a definite plan to conduct a terrorist act had just bounced this investigation into high gear. Wiring their homes and devices would give reams more information than these recorded meets.

Chaz stretched back in the van's ergonomic chair. "I thought the Race was supposed to be action-oriented. That was like pulling teeth."

"Thomas Bradley must have been the leader behind the mosque bombing, and these two were his hapless underlings."

Chaz snorted. "Those turkeys? We shoulda caught 'em days ago."

She studied the dichotomy of his sprawled body language versus his tense expression. Interpreting him was a challenge. "Are you criticizing Jace's handling of the op?"

He gave a dismissive shrug. "It's his rookie debut, and thankfully, he's being cautious, so no. But had I not been born Black, I'd have already tied a big red bow around this racist op and plunked it right on the AUSA's desk."

"Nice ego." She softened the remark with a grin.

He spread his hands. "Can't help it if I'm the best."

"Have you ever done a white supremacy op?"

"Hell no. Mostly high-level drug cartels and gang infiltrations. This"—he waved at the screen, where Jace's ball-cap camera was displaying another uneventful walk home—"is a piece of cake. Jace should not be in any personal danger."

"Yet." Anything could go wrong and jeopardize Jace's safety.

Chaz cocked his head and studied her for a long moment. "You really dig him."

Here we go again. "I care very much about his success and safety, if that's what you mean," she snapped.

"You know I don't." Chaz jerked his head at the monitor, where Jace waited on the El platform. "Hot young guy like that, risking his life for national security. I bet you're a sucker for heroes."

"Who isn't?" Hopefully the blue light from the monitors masked her blush. "But I'm not the kind of agent that sleeps with subordinates. And if I were, his arrogance would be a real turnoff."

The only movement in Chaz's preternaturally still face was a slight crinkling around his eyes. "You'll end up with him. I'll bet my piss-poor salary on it."

His confident tone had the effect of a steel rod being jammed down her spine. "Well, you'd lose," she snarled, punching the keyboard to shut down the surveillance. "Let's wrap this up. It's been a long night." And she had a lot left to do.

"Fine by me. Want me to drop you off at his house?" Chaz was already on his way to the driver's seat, so thankfully, she missed whatever knowing look was probably plastered on his face.

Still, it took everything she had to keep the defensiveness out of her tone. "Sure. Thanks." Acknowledging, congratulating, and celebrating Jace's incredible inroad tonight could be accomplished without crossing forbidden lines. So why was her heart thrumming such a giddy beat?

17

"What part of this op would you say is the most difficult?" Heidi asked, studying Jace lounging on his bu-house sofa, feet on the cocktail table, beer on a coaster by his side. On the surface, he gave every indication of kicking back after a successful day at work. What ruined it was the defensive posture—tightly crossed arms, fisted hands. Visceral cues for uncomfortable, closed off.

"Same answer as yesterday and the day before," he said casually. "The mental challenge of evaluating every sentence before I say it."

It was becoming apparent he wasn't taking the hot washes seriously. She'd better dig deeper. "What about psychologically?" She tapped her temple. "Every evening this week, you've been immersed in hate and paranoia."

Jace scoffed. "I've been around hate and paranoia my entire adult life." His flippant tone was getting on her nerves. "I fought ISIS as a career, and they're a hell of a lot more dangerous than these two whack-jobs." He uncrossed his arms and wiped his palms down his thighs.

Pacifying behavior. The guy's body language made him an open book. Why wasn't he admitting to this anxiety?

"But you made amazing progress tonight, so it's different," she said. "You're officially off the sidelines and in the game."

"Hoo-ah." A gleam entered his eyes. "Let's get this show on the road." He grabbed his beer and kicked forward, resting his forearms on his knees. So when she pointed out actionable danger, his inner feedback showed confidence and full engagement.

Barely able to keep from shaking her head, she tapped his answers into her iPad. "What part of this op causes you the most anxiety?"

"That's not a hot-wash question."

"It is now."

He sipped beer thoughtfully, and hope rose. These sessions were designed to let him decompress, and yet night after night, he still wasn't acknowledging the covert negativity his limbic brain had on full display. She wasn't making the same mistake twice—even if she had to browbeat Jace, he was going to learn to get it out.

He thunked his beer on the table and spread his hands. "I got nothing."

Damn it! "Dig a little deeper, Jace. What causes you anxiety?"

"I'm not anxious. If anything, I'm impatient."

Sighing quietly, she saved his responses and clicked out of the app. Overall, another hot-wash failure. He'd swallow down whatever trauma lurked within and soldier on, while she would toss and turn most of the night, wondering if she should have asked this or said that.

"My turn," he said softly.

She didn't bother looking over. Boy, had she ever

opened a can of worms allowing him one question per hot wash. She nodded reluctantly as she ordered her rideshare.

"Why is my undercover op still being kept secret?"

She wasn't answering that until she found the leak, which was currently at a dead end. "It's not a secret. Your SAC, ASAC, and Heather know."

"You know what I mean."

"And *I* mean, the people who need to know do." Heidi pocketed her phone, her lips firm. "This is a long game that requires intricate strategy and one commander to keep all the plates spinning in the air." She'd barely held it together managing Wastewater, and this op was growing much more complex.

"Are you going to tell me one day?"

"You can count on it, Jace." With the pending terror attack shifting into high gear, he did not need to spend a nanosecond worrying about a task force betrayal. Lord knew it kept her awake enough for the rest of the team.

Heidi gazed out the window, which reflected her lined, frowning face. Who *was* this tired frump? How pathetic that she had the hots for a smoke show like Jace. She turned back with an inner sigh. "I worked with an agent who resembled you in a lot of ways. Intense, competitive, impatient to succeed."

"Yeah? How'd it turn out?"

Evan's face, peaceful in death, flashed before her. She bowed her head and checked her watch so Jace wouldn't catch the hard swallow. "I learned a lot of hard lessons." This op would be her redemption. She braved his steely gaze again. "You need to dig much deeper and get what-ever toxicity is in there out." She stood abruptly, joints creaking, while he rose with the grace of a jungle animal.

"You know," he said, one side of his mouth quirking

up, "you suck at this hot-wash thing too. That's three nights in a row you've deflected my allotted question."

Because he kept asking for secrets or digging into her childhood. Things that were none of his business. She opened her mouth to tell him so, but he was already stalking toward the door. He slumped against it, folding his arms. "I'm not opening this until you tell me one honest fact about yourself."

Maybe it was the chronic weariness of so many late nights or the odd standoff over such a stupid issue, but the intensity he wore like a second skin suddenly seemed to morph into something smoldering and powerful. The last time she'd glimpsed this seductive look, he'd had his hands up her skirt, and she'd been pretending her girlie parts weren't dancing the cha-cha.

She wrenched on her coat to signal her contempt, but her nerves blitzed in panic, and the Flirt roared awake. Better get out of here before she did something stupid. "How's this for honest? I'm not into silly games."

"Is this a silly game, Heidi?" he asked softly.

Heat shot through her. Trembling muscles threatened to drop her into a limp puddle. She all but staggered to the door and gazed up at him. Putting on her coat had been a strategic error. She was on fire. "Enough." The whisper came from parched lips. "This is reckless."

He studied her lips through hooded eyes. Gone were the subordinate and supervisory roles, swept aside by a guy who took charge with panty-dropping confidence.

Her belly fluttered with longing. Oh, to be his age and not his boss. To have the freedom to act on her desire without a shit-ton of career-ending bricks descending on her for the lapse. She could imagine the look on SAC Webb's face now. The demotion, the ruined reputation, the whispers that would follow her wherever she went.

The horror of that alternate future was the cold shower she needed. "See you tomorrow," she said tersely.

He blinked like he was snapping out of a daze. "Right." His grin seemed forced as he straightened from the door. "Thanks for using a precious half-hour trying to nudge some feelings outta me. You honestly don't need to waste your time."

"You're never a waste of time, Jace." Oh, Lord! She'd meant to sound reassuring, but it came out like a husky come-on. She rolled her eyes and swirled a finger in the air. "Rewind. I mean your psychological wellbeing is crucial to this op and therefore to me," she said formally. "You're out here alone on the front line. I'll spend whatever time is necessary to keep you in optimal shape."

He slapped his steely abs twice. "Shape doesn't come more optimal than this." His genuine grin softened those features that had been taut with desire a moment before.

She jerked her head toward the street. "My ride probably arrived half an hour ago."

"Yeah." He pulled the knob, and frigid air embraced them. A dark sedan with its hazards flashing was parked at the curb. Shoving his hands into his pockets, Jace walked slightly sideways, taking the brunt of the north wind. "Say. Do you have plans for Thanksgiving?"

She hurried down the walk. "What?"

"You're from out of town. I have a gigantic extended family. You'd be a welcome addition." The words were light and teasing. His stiff posture could be from the bitter cold. "Unless you're flying back to D.C. for a long weekend or something. Or have plans with Dave?"

"I don't." Heidi paused at the car door, shivering. "And I'm in town." The biting wind was making her nose run. "Sure, thanks. Just text me the address."

He opened her car door with a quiet chuckle. "It's Thanksgiving, Heidi. I'll pick you up."

Too date-like. Too dangerous. "The takedown is the next night, so I'll be knee-deep in plans at headquarters all day. I'd better rideshare it."

"Suit yourself."

She escaped into the heated car, continuing to tremble long after she'd warmed back up. These hot washes were turning into the riskiest part of her day.

18

"I'm happy to report the undercover operation is in full swing," Heidi said authoritatively the next morning. "Jace Quinn is firmly entrenched in the Race, and after seven days of feeling him out, the cell seems to have accepted him. The task force is thoroughly investigating links between these two additional members and Bradley or the bombing."

"Excellent," Webb said, while Garcia nodded in unison. "And how are you feeling?" He nodded to the yellowing bruise on the corner of her mouth from the airbag.

"Perfectly fine, sir."

"Just so you know, the government insurance agreed to pick up the damage from your little, er, incident last week, without outing that it was bureau-related."

Presto change-o, she was a newbie klutz standing before her superior after another impulsive disaster. Fighting the blush, she maintained direct eye contact. "It was my only course of action at the time, sir."

His smile didn't reach his eyes. "Assistant Special

Agent in Charge Garcia agrees with you. That's the only reason you're still here."

"Understood, sir." The warning was clear: no more fuck-ups.

He nodded magnanimously. "Go on with your report."

She collected her suddenly frazzled thoughts. She'd come in here with such confidence and exceptional news... *Oh, yeah.* The news. "Last night the Race cell discussed plans to blow up a Pakistani restaurant." She'd recaptured their attention. She was back in the game. After clearing her throat, she said, "If this becomes an active plot, we'll need to move fast. Their target date is next Friday."

"The day after Thanksgiving?"

"Yes, sir. It happens to be Mohammed's birthday."

Garcia and Webb exchanged grim glances. What kind of pressure did they face from the mayor and governor? The daily protests from the Muslim community out on the sidewalk had only grown since she'd been here, and now a Race cell was technically planning more destruction. If it had gone down for real instead of as a sting operation, this city would have erupted in chaos. Even if the takedown went like clockwork, the media coverage would probably point out the potential for violence still existed, that the divide was as wide as ever. It would take more than arresting one terror group to soothe Chicago's polarization and fear.

"What resources do you need?" Garcia asked in his gentle, supportive way.

"It's a fluid situation at the moment, sir, but as the sting continues its forward momentum, I'm authorizing my entire team to work whatever hours needed over Thanksgiving." Not only had she proclaimed her decision rather than requesting it, but she was trampling all over the administrative component. If the FBI was anything like ATF, holiday pay was a sore point with supervisors. Once again, she was poking the bureaucratic bear.

Surprisingly, Webb and Garcia gave their blessing without hesitation. "And I'd recommend SWAT on stand-by," Garcia said.

Heidi spread her hands. "At the moment it's a small takedown of two members, but their cell leader is requesting more men. I'll keep you appraised." Without more Race members or at least linking Nate Henderson and Dennis Howe to the mosque bombing, these arrests were a tiny, side success—not even close to what she'd been brought in to do.

"What do you have for us on the counterintelligence side?"

Not enough. "I'm beginning to suspect the leak may not be on my team."

Webb cocked his head, and Garcia's eyebrows lifted.

Heidi slipped a list from her briefcase. "I reviewed this database showing employees who were still in the building the night the call was made from Hennessey's office." She passed it to Garcia, seated on her right. "As you can see from the highlighted names, my associates were a handful of women, two Black agents, and Josh Peters, a rookie agent who's low on my list of suspects. He's white and the right age to be recruited, but he comes from a long, distinguished FBI lineage." Garcia handed the list to Webb as Heidi went on. "I'm certainly following up on him, but I suspect we're looking for someone with a tertiary association to the case." Hell, it could even be the nightly janitor who'd come across the information.

Technically, it could be these two men. Webb and Garcia had both been in the building that night, and no doubt they had high enough security clearance to look up the cypher code to get into Hennessey's office. Requesting their files was a nonstarter, though, and honestly, given the number of names she was working her way through, they would be the last two she'd investigate.

Webb handed the list across the coffee table. "Very good, Heidi. Overall, I'm pleased with your progress, but given the depth and cost of this investigation, let's hope we can arrest more than two measly members." Again, back to the underlying warning.

"My thoughts exactly, sir," she said, but it didn't negate the sting. Hennessey had come up with squat after almost five months in command. It was a testament to Calvin Sheer's brilliance in making his teams so small and the harm done by whoever here was warning those soldiers. She wouldn't get far ferreting out terrorist cells until she found the traitor.

"Sorry for the late notice, but I invited someone to Thanksgiving dinner."

"Isn't that nice," Mom said absently. "What's his name?"

Jace paused. He probably deserved that. He'd never brought a woman home before. His relationships were too fleeting. "Heidi Hall," he said shortly.

The silence on the end of the line was ripe with astonishment and questions. Trust Mom to completely misread the situation.

"Don't make a big deal about it. She's my supervisor, and she's from out of town. I felt sorry for her." Which wasn't true, but damned if he knew what had spurred his impromptu invitation last night.

"I see." The two words held fathomless disappointment, and Jace ignored the impulse to engage further. Trick was the perfect son, the only one who'd managed to marry and reproduce, which were Mom's loftiest hopes for her five sons. Coming in second to Trick in any area was a poison-coated thorn in his side.

Time to change the subject. "Have Kevin and Gage found an apartment yet?"

"I think Gage's behavior lately put the kibosh on living together, so Kevin's decided to look for a one-bedroom."

"At least you're down to one final son living at home, Mom."

"I don't know how much longer your father can take having Gage here. They fight all the time."

The impulse to jump into the savior role and fix the latest family crisis pulled at Jace. The silence over the line meant Mom expected it too—in a wave-a-magic-wand way, when it would take months to pull Gage out of the hole he'd dug for himself. Under no circumstances could Jace whip him into shape right now. The training with Chaz, the avalanche of documentation for Heather's prosecution, and the actual hours spent with those imbecilic cell members took up every waking moment. "I'll talk to him at Thanksgiving," he said reluctantly. More hours out of his one day off. Just the simple task of leaving this bu-house would require over an hour of the stealthiest backtracking.

"You can call him anytime," Mom pointed out. "I really am worried something will happen between him and your father if someone doesn't step in."

"Yeah, sure, Mom." He was so sick of this role, but who else in the family could do it? "I've got a few minutes. Put him on."

A puff of exasperation sounded in his ear. "Now isn't good. He's sleeping like the dead."

"Mom." Jace glanced at his watch. "It's after ten. Wake him up already!"

"He only got home a few hours ago. Why don't I text you when he wakes up?"

Jace paced a tight circle in his kitchen. "He's never going to get a job *or* get a life if you keep coddling him like this."

"I'm not coddling him, Jason Robert," she snapped. "I'm giving him a supportive environment while he adjusts back to civilian life, and I'll thank you to keep your childrearing opinions to yourself."

Chest burning, he didn't fight this second pull to rise to her expectations. She was the one decent relationship he had with a female. "I'll try to call this afternoon, okay?"

"And you won't forget?"

"I won't forget." Hanging up, he rubbed at his chest and gulped a breath. It was getting mighty hard to prioritize the dual expectations from the women in his life. There were only twenty-four hours in a day, so one of them was getting let down, and his body was alerting him that was totally unacceptable.

19

The caller ID on the bu-phone read *unavailable*, but Jace answered. Even if it was a robocall, it was being taped and transcribed. "Speak."

"Nate's been telling me great things," Calvin Sheer said in lieu of a greeting.

"He's inept." Jace made sure his tone was biting. "He'll bring down this celebration if you keep him in charge." One of the first things Chaz had instructed him on was lingo. Keeping nouns vague. White supremacists were as paranoid as drug dealers about being infiltrated and wiretapped, so conversations carried vague references or substitutions like "cake" for "C-4" or "celebration" for "bombing." When Sheer didn't respond in the prolonged transatlantic silence, Jace continued. "And I'm sure as shit not letting him take credit. What other help do you have locally?"

"What do you need?" The leader's tone was more subdued.

"I can get my hands on the supplies, but I need men who have experience pulling it all together. Nate not only doesn't have the required skills, but I'm wondering about an undiagnosed mental illness."

"He can be a loose cannon," Sheer conceded.

Jace barked out a humorless laugh. "He's using your men to settle personal vendettas at great risk to themselves. He's giving your organization a bad rep and harming whatever hopes we have of growing in Chicago."

Sheer's sigh was mixed with condescension. "When you're gathering an army of men who have nothing else in common besides their beliefs, you quickly learn you can't be choosy. A soldier is a soldier, and Nate's intensity is an asset. He gets the job done."

Jace let the topic die. If he insisted on transferring to another cell, Sheer might grow suspicious. Or worse, might actually transfer him. What if Nate ordered the replacement recruit to rape Zamira?

But more local cells had to be uncovered, and Sheer had to be lured back to the States. There was no extradition clause with Russia, and this snake needed beheading. "I'll take care of the supplies," Jace reiterated, "just connect me with some brains."

"I'll be in touch." Sheer hung up.

Jace stood and stretched, then glanced at his watch. He had a whole hour to kill before going to Nate's for the evening meeting. After that, he'd be right back here in this living room, going through the hot wash with Heidi. He despised how she needled him mercilessly until he coughed up some vulnerability about the role he was playing. But it was also a chance to see her again. And these private moments were fast becoming the best part of his day. Especially last night...the "silly game" at the door.

He shook off the already spinning fantasy. That his thoughts turned to her every spare moment was as irritating as an unreachable back itch. It had to be because she kept herself wrapped in a shroud of mystery. What made her tick? What turned her on? How had she navigated a male-dominated field that had drummed so many other women from its ranks?

Josh couldn't be right—Heidi hadn't slept her way up the chain of command. Her brains and balls were evident to anyone who worked with her for more than half an hour. But there was also Alma's cryptic mention of Wastewater during that first meeting, and Heidi almost flinching...

An internet search had uncovered little except that a task force had investigated a series of pipe bomb incidents last year at a waste treatment plant in Atlanta. Although the perps had been arrested and successfully convicted, one plant employee and an ATF agent had lost their lives. All Jace's attempts to find out more had hit brick walls. Wastewater was a lure he could no longer ignore.

Scrolling through his phone directory, he tapped Alma's name. She answered on the first ring.

"Hey, you got a minute?" At her assent, he sat back down, dragging a pad and pen closer. "Can you give me the gist of that ATF op you mentioned a few weeks ago? Wastewater?"

"Why would you want to know?"

Well, shit, this hadn't been well thought out. In her eyes, he was no longer on the MOSQMO task force. Would no longer be working for Heidi. So why ask about an investigation she'd headed? Thinking fast, he said, "We're looking into a similar MO at a treatment plant in Indiana. My boss is in talks with the original SAC who oversaw Wastewater, but I wanted the unofficial version. Figure Heidi's up to her neck in MOSQMO, but I remember you mentioning it a few weeks ago."

He stopped for breath, suddenly cognizant that he'd

been rambling, and his skin was damp. Lying did not come easy. Ask him to penetrate enemy lines in an Afghan desert, and he wouldn't break a sweat. This? He could have just gotten out of a swimming pool.

"I was a tertiary member," Alma said apologetically. "I don't know much."

"No worries. Whatcha got?"

"A disgruntled employee at the Utoy Creek Water Reclamation Plant set off a couple of pipe bombs that effectively shut the entire facility down. Heidi headed the investigation and came up with the idea to have an undercover agent act as a trainee plant operator. I'm not sure of the details, but a plant employee was held hostage and the negotiations didn't go well. He ended up dead."

"Didn't an agent die too? Was that the UCA?"

"Yeah. His name was Evan Cartwright. It happened *after* the arrest. The investigation was successful and winding down."

"What happened?" Jace asked.

"He committed suicide."

Jace halted his note-taking. "Suicide?" he blurted. *After* a successful op? "Why?"

"No clue." He could hear the shrug in Alma's tone. "That's as far as the rumors go. None of the other agents knew if something happened on the op, but as the team's case agent and Evan's handler, I'm sure Heidi does."

Jace thanked Alma and hung up. Suicide... Shit. He slouched back on the sofa, staring at the ceiling, tap-tapping the pen on his thigh. Was this why Heidi was so button-lipped about her past? Why she showed up every evening trying to excavate his emotions? Was she afraid of a reoccurrence?

Or did she blame herself for Cartwright's death?

HEIDI STRAINED to hear what Jace was saying. Based on tone alone, he was defensive. Adjusting her earphones didn't help, and given Chaz's knotted eyebrows, he was experiencing the same difficulty.

"Something's wrong with the audio on his baseball cap," she said. "But I'll bet their argument is related to the Sheer call."

"Probably." Chaz stared at the screen, where the microscopic camera in Jace's cap was at least recording Nate Henderson's thunderous expression. "I'd be pissed, too. Jace totally overstepped his bounds again."

Heidi swiveled in her seat. "Oh, come on." This infernal need to criticize Jace's every move was too much. "Sheer called *him*."

Chaz glanced over, lips thinned. "Sheer called to compliment him, and Jace immediately put it upon himself to trash someone above him in the hierarchy."

"Yeah, to get more Race affiliates." Surely Chaz saw the bigger picture. "Taking down one cell of two men is not going to look good given all the time, money, and resources we've sunk."

"I'm just saying." Chaz waved a hand at the screen. "What do you expect?"

Nate jabbed a finger near the camera, his fury visible in the glint of his eyes and spittle forming at the corners of his mouth. The words remained muffled, but lip-reading obscenities was effortless. A tightness entered Heidi's stomach. Even Sheer thought Nate was a loose cannon. Had Jace overstepped bounds to the point of danger? This was Wastewater all over again—watching a smoothly run op suddenly careen out of control and being stuck in the cocoon of a warm van. Damn this bad feed! Were they arguing about more than the hierarchy structure? "Call him," she said quietly. "Tell him to get out."

The picture onscreen jolted, like Jace had abruptly stood. More muffled dialogue and the scene changed to the front door growing closer. *That's right, Jace, withdraw and regroup.*

"I'm at your hot wash tonight," Chaz announced, not even remotely asking permission. "I need to review his recording of this to assess how badly he's damaged the op."

20

J ace grabbed another beer and chugged half of it, still anchored in front of the open refrigerator. He hadn't been able to tolerate one more second of Heidi and Chaz hunched over tonight's recording. Despite being a room away, though, Nate's obscenity-laced rebuke floated in, rekindling a deep-seated fury. The guy was a deeply insane dick. Arresting him at the end of this would be such a goddamn pleasure.

Jace guzzled the rest of the beer, his anger pivoting inward. He never failed at anything, and he sure as hell didn't fuck up *this* badly. How hard could it be to spout white supremacist shit and gather evidence? And yet acting on his instincts to move the case forward was having the exact opposite effect. The disgust and disappointment on Chaz's face tonight had been easy to take compared to his dismissive "I knew you wouldn't be able to handle this."

"Jace?" Heidi called. "We're finished."

Snatching another bottle, he slammed the refrigerator door. Showtime. Drawing in a breath, he strolled into the living room and sat military-erect in the wing-back. Being defensive would be a waste of time. He was tired and wanted them out of here.

He faced the two of them on the sofa like he was facing Mom and Pop after blowing through a curfew, mea culpa expression and all. "I screwed up," he said bluntly. "I get it."

"We told you to pass any ideas by us before acting on them," Heidi said. "Sheer doesn't know Jason McGowan yet. He's not going to appreciate you trying to divide his men when his goal is to simply amass an army."

"That was apparent the second I faced Nate's wrath."

Chaz frowned. "Then why'd you do it?"

Jace raked a hand through his hellishly long hair. "Because I'm right." He checked the defiant tone. Ever since he'd met the man, something about Chaz rubbed him the wrong way. "Look, the conversation with Sheer was a calculated risk. I need access to more members, and more importantly, I was telling him the truth. Nate doesn't have the smarts to pull off a terrorist act, so we need to rope in other members to plan and plant my fake C-4. If the ideas come from me, it's totally entrapment."

"Then you brainstorm with us," Chaz snapped. "I'm not taking time off from my cases to train you, and advise you, and wipe your skinny white ass just so you can go rogue whenever you *think* you know better." His scowl mimicked Nate's from earlier. "You still think this is a game. You still act like it's no big deal if you make mistakes. Let me tell you, undercover work is a high-wire act. No safety net. Forget the damn balance pole. Every sentence you utter has life-and-death consequences."

Sheesh. "That's a bit extreme—"

"They're hyper-paranoid, Jace. A *real* white supremacist just accepted into the Race would never sow seeds of discord, at least not this early."

Jace slumped back, scrubbing a palm over his face. "Yeah, yeah, I got it."

"I don't think you do." Chaz leaned forward, the next berating syllable already forming when Heidi placed a hand on his forearm. The touch was tender, her expression that of a colleague.

Jealousy pierced Jace's chest like an industrial-sized ice pick. Clenching his jaw, he looked away.

"That's enough, Chaz," she said softly. "I think we've all said what we needed to say. Let's call it a night."

Even though Chaz's expression indicated he could've gone on for several hours, he raised his hands in surrender. "Whatever." He rose, a tall, muscular badass exuding homicidal fury. No doubt he was extremely authentic in his underworld drug character. "See you both tomorrow."

Jace picked at the beer label until the door shut, then squinted wearily over at Heidi. She was busy packing the recording equipment on the cocktail table, but her troubled look gave him pause. Was she considering taking him off the assignment?

"I got the message," he said. "I'll toe the line."

She shook her head like he'd misread her. "I'm beginning to wonder if you have that in you. We ask for stealth, and we get a lit fuse."

"That's a bit dramatic, Heidi." Yeah, his condescending tone was straight-up insubordination, but he didn't give a flying fuck.

"*Is* it dramatic?" She waved her hands like an agitated choir director. "You have two superiors constantly advising you, you've read through a huge list of scenarios with suggestions of what to say, and yet over and over, you go rogue at the drop of a hat. Isn't this what you pulled with Agent Hathaway earlier this year?"

Jace exhaled in a low hiss. Margo, again. Wherever she was, she had to be laughing at how much she was haunting his career. Well, screw this! "Tell me about Evan Cartwright, Heidi. Tell me why an agent in your command took his own life."

Heidi stiffened, color draining from her face.

A hollow ache spread in his chest. Fuck, had he screwed up. "I'm sorry. I didn't mean it to come out like that."

She stared at him in horrified silence, a death mask with wide, unblinking eyes. He tried apologizing again, but she was up and stumbling toward the door, briefcase still open on the table.

"Wait," he said, catching her in two long strides. "Heidi, wait." He grabbed her bicep, but she spun around and shoved him away. Her chest heaved with gulping breaths. The glistening in her eyes couldn't be tears; she looked too livid to cry.

"How dare you bring up his name." Her voice shook, the tone an octave higher than usual. "You could work thirty more years and never acquire his experience and intuitive skill."

More ice picks to the chest. A part of him wanted to take exception, to trot out his elite military past, but the larger, competitive-oldest-brother side wanted to exceed her regard for Cartwright, no matter what it took. "I deserve that," he said stiffly. "Please sit back down."

Emotions warred across her face. Stubborn refusal, dread, maybe a flicker of relief?

"You forgot your briefcase." He pointed at it like a game show host. "And we still have the hot wash."

The questions he hated might be his saving grace. Avoiding eye contact, she brushed by on her way back. In his mind's eye, he grabbed her, backed her into a bear-hug embrace. Whispered...well, *something* in her ear. What could he possibly say to defuse the situation? Interpreting women was so not in his wheelhouse. All that mystery and moodiness—dual pits of quicksand. And the depth of a woman's anger? Shit. He'd rather dodge a rocket-propelled grenade. Trick and Kevin not only read women correctly, but responded in ways that gained adoration, a skill Jace had given up on acquiring long ago.

So instead of expertly repairing the damage, he gestured to her empty glass. "More club soda?"

Heidi shook her head, sinking onto the sofa. Exhaustion etched deep lines around her mouth. "Let's just...get through the questions. I still have work—"

"Back to the office," Jace finished, reclaiming the wing-back. "How long do you think you can keep working eighteen-hour days?"

"We're making great headway." She dug into her briefcase and retrieved her iPad. A couple of swipes and taps and she looked up, finally gracing him with a wan smile. "What went well tonight?"

He settled back in the chair, exhaling through pursed lips. "I wasn't kicked out of the cell." The word *yet* hovered in the air between them, and he hurried on. "Nate may be mad that I went over his head, but A, he can't do anything about it because everything is Sheer's call, and B, I think I've convinced both of them we need to gather more manpower, so hopefully we can take down more cells next week."

Her fingers tap-tapped, but her nod seemed distracted. He couldn't think of anything else, a testament to how shitty the night had been. How well had Cartwright done in hot washes? "That's it," he said shortly.

"What are your immediate goals for improvement?"

To stop competing with a dead agent. He grabbed the now-lukewarm beer and twisted the cap. "Come up with a plan to lure Sheer onto a plane." He took a bracingly long chug, and his parched throat thanked him. He rested the bottle on his knee. "I also need to do something to gain Chaz's respect. Maybe walk on water? Turn that water into wine? I'm still debating my options." He jerked his chin at her iPad. "Maybe swap that with the first goal."

The ghost of a grin softened her face, and he sucked in a breath. Alongside the overwhelming relief, something else surged inside him. A need to regain her esteem? To be forgiven for his jackassery? Anything to return to last night's camaraderie and that almost-kiss by the door. There was only one way forward—he owed her something of himself. A nugget he'd never told anyone.

He drank another long pull, watching her type while he gathered his courage. By the time he swallowed, her fingers rested lightly on her device, waiting. "It's not like I go rogue to piss either of you off or damage to the op," he said slowly.

She nodded, brows knitting in curiosity. Jace put down the beer and wiped his palms vigorously along his thighs. She glanced at the movement, and he quickly crossed his arms. "I get this gut instinct, see, and if I—if I don't act on it—if I don't seize control, then something bad might happen."

"Can you give me an example?"

God, this was hard. "That whole Margo thing. She was the kind of agent that wanted to double down on research and study the investigation from all angles before even beginning to draw up a plan of action. A fluid situation made her downright freeze, but God forbid she listen to me." He spread his hands, warming to the topic. "Because even though I came from a black ops background, I'm now a special agent *associate* until I finish my college degree. Do you know how frustrating it is being told what to do by a timid boss when I know better, faster, more effective solutions?"

Heidi stopped typing and studied him intently.

"My insubordination had *nothing* to do with Margo being a woman," he said. "It was her dragging her feet while Syrians were planting bombs around Chicago. It was my kid brother being kidnapped because of *my* case." The case Jace had dragged him into. He blew out an exasperated breath, keyed up as if six months hadn't passed.

"When I'm not in control, people get hurt." The impulsive comment was out of his mouth before he could stop himself.

Something in Heidi perked up. Maybe her straightening imperceptibly, or a dawning in her eyes. It happened too fast for him to catch. Thankfully, she hadn't typed any of that last part. *Yet.*

"I don't know why I said that. Please don't add it."

"Taking responsibility for everything and everyone would make anyone anxious, Jace."

"I'm not anxious," he corrected her, reclaiming his grip on the beer. Trust her to fixate on the dumbass remark he hadn't meant. "I'm telling you why I can't sit around like a stooge and leave the planning to others."

While she acknowledged his remark with a nod, that perked-up quality remained, like nothing he said in his defense would matter further.

"I have the experience and intelligence to be two or three ranks further up in the FBI," he said, trying anyway, "but I'm pigeonholed by the narrow-mindedness of this organization."

"I never thought I'd say this," she said, looking down at her iPad, "but we have a lot more in common than you know."

"Like what?"

"We should both be much further along in our careers."

What had held her back? He held his breath, waiting for her to elaborate. Her color had returned, and a strand of hair had escaped from behind her ear to curl against her cheek. In the glow of the living room lamp, she resembled those smart, shy girls in high school that would hide deep in the library carrels, peeping up at him as he passed by with his friends. Back then, their mysteriousness had made him ill at ease. They were so different from the sassy, in-your-face cheerleaders—like the side of Heidi he'd met at the wedding. The signals were damn clear that night. If not for misunderstanding who Dave was to her.

But this woman—this softer, more vulnerable Heidi —was powerfully sexy. He wanted her. And he was tired of hiding it for the good of the op.

As the silence lengthened, it became obvious that was all she would be sharing of herself. Well, there was always tomorrow's hot wash.

She raised her head, her deep brown eyes back to professionally attentive. "Any other goals, Jace?"

"Yes," he said. *Fuck tomorrow.* "I want to kiss you."

21

Heidi's heart flitted straight into her throat. "Excuse me?"

"You heard me." His quiet authority shot lightning through her veins while, fantastically, goosebumps skittered along her arms. Such a shredding of her equilibrium caused a deep shiver, overt body language no words could camouflage. To Jace's credit, he read the signal right. Clunking his beer on the cocktail table, he moved in. His weight displaced the sofa cushion, dipping her toward him. "Kiss me, Heidi."

This was the first time reading visceral cues felt like a curse. If only she were ignorant of what darkening pupils signified. Or why his head slanted to the perfect angle of its own accord. If only he'd stop giving her such a scorching Big Bad Wolf look. But most of all, if only she could close the distance and feel the crush of his mouth.

"I can't."

A muscle fluttered along his jaw. "Can't or don't want to? There's a big difference."

She owed him honesty. That he'd finally admitted to his anxiety at maintaining his superhero status had taken massive guts. "I can't. I'm your supervisor. It would put your op and my command at risk." She was also older and devoid of the taut body and bunny-rabbit enthusiasm he was no doubt used to.

"But you want to," he said.

She let her face answer. For weeks her struggle of wanting-to versus should-not had been tearing her apart.

"Okay, then."

A dare flared to life, hovering between them. He laced an arm around the back of the sofa and leaned in, his lips inches from hers. She breathed in the scent of beer and his fabric softener. "For the next two minutes," he said, "we're no longer UCA and handler."

Something about having a time limit made it seem feasible. Less forbidden. What trouble could they get into in two minutes? Hell, that was the time it took her to brush her teeth. She inhaled unsteadily. "Two it is."

"And that's *all* you get." The severity of his tone was adorable. "Kissing only. No copping feels or mashing body parts together, *comprende*?"

This teasing was a side she hadn't seen before, and it was charming enough that a snort-giggle escaped with her "yes."

"That's attractive," he murmured, grasping his phone and summoning his virtual assistant. "Set a two-minute timer," he ordered, and the disembodied female voice repeated his command.

He placed the phone on the coffee table and slid the remaining inches, his expression fierce. Long lashes lowered as his mouth closed over hers. His lips were damp from the beer and surprisingly gentle, even tentative. Shifting closer, he wrapped an arm around her waist, and she clasped shoulders that felt like carved rock under soft cotton. With a whispered sigh, she nestled further into his body heat. He might have his flaws, but kissing wasn't one of them.

He slanted his head, his mouth seeking another angle. His strong fingers threaded through her hair as his tongue swept the seam of her lips. She accepted it willingly, emitting a soft moan. The kiss grew deeper, hotter. Their tongues tangled in an erotic duel, and the Flirt, who'd been ravenous since that garter seduction, greedily absorbed this sensual invasion.

The blaring alarm jarred her like an electric shock. No way could that have been two minutes.

Jace withdrew slowly, repeating her thought aloud in a husky growl as he shut off the horrible ringing. His eyes were heavy-lidded and hypnotic. The naked desire on his face had to mirror hers. Years dropped away and she was young and vibrant again, every cell sparkling and tingling and crying out for more. The burdensome weight of the investigation and her smothering exhaustion had disappeared. She could do this all night. God, it would be so easy to lean in and continue, even take over... He wouldn't resist—look at that longing.

Jace inhaled deeply, a faint grin appearing, which bloomed into a captivating smile. "That was something," he murmured. "Thank you."

"Time flies." Her words came out much more regretfully than was appropriate, and she huffed out an embarrassed laugh.

"You look so different when you smile." One rough palm cradled her cheek, his other arm still draped along the sofa. He didn't retreat any further, so the flow of his breath streamed on her. "So soft and vulnerable."

"Yeah." She waggled her brows. "Me in a nutshell." She took her time studying his handsome features, then boldly traced his eyebrow with her thumb, skimming it along the edge of his razor-sharp cheekbone to the corner of his supple mouth.

He eyed her lips leisurely, like a wolf would a sheep. She paused, thumb pad about to outline his plump lower lip. She'd be sending him a direct signal, and he raised his gaze, daring her. Once again she was back to the thousand reasons she should gather her things and go. Retreat. Flee.

Her thumb trailed away; her hand dropped in her lap. "I'm going to call it a night," she said. "And we won't mention this again."

Regret flitted across his face, but he dipped his chin. "Yes, ma'am."

Good. The "ma'am" brought enough formality back that it was the final push she needed. Heidi retrieved her phone and summoned a rideshare with trembling fingers, then dropped the device in her coat pocket and gathered her things.

"I'll walk you out," he said, standing alongside her, but awkwardness was already setting in. Something about holding her briefcase with all the files and Jace's tape of tonight's events...

"That's okay," she answered, "the car was a few blocks away when it confirmed."

"How much longer?"

"Not long."

"How much?"

She barely avoided the eye roll as she dug out the phone and glanced at the screen. Exhaling a soft laugh, she glanced up at him. "You're not going to believe this. Two minutes."

Fire lit his eyes, sucking her breath right back out of her. *Oh, what the hell.*

Heidi dropped the briefcase.

22

Heidi yawned loudly as she sifted through the final pages of Mark Hennessey's thick personnel file. The former MOSQMO case agent had a long history as a dedicated street agent who closed cases efficiently and readily volunteered his help to fellow agents' investigations. Mark was liked by all, just as Alma had said during that initial dinner, and he'd racked up annual reviews full of praise. Nothing in here pointed to white supremacist views or a dubious secondary life. Another waste of time.

Pushing the file aside, she leaned forward in the ergonomic chair and studied the wedding photograph she'd never gotten around to stuffing in a drawer. "Who's the leak?" she asked in the silence of the empty federal building. Maybe she'd call him again tomorrow, pick his brain in more depth, but then again, that might prompt him to call Garcia to claim the woman in charge wasn't handling the job. It had happened before when she sought out advice from friendly colleagues. What she considered requesting an opinion, they saw as inept. The alphabet soup organizations were notoriously cutthroat. She'd figure this out on her own.

Heidi scanned down the list of Caucasian males on her team, sipping coffee that had grown cold hours ago. Could she be wrong? Was it tunnel vision to narrow the leak down to only that parameter? White supremacists weren't known for their supportive feminist views, so it was hard to conceive any female agents, analysts, or the AUSA, Heather, as the betrayer. All of them strove to push through the glass ceiling daily, the more aggressive ones tromping on others to get a rung further.

There were two male agents with Latino backgrounds, but again, white supremacists didn't welcome anyone of color or a record of immigrating even two generations ago. The motivation wasn't there to tip off Bradley.

No, her instinct was right. She would go back through the files of the white guys: Bill Fontana, Josh Peters, Arron Gibbs, the two Jims, three Bobs, and seventeen analysts. And Jace. Although reviewing his file was sheer nosiness. He was so uncomfortable spouting neo-Nazi views that he was almost blowing the op.

Heidi closed her eyes, luxuriously surrendering to the image of Jace the nanosecond before that second two-minute kiss tonight. The erotic promise in those eyes, the way those steely arms gathered her into the hard length of him. His seduction of her mouth had left her limp as a noodle.

She gazed unfocused at the ceiling. Slicing through the glow of this pulsating desire was abject fear. If Garcia ever found out she'd entangled with a subordinate, she could kiss this coveted position goodbye. This old boys' network extended to ATF headquarters in D.C., and men she considered friends often acted like sharks at the scent of weakness, especially weaker women not living up to their double standard. It would take so little to ruin her career. And without that, she was nothing.

Getting together with Jace made no sense, so why did she keep recalling his kisses, fantasizing about taking him in bed or up against a wall, his naked body so deliciously forbidden? She blinked and bolted upright. Enough! All this goopy idiocy was eating into her precious investigation time. It was almost one in the morning, and she was no closer to finding the traitor. This failure could cost her the op. Cost Jace his life.

Heidi rifled through the stack of personnel files until she came to Bill Fontana's. He was respectful to her face, but instinct made her reselect his file first. Yes, he was a bit of a sad sack, and the divorce was obviously a factor. Yes, he struck her as a desk jockey, and she held a contemptuous bias toward all officers of the law who were just marking time until retirement. But most of all, the CPD officer hadn't come up with anything substantial to move the Bradley murder investigation forward, and that struck her as odd.

Heidi flipped through the pages. Nothing had stood out the first time. He'd started with the Rockford PD before transferring to Chicago eleven years ago. An old resumé, stapled to the back, highlighted a criminal justice degree from Keiser University, followed by thirteen months of supervisory probation as a guard at USP Marion, a medium-security penitentiary in Illinois.

He'd certainly have encountered white supremacy gangs as a prison guard. The Aryan Brotherhood had a huge presence in the penal system. "Wait a minute," she muttered, digging for her notes from the team meeting— gosh, was it only sixteen hours ago? She flipped to the page where Josh had mentioned Thomas Bradley's incarceration at... Here it was. *Marion*. No dates to compare with Bill's thirteen-month supervision stint. Was it possible they'd been there at the same time? Known each other? Guard and prisoner. According to Josh, Bradley had joined the Aryan Brotherhood. Heidi frowned, tapping the pen rapidly on the pad.

When Josh brought up the Marion Pen detail, Bill hadn't uttered a peep. That was peculiar, right? To not acknowledge he'd worked there as a guard? Or ask Josh, "Hey, when was Bradley incarcerated?"

She glanced around the room, heart pummeling her ribcage like she'd guzzled a dozen espressos. If Bill was the double agent, she'd alerted him to two more Race names they were investigating. And if that information got back to Nate and Dennis, they'd immediately suspect the link had to be their newest member.

"Shit, shit, shit," she whispered. Her intuition had failed her. She'd compromised the op...

No. She hadn't. Her exhaustion was triggering wildly unsubstantiated thoughts. Closing her eyes, she willed the return of commonsense. First thing tomorrow she'd get Bradley's incarceration dates and compare them to Bill's resumé. No need to panic ahead of time.

The self-talk worked, and she jotted an email to Josh, marking it urgent and confidential. Yawning, she closed Bill's file and signed off the computer. One fifteen. Her phone rang, shrill and overly loud in the silent building. She jumped like she'd been shot. Caller ID: Jace.

"What's wrong?" she asked, kicking herself for the worry in her voice.

"Sheer just called."

Heidi frowned at his excitement of getting a call in the middle of the night, her sluggish mind taking too long to calculate it was nine fifteen in the morning in Moscow.

"And?" she sputtered.

"He said he'd slept on it and agrees with me. He'll call in two other cells to help us blow up the restaurant."

She slumped back, expelling a sigh of relief. "Excellent. Six to eight more supremacists to incriminate." Heather would be thrilled.

"He also said one of the men has working knowledge of explosives and commercial construction. Sheer's already called Nate and told him to host the entire group tonight."

Her exhaustion turned to giddy glee. "That's fantastic! Your instincts were right."

"And here's what my instinct says now." Jace's voice was clipped and authoritative. "I don't think I should wear a wire tonight. There was enough paranoia at that initial meeting with Nate and Dennis. Add in more suspicious personalities, and it'll be too easy to get tagged."

Heidi frowned. "You think everyone's going to pat each other down even when they've all been handpicked by Sheer?"

"Until trust is established, I can guarantee it. What about the ball cap I used the other night?"

"The audio part is still being fixed." No way was she agreeing to valuable information becoming hearsay. "What about a recording device in a pen or a watch? There are even ones that look like a thumb drive that can record for hours."

"I don't know what a construction supervisor would be doing with a thumb drive in his pocket."

Hearing her ideas rejected in that dismissive tone stiffened her spine. She'd opened her mouth to demand he obey when he said, "The watch sounds feasible."

She exhaled and collected her thoughts. "Chaz and I won't be able to listen in real time. Your emergency word or gesture won't work if you get into mortal danger."

"A, I'm a former SEAL. B, how much mortal danger can I get into at a meet-and-greet?"

A meet-and-greet that frisked each member at the door.

Heidi kept the thought to herself. "I'll send the requisition right now." She toggled the computer awake and typed in Garcia's email address. Not only could he acquire the equipment faster, but the MOSQMO case agent requisitioning a microscopic recording device would raise too many questions.

"Call Chaz first thing this morning," she said, fingers flying across the keyboard, phone awkwardly tucked between her chin and shoulder. "I'm sure he'll have a ton of advice."

No response.

"That's an order." She hit send as more silence filled the line. "Jace?"

"I heard you," he said shortly.

She paused at the insolence in his tone, then checked herself. His admission tonight on why he grabbed control brought a different perspective here. He wasn't dissing her authority; he was bucking the constraint she and Chaz kept putting on his gut instinct. She needed to acknowledge when he was right.

"While I understand Chaz's concerns tonight and why he said what he said, I also think your instinct to push Sheer was right. I'm thrilled it worked out in our favor."

"Thanks." The warmth in the lone word reverberated through her soul.

"I'll touch base with you midmorning to coordinate your evening."

"Copy," he said. "And please tell me I've reached you at home."

"I'm heading there now." She murmured a goodnight after he did and disconnected the call.

Jace's sleep-interrupted voice was deeper than normal, which dredged up an image of him sitting up in bed, the sheet crumpled at his waist. Heidi dropped her head onto her folded arms and welcomed the fantasy. Moon rays slanting in the window would illuminate that naked chest, accentuate all those hard muscles, while keeping his tousled hair and the sharp angles of his face in the shadows. Those firm, talented lips shaping each word in the darkness...

Oh, to seduce him right now. Straddle his slim hips. Take her time caressing the ridges and valleys, then lick every burning, writhing, sinuous inch until she knew him blind.

The tingling in her belly had grown into an uncomfortable ache, breaking the vision. Heidi sat up groggily, her breath ragged. Instead of Jace's warm bed, she was in Hennessey's office, lit with a too-bright desk lamp. Her pounding heartbeat began to slow, leaving her with both a wish and a fear. The wish was one night with Jace, no holds barred. No worries over all the reasons their liaison would be the death knell to her career. Which was impossible.

So fear it was: could she finish this op without giving in to her craven temptations?

23

Turned out the Race had recruited a big-time mover and shaker in the city. Ken Nash, friend of the mayor, philanthropist, and owner of the largest commercial construction company in Chicago stood across from Jace, along with six other men encircling Nate's dining table. Before them lay the architectural floor plan for Johnny's Steakhouse, courtesy of Ken. He was flanked by his own cell members, John and Hank, who listened intently to his quiet words and followed his finger as he pointed out key trusses in the structure where they could affix the C-4.

"So, we've got a Howe Design truss bridge here," Ken explained. "And these load-bearing walls here and here. A straight truss like that is the strongest part of the ceiling and holds the most structural weight. If it's compromised, the whole building collapses like a bunch of matchsticks."

Jace nodded absently, his hands stuffed in the front pockets of his jeans, which pointed his watch face directly at the speaker and captured each word. His gaze flicked back and forth among those three men. This was the cell to watch. Unlike the schmucks he'd been paired with, Ken and his soldiers had shunned the whiney complaints and wild conspiracies. Their interaction focused solely on the project, in a deadly, vengeful kind of way. Hairs rose on the nape of Jace's neck at this cell's display of leadership and intelligence. They'd be formidable to take down. And outing Ken Nash as a white supremacist terrorist? That would rock Chicago to its core.

Ken stroked his chin, like an old wizard deep in thought. "I'll need to do formal calculations, but I'm thinking, oh, say five and a half, six kilograms cut into thin sheets should do it. Mold it right up the flange near this cross section—"

"How many kilos are in a stick?" Nate interrupted, looking at Jace.

"About half a kilo."

As Ken nodded in agreement and continued his pointing tour, Jace sent a grudging prayer of thanks to Chaz. The undercover agent had harped long and loud about the importance of understanding every last detail of a career in construction. Several times tonight the op would've gone belly up if it hadn't been for the more experienced agent's advice, a stark lesson to do a better job of respecting Chaz's suggestions.

Jace concentrated on steadying the thump of his heart. He'd passed another test—from his own cell, for fuck's sake—but there'd be more. The paranoia in this room was palpable. As predicted, the evening had begun with mutual frisks at the door. The cells had never met before, that much was clear. And based on Ken's ease in acquiring C-4 for his construction projects, this was also not the cell responsible for the laborious accumulation of ammonium nitrate used in the Mosque Mohammed bombing.

Jace turned his attention to the third cell, a two-man operation, who'd immediately claimed the dominant positions at the head and foot of the table. Chris and Craig. He'd already forgotten which one was which because they looked nearly identical. Similar height and weight, scraggly, chest-length brown beards, and male-pattern baldness. Probing for more intel ended there, because Ken had immediately assumed the leadership role and begun the presentation. But based on the hard eyes and sullen expressions, this third cell was loaded for bear with violent blood lust.

"The blast may result in cracked foundations in neighboring structures, but for the most part, the explosion should be self-contained," Ken said. "Any questions?"

Dennis held up a hand. "How much C-4 can you lay your hands on without raising a red flag?"

"That depends." Ken turned to Jace. "I understand you work at Whitehead?"

All eyes swung to him again, and Chaz's reminders to play it cool reverberated in his head. Jace shifted his weight, nodding. "I can get the supplies."

Ken shook his head. "No need. We'll split it fifty-fifty. I'll get you the precise calculations tomorrow."

Sweat broke out on Jace's upper lip. Fifty-fifty was a complete no-go. It meant fifty percent of the C-4 would be real. But how to insist on supplying the whole share without looking suspicious? "I got this," he said casually. "My contribution to the cause."

Ken studied him with an alertness that dumped more adrenalin through Jace's system. "I appreciate the gesture, but that's taking too much of an inventory hit. Splitting will ensure less chance of detection."

"Jason's got this," Nate said forcefully. "Just tell him the quantity." It finally registered what Nate's participation boiled down to tonight. He thought the cells were in competition.

No surprise, Ken turned that all-encompassing gaze his way. In the subsequent standoff and prolonged silence, Jace held his breath. How odd to be rooting for Nate.

"Fine." Ken grabbed the edge of the floor plan and began rolling with swift expertise. "I suggest we each purchase burner phones tomorrow and plan to meet again later in the evening." He glanced around Nate's sparsely furnished condo. "For security purposes, I suggest someone else's place."

Jace immediately raised a hand. "I'm two blocks from the Kimball stop."

"No kidding," said the guy at the head of the table. "I am too. North Bernard."

"Shit, you're almost next door. West Leland." Jace grinned without humor. "Love that six a.m. garbage pickup at Chan's."

"Every fucking morning like clockwork." The guy gestured a couple of masturbatory strokes. "Fucking chinks."

"All agreed?" Ken's utter disregard for the embryonic interaction was both a snub and the kind of power grab Jace hadn't seen since his early boot-camp days. Beside him, Nate stiffened, but the others didn't seem to notice and nodded unanimously.

Jace gave out his street address. The bu-house had been wired for such an event, so tomorrow he'd capture video evidence. And the sound quality would be a whole lot clearer than this watch. He dared Chaz to find fault with his invite.

"Assignments for tomorrow." Ken pointed to the guy at the foot of the table. "Chris, you're in charge of reporting where all the security cameras are located within a four-block radius from Johnny's. Craig, you're a locksmith, right?" At the curt nod, Ken said, "Find us a way in. And find out if the new owners have installed a new security alarm."

"Will do."

"What's our role?" Nate said sharply, thumbing in Dennis's direction.

"Sit there and look pretty."

Jace barely avoided wincing. How could he neutralize this struggle for dominance before it sank the mission? "If the Race is gonna take credit, Nate and Dennis can draft a manifesto of some kind. Pass it by Sheer."

Ken shrugged and held up the plans like it was the staff of Moses. "See you all tomorrow at Jason's. Let's say eight o'clock?" When no one objected, he nodded to John and Hank, and the trio left.

"What an *asswipe*," Nate muttered.

Jace quickly turned to Craig, the locksmith neighbor, and held out his hand. "How long have you been in Mayfair?"

"Thirteen years. You?"

"Just moved there." Per Chaz, Jace stuck to the truth whenever possible. "That bakery on West Lawrence is the GOAT."

They followed Chris to the door. Dennis hung back with Nate, a show of brotherhood Jace immediately rejected. He could predict what came next. Ken's power grab had been a declaration of war to Nate, whose easily triggered inferiority complex would demand a destructive response targeted at a "lesser than."

A couple of days ago it had been the pizza delivery guy who handed over the wrong box and had the audacity to barely speak English. A week ago, a clerk had bagged Nate's sugar in with his detergent. His instantaneous, obscenity-laced tantrum was so excessive that the white manager and a small crowd of witnesses had ganged up on Nate and comforted the sobbing woman, an even bigger betrayal. The aftermath of Nate's sulking rage back in his living room, the insistence that this disrespect never happened a generation ago, and how one day he'd get the damn deference he deserved had been exhausting.

No, thank you to that replay. Jace closed Nate's door firmly behind him and waved goodbye to Chris climbing into his Camaro. "How long have you been with the Race?" he asked Craig, as they hung a right and walked briskly toward the Brown Line.

"Two years." That was almost as long as the Race had been in existence. Maybe Craig knew about Bradley's cell.

"Have you guys worked with other cells before?"

"Rarely. Only when Sheer says so." They turned the corner. The El station was one block up.

"Back then, did Sheer personally assign you and Chris to a cell?"

Craig sniffed and spat a thick stream. "Yeah, but it was more informal. Like, Chris and I have been friends since grade school and joined the Race together, so Sheer kept us together."

Made sense, but there'd been no leadership dynamic or jockeying for power from the two-man cell tonight, which was unusual. "Which one of you takes the lead?"

"Neither." Craig shoved his hands in his pockets. "We had someone, but he died."

Jace glanced over, every brain cell sparking to attention. Could *they* be Bradley's missing cell? All the manpower, all the months of investigating, and this final clue just plummeted in his lap? He blew out a breath to equalize the rush of adrenalin. "Jeez. My condolences." He scratched his ear and centered his ball cap to make sure the watch was as parallel to

Craig's mouth as possible. "Did he die in the Race line of duty?"

"Naw." Craig stared at the ground in front of him. "We didn't have anything in the works, so Chris and I went camping up in Wisconsin. We got back a week later and thought it was odd he hadn't called. Next thing we knew, the FBI was raiding his house, and he'd been dead for days."

"Nothing in the works and FBI was still targeting him?"

Craig shrugged without looking over.

Jace whistled in sympathy, chills coating his skin. He had to tread carefully. They swiped their El passes and walked into the station, which was warm and muggy compared to the chilly night. "Since you're a man short, maybe Sheer will put me in your cell. The one I'm in doesn't do squat." He made sure to sound glum.

Craig frowned at him. "I thought you guys came up with this restaurant deal."

"*I* came up with it," Jace lied. "It was immediately apparent those two didn't know squat about planning and organizing an operation this size, which is why I insisted Sheer bring in cells that could help. I need a cell that's more active."

"We used to be active." The tone was nostalgic. "We were tight, you know? Right now, we've kinda lost our mojo."

"Like, what did the three of you do?" It was pressing too hard, but he had to get something on tape.

Craig shrugged, his face shutting down. "Sheer's number one rule is we don't take credit and we don't brag. By the way, your suggestion tonight for a manifesto? Won't wash. We keep our victories to ourselves."

But if they'd pulled off the deadliest terrorist act in Chicago, surely Craig's ego would eventually slip up. "Do you have experience in a massive op like this? Know how to rig explosives?"

Craig threw him a look like he'd just asked Sammy Sosa if he'd ever hit a home run. "Sheer put us on your job for a reason," he said.

The rumble of the train came from the right, and they tracked the headlights racing toward them. Excitement sped through Jace's veins with the same rushing speed. This was huge. This was the cell. He had to convince Sheer to switch him. As much as he didn't want Nate to have a new recruit to initiate, the immediate focus had to be getting tight with Chris and Craig, gaining their trust and collecting evidence that they'd been behind the killing of two hundred and forty-five Muslims.

"I'll request a transfer." Jace raised his voice to be heard over the squeal of brakes as the train hissed to a standstill. "I want real accelerationists, not just guys who talk about it with their thumbs up their asses."

Craig grinned over his shoulder as he climbed aboard. "Hope you get it, man. You remind me a lot of our old leader."

24

Heidi's quick steps rang down the Bureau hallway, her spirit so jubilant it was hard not to twirl like Maria von Trapp ascending a mountain. Despite another night of little sleep, her wide smile and hellos to everyone she passed were heartfelt. Life was great! Jace's huge lead last night meant the op would be over within days, the perpetrators behind the mosque bombing finally arrested and eventually prosecuted.

She pictured the ecstatic looks and gushing compliments from Garcia, Webb, and Heather when she met them in twenty minutes. After handling three simultaneous investigations in this joint task force, she would truly earn her stellar reputation, which would go a long way to dull the guilt from Wastewater.

Josh got off the elevator ten feet away, and she called out to him. He pivoted and headed her way. Here was an agent whose attitude had taken a giant leap forward, although improvements were still needed. "I haven't received an email from you," she said. "I need the specific dates Thomas Bradley was in the pen ASAP."

"Sorry, ma'am. Home yesterday with a head cold." He did sound stuffed, and she stepped back, holding up both hands.

"I'll thank you not to get me sick the Tuesday before Thanksgiving." Or before she wrapped up the case of a lifetime. "Just email me the information within the hour, please."

"Yes, ma'am. Give me two minutes." He scurried off as she entered her office and dumped her briefcase beside the desk.

Glancing at the full inbox on her desk, she dismissed the instinct to get caught up in that quagmire so close to the meeting. Instead, she signed in to her email, which took several minutes and multiple passwords, each allowing her access into a higher-tiered security level. Dozens of messages popped up, mostly email to other personnel that she'd been copied on, and her eyes skimmed down the page until she registered her old boss's name and the *urgent* subject line. Heart leaping to her throat, she plopped in her chair and clicked on the email.

> *Heidi,*
> *Yesterday Evan Cartwright's family filed a wrongful death suit against ATF. I'll need your case notes and all emails pertaining to Operation Wastewater immediately. Specifically, our attorneys are looking for any indication that you were aware of his state of mind in the days before. Sorry to be abrupt; this has turned the entire office on its head.*
> *—Roger*

Heidi slumped back, throat thickening as memories flooded back. Evan sitting in her car as she pleaded with him to seek professional help. How he'd stoically refused the lifeline or acknowledged anything was even eating at him. *Any indication you were aware of his state of mind...*

Roger's email blurred, and she blinked rapidly. Yes, on a visceral level she'd known Evan had been sucked into some tortured, self-destructive tunnel, but had she documented her fears? Told anyone about the distressed body language? She racked her mind. She definitely hadn't alerted Roger. Hadn't wanted her boss to think she couldn't handle every detail of the op, and that was a regret she wore like stale perfume. Before the surprisingly successful conclusion, her progress reports had marked a case gone flat and an undercover operative who was not getting anywhere close to the targeted evidence.

She swallowed hard as the haunting old mantra resurfaced: she should have gone against the wishes of the higher-ups and pulled him out. Instead, she'd covered for his decompensating behavior and gone along with Roger's insistence to delay the takedown until more players could be pulled in. Her ambition had easily trumped instinct and compassion. She'd never forgive herself.

Heidi exhaled shakily. It had been a while since the self-blame and second-guessing had swamped her like this. Funny how working with overly decisive, confident Jace shielded the guilt and grief.

The blinking cursor caught her attention, and she hit Reply. It took several drafts to acknowledge Roger's note without defensiveness and to authorize the IT department to pull the Wastewater files and emails off the server. Even if the MOSQMO task force wrapped up arrests next week, she'd be sticking around to help Heather build an airtight case, which meant leaving her old office staff to gather the records and battle the civil suit. That left a bad taste in her mouth. She should travel back there. This was her mess.

Heidi signed off and headed to Webb's office, her mood a complete one-eighty from the previous airy glee.

"There she is," Webb said in that expansive but shrewd way, like he was delighted to see her, while noting she was two minutes late. Such a disconcerting man.

Heidi greeted all three, apologized for the tardiness, and claimed a seat on the luxurious sofa beside Heather.

"I have some great news." She quickly summarized the updates on Jace's success gathering two more cells into the sting, one including philanthropist and construction mogul Ken Nash.

"Nash?" Webb said, with a startled look. "He's a member of my club."

"He didn't strike me as a run-of-the-mill supremacist, sir," she replied. "He spent no time belittling minority groups or using racial slurs, and he ignored other members' attempts to go down that path. But he very much grabbed the reins of the operation and divvied up the duties."

Webb tilted his chin once in acknowledgement, but she'd struck a nerve.

"I've emailed his name to Alma Reyes, our ATF liaison from TEDAC, who specializes in identifying signature ingredients in explosive devices. Our group hasn't been successful in matching the MOSQMO ingredients with other known groups in the database, which could make sense. If Nash was involved, his respectability as a Chicago developer would bump him off our radar. Literally hiding in plain sight."

Webb's face turned a ghastly ashen, and based on his white-knuckled grip on the armchair and his drifting gaze, the wheels were turning as he tried to make sense of a wealthy acquaintance plotting a terror attack.

She glanced at Garcia in hopes of some direction. "Go on," he said softly, side-eyeing his boss too.

Heidi moved on to her task force members cross-referencing Bradley's unopened burner phones and the receipts to cross-check the remaining phone numbers he'd used and tossed. "Once this is compiled, we should be able to gather his phone and text data with ease. We believe two of the new members Jace met last night were the remainder of that cell. If he can get closer to them, it'll really help our case."

"Outstanding," Webb said solemnly, deflated.

Heather's pen flew across her legal pad as she, too, nodded.

Garcia crossed his legs and asked, "And what about the leak?"

Heidi paused, her smile freezing in place. In her shock over the wrongful death suit, she'd forgotten to check if Josh's dates had come through. Thirty more seconds of tardiness would have either pointed to Bill Fontana as the stooge or cleared him. Damn it!

Her instinct was to keep Bill's name quiet for now—why ruin a man's reputation on what could be an odd coincidence? If she mentioned him as a potential suspect and turned out to be wrong, it would make her look impulsive, gunning for innocent blood just to solve the case. "I have no hard evidence at this time, sir," she said carefully. "However, five of our members are checking out the two men in Jace's cell, and I'm happy to report that this new information doesn't seem to have gotten back to the Race." Another reason the leak couldn't be Bill.

The three asked more detailed questions, which Heidi answered, then Webb glanced at his watch. "Very good work, Heidi. Keep us apprised."

"Thank you, sir." She stood and smoothed her pants.

"The takedown is scheduled for this Friday, so I'll keep you all in the loop as details evolve."

She hurried back to her office and logged in to her computer again, impatient at all the security levels she needed to bypass just to find Josh's answer. There it was!

Hi Heidi,

Thomas Bradley was at Marion May 5, 1998–2001.

–Josh

Heidi flipped to the back of Bill's file where the resumé was stapled, lifting the corner of the first page with trembling fingers. At the bottom of the second page, where his education and degree were listed, was the thirteen-month supervision at USP Marion. May 1999 to June 2000. His time there overlapped with Bradley's.

She pulled up the penitentiary info from the national database and called the warden's direct line, but a secretary answered. Heidi offered her name and credentials then added, "I have two questions. Is there a way to identify which cellblock one of your prisoners was assigned to back in oh-four?"

"Yes, we keep those records on the computer."

"Great. I'm requesting data on a Thomas Bradley." Heidi's ribcage was so tight that it seemed to squeeze her chest, blocking her breathing. "My second question is do you also have a record of which guards were assigned to his cellblock? Did they do shifts in different locations or stay in one spot—"

"That information would be a lot more difficult to find," the woman said apologetically. "We might have it, but it'll take days to find and compile."

"It's just that…" Heidi massaged her temple with one hand. "I need it today. It's a very integral piece of information for a high-profile case." Summoning her politest tone, she said, "May I speak to the warden?"

The secretary put her on hold, and Heidi drummed

her fingers on the desk. If Bill had spent his supervision months guarding Bradley's cellblock, then the connection was enough for Jace's op to be in jeopardy. Of course, she could always haul Bill into her office, confront him with what she had, and word it like she had proof of his cell-block assignment until he acknowledged it. If a highly successful philanthropist like Ken Nash could gravitate to the underbelly of society, then it was certainly feasible for someone sworn to protect Chicago citizens to do the same.

The warden picked up and greeted her by name. "Tanya said you need some kind of urgent information for a case?" Although his tone was respectful, it held the shadow of refusal.

Heidi drew a deep breath and, without naming Bill, explained her predicament. She ended, "It's critical to discover the identities of all the guards assigned to Thomas Bradley's cellblock during those years. We have an undercover agent in the field, and his role might be at risk."

"I see."

Silence followed, and she found herself gnawing another fingernail. Wrenching the finger out and clenching her fist in her lap, she glanced up to see Kelly at her doorway. That apologetic expression could only mean Heidi was late for another meeting. "I'll be right there," she mouthed.

Kelly nodded as the warden said, "I'll put an inmate on this, but it'll take a while. Back then the cellblock schedules were done by hand weekly, and we haven't yet computerized those archives. He'll have to manually go through notebooks."

"I appreciate this," she gushed. "We just need the data as soon as humanly possible."

After making sure he had her contact information,

Heidi hung up and headed down the hall. Now she had another problem to solve. Even though she hadn't voiced her suspicions to Webb and Garcia on the off chance that Bill was innocent, that didn't mean he was welcome in the inner sanctum of this task force anymore.

Inside the conference room, Bill was in his usual seat, slouched back with a hand on his belly, an uninterested expression on his face. In days past, she'd chalked it up to the desk-jockey factor. But maybe it was a cunning ruse to sit here, absorbing every last detail for Sheer. The only saving grace was that Bill didn't know Jace had infiltrated them, so Sheer didn't know Jason McGowan's real identity.

"Good morning," she said briskly. "Before we begin, I have a special assignment that needs immediate attention." She took her seat, pretending to peruse the alert faces around the table. A mindless busywork task would keep him separated from the team. "Bill, I think you'll be perfect for it."

"Oh." He rubbed an eyelid and slowly sat up. "Happy to help." His tone, along with body language, communicated grudging reluctance.

"We've received a crucial tip that Thomas Bradley received backup assistance the day of the bombing from another Race cell. The only detail we have is that they were driving a dark blue commercial van. I need you to review the June second surveillance footage again for all the surrounding streets and report back on your findings."

Huffing a breath, he stood laboriously, knees creaking loudly. "Will do," he said, and lumbered out.

"Now," she said when the door closed behind him. "Let's start with progress reports. Josh? Why don't you go first?"

As Josh began his update, Heidi's thoughts strayed

back to Bill. If he'd had any part in the mosque bombing, he knew there were no backup cell members in a dark blue van. Let him share that tip with Sheer. Let them have a good laugh that the task force was chasing a dead lead. As long as Bill didn't discover this was a fool's errand and he'd actually become her primary suspect.

25

"It's only nine fifteen in Moscow," Jace said, glancing at his watch. "Sheer should definitely still be up."

Chaz lounged in the blue plastic chair across from him in the rented office of Whitehead Construction. "Place the call. Don't go off script. We want to lure him to the U.S., period."

"I still think I should request a transfer to Craig's cell. The only way we'll get evidence that they were part of the bombing is to get in tighter with those two."

"They'll be close enough in a CPD interview room after we arrest them. You'll have an opportunity to ask them anything."

"Not after they've lawyered up," Jace said, his voice rising.

Chaz sat forward, forearms on his knees. "We've been over this, Quinn. It'll look too suspicious for you to ask Sheer for a transfer. You're too new. Just be eager to commit violence. Period."

Jace waved off the rest of the lecture. "Yes, Master Yoda," he muttered.

"That's more like it." Expression softening, Chaz motioned to the landline.

Jace punched the speaker button stiffly. If only he'd had undercover experience, so he didn't need this damn babysitter. He dialed the international number. If caller ID was available in Russia, Sheer would see the company name, backing up the cover story that Jason was a construction supervisor here. The secretary out in the foyer knew nothing but his undercover name and had been instructed to direct any calls his way if he was in, or let the caller know he was touring a site if he was out. So far, no one in the Race had called here for verification.

Sheer answered on the first ring. "Jason. Give me the good news."

Jace paused. That was not the question he'd expected. "Ken didn't update you?"

"I understand he's winging his way to a crucial meeting down south. He sent an email that you all had a productive night."

Chaz held up a thumb, gracing Jace with one of his rare smiles.

"We did. There's going to be quite a fireworks display here this Friday." Jace tilted back in the swivel chair and crossed his ankles on the desk. "It would be great for morale if you booked a flight and watched the show."

Sheer laughed. "God, I'm tempted. Glad to hear the dynamic worked. I thought you all would make a good team."

Jace filled him in on the meeting and the assigned duties, making sure to sound eager, angry, and unrepentant. He ended, "My only regret is that the restaurant isn't open and packed with people yet."

"Too much diversity," Sheer said dismissively. "We're not in the habit of killing off whites as collateral damage.

If we were to target a packed venue, we'd study the victim population carefully."

Like Mosque Mohammed. Two hundred and forty-five Muslims dead and close to four hundred injured. Not a white Christian among them. Jace clenched his jaw. It was going off script, but he was on a roll, and Sheer was in a good mood. "Did you travel back here for the mosque bombing?"

Chaz waved his arms like a referee, vigorously shaking his head.

Jace kicked his feet off the desk and pivoted so the antics were peripheral. "Wasn't the Race involved in that triumph?"

"Why do you ask?" Sheer's hushed tone held a shade of outrage, as if Jace had asked what his wife's clit looked like.

Jace hunched forward. Every nerve in his body hummed with adrenalin, which sharpened his mind and fed him creative options to achieve his goal. "Because I want a repeat of that terror attack. I want a large target, filled with lots of people. I'm a leader, Calvin. I intend to be your most valuable asset in Chicago, and if providing the supplies to blow an *empty* restaurant gets that across, fine, but I think Nate and Dennis set the bar too low."

"An empty restaurant is big for them."

"Then transfer me to a cell that thinks large scale. Chris and Craig seem to have the balls for bloodshed."

Chaz paced the small office, furiously typing a text. Fucking tattletale.

The silence at the end of the line grew. "Let me sleep on it," Sheer said finally. "I like the way you think, but you haven't built up the trust."

The call disconnected. Jace swiveled around and lowered the receiver back in its cradle, bracing for wrath.

Chaz stood before the desk, legs spread, arms crossed,

a thunderous expression on his face. "You think he doesn't smell a fed?" he said in a chillingly quiet voice.

"If he's suspicious, he'd have kicked me out just now." Jace rose and adopted the same stance. "You told me to be authentic, and I was. I'm results-oriented. I assess risk and secure solutions. I push. In this case, it means I want to solve MOSQMO. I want Sheer in the city, and Chris and Craig's confession that they helped Bradley."

Chaz pointed toward the door like the men were right outside. "How is transferring to that cell three days before the takedown going to give you anything? Three days to establish brotherhood? Seriously?" His arm dropped heavily, slapping his thigh. "I know you're not that stupid, but your arrogance? It's off the fucking charts. You took a worthless gamble, man. I can't watch you destroy this op any further."

"You can't quit. It ends in three days."

"It ended just now." Chaz jerked his head at the phone. "He got off that fast because he needs to strategize. He's sitting in Moscow right now weighing the odds of you being a fed and this restaurant deal being nothing more than a sting." He held up an open palm. "If he's wrong, he loses a chance to blow up an empty building— big deal." The other palm came up, like Lady Justice's scales. "If he's right, he just saved seven of his men, including his most significant asset, Ken Nash."

Both hands dropped and his face got that contemptuous look, like Jace was something he'd peeled off his shoe. "My gut? He ain't stupid. He's calling you back within the hour to pull this op and kick you out of the Race."

"Then be man enough to wait for that call," Jace growled, pointing at the chair. "Because when he says the restaurant's still a go, and I'm in with Chris and Craig, I want you right there admitting that *maybe* I know what the fuck I'm doing."

HE'S JUST BLOWN the op.

Heidi pushed the cell phone aside. If she'd gotten a dollar for every time Chaz said or texted that... In her eighteen years of teaming with every variety of law enforcement personnel, she'd never encountered two men with such identical personalities and goals fighting to the death as adversaries.

She refocused on Alma, who was wrapping up her report on Dennis Howe's guilty plea and five-year sentence for conspiracy to use a pipe bomb at a Muslim-owned laundromat in 2001. The device had been a dud, the only reason he wasn't serving thirty-plus.

"Just for kicks," Heidi said, "where was he incarcerated?"

Alma rifled through pages. "Marion. Southern Illinois."

Bill had finished his guard supervision, but Bradley had still been there. "Let's cut to the chase. Did Nate Henderson serve time there too?"

Alma switched files, and in less than a minute confirmed the same penitentiary and same year.

"So, what we have here," Heidi said, "is a high degree of probability that Bradley, Nate, and Dennis either knew each other beforehand or found each other on the inside. The Race was not in existence at the time, but the three could've stayed in touch once they were released and recruited together to form a cell."

The only problem was Jace thought Chris and Craig were the ones that had helped Bradley pull off the bombing. "I have five more names," Heidi said. "One of them is big."

The team reacted with varying degrees of surprised attentiveness. "How are you coming up with all these new suspects?" Alma asked.

"It's classified at the moment, but their link to the Race is indisputable. Once again, I insist this information stay within the confines of this room and this core team." *Wait*. Bill was considered part of this group. How to make sure he was eliminated from any updates without sowing curiosity or mistrust? "Just the four of you at this juncture," she added, eyeing each member. "It's vital to the investigation."

The surprise on their faces morphed to confusion, curiosity, and, in Alma's case, suspicion. She seemed to be the one with the most experience and analytical perception. If her career was anything like most female agents', she'd probably been overlooked for promotions more than once and now lagged way behind male colleagues with comparable skills.

Heidi named the remaining men who were planning to bomb the restaurant, and once again a shock wave went through the room when she identified Ken Nash.

"Wait," Alma said, brow furrowed. "Wait just a minute." She dragged her iPad closer and tapped her screen. "I thought so," she murmured, and looked up. "Nash's name came up in the explosives evidence portion of my team's investigation. He owns a Formula One racing team. He'd have access to the nitromethane fuel used in MOSQMO. Given who he is, we never checked any further."

"*This*, people!" Heidi exclaimed. "This is the kind of investigative detail I want from all of you. We're up against a tight deadline, so each of you take a name and email me with whatever you've found by the end of today.

Alma, you take Nash." She scanned the four solemn faces again. "I repeat, your results are for my eyes only. We're breaking up team communication on these particular individuals, is that clear?" At their mystified nods, she gathered her iPad and mug. "That's all," she said briskly. "Thank you for your time."

———

HEIDI HAD MADE it halfway down the hall when Alma calling out her name stopped her. Suppressed the crawling dread, she turned with a smile.

"May I speak to you in your office?" Alma's tone was respectful, but the set of her jaw and pressed lips were signals representing confrontation.

"Of course." Heidi gestured to the open door a few feet away. Once it was closed and they were both seated, she asked, "What's up?"

"That's actually what I'd like to ask you. You're dividing a task force with morale problems into smaller and smaller core members, and now we're not even allowed to collaborate. I think we deserve an explanation." Short and to the point—had to respect that.

"I acknowledge your concerns," Heidi said smoothly. "Unfortunately, it's a highly classified matter."

"There's a leak, isn't there?"

Yes, a very perceptive agent. Instead of answering, Heidi stared hard, letting the silence build. A critical error, because Alma's gaze dropped in deference, landing on the open file on the desk. Bill's personnel file. Her eyes scanned the boldly centered name at the top of the resumé page before Heidi slapped the file shut. Shit! Her stomach cramped tight.

Alma's expression turned thoughtful. "Well, that makes sense."

"What does?" Did she know something about Bill? Would it prove the leak?

"I've interacted with Bill almost daily for the last six months, and his heart has never been in this investigation. His contribution has been minimal, and his attitude is a chronic mix of surly contempt."

Characteristics Heidi had blamed on the divorce or excused as desk-jockey behavior. "There's no confirmation, Alma. I'm looking into everyone's background."

"Don't waste your time."

"I can't ruin someone's career because they don't play well on a team."

Alma waved a hand impatiently. "All you have to do is watch him interact with minorities and women. He can't hide his bias. We're not equal. We're not worth his time."

"That doesn't mean he leaked strategic information to Bradley."

Alma lips parted in surprise, but she clamped them shut and shook her head. "Yes, ma'am."

"I'm ordering you to keep this entire conversation private," Heidi said in a severe tone. "Bill's had days to leak our leads, and there's no indication Nate Henderson and Dennis Howe know they're under investigation."

"How do you know? Are they under surveillance?"

God, she was good. "That's confidential."

"If they don't know, then why shut Bill out of today's meeting and hearing those five additional names?"

"Only as a precaution."

Alma's chest expanded with a long inhale. She blew it out through pursed lips. "I hope you know what you're doing."

I hope I do, too. "I appreciate your candor and that you came to me with your concerns, Alma. This conversation has to remain confidential."

Alma nodded, standing. Her face was noncommittal,

her body language closed down. "I heard you the first time."

Heidi waited until the door closed to expel her own long breath. This case was unraveling faster than a snagged sweater. She snatched up her cell and tapped Chaz's number. As if she had time for these two and their antics. He answered on the first ring, and she snapped, "What's up?"

"We've got a mess of problems."

"Let me guess. Jace did not take your direction and his impulsive brashness has somehow put the op in jeopardy."

The long pause was filled with condemnation. She closed her eyes and let her head fall back on the headrest. Her excessive lack of sleep was turning detrimental. She was beginning to make errors in judgment and blowing off the best people on her team. "I apologize," she said stiffly. "Is Jace with you still?"

"Yes."

"Put me on speaker, start at the beginning, and catch me up to speed. After you're through, he can do the same. Let's get everyone back on the same page."

"That ship has sailed, Case Agent Hall. I'm hereby resigning from this op."

26

Jace raised a clammy fist and knocked on SAC Webb's door. First-day advice to all newbies who worked in the bullpen was: you don't ever want to see the inside of his office.

"Enter."

He set his shoulders, walked in, and faced three identically grim faces. The SAC, ASAC, and Heidi sat in thick leather club chairs in an alcove of the spacious office. SAC Webb greeted him and motioned to the final chair. "Have a seat, son. Heather's in court, but we'll keep her apprised."

Jace sat across the cocktail table from Heidi. Every muscle in his body was drawn taut, like those times Pop would gather various brothers for a blistering reprimand and brutal grounding. The only difference here was that his job might be handed to him at the end.

Webb crossed his legs. "Let's clear the air and develop a strategy going forward."

That sounded encouraging. "Sir, I'd like to explain—"

Webb raised a palm. "It's not your turn to speak." He nodded to Heidi. "Why don't you begin?"

She looked beyond exhausted and more vulnerable than Jace had ever seen her, which tugged at his heart. He'd done that to her and still hadn't had a chance to explain. Now, in the midst of displaying deep disappointment, she threw him what seemed like a hint of apology. Like she was sorry she was ratting him out, even though he was in the wrong.

Clasping her fingers in her lap, Heidi reconstructed the fractious alliance of an experienced and decorated undercover agent attempting to train an inexperienced, headstrong operative on the fly. Although she assigned blame to neither, Jace clamped his jaw tight at the descriptors she used and the shade she was throwing at his career. Yes, he deserved it. Didn't mean he was going to lie back and take it.

When she was through, she unclenched her hands and smoothed her pants. Her gaze stayed fixed on Webb's face, and by the complete stillness of her silky blouse, she had to be holding her breath.

"Correct me if I'm mistaken, Case Agent Hall, but wasn't it your call to assign this role to Jace?"

Her nod was jerky.

"Right," Webb said. "Well, we'll get to that later." The powerful man adjusted in the chair to face Jace, then recrossed his legs. "You've been here almost two years now, Jace, and achieved quite a golden-boy status in an incredibly short period of time."

Jace blinked, waiting for the "but."

"On the other hand," Webb continued, "you have a troublesome history of not being able to follow direct orders from women and minorities."

Jace clenched his jaw as the urge to defend himself built like a scream in his throat. Unwilling to be shot down again for speaking out of turn, he stayed motionless, staring the formidable man down.

"Last spring, Margo Hathaway complained about you going rogue, and now Case Agent Hall and Charles Jackson are leveling the same accusation. What do you say on your behalf?"

Finally. "My background has given me ample experience to formulate strategies and mitigate—"

"Yes, yes. Your distinguished career as a Navy SEAL. That also would have given you the same years of experience carrying out orders from superiors without question and working within the structure of a team. In your career as a SEAL, did you ever answer to a superior who happened to be a woman or a minority?"

Jace flushed hotly at the implication. "Sir—"

"Answer the question, son."

"No, sir. I did not."

Webb nodded as if expecting the answer. Garcia, who'd remained basically motionless and expressionless since the moment Jace walked in the door, now shot him a look of pure sympathy. Like he'd answered wrong and would reap holy hell. Heidi just looked like she wanted to throw up.

"The thing about being back in the civilian world," Webb said, "is that you have to get over your glorified sense of self and know that people who are not white men are just as, if not more, capable than you or I. It does you a great disservice believing otherwise."

Jace clenched his teeth so hard that a shaft of pain knifed into his skull. He winced, which they probably took as his reaction to Webb's words. Having been deep in the belly of white supremacists these last weeks, though, the SAC's inference was unacceptable. "I can assure you, any insubordination has nothing to do with bias," he blurted. "I had just as much trouble taking orders from white men. It's who I am—it's ingrained in my DNA to lead and to win. I'm the oldest brother, the captain of the football team, the most competitive SEAL in my outfit. *I'm* in charge..." He slapped his chest, which jolted his brain to catch up to his runaway mouth. Oh, shit! How could he take it all back?

"That explains a lot," Webb said quietly, his expression already reaching the obvious conclusion. "But how on earth did you get an honorable discharge?"

And there it was. Jace's gaze dropped to the fists resting on his knees. Shame rose like bile, bitter and corroding. He slumped against the cushion weakly, as if he'd just awoken from a long fever. "I received an honorable discharge with an early release."

"Meaning your work was stellar, but they were sick and tired of you."

"Yes, sir." The secret he'd planned to take to the grave. He'd never even told his best friend after returning stateside. Had meant to, but then Dirk got killed in the warehouse explosion.

A long moment of silence passed. "Thank you for your candor, Jace," Webb said, the gentle tone adding to Jace's shame. He couldn't bear to look over at Heidi.

"I'd...I'd appreciate it if that detail never left the room, sir."

"Everything about this meeting will remain off your record and within these walls," Webb said briskly.

Jace stared at him blankly. "Off my record, sir?" He didn't deserve the luck.

"To be perfectly honest, both ASAC Garcia and I benefited from the national recognition your cases earned this field office last spring. We owe you one favor, but this is it, and it comes with your final warning, son."

Jace's limbs went weak with relief. He swallowed hard. "Thank you and understood, sir."

Webb clapped his hands together and rubbed them as he turned to the others. "Now, let's problem-solve this operation back on track, shall we? Felix? What are your thoughts?"

"We're three days from the takedown, so acquiring a new UCA to supervise Jace will be more detrimental than helpful," Garcia said decisively. There was a pause, and no doubt they were all thinking that another supervisor would be pointless after the blathering confession of Jace's inability to take orders from anyone. Jace closed his eyes briefly. He'd give his left nut to be out in the hall, rapping on the door again. Start this whole thing over...

Garcia nodded to Heidi. "We'll need someone for surveillance and backup in the van with Heidi—"

"I recommend Alma Reyes," she said immediately. "She's an ATF representative on the team and has shown herself to be a brilliant and perceptive investigator."

Webb nodded. "Done. What else?"

"We're good, sir," she said. "Jace is hosting the men tonight, so he probably needs to head out."

"Fine. Best of luck, son. Heidi, why don't you remain behind?"

Jace stood, slightly dazed. His shirt was plastered to his clammy back. "Thank you, sir." He still had his career. He was still on this op. But the damage was catastrophic. His golden-boy image was over. He nodded goodbye to everyone, but Heidi looked away. Her pale complexion was back, and her wide eyes held profound dread, like she was being sent to the gallows. And it was his fault.

THE RACE CELLS gathering in Jace's living room were in high spirits. Tonight's meeting, nailing down details and assigning further tasks, had gone smoothly. Now the men were kicked back, drinking beer and trash-talking about the glory that would rain upon them after the restaurant blew to smithereens and Chicagoans entered a dark era of fear and distrust.

Heidi took off her headphones and swigged some water. Sporadically during the uneventful hours, she'd updated Alma, who was understandably shocked that not only was the overall investigation much farther along than the team had imagined, but there was this cloak-and-dagger side op led by Jace Quinn, who'd never actually left the task force.

"So this morning," Heidi concluded, "the Marion warden assigned an inmate to check Bill's cellblock assignments. If there's a link, I'll confront Bill with the proof. Until then, he's down in the AV forensic lab reviewing security tapes for an imaginary second van."

"An assignment he's well suited for." Alma's eyes sparkled mischievously. "When will you hear from the prison?"

Heidi shrugged. "We're two nights away from the sting, and if the leak isn't Bill, then *we're* being set up." The urge to bite her fingernails came roaring back. Ever since the scathing dressing-down from Webb this afternoon, her mind had been scurrying through every aspect of this op, searching for problems, second-guessing decisions, forecasting hitches. This Bill element was her biggest fear. If she was wrong and he wasn't the traitor...

Alma pursed her lips. "You know, if the Marion info doesn't come through tomorrow, you might want to create a backup task for Bill, just in case. He's got a big ego, bores easily, and has a ton of connections."

"Sounds like a lot of the men I've worked alongside."

They shared a laugh. "So many of these guys should've drowned in the hashtag-MeToo wave a few years back," Alma said in a scathing voice. "But you know how some men are lucky enough or slimy enough to slink away from the spotlight? That's Bill."

"Bill sexually harassed women?"

"Not me. He targeted the analysts and support staff."

Heidi shook her head grimly. "If I had a dime..." She didn't bother finishing the worn phrase. Very few of the men who harassed women in her Atlanta office had been dealt with in a manner she considered just. Somehow it was not surprising that Bill, riding his law enforcement reputation, would also be someone who made women feel uncomfortable.

Onscreen, a burst of laughter captured Alma's attention, and she swiveled on her stool, reabsorbed in watching the feed from Jace's.

Heidi rolled shoulders that were a lot less tense than with Chaz. These hours in the van had a completely different vibe. Gone was the undercurrent of his constant disapproval that had wrought self-doubt over the op's success and anxiety for Jace's overall safety. Alma had a great sense of humor and an eager generosity of spirit. The laughter and lack of friction in this tiny, confined area was more effective than caffeine. Heidi's chronic exhaustion had disappeared like a puff of smoke.

"Looks like they're wrapping up," Alma said, and Heidi noted the time: nine twenty-five.

"We don't leave the scene until Jace gives the word," she said. A strategy Chaz had set up after the numerous times he'd been left solo by a departing van only to have the drug dealers or killers return to the scene for a forgotten item or final thought. It was also one piece of advice Jace had adhered to without arguing.

The women watched the cell members drive off or walk away one by one. Jace stood on his front stoop in the dark, quiet neighborhood for several minutes then turned back inside. "We're good," he said. It was always disconcerting hearing his more relaxed, deeper voice, after Jason McGowan's forceful enthusiasm.

Alma pulled off the headphones. "Thanks for letting me be a part of the real action," she said, tightening her ponytail. "This is a whole lot more fascinating than the desk work."

"Hopefully, you'll still think that way by Friday, because you have a mountain of strategy and background to catch up on."

Alma's laugh was short and dry. "No one's waiting up for me. I'm seeing a lieutenant over at CPD whose hours are crazier than mine, so give me all you got."

"Great." Yes, Alma was a great addition. "Let's meet in my office at eight, and I'll go through our roles for Friday's takedown."

"Will do. Want me to drive again?"

"Actually, if you don't mind dropping me at Jace's? After submerging him in this filth, I make him go through an informal hot wash."

"Jace?" The name burst out in another puff of laughter. "He wouldn't admit to a vulnerability if you offered him a million dollars."

He'd admitted to anxiety at not being the one in control the prior night, just before they'd kissed. And then admitted that same need to be in charge had cost him his SEAL career earlier this afternoon. There'd been no chance to speak to him after he left Webb's office, so who knew where his head was right now? She was betting on anger. On him lashing out like a wounded animal. Could be he'd surprise her by remaining locked in that commanding, intense alpha persona as if nothing had happened. Either way, tonight would be tricky. "I don't offer him a million dollars, and I don't give him a choice. I've learned the hard way that men with super-hero tendencies hold in a lot more toxic anxiety than is healthy."

Alma glanced at the monitor that had gone dark

when Jace turned off the living room switch. "Every woman on that task force wants a piece of that guy," she said quietly. "Even me, happily dating Manuel. Jace checks off all the boxes—hotter than fire, driven, indifferent to our flirting." Her smile had a faraway wistfulness. "Trying to figure him out used to be our favorite topic hanging out at Mickey's. Which of us could bulldoze through that blind ambition to what really makes him tick?"

Her smile slipped away. "None of us were ever stupid enough to start an office pool, though. We know a lost cause when we see one."

27

J ace checked his phone again. It was on, the silencer was off... Why hadn't Sheer gotten back to him? It had been over twelve hours since this morning's call. How much thought was required to transfer him to Chris and Craig's cell? It wasn't like he was asking Sheer for a kidney.

Tossing the phone on the sofa, he muttered an obscenity. His instinct to go off script had been right. It was the only way to get proof that other people had had a hand in the bombing. He'd mentally written I-told-you-so emails to Chaz all day, ready to fire off a real version the second Sheer called back. But the longer the Race leader remained silent, the more Jace questioned his own judgment. And any soldier knew that was a slippery slope.

A soft knock sounded at the door, the familiar tap-tap instantly triggering a visceral struggle. His pulse accelerated at the promise of the nightly alone time with Heidi, while his stomach roiled at the subject matter ahead. What sane man willingly explored his weenie feelings? How did anything get accomplished that way? No male superior had ever put him through this so consistently and relentlessly.

He ran a hand through his hair as he walked to the door. He'd managed to dodge her psychobabble questions so far. Why should tonight be any different? As he reached for the knob, his inner voice piped the answer: *'Cause now she knows what a loser you are.*

In the renewed flush of humiliation, he wrenched the door open so violently that Heidi hopped backward. "Yow! Are you okay?"

He forced a grin, waving her in as he stepped aside. "Does that count as your first question?"

She shed her coat with a bemused expression, like she was considering it.

"I was kidding," he said, taking the coat and folding it over the nearest chair. Women. Everything was so overly serious. "Have a seat. Club soda?"

"Thank you." The late-fall chill had colored her cheeks baby pink, and her brown eyes snapped with purpose. "And yes, why don't we make that the first question?"

He didn't bother to hide the flash of annoyance. After the meeting with Webb and Garcia, he was completely unwilling to reveal anything more. Ever.

He headed into the kitchen and stood motionless for a few seconds to regroup. During the worst of BUD/S training, when death was such a better option, the only way through had been to focus on completing one more second. Then one more second. He could do that here too, until she wrapped up the last question.

After pouring the club soda over ice and grabbing a beer for himself, he returned to find her in her usual place—tucked in the far corner of the sofa, iPad on her thigh, her face alert and expectant.

Here went nothing. "What's the question again?"

"Are you okay?" She stretched the words out, making the question sound like she searched for deeper truths and hidden meanings.

"Tonight's meeting went great," he said, placing the drinks on two of the coasters scattered along the table and sinking into the armchair with an exasperated sigh. "You were listening in. Didn't you think it went good? I've got no buried emotions about that."

She sank an elbow on the back cushion and rested her head into her palm. "Regarding the Race, yes. I meant with what went down earlier. Chaz walking out. Your meeting with Webb and Garcia. Your insight into your control issues—"

He held up a hand. "See, I don't complicate my life navel-gazing like that. I appreciate all Chaz did for me, but now he's out of the picture. This afternoon, I thought I'd be pulled off the op, but my superiors gave me another chance. Why would I wallow in any of it?"

"Because it all highlights your fatal flaw."

Inwardly, he flinched. Outwardly, he barked a laugh. "Being competitive? Controlling? I don't call those flaws."

"Taken to the extreme, they are. You don't just want control; you need it. You annihilate anyone who gets in your way. Your overly competitive streak hinders any growth in meaningful relationships—work or social."

Sweaty heat pricked up his neck and burned his ears. "I have no complaints, Heidi."

"Of course you don't. You're stuck, and not even aware of it. Even before we isolated you here, when was the last time you hung out with fellow agents? Went to a ball game? Called up a woman for a date?"

The answer to all of those was: hardly ever. It was how he rolled. Apparently, he was supposed to feel bad about that, but he didn't. If he answered honestly, though, she'd think worse of him than she already did. And for some reason, that was unacceptable. It was slimy bringing up Dirk's name this way, but it would slap down any further harping over his preference to be alone. "I had a close friend who died in the warehouse bombing last spring," he said. "Which led to the retaliatory bombing of Mosque Mohammed a week later. Which is why I've focused on solving the case ever since."

Her eyes softened in sympathy. She pressed her lips together like she was observing a moment of silence for Dirk. Jace scraped a palm over his face, biting back the urge to redirect the narrative, even if it was an insult that started an argument. That pathetic side she was awakening in him pointed out those impulses were also controlling. He could do better.

"We joined the SEALs together," he said instead. "And once we were stateside, he talked me into the FBI."

Heidi laid her iPad aside. That couldn't be a good sign. "What was his name?"

"Dirk Jameson. His death... It's been hard. I don't know if you've ever had a friend die, but"—he shrugged —"it's like a piece of you dies too, which makes no sense."

"It makes sense." She swiveled her head and looked out the window, even though the tiny backyard was pitch-black. Sadness etched the corners of her eyes, and she blew out a breath through pursed lips. "Evan Cartwright shot himself the day after a successful takedown last year."

Jace froze, the beer halfway to his mouth.

"He'd been deep undercover for so long that the suspects became like family to him. He attended their weddings and christenings, backyard barbecues and weekends at the Wastewater CEO's cabin on the lake." She turned from the window and looked at him with eyes so large and vulnerable that she looked like a wounded fawn, huddled in the corner of the sofa. "Somewhere along the way, he lost perspective. He became torn between his duty to take these men down and his genuine affection for them and their families."

"Let me guess," Jace said. "He didn't tell you any of this during your nightly hot-wash talks."

Her gaze slid over his shoulder, searching much farther than the dimensions of this room. "I didn't do them routinely back then." She crossed her arms like she was cold. "I read his body language, though. The closer we got to the takedown, the more anxious he became. He stopped sleeping, barely ate. I did confront him then, but he hid behind all that alpha bullshit." She jerked her chin, including Jace in her scathing description.

It wasn't worth objecting to or defending against. He wasn't remotely invested in those Race members and their shitty views and had no plans to off himself—nothing could get him to that mental state.

"Anyway," Heidi said with a bit more energy, "the takedown happened, the evidence was rock solid, and the suspects were suitably shocked seeing Evan among the sea of law enforcement. The whole task force went out that night to celebrate him, and he acted...so normal. He fooled me." She shook her head as if being duped by someone's behavior was inconceivable. "I found him in his office the next morning."

Jace put down his empty beer and somehow kept the forward momentum going until he was next to Heidi on the sofa. He clasped the hand closest to him. "That's not your fault." He winced at his own words. He'd been miles away from Dirk's warehouse raid, desperately searching for clues into his brother's kidnapping, when the bomb detonated. On sleepless nights, he still searched for something he could have done to stop the blast or save Dirk in some way. But realistically, had Sean not gone missing, Jace would have been at that warehouse right by Dirk's side. Dead.

"Survivor's guilt is pretty destructive, huh?" he said, and she blinked like she'd woken up.

"Listen to you spouting psychology." Her smile began in her eyes, crinkling with laughter before curling her lips. He tightened his clasp on her hand.

"You're so beautiful, Heidi." His voice was a husky rasp. "So different..." How could he finish that sentence without her nailing him with the misogynist label? But she wasn't like any other woman he'd come across in his lifetime, because no woman made his heart swell like this.

"I'm not different, Jace. You haven't looked deep enough at any other woman before tagging her with a label and running for the hills."

He let her ribbing float away. "The fact that I can't tag you at all is what makes you different." She was a combination of everything. And rather than that being a turnoff, he was fascinated.

"Maybe I don't fit because I'm a generation older than your usual dates. I have money, I've got my act together, and I'm perfectly happy with my independence."

Nope. It wasn't age or her career achievements or even that unpretentious personality. It was *her*. Was he in this by himself? "Is it time to ask my hot-wash question?"

Her smile morphed into caution. "Sure. Go for it."

Here went nothing. "Do I have a shot with you?"

The caution turned to dread, and her gaze slid to something over his shoulder again. He might not be great at reading women, but this was a real bad sign. She'd found out what a loser he was and wanted nothing to do with him. The awful, hollow ache returned to his chest. See, this was why he never put himself in such a shitty vulnerable position.

"Forget it," he said, mustering a grin. "Just thought I'd ask."

He tried to slip his hand from hers, but she gripped it tight. "It isn't you, Jace," she said. "I happen to have indisputable evidence that I'm not great girlfriend material."

The old *it's not you, it's me* excuse. He'd used it a thousand times but never knew it hurt like this.

"Besides," she continued, "I don't plan to hang around long after we wrap this up for Heather." She squeezed his hand and let it go. "It's better if we keep this professional."

Numbly, he watched her slip out her phone and tap the rideshare app. So this was what rejection felt like. Too bad it wasn't in his DNA to accept that status quo. But how could he convince her he was worthy of a relationship? The only thing that came to mind was to wrap up this op swiftly and successfully, and hand it to her on a silver platter. She'd feel differently about him then. Everyone loved a hero.

JACE AWOKE to his bu-phone buzzing across the bedside table. Beyond it, the digital clock flipped to three forty-two. This had to be Sheer. Jace blinked alert and grabbed it, frowning at the caller ID. A Chicago area code. Who else had this number?

"Speak," he said in a rough rasp.

"I've got good news and bad news." Sheer?

Jace squinted at the number again. "You're not calling from your usual number."

"You are correct, sir." Sheer chortled with glee. "I'm in the States."

Holy shit! Adrenalin shot through Jace, waking him faster than a slap in the face. He sat up and pinched the bridge of his nose, trying to summon Jason McGowan. "I'm assuming that's the good news?"

"I decided you were right. I need to visit the troops and meet all these new members."

All these? "I'm not the only one?"

"Hell no. Our Chicago growth was the largest in the nation after that mosque bombing got worldwide sympathy. Misplaced compassion for a bunch of jihadists who don't belong in our country in the first place was a fucking call to arms to men like us."

"What do you expect?" Jace thankfully lurched back into character. "Fake news designed to make your heart bleed."

"We've even had five new members join after you did this past month."

"Glad you're here to give us a pep talk, then." It was highly unlikely Sheer would gather the entire Race clan together in Chicago, but what an FBI dream. Arrest a ballroom full of them. Somehow Jace needed access to a master list, which was probably in an encrypted file in Sheer's possession. "Where are you staying?"

"The Race rented a safe house last year just in case."

Chaz would've had his head for that probing question, but he'd had to try. Sheer was mere miles away; what clues could Jace ferret out? By the time the MOSQMO team locked on to this new phone number, the device would've long since been tossed. "You said you had bad news?"

"I'm denying your transfer request. Nate needs a strong member like you in his cell."

Jace scrubbed a hand over his face. "Nate has a problem with me elbowing control."

"Then I'll put you in charge." Sheer said it simply, like the political blowback and infighting would not be an issue to his master vision.

Jace slipped from the bed and began pacing. "With all due respect, Calvin, inserting me into a power cell like Chris and Craig's will give us unlimited opportunities to do Race work around here. Don't rein me in with two weenies."

Sheer laughed heartily. He was clearly in a great mood and wide-awake. "I agree that you three would make a formidable force, and maybe it's a request I can grant later in the year, but right now I need to spread the stronger warriors around. Besides, we just got a new recruit with a go-get-'em spirit like yours, so I'm training him with Chris and Craig."

Jace let silence be his answer. He couldn't push any further.

"Guess I'll see you at Nash's tonight," Sheer said, with that pumped-up fervor so at odds with the hour. "Looking forward to meeting you."

"It'll be an honor, sir." Somehow tonight, when they all met at Ken's home for the final prep, Jace would figure out a way to get taped proof from Craig that he and Chris had teamed with Bradley last June. Although now that Sheer was here, there'd probably be more thorough pat-downs for wires, which meant the less effective watch recorder again. Shit. Too much was up in the air suddenly.

Could the task force arrest Sheer at Ken Nash's house, since they knew exactly where he'd be? Had the task force accumulated enough evidence for Heather to charge him in connection with MOSQMO? Jace grabbed a water from the refrigerator and downed the entire bottle in gulping swallows. He should wake Heidi and begin brainstorming.

28

Heidi sent out an urgent group text to all task force members except Bill Fontana, summoning them to a meeting at eight. She texted SAC Webb and ASAC Garcia requesting their presence, then checked her email for an answer from Marion Penitentiary, but nothing was in her inbox. Time was down to the wire. She had to get her team organized for the pending sting, but to do that when she hadn't verified who the traitor was meant tipping her hand to the Race. She rubbed her hands vigorously over her face, groaning. There was only one option left: she'd have to confront Bill on supposition. Since he was an early bird, her final text ordered him to report to her office as soon as he arrived.

Next came organizing today's presentation and pairing agents for surveillance around Ken Nash's house hours before tonight's eight o'clock meeting. If Sheer showed up early for some one-on-one time with Nash, the team would be ready.

There were very few photos of Sheer circulating on the internet, and except for a prominent Roman nose, his features were easily disguisable. The latest photograph showed a pale, blue-eyed, bald man with the full lumberjack beard, all of which could be easily altered this evening. He must have acquired a passport under another alias to have gotten back into the U.S. His other five aliases were flagged on the CBP consolidated terrorist watch list.

Alma knocked on Heidi's open office door. "Got your text—" Her eyes widened as she scanned Heidi's rumpled outfit. "Jeez, how long have you been here?"

"Since four." Heidi slumped back in her chair with a long exhale and studied Alma with bleary eyes. "I know we arranged to meet later this morning, but I've got a massive emergency on my hands."

Alma slipped into the chair across the desk. "What?"

"I honestly don't have the time to explain it more than once. Suffice it to say I've texted Webb and Garcia asking them to attend the meeting." Heidi checked the time. "In an hour. What are you doing here so early?"

"Finishing some reports I put aside to be in the van last night." She eyed Heidi with concern. "No offense, but if the big kahunas are coming, you need to take a few minutes to freshen up."

Heidi looked at the notes, files, and to-do lists scattered around her desk. "I don't have the time."

"Take the time, Heidi," she pressed. "You need to look fresh and confident. The good old boys are waiting for you to buckle under the pressure."

Alma was right. Saying there was no double standard around here when it came to appearances was naïve, but the added pressure to devote time to something so inane was exhausting. Heidi patted her hair self-consciously. "All right, thanks. I appreciate the advice."

Another knock on her door. "Come in," she called, and Bill poked his head in.

"You wanted to see me, boss?"

Alma jumped up. "I was just leaving."

The two murmured a greeting at the door, and then Bill sat heavily, knees and duty belt creaking. The full accessories on it forced him into an uncomfortable forward position, his legs spread wide in alpha dominance.

"Thank you for coming in so early," Heidi said, rummaging around for his personnel file. "I was reviewing everyone's records and happened upon your supervisory stint as a guard at Marion."

He nodded, a puzzled knot forming along his brow.

Hell, the stakes had been pushed too high to beat around the bush. "Were you assigned to Thomas Bradley's cellblock?"

"Excuse me?"

"You were both at that facility during the same time period. Did you guard him? Please know, before you answer, that I have the warden pulling your schedule for that year. I'll verify this one way or another. Also know that if you cooperate with me now, I'll make sure the higher-ups know."

Bill sat in stunned silence. The limbic survival reactions were fight, flight, or freeze. It was clear which one Bill was experiencing. A long moment passed. From out in the hallway, sounds of employees greeting each other, elevator doors dinging, and the muffled ringing of phones filtered in.

"Bill—"

"Yes," he said in a subdued voice. "I was assigned to his cellblock."

Heidi's heart hammered in her chest. She took a steadying breath. "What was the extent of your interaction with Bradley, Sergeant Fontana?"

"He was part of the CMU experiment." Bill focused

on his index finger, ironing the crease in his pants back and forth. "Communications management unit. A lot like solitary confinement. Everyone has tiny cells and no roommate. We severely limited the inmates' abilities to communicate with each other and the outside world. Marion was one of the first USPs to implement that."

"Solitary confinement? Aren't they medium-security?"

His nod was dismissive. "It was downgraded in oh-six, but before then, the cellblock I worked was mostly Al Qaeda convicts and neo-Nazis. If we'd allowed any inter-action or put in bunk beds or community yard time, there would've been a bloodbath."

"What kind of interaction did you have with Bradley?"

Again, he hesitated. Probably looking at the time of death of his career and wondering how he could limit the damage to his pension. The stunned look hadn't quite disappeared from his face, but it was mixed with resigna-tion now. "There are some who adapt easier to the twenty-three hours of isolation, but Bradley wasn't one of them." His eyes strayed to the window, his gaze far away. "I was right out of college and idealistic enough to think I could make a difference or rehabilitate some of the more remorseful ones."

"Bradley was remorseful about the pipe bombs?"

He gave a short chuckle. "In hindsight, no, but he was a master manipulator, so I thought he was repentant and befriended him. I was also dirt poor and newly married. He bribed me to smuggle communications in from the outside, allow him to interact with a few inmates, stuff like that."

"Stuff like meeting other white supremacists? Dennis Howe?" The sordid tale was too familiar. "Did they keep in touch after they were released?"

"Casual acquaintances. Look, I swear to God, they were on the up and up after release. They had good jobs, got married, Dennis has kids now..."

"And both joined the Race. Do you know Nate Henderson?"

"Never heard of him until this task force."

"Tell me, Bill, are you a member?"

His belt creaked as he shifted in the chair. "God, no!"

"But you're sympathetic to the cause. At least when the cause targets Muslims."

She recognized the look of hate he threw her. In a world where everything was polarized now, it was the silent condemnation that a woman, even a Caucasian one, was a bleeding-heart liberal who would never understand. "I doubt there's a white man alive who lived through nine-eleven and isn't somewhat biased toward Muslims," he rasped.

Heidi exhaled a soft sigh. Trying to keep the disgust off her face was taking all her energy. She spied the time on her monitor. Shit, she was due to present to the team and her superiors in nine minutes. "Let's skip to the part where you tipped off Bradley that the task force had ID'd him for MOSQMO."

Bill looked down at his feet, shoulders slouching, mouth pressed into a straight line. Regret. Shame. "I called him from one of the agent's phones—"

"Mark Hennessey's," she interrupted briskly. "Your case agent and superior. How did you know his cypher-lock code?"

Bill shrugged. "I spied him earlier that week inputting it. Not hard to remember. One, one, one, one."

"You weren't on the database as still in the building."

"I used the end-of-day chaos in the lobby to scan my ID out but turned right around like I'd forgotten something and followed someone scanning in. Waited in the john until the bullpen emptied, keyed in Hennessey's code, lowered the blinds, and made the call." He spread his hands impatiently. "I confronted Bradley, is all. Wanted to get inside information I could present to the team."

"You told him of the pending warrant for his arrest."

"He put two and two together," Bill hedged.

She waited a beat, her hands fisted in her lap. "Did you murder him, Bill?"

He jerked like she's poked him with a cattle prod. "No!"

"Then what have you found out in your murder inquiry?"

His tight-lipped silence was her answer, and she buried the urge to lunge across the desk. Bradley's death had severed any connecting ties, so why open Pandora's box? In the weeks Bill had been assigned to investigate, he'd done anything but. This was all on her. Taking Hennessey's advice to have Bill head the murder inquiry had been assigning the fox to the henhouse.

"Have you been in touch with Dennis Howe since the bombing?" she asked stiffly.

"No. I had no idea he'd joined the Race too. We thought Bradley acted alone until you came."

"Where's the Race safe house?"

"How the hell should I know? I'm telling you, I only dealt with Bradley!"

Heidi stood abruptly. She had to get him out of here before she did something truly unprofessional. "I'm sure SAC Webb will want to speak with you after the task force meeting. I'm alerting security not to let you leave this building. Wait in the bullpen until further notice."

His belt and joints creaked just as loudly when he rose. He stayed in an aggressive cop stance, arms hovering at his side, like an old-fashioned cowboy getting ready to draw. "You said you'd put in a good word for me."

That he would use his body language to intimidate her was the last goddamn straw. "I said I'd tell them you cooperated." Her voice shook with fury, and she no longer held back her contempt. "I don't have any *good words* to describe your disloyalty to your own joint task force or your betrayal as a cop and a human being toward the entire Muslim-American community."

Still he hesitated.

"Give me your Glock and go," she said between clenched teeth.

His scowl was formidable, but after a few tense seconds, he handed over his weapon, turned, and lumbered out the door.

After notifying security, she stashed his gun in her briefcase along with her files and laptop, then lugged it into the ladies' room. Instead of celebrating solving the leak, she was spending precious minutes creating the illusion that she was stylishly calm, composed, and confident. Sometimes being a woman sucked eggs.

29

H eidi scanned the eager faces of the murmuring crowd. Her team. She'd shaped them for weeks, they'd risen to her expectations, and collectively they stood at the precipice of this final stage. Excitement buzzed through the air at the impromptu meeting, and many nervous glances fell on the SAC and ASAC, seated on her right and in deep conversation with Heather.

The core team lined the left, followed by scores of other agents who assisted part-time. All the analysts and several techies sat in the remaining chairs along the table or grabbed stacking chairs from the far corner and sat wherever they could. There had to be close to fifty people in here.

"All right," Heidi said authoritatively, "let's get started. There have been other elements of this investigation most of you aren't aware of, and it's time to bring everyone up to speed." The surprised silence was all-encompassing. She began with her decision to choose Jace Quinn to infiltrate the Race as an undercover operative, then explained the terrorist act the group was planning two days from now at the Pakistani restaurant.

Josh raised his hand. "Why wouldn't you tell us Jace was still on the team? We were led to believe he was on a case in another state."

"It quickly became a classified assignment for reasons I'm not going to go into today. I assure you, the people who needed to know did." She motioned for the analyst closest to the light switch to flick off the overhead fluorescents, then projected various photographs she'd spent the predawn hours organizing onto the enormous screen.

"These were culled from Jace's videos. Let me introduce you to the Race members involved in this sting." She went through each of the men in the three cells, listing the bios and pertinent background that had already been collected on Nate and Dennis. As expected, there were gasps of shock when the photo of Ken Nash appeared. "Alma, I know you've been preoccupied helping me in the van, but what have you found on Nash so far?"

"We haven't issued warrants because of Jace's clandestine op, but we do know Nash uses three of the Race members Heidi just showed as subcontractors for his construction business. Nash is the sole owner of his firm and has an updated ATF E-Form fifty-four hundred permit to store and use C-4."

"Any social media connecting him to the Race or Calvin Sheer?" Heidi asked.

"So far, not a peep. By all accounts he's an upstanding citizen, but upon further study, all his philanthropic measures are directed toward affiliations that benefit whites."

Heidi noted Webb's grim face, like he still hadn't come to terms with a good acquaintance from his posh country club being a part of anything so heinous. Moving forward in her slides, she shifted her presentation to Calvin Sheer. She listed his aliases and showed internet file photos of all the different metamorphoses of his appearance. Skinhead bald, full head of hair, clean-shaven, trimmed beard, or so heavily bearded that the lower half of his face was no longer visible. By the end, the expressions around her displayed degrees of shock or dismay. It was hard to reconcile that all these photos were the same man. He would be hard to identify.

"We found out early this morning that Sheer arrived in Chicago sometime overnight," she concluded, then waited for the hum of excitement to die down. "He's hiding in a Race safe house somewhere nearby and is expected to attend tonight's final meeting at Ken Nash's residence in Wilmette."

Javier raised his hand. "Do we have enough to arrest him tonight?" The million-dollar question.

She glanced at Heather, who shook her head.

"We've established a solid connection that he's the head of the Race," the AUSA replied, "but nothing connecting him to a specific felony like MOSQMO."

Webb frowned. "Sheer would've been actively involved in the planning and recruiting prior to the June second bombing. What digital forensics have we uncovered for Thomas Bradley?"

The crack analyst, Christine, raised a hand. "That would be me, sir. We finally identified the burner phone numbers Bradley used and have issued warrants for all calls and texts he made. Unfortunately, some wireless companies are very uncooperative with law enforcement, and Bradley's carrier has the worst rep of them all. They won't be in any hurry turning over the requested information."

"We've uncovered solid evidence linking Sheer with Bradley all over social media," Kelly added, bright spots staining her cheeks, "but we can't arrest someone for exercising their First Amendment right to agree with someone else's hate speech."

"Which leaves Jace," Garcia said softly. "Tonight, he'll collect the crucial surveillance of Sheer colluding to bomb Johnny's. We need to be ready to move in with an arrest."

Before Heidi could strenuously object, Heather's hand shot up in the universal halt sign. "No, sir. With all due respect, taking them down tonight in their planning stage only gives us conspiracy-to-commit charges. We need them to go through with the attempted bombing on Friday to rack up substantial counts."

"But what if Sheer isn't on site Friday?" Webb asked Heather. "What if he's already escaped back to Russia?" He looked over at Heidi. "How did he even get past customs?"

Perfect segue. Heidi looked down at the task force to-do list. "I'm assigning Howard Kennedy, Kate Collins, and John Devine to O'Hare. Find out which flights Sheer could have connected on to get here overnight from Moscow. He swept through customs with a new alias and false passport. Comb through TSA surveillance, find out what his name is and what he looks like now."

She continued down the list, assigning twelve SSG members who specialized in clandestine surveillance to pair up and begin shadowing Nash's house for any sign of Sheer, and tailing when they had "eyes on." Next was allocating analysts to canvass banks for any ATM withdrawals in any of Sheer's known aliases, and tasking two more analysts to each of the team heads investigating the newer cell members. The rest of the team would set up and man the command center in this room and compile all information coming in from the field.

Heidi closed her laptop with a decisive snap. "I'll be in

this room overseeing everything until this evening, at which time Alma Reyes and I will be in the surveillance van—"

"As will I," Garcia interrupted.

Heidi blinked, mouth still open as if going on with her next point. He was horning in on her op. The one bureaucratic move that had been her line in the sand. She glanced at Webb. Surely he would object. Once again the pleasant smile was a jarring mismatch to the hawkish eyes. He was daring her to refuse or contradict the ASAC in front of her team.

"Yes, sir," she managed, her gaze returning to Garcia. "I'll bring you up to speed as soon as we're through."

She finished the assignments with a level voice and calm demeanor, but her throat was thick with choking anger. This was exactly how Wastewater had flown out of control. Too many chiefs before the takedown, which made for too many commands, and counter-commands, and delayed arrests, and a messy ending. Too much covering of individual asses after Evan's suicide.

As her troops filed past, Heidi smiled, answered questions, and made notations, but her ricocheting thoughts were stuck on this crisis. Once the room emptied, Webb and Garcia stood up. "Excellent work, Case Agent Hall," Webb boomed, leaning in and holding out his hand. "What a coup if we can get Sheer in on this sting too."

"Sir," she said quickly, cutting her gaze to include Garcia too. "I have an update on the leak."

Both men promptly sat back down, faces grim. Steadying her breath, she filled them in. "My gut tells me Sergeant Fontana is telling the truth—he had nothing to do with Bradley's murder, but we're basically starting from square one on that part of the investigation, since he's sat on his hands this whole time," she concluded. "I told him to wait for your summons in the bullpen."

"What's his state of mind?" Garcia asked, always the supervisor who looked beyond job performance in individuals. Before he horned in on her op tonight, she'd have rated him one of the best supervisors she'd worked under.

"To be honest, I didn't get a sense of remorse other than how it will reflect on his career."

"His career is finished," Webb snapped, and huffed like a bull. "I'll speak to the commissioner. Again, great work flushing him out, Heidi."

"Thank you, sir."

Garcia looked at the ceiling as if in prayer. "Thank God it wasn't one of ours."

Now was the time to confront them. "About the surveillance tonight—"

Webb waved her off. "The closer the lead-up to an FBI sting, the more the bigwigs want to experience the excitement too. Can't imagine your agency does it any differently."

She knotted her fingers in her lap. "It's very similar, sir. Which is why I was up front in the interview that I would only take this job on the condition of sole autonomy."

"And yet Chaz Jackson returned to New York."

And there it was. They didn't trust her on her own. "The personality clash between him and Jace was insurmountable."

"Nevertheless. ASAC Garcia will take his place in the van tonight. Think of him as a ride-along. He's not there to take over."

Her lips felt stiff as she smiled. "I worry about differing opinions interfering at such a vital time—"

"I have no intention of hindering your investigation or stepping on your toes," Garcia said kindly. "I'll remain a silent observer unless you decide otherwise."

Webb nodded. "This op is too important, Heidi. The pressure from the mayor and governor, the scathing media stories, the public distrust... It's taken a great toll on this task force and the entire field office. We'd like to stand alongside your outstanding team when you wrap this all up."

Translate that to "seize all the credit." The rigid set of Heidi's shoulders was giving her a headache. Had this power play happened earlier in the week, she'd have been on the next flight back to D.C. Now she was too invested. Too close to Jace. They had her over a barrel.

"Am I making myself clear?" There was no mismatched smile this time on Webb's face. His eyes had turned deadly.

She lifted her chin, refusing to cower. "Very clear, sir."

30

J ace had the rideshare drop him a couple of blocks from Ken Nash's house. Hopefully the walk in the brisk night air would jolt his mind to the task at hand instead of rerunning last night's let's-keep-this-professional disaster. *Stop thinking about Heidi!*

He jammed his hands in his pockets and quickened his pace. Sheer was in Chicago and in his sights. The prospect of taking down the head of the Race generated the same adrenalin buzz as those deadly ops in Kandahar. The role of hunter was a comfortable second skin. It also led to making riskier choices, like only donning both the watch, that recorded audio, and the repaired baseball cap that captured audio and visual, because there was bound to be an even more thorough torso pat-down tonight.

Capturing anything Sheer might say about Friday's plans or, better still, June's mosque bombing made it important enough to wear both. He glanced around the street that was empty and quiet. According to Heidi's most recent text, the various SSG surveillance teams who'd blanketed this area all day had not picked up on Sheer arriving at Nash's house yet.

Jace turned onto Washington Avenue, automatically scanning this new environment for threats. Didn't matter if a quiet neighborhood lay before him—a soldier parsed out every detail of the scene. Any sudden change in the shadows? Any bodies sitting in parked cars? Any exhaust pipes running? Every location was a potential combat zone.

In this case, the only element of note was the nondescript FBI van, parked four houses down, deceptively dark and unoccupied. The SSG vehicles were doing an exceptional job of blending in, because he couldn't identify any in the vacant parked cars along the street.

His steps slowed as he approached the back of the van. Heidi, already monitoring the feed captured by his hat, knew he stood there. Had her heartbeat just rocketed into the cosmos too? What if he wrenched the door open and climbed in? Wordlessly lunged by Alma Reyes to get to Heidi, who would be open-mouthed in shock.

Damn it. Way to get sidetracked again! He strode on by, gritting his teeth. There was going to be a goddamn standoff at the hot wash tonight. Jace shook his head. This was exactly why he didn't do relationships. The tangled, irrational emotions... Life was too short to deal with the bullshit and this aftermath of obsessively going over what he could have said to make her want him.

Up ahead, a couple of vehicles eased to the curb in front of Nash's. Headlights blinked off. In the faint light from a streetlamp farther down, Jace recognized Craig's locksmith decal on the light gray pickup. He paused again, this time in the shadow of a giant elm.

Chris got out of the Camaro at the same time both doors on Craig's cab opened. Sheer had mentioned that their cell had a new member tonight. The trio didn't seem aware of Jace as they gathered on the walkway to Nash's. Jace squinted at the newbie's familiar build and loose-limbed gait.

Shit. Please let him be hallucinating. Heart beating like a sledgehammer, Jace slipped further behind the tree.

The men spoke quietly as they approached the threshold to Ken's well-lit house. Craig's larger body blocked a clear view of the new guy walking beside him. Jace craned his neck as the men climbed the three steps into the flood of Nash's front-door light.

His breath stalled and prickles covered him like hives. Standing perfectly illuminated with the other Race members was Gage.

"What's he doing?"

Heidi raised her head from the notes she'd buried herself in the moment Jace stopped feet from the van, basically outing their attraction to ASAC Garcia. Face still burning, she glanced at the monitor Garcia was pointing to. Jace's ball cap displayed a hurried route *away* from Nash's house. He crossed the street, then turned in the direction he'd come from, like he was leaving. She frowned. What *was* he doing? Why wasn't he talking aloud to provide an explanation?

A second later her phone dinged, and she grabbed it off the van's custom-built counter, heartbeat skittering against her ribs. She read the text aloud. "Massive FUBAR. Meet at corner of Washington and Ridge Rd."

"That's a couple of blocks away," Alma said from the driver's seat.

"Why?" Garcia said, anger lacing the word.

How typical of Jace to go rogue and make her look

like an imbecile in front of Garcia! "He wouldn't do this unless there was a reasonable explanation," Heidi said evenly. He'd better have the world's best reason! She swallowed hard as she tore off the headphones and swiveled to Alma. "Drive. Let's find out what the threat is."

She hadn't seen anything out of the ordinary, but then again, she'd taken her eyes off the monitors for a full minute. What had he seen when the pickup and Camaro parked? How fast could she talk him down so he could return and make his excuses for arriving late to the most important meeting of the entire op?

Alma crept past Nash's house and reached the designated corner just as Jace slipped from behind a maple. Heidi lurched to the back door, and as Alma began to slow, she swung open the panel. Without waiting for the van to fully stop, Jace leapt in, landing in a smooth crouch. Impressive, given forward momentum, the moving vehicle's tight space, and a fourth body jammed in here. She'd have propelled right into something.

"What the hell's happened?" Garcia said instantly.

Had it been any other time, the dumbfounded look on Jace's face would have been priceless. "Sir," he said, slightly out of breath, "we've got a situation. If I go in that house, my cover is blown. They've recruited my brother."

Heidi barely suppressed a string of obscenities. Alma and Garcia let them fly.

"His name is Gage." Jace tore off his ball cap and scraped a hand through his hair. Shock was still written all over his face. "He's had a tough time adjusting back into civilian life, but I didn't think..." He shook his head. "I can't believe..."

The man crouching before them was helpless, and by the darting eyes and pale complexion, he was also terrified. Clearly for his brother. The real Jace she'd discovered through the hot-wash questions was fearless, irrationally owning all the responsibility for solving problems and saving the world. No doubt he was trying to figure out how to save the op *and* protect his brother, diametrically opposed goals and, in this case, impossible to achieve. She ached for the man she'd come to know, but as his supervisor, she owed it to him to suppress any sympathy. He needed to get his head back into the Jason McGowan role, pronto.

Heidi tore her gaze from his open distress to Garcia, whose stony expression was just as alien. The gentle administrator had been replaced by a battlefield commander. "The first thing you do is text Nash you'll be late. Be vague on arrival time."

Jace's expression instantly cleared. He whipped out Jason McGowan's phone and complied.

When he looked up, Garcia continued. "Now we find a way to extract your brother from the scene, so you can get back in there."

"What would make Gage tear out of the house?" Heidi asked Jace.

Those powerful shoulders lifted in the faintest of shrugs. He wasn't thinking clearly. The sight of his brother had blown his concentration.

"A family emergency?" she asked.

He was already shaking his head. "We have too many first responders in the family."

Even Alma was frowning at his obtuse reasoning. "No. You call and tell him your mom has had a heart attack and is being rushed to the hospital. You're all gathering there to say goodbye."

He swiveled, peering at her like she'd just appeared out of thin air. There were too many echoes of how Evan's op began to flounder. Amid her own clawing anxiety, Heidi mentally commanded Jace to snap out of it. What were they going to do? Even if they could get Gage out, Jace was not mentally prepared to stroll in as Jason McGowan anymore. Especially when a brilliant sociopath like Sheer was due to arrive.

"I don't have my personal phone," Jace sputtered. "I can't call Gage from the number the Race recognizes."

Alma's phone appeared in her hand like a magic trick. "I'll call. I was a certified paramedic before joining ATF. I can pass myself off as an ER nurse calling the whole family to gather."

A crank call would only buy them an hour at best. "What do we do when he gets to a hospital and no one there knows what he'd talking about?"

"We have agents waiting," Garcia said.

"And hold him on what charges?" Jace shook his head, eyebrows knotted. "Besides, he'll notify the Race the second we let him go. I'm telling you, the op is compromised."

It couldn't be. They just needed to think with clear heads. Heidi yanked the damn fingernail out of her mouth again. "Have your other brother, what's his name —Trick?—meet Gage at the ER and keep him waylaid. Or that other brother—you were standing with him in the hotel hallway when we first met. Whichever one is available or that you trust."

The four looked at each other, the silence filled with furious thoughts. Maybe, like Heidi, they were searching for loopholes.

"You met in a hotel lobby?" Or maybe, like Alma, they weren't.

"Wedding," Heidi spat out. "Long story."

Garcia finally nodded. "Do it. Which hospital would your mom be brought to?"

"Evanston."

Heidi handed Jace her cell phone. "Call one of your

brothers first and find out if they're available to go over there before Alma calls Gage."

Jace hesitated over the keypad on her screen. Whether he didn't know his brothers' phone numbers or he was centering himself to push through this was unclear. Tension locked Heidi's shoulders up near her earlobes. "Jace?"

"I'm rehearsing what to say."

Heidi wrenched the headphones from around her neck and tossed them on the console. "Can I see you outside?" Even as the request left her lips, she regretted the polite tone. Jace reacted exactly as expected, with an irritated shake of his head.

"I need to make the call, and I want to hear what Alma tells Gage."

"Negative," Heidi said, this time in her drill sergeant tone. "Step out of the van." All three faces registered surprise.

One thing about observing Jace all these weeks—on the van's screen in his undercover role, interviewing him as he struggled through hot washes, and last night's glimpse of his vulnerability—she *knew* him now. Intimately. The infuriated glare in his eyes wasn't because he was being ordered about by a woman. His anger was directed inward. Maybe because he'd had this unusual meltdown between his private and professional lives in front of an associate and two superiors. Or his presently unsuccessful attempt to regain his über-cool SEAL persona. The reason didn't matter. They had very little time to turn this imploded op around. *She* had very little time. What an awful night for Garcia to have sat in on surveillance. Faced with this wrench in their plans, both she and Jace looked like they didn't know what the hell they were doing.

Heidi turned to Garcia. "Give us two minutes."

Brushing past Jace, which had the same impact as brushing by a brick wall, she opened the panel door and hopped out into the cold night air. Jace followed and shut the door. She spun around, breath streaming in a mist, and put her finger to her lips. He stilled. Motioning to his cap and watch and then the area under the van, she stepped back and waited for him to strip himself of the surveillance and recording devices.

Jace placed them neatly by the tailpipe and followed her down the block. She clenched and unclenched her fists. "You've got to pull it together, Jace."

"My brother was not brought up like this," he said between clenched teeth. "I can't decide whether to rescue him or wring his goddamn neck!"

"We'll handle it from here." She stopped and laid a hand on his arm. "Breathe. You need to get your head back in the game. We don't have a lot of time."

He scrubbed a palm over his mouth, but then followed the impatient gesture with a noisy inhale and exhale. "Okay," he said. "Let me call Trick."

"Take another minute."

"No." He raised Heidi's cell phone. "I gotta fix this now."

The conversation was short, his brother's questions rebuffed. "I'll tell you later," Jace kept repeating. "Just get the hell over to Evanston ER and wait for Gage. I don't care what you have to tell him, but don't let him out of your sight until you hear from me again."

Heidi hopped up and down, blowing on cupped hands. She hadn't thought to grab her jacket before jumping out.

"Okay," Jace said with relief. "I owe you." He clicked *end*, the cell phone light throwing his chiseled jaw in sharp relief. Handing her the phone, he said, "Tell Alma to make the call. I'm heading back there now."

"Jace, wait for your brother to leave the neighborhood."

"He won't see me." He walked back to the van and snatched up the cap and watch.

"At least give yourself a moment to get it together."

Jace wordlessly tugged the cap on, snapped the watch in place, and strode away without a backward glance.

Heidi gripped her phone. His body language! The confident swagger was gone, his posture emanated defeat. He was going back in before he was mentally prepared. It was Evan all over again, and all she could do was stand here helplessly. "Jace," she called. "Stop. That's an order."

"I'll see you at the hot wash, Heidi." He turned the corner out of sight.

31

J ace jogged up Nash's walkway, wiping sweat from his upper lip. There was nothing he could do about the icy version clinging to his torso, and it would only distract him to keep thinking about the damp discomfort.

Thankfully, Gage was long gone. His brother had split at a dead run in the direction of Milwaukee Avenue, the closest main thoroughfare, where no doubt SSG surveillance made sure he'd hailed a cab. *Forget about him. You're Jason McGowan now.*

He rearranged his expression just as the door opened. Warm air spilled onto him. "Jason," Ken boomed, "come on in. We were getting worried." He wasn't smiling. Arriving half an hour late was newbie fuck-up 101.

"Sorry." Jace tugged the lip of his cap in deference. Per Chaz's lectures, the tardy excuse had to be unverifiable. Saying his phone died and yet there it was, working in his pocket, wouldn't fly. Saying he was caught in traffic this late in the evening when most map apps showed real-time traffic patterns was risky. "I left my phone at our Belvidere construction site." He stepped into the foyer.

"Had to go all the way back and get it." There was a Whitehead Construction project in Belvidere, a farm town over an hour away.

"You know the drill."

Jace nodded and raised his arms out to the side. Ken performed a quick pat-down, then motioned to the baseball cap. "Sheer isn't here yet, but out of respect I've asked all the men to remove their ball caps. You can leave it here." He motioned to the Shaker-style bench, lined with three caps.

How would Jason react? Jace covered his hesitation by nodding, but the moment was over. No one fought to keep their hat on inside a house. During the previous evenings, the cells hadn't thought twice about manners. All the members, except Nash, were blue-collar workers who generally wore caps indoors. Jace slowly removed the FBI's only visual surveillance and tossed it next to the others. Hopefully the team had gotten a warrant and somehow planted bugs in here today.

Ken motioned down the hall. "Second door on your right. Drink?"

"Just water, thanks. I want to be sharp for Sheer." Jace walked toward the final meeting place like it was his own hanging. Seeing Gage arrive had been a body blow. The realization of how far his war-damaged brother had sunk was interfering with his ability to get into character. Or think. Or react in any sort of pivotal fashion. Of all the nights.

Jace turned into the spacious living room, greeted the others on rote, and apologized again. He gravitated toward Craig on the sofa when Nate Henderson waved him over to an empty armchair between him and Dennis. A quick survey of the room showed that each of the cells had clustered together. Shit.

Jace murmured a final apology as he sat next to Nate,

shoving down the adrenalin-induced urge to fidget. Ken returned with his water, and then addressed the room. "Let's get started. Calvin will arrive shortly, and we'll run through the whole plan one final time. In the meantime, Jason, how are you doing with the materials?"

"The bricks are in a backpack, ready to go."

"And how are you accounting for the loss of supplies to your employer?"

Jace hesitated. Ken's tone was all wrong. And why the sudden third degree on covering his ass? "I oversee inventory. All I did was alter a previously paid purchase order to reflect four fewer blocks."

His brain was rebounding under the full attention of seven men. This was the kind of night Trick would refer to as bad karma—there was no further room to make a mistake. Jace looked Ken in the eye. "Based on your logistics, I still recommend a soldering iron, tungsten carbide tip, and titanium drill bit. We'll need the flexibility once we see the structure up close."

Ken nodded absently, the scrutiny still chilling. When the moment had gone on a fraction too long, Jace abruptly turned to Nate. "How are you coming with the declaration?"

Nate leaned forward and plucked a folded wad of papers from his back pocket. "Figured we could send this to the *Tribune* right after the explosion," he said self-importantly as he unfolded it. He paused, squinting. "'On behalf of the white population of Chicago, we strongly object to our historic American restaurant being stolen by Pakistanis who have no right to be here. Since the space will no longer be used by and for our pure species, we've rightfully chosen to obliterate it from the earth—'"

The doorbell rang. "Hold it right there. Sheer will want to critique it anyway." No surprise, Ken sounded under-impressed, and missed Nate's murderous scowl as he turned toward the hallway.

At the sound of the door opening, effusive greetings, and the door closing, Jace concentrated on normalizing his heart rate. This was it—he was about to lay eyes on Calvin Sheer, no doubt the terrorist mastermind behind the Mosque Mohammed bombing.

Ken turned the corner, grinning proudly like he was hosting the president of the United States. "Gentlemen. Meet the ingenious inspiration behind the Race, Calvin Sheer." The group stood up, expressions ranging from awestruck to overcome.

"Good evening, everyone." Although Sheer was surprisingly short and stocky, he held a larger-than-life magnetism. Keen intelligence shone from bright blue eyes, and he had a swagger of energetic confidence as he shook hands and engaged in individual introductions.

"Jason McGowan." Jace gripped Sheer's palm. "This is a real honor."

Sheer came to his chin and sported a shaved dome with a shadow of growth along the crown and a bushy brown beard. His gaze was shrewd and psychotically cold. "Good to finally meet you," he said in a toneless way. Given the multiple crises this evening, Jace's suspicion escalated another notch. Something definitely wasn't right.

When Sheer finished shaking hands around the circle, Ken gestured to the armchair adjacent to where he stood. Sheer claimed the seat. The rest took their cues and sat too, shifting uncomfortably in the formality. Celebrity reverence still hung heavy in the air.

"We were going around finalizing everyone's role," Ken said in an overly pompous tone.

Nate crossed his arms, emitting an audible exhale that both leaders ignored.

"Before you all continue," Sheer said to the men, "let me just congratulate each of you on your bravery and willingness to step up on behalf of your race. The greatest tragedy is that most whites don't even realize how much they need us to fight for them and uphold our dwindling rights. We were born the superior race, but our freedom has been rapidly eroded by media-driven socialist agendas, uncontrollable immigration, and the gross atrocity of interracial unions."

Ignoring the waves of disgust sweeping through him, Jace nodded alongside the others. Chaz had been reluctant to talk about his vast experience in undercover work, but he had admitted to hating the arrest part of the process, when the criminals finally clued in on who was behind the sting. The shocked looks of betrayal sat heavily with him. Jace had understood the reasoning at the time, but in this instance, he lived for that expression on every single one of these faces. Especially Nate, Ken, and Sheer.

Sheer held up his right fist. "White power." They chanted it back. He rubbed his palms together, beaming. "All right, let's hear the details of your attack."

Ken nodded to one after the other, and they brought Sheer up to speed. Craig had made a key that would fit the lock for the building. The new security alarm had not been hooked up yet. Chris passed out copies of a hand-drawn map of four surrounding blocks with notations of all the security camera locations. They brainstormed how to bypass some and disarm others. "I've instructed our new guy, Gage Quinn, to secure hooded masks for all nine of us—"

"Wasn't he supposed to attend tonight?" Sheer interrupted.

"He was, but had a family emergency," Ken said

shortly. "He assured us he'll be at the meeting place on Friday."

Don't count on it. Jace sipped his water, too immersed in his role to brainstorm how the hell he was going to get his brother out of this or even let Gage know how he knew of the Race involvement. But sure as shit, his brother would be nowhere near Johnny's on Friday night.

"Unusual name, Gage," Sheer mused.

It was French for *one who was defiant*, and the second Gage learned to walk and talk, he'd lived up to that. Jace adopted a bored expression to cover the creeped-out vibes from his brother being so openly discussed by these fucktards.

"He's had it rough since he's been back stateside," Craig said. "The job interviews haven't panned out because most companies are looking for minority hires."

The jobs hadn't panned out because Gage walked in hungover, undereducated, and with a massive chip on his shoulder. "Can we get back to the plans?" Jace rode out the awkward silence at his snapped directive and ignored Sheer's contemplative gaze.

Nate raised a hand. "I'll finish reading the Race declaration we're sending out after the bombing."

Sheer waved him off. "No need. We don't advertise our victories. Unlike others, we're in this to save whites from themselves, not seek publicity." On the other side of the room, Craig was nodding, unsurprised.

Inwardly, Jace cringed. There was no love lost between him and Nate, but the slap of that dismissal, after Nate had labored so long over the damn thing, was brutal. He didn't need to look left to confirm Nate's fury—the space around his stiff posture was clogged with tension.

Jace glanced at his watch, the only recording they'd have

of this meeting unless MOSQMO had gotten a warrant to wire the place. Were Heidi and Garcia discussing the possibility of turning Nate right now? They didn't know him as well as Jace did, but the stunt with Zamira should have shown them this man fed on his need for revenge. Pair Ken's week-long contempt and now Sheer's lack of respect, and Nate was ripe for trading evidence for federal immunity.

Ken rolled out the floor plan and went over the logistics in that gratingly pompous tone. On the other side of Nate, Dennis shifted restlessly. Clearly, organizing mayhem wasn't in his comfort zone. He was geared toward pounding beer and reviewing all the daily slights he'd experienced solely because he was a white male.

Jace scanned the rest of the members. John and Hank watched their leader explain trusses to Sheer with the kind of worship that set off an inner shiver. Heidi had emphasized that the core of a white supremacist was the desperate need to belong, to take orders from someone they idolized, even when provided with concrete evidence that the leader was downright evil or batshit crazy. These two embodied that theory.

Chris and Craig, on the other hand, contemplated Ken with the hardened eyes of stone-cold killers. Soulless lizard eyes. Jace had seen enough soldiers overseas like this to recognize the look. The only thing these two got off on anymore was ending the life of another. The ultimate control. Without a doubt, these two had helped Thomas Bradley bring down a mosque.

The sudden glaring reality of this op started a low buzzing in Jace's ears, his body's red alert system. He had infiltrated a nest of adversaries that ranged from incompetently harmless to full-on homicidal. One misstep, one hint of his real thoughts or an expression flashing across his face, and he could kiss his life goodbye. The only thing white supremacists hated more than non-whites was the Deep State government.

He fought the irrational surge of panic. He didn't do insecure. He was a goddamn SEAL—could single-handedly take down half these men in under a minute. He'd be fine. In an hour he'd be answering Heidi's soft knock at his door.

For once, the hot wash was a godsend. He'd fully unload tonight. Gage becoming a white supremacist, Garcia's sudden presence in the van, Sheer's and Ken's peculiar behavior tonight... He was unpacking it all, until this David-facing-Goliath feeling was a distant memory of an overblown overreaction.

Jace blinked and sat up straight. All he had to do was pay sharp attention to the remaining plans, make suggestions, and maintain Jason's wholehearted, eager support. Piece of cake.

When Sheer concluded the meeting, Jace was first in line to shake the man's hand once more. "An amazing honor," he said, and this time Sheer's smile reached his eyes.

"You'll go far, McGowan."

Jace sent a half salute to the rest of the group, reclaimed his baseball cap, and ventured out into the crisp night. He purposely chose the opposite direction of the dark van, a slightly longer way to the Linden Ave station. Near the Camaro, he stopped and shot off a text to Heidi, giving her the all-clear to leave, and another letting Trick know Gage was safe to be let go. What reason had Trick thought up to contain their squirrely brother?

A sharp laugh sounded back by Nash's house. Jace glanced over, then ducked behind the left rear bumper of Chris's vehicle. Half a block down, Chris and Craig strolled toward him, talking in low voices. On instinct, Jace hit the record app on his phone.

"Yeah, remember how Tommy almost shat bricks?" Chris said with a chuckle.

"Wouldn't put it past Sheer to do it again. Did you notice how he barely paid attention to any of the details?"

"And I don't think he'd come all this way for a shitty little job like Johnny's. He's got his eye on something way bigger."

Jace frowned into the night. The sound of palms slapping. "Check ya later," Craig said. Chris grunted.

Jace slid to the right side of Chris's back bumper, where he wouldn't be detected. People who parked on a curb generally only checked over their left shoulder before pulling out. Plus, the Camaro was behind Craig's pickup, which meant Jace had a split second while Craig was driving off and Chris was checking his left mirror to somersault behind that tree at the curb. If he didn't time it right, Chris would see him tucked back here.

Heart thrumming steadily, Jace waited for the pickup to drive off. At the glare of brake lights indicating Chris had shifted into drive, Jace propelled sideways, rolling behind the thick tree trunk. The heavy engine roared off into the night.

More voices came from Nash's walkway. Jace rose to a crouch and pretended to tie his shoe a second before Nate and Dennis came into view. John and Hank were still in the doorway, backs turned as they said something to someone inside.

"Hey, guys," Jace said, rising to meet his cell. "Good meeting, huh?"

"If you call hijacking my original plan good," Nate snarled. "Not one ounce of thanks or credit tossed in our direction for coming up with the idea in the first place."

Perfect timing to nurse that bruised ego. "That manifesto was a whole lotta work for nothing."

Nate spat on the ground. "I'm going to talk to Sheer. I'm not working with Nash."

Jace's senses went on full alert. If Nate backed out of the plan, he'd take his three-man cell with him. "Ignore the mofo, Nate. *We* know Johnny's was your idea. Right, Dennis? Sacrifice for the team. Think of the glory when we pull this thing off."

Dennis nodded, shoving his hands in his pockets. "And we'll be part of a message to the Pakis to get the fuck out of our country."

Nate looked slightly mollified. "I guess."

John and Hank waved goodbye from the walkway and headed in the opposite direction. That left Sheer still inside. It was pure instinct to follow the man and find out where his safe house was, but there were teams of specialists hiding in the dark waiting to track him. Besides, the van was gone, so Jace had no backup. It was time to get home—definitely time to unload the sickness in his gut.

"You guys have a happy Thanksgiving," he said, purposely changing direction again, so he was heading back the way he came. It was quicker to the metro station this way, and he wouldn't have to walk with Nate and Dennis and listen to the endless spew of self-pity.

He set a slow pace so he wouldn't catch up to John and Hank, and shot off the recorded audio to Heidi. What kind of change had Sheer pulled on them before? Jace typed his thoughts to Heidi in a second text.

Maybe the mosque wasn't their original target? What do you think?

Half a block down, her return text dinged.

Interesting, thanks, will review. Cancelling the hot wash.

Garcia and I are evaluating the takedown strategy with SWAT.

The lancing disappointment rocked him to a standstill. Not seeing Heidi? Not talking about the toxic shit bubbling up? Tonight of all nights? He shook his head. He had to see her. Find a way to talk through this mess of fear in his head. Gage had destroyed the illusion that Jace had any of this under control, and that needed to change, ASAP. Whenever he couldn't fix stuff, people ended up hurt. Or dead.

He texted back with a tremor in his hands.

I'll come too. Office?

Chaz had participated in every aspect of the backup plans. It was more than time for Jace to pull that kind of weight too. His phone dinged immediately.

Get some sleep. See you at Thanksgiving.

He lowered his phone slowly, the night air misting with his harsh exhale. This. This moment here was what true powerlessness felt like. He was really in a bad place.

32

"I'm hoping sons three and four begin assimilating back into society, Gage. Is that too much to ask?"

Jace closed the front door silently, standing motionless in his parents' foyer. Pop's angry voice came from the living room, along with the sound of a cheering auditorium and a sportscaster calling a play on fourth and five.

This effective torture was known around here as Pop's selective attention test. The son in question would be on the sofa, while Pop, intimidating and red-faced, paced back and forth, listing all the ways said son didn't measure up. The torture angle? A game of some kind would be on, directly in the son's line of vision, and so help that boy if his eyes strayed to it. Evidently, focusing on a blistering lecture while ignoring touchdown cheers built character.

Even though Jace was forty and not on that sofa, an echo of apprehension slithered into his gut. He strained to hear his brother's answer. There was none. The Steelers got the TD and the crowd went wild.

Jace popped silently around the corner into the

kitchen. Mom held a dripping colander of green beans, her lips pressed into a strained line. "You never called Gage, did you?"

Oh, shit. "I forgot, Mom. I've been so—" There was no busy-at-work excuse that would stand up to the look on her face. "I'm sorry."

"Stop your father," she said quietly. "It's Thanksgiving."

Jace nodded once, braced himself, and strode into the living room.

"Speak of the goddamn devil." Gage was slumped on the sofa, legs spread, arms crossed. The bloodshot eyes were a dead giveaway. Another night of hard drinking. What had happened after Trick let him go?

"Let me guess," Jace said, eyeing the scraped and swollen knuckles. "A random fistfight and a night in the pokey?"

"Fuck you, Jace."

"Watch your mouth," Pop snarled, then turned to Jace, jerking a thumb in the direction of the patio. "Go join the others. We're almost done."

Jace lifted the remote and snapped off the TV. His tough-as-nails father blinked in astonishment. "My guest is on her way, Pop. Time to give it a rest."

"We're in the middle of something."

"You're a sentence away from ruining Mom's Thanksgiving. Can you finish after everyone's gone home?" He looked Pop in the eye and rode out the emotions flitting across his father's face. This would end one of two ways: either Jace would be taking a seat beside Gage and the TV was going back on, or Pop would grab a thread of reason and know that pissing off Mom today would be detrimental to everyone's dinner.

The silence stretched like a thick rubber band. Thankfully, Gage stayed silent. Any pipsqueak back talk, and this house of cards was going down. "Fine." Pop scraped a hand over his mouth, a tell Trick had picked up of symbolically holding back words that wanted to stream out. He pointed a finger at Gage. "You're not going anywhere tonight. You're mine. Now let's all go enjoy the rest of the family."

Gage's response was to pick up the remote and turn on the TV. If he felt as shitty as he looked, then he was a warrior just to have hauled himself out of bed. Jace set aside his own bullet-pointed lecture and sat next to him.

With a double wave off and disgusted shake of his head, Pop followed his own command and walked out onto the deck. Trick's girls were shrieking over by the tire swing. The door shut hard and muted the glee. The commercial ended, and Jace watched the game in silent solidarity with his mess of a brother. Irrespective of reality, men who felt lonely, underappreciated, or deeply misunderstood reached out to white supremacists. Instead of confronting Gage on joining the Race, maybe the first step today was just to be supportive.

"You don't need to stick around like some kind of hero," Gage muttered. "I'd rather be alone."

Well, that was right on cue. Jace bit back the reflexive, obscenity-laced response. "I'm waiting for my guest to arrive," he said, without looking away from the screen. "In the meantime, if it's okay with you, I'll watch the Steelers kick ass."

Within ten minutes, Gage was grudgingly participating in referee bashing, critiquing the wisdom of trading Kerns, and cheering on the wide receiver sprinting down the field.

The doorbell chimed and Jace rose, heart rate doubling, nerves prickling in anticipation. "I got it," he called to Mom, and headed for the door.

Heidi stood on the doorstep in the same floral dress

she'd worn to the wedding. He hadn't seen her out of a pantsuit since that evening, and his gaze strayed in appreciation to her hot, shapely legs.

"Eyes up here, Buster." But she was smiling, and for a moment his world was all right. Man, he had it bad. He needed to snap out of this.

Jace extended his arm. "Welcome to our insane asylum."

"Bet it can't beat a revolving foster family of nine." The impish twinkle in her eye was also a throwback to the wedding reception, when her carefree happiness had stolen his breath.

Something in his chest thickened, making it hard to breathe. The last time he'd grinned like this, he'd been a teenage sap. "You look nice."

Her softening expression obliterated the usual stress lines. She held up a bouquet of autumn-colored flowers. "For your mom."

Why hadn't he thought of flowers? "She's going to love you. Come on in."

Heidi stepped past him, the scent of something fresh and tart trailing her. He inhaled as he closed the door. By the time he turned back, she was already in the kitchen, introducing herself to Mom. He eased to her side, throwing Mom an apologetic half-shrug. She'd ingrained gentlemanly manners in each of her sons, but Heidi waited for no one and, as far as he'd seen, confidently held her own against anyone.

"Jace, put these in a vase, will you?" Mom handed the bouquet over and went to check on a boiling pot.

Heidi looked at the pots and pans and controlled chaos of a Quinn holiday meal, and grimaced. "No one's helping you?"

Mom laughed. "Oh, I made sure each of these boys knows how to cook, but Thanksgiving is sort of my day."

Heidi paused, clearly unhappy with the response. "Why don't I give you an assist?"

Jace's heart fell. Guess he should, too, given she was his guest, but it sure wasn't how he'd envisioned their time together.

"No, no." Mom waved them off cheerfully. "The whole thing will come together in about ten minutes. I'd love your help transferring it all to the table then."

"Sure." Heidi checked her watch. "Ten minutes."

"Come meet the rest of the clan." Jace led her into the living room. "This is Gage, the fourth of five."

Without missing a beat or remarking on Gage's ravaged, sullen face, Heidi swept over, holding out a hand. "That Kerns trade is going to come back to haunt the GM," she said in lieu of a hello. Gage's mouth popped open, but he automatically shook. She sat down uninvited, her purse perched on her bare knees. Her high heels were spikes. Jace swallowed hard. She sure could do feminine when she wanted to.

"Jace tells me you just got back from Afghanistan. I can't tell you how much I appreciate your service on behalf of our country. It must be hard transitioning from such a tight brotherhood back into this self-centered society." She waved a hand like the society was here in the living room.

Gage, still looking dumbstruck, didn't answer. Heidi opened her purse and handed over a business card. "If you're looking into any of the agencies, I'm a senior special agent with ATF. We're a close-knit group that prefers hard work to grandstanding glory." She glanced swiftly at Jace during the last two words, then winked at Gage. Everyone knew of the friendly hostility between ATF and FBI, and she was roping in Gage's interest by openly dissing Jace's choice.

Gage's faint grin was so much more poignant than

words. How the hell had she cut to the chase and established an authentic connection so fast?

"We look after our own." She rose with a smile. "Contact me anytime, Gage."

"Yeah, sure. Thanks."

Trying to ignore those sexy legs and killer heels, Jace ushered her out to the happy family scenario in the backyard. Trick pushed a squealing Tina on the tire swing. Sean, earbuds isolating him from the laughter, skimmed leaves from the pool. Amy tossed a beat-up tennis ball to Blaze, Trick's Irish setter, and Zamira and Gretch rocked gently on the glider sofa, talking quietly.

"I remember you," Gretch called with a smile. "The woman who made Jace blush."

"And I remember your smooth lateral glide," Heidi said, "that got me into the garter mess."

Jace swallowed the inner groan and ushered Heidi over. These two could potentially be deadly together. "Gretchen Allen," he said to Heidi, "Sean's girlfriend. Gretch, this is my case agent, ATF Senior Special Agent Heidi Hall."

"How formal of you, Jace," Gretch teased, shaking her hand. "Too bad you ruined with your bright red ears." Yes, this could be catastrophic.

"Are you and Sean in a fight?" He nodded to his brother, still unaware of the activity and noise swirling around him.

Gretch shrugged. "There's a complicated Raphael painting he's restoring that's giving him fits. He's probably brainstorming color combinations in that introverted head of his."

"What an interesting field," Heidi exclaimed, studying Sean with curiosity.

"And you remember Zamira Bey," Jace said hurriedly.

"Of course. Good to see you again." Heidi shook hands. "Any further problem with Nate?"

"No." Zamira, the antithesis of Gretch, spoke softly and smiled shyly. "The custody hearing was uneventful, and the judge had some harsh words about the conduct he expected before the next hearing, so strict parameters have been set."

Jace and Heidi exchanged a glance. Tomorrow Nate would be arrested red-handed in a sting operation. Committing a domestic terrorist act was probably not within the judge's parameters.

"I imagine you won't have any further problems," Heidi said confidently, then Jace led her to the ice-packed cooler and they helped themselves to beers.

"That was some kind of wizardry in there," he said, nodding toward the living room, where the flicker of the TV glowed beyond the sliding glass door.

Her lingering smile turned pained. "Something in Gage's eyes reminds me of my brother Dave growing up." She tilted her head in the direction they'd come. "He's rudderless, and there's no help in sight."

No help? Gage had four brothers and a lecturing father. The help was there. It was called tough love.

Maybe they were going about it wrong. "We need a strategy to keep him away from tomorrow's attack and a long-term plan to keep him away from white supremacists."

"Yeah, I was up most of the night thinking about it. That"—she did the head tilt again—"was the initial step."

He puffed a laugh. "You're going to get him a job with ATF?"

"I'm planting the seed that the kind of camaraderie he's starved for can be found in a law enforcement career."

Jace grinned down at her. A dozen yards away, the

Quinn generations were still shouting and playing, but he stayed in this pleasant bubble of sheer admiration and building desire. He wanted her so badly. If she'd stopped by last night, he wouldn't have had the strength to hold back from making a move again, despite the boundaries she'd set. "I missed ending my night in a hot wash," he admitted. "I was prepared to unload."

She morphed into case-handler serious, so as usual, his stupid admission had ruined the moment. "I couldn't get away, Jace. I know seeing your brother was a massive shock. Do you need talk about it?"

"Not anymore." In the cold light of morning, the anxieties and regrets had somehow compartmentalized themselves back into the airtight mausoleum. He could handle the crises same as he always did, like a matador facing down a charging bull.

"Jace, if you're feeling—"

"Skip it." He wanted to be with her, not talk about feelings. "Seriously, I've got it under control."

A high-pitched squeal drew their attention. "Throw it, Uncle Kevin!"

Jace winced, pretending to clean out his ear canal. "That's Trick's eldest, Amy. She's eight going on twenty."

"Yes, I remember her from the conga line. And who could forget Kevin?"

"You're not to talk to him today," Jace ordered her, and then flushed. "Just kidding."

"No, you're not."

Kevin pumped a fake throw at Amy. "Go long!" he called.

"I don't know what that means," she yelled back in a stricken voice.

"Go that way as far as you can... Further!" Kevin threw such a slow, anemic spiral it was a wonder gravity didn't claim the football halfway through the arc. At the last second Amy spun away from the hurtling object, arms shielding her head. The football bounced twice on the grass before Blaze leapt on it.

A footstep on the wooden deck made them turn. "Hi, I'm Sean."

"Oh, hi. Heidi Hall. I work with Jace."

Surprisingly, Sean, the shyest of the clan, maintained eye contact through the handshake. "Jace has never brought a woman home before."

And there it was—vintage Sean, verbalizing whatever popped into his head. Jace prickled with humiliation and the urge to cuff his brother on the back of the head, but Heidi gave a soft, girly laugh. "I think he felt sorry for me. I'm away from home."

Sean looked at Jace in that odd, fathomless way, then back at her. "That's not it—"

"I think Mom needs help," Jace barked, waving Trick over. It was past time to hear what happened at the ER last night.

"I promised your mom I'd help." Although Jace sputtered a protest, Heidi walked in with Sean, and Zamira and Gretch followed. That brother's mouth could do a lot of damage in very little time... Never meaning to, of course. Jace frowned after them as Trick walked up, six-year-old Tina riding piggyback.

"Hi, Uncle Jace!"

"Hey, little girlfriend. Can I talk to your dad a sec?" As she slid off Trick's back, Jace dug out a dollar and hunkered to her height. "Here. Go keep Uncle Sean talking. Ask him a bunch of questions, okay?"

With a determined nod, she headed inside.

He straightened. "Thanks for helping out last night."

"What was going on?" Trick was the kindhearted son. Hard to believe that quality also made him the apple of Pop's eyes.

"Gage is mixed up with a crew we're about to take down. I've gotta find a way to keep him far away tomorrow."

"Sorry, I'm on duty."

"How'd you get him to stick with you last night?"

"Bribed him with beer. Nothing else worked." Trick flitted a troubled glance through the glass door. "When I got your all-clear text, I hung out another hour, then poured him into a rideshare. He *was* on his way home. I don't know what happened that caused him to look like that."

"I doubt he does either." Knowing Gage, he probably got into it with the driver. Alcohol made him a combative drunk. "We'll need to sit him down real soon."

Trick lifted a shoulder as he reached for the door handle. "Pop's gotten nowhere."

"Pop may be part of the problem. He's coming down on Gage like a ten-ton brick."

"I remember the treatment." Trick's face looked pinched. He'd never shared details of the horror he lived through last May, but somehow even his relationship with Pop had floundered for a while. Their rapport was different now. More mature. Jace swallowed down the sour envy.

"I'm just saying, maybe Gage needs a little space." Someone more sympathetic, like this other side of Heidi, because the more Pop rode him, the more the welcoming acceptance of a neo-Nazi brotherhood would look like the only option.

"So, what's with you and Heidi?"

Jace opened his mouth to dispel anything more than friendship when Trick raised a brow. This was the brother who'd always called bullshit and nine out of ten times been right. Jace sighed. "I've got it bad, and she's my boss."

His brother threw back his head and laughed. "Way to make a budding relationship sound like torture."

Torture. That was a great descriptor. "She's on loan from D.C., she's much higher up the federal agency food chain, not to mention older..." Jace petered out as he gazed around the lawn. Kevin was throwing that chewed-up tennis ball to Blaze.

Trick patted his shoulder. "None of those excuses mean much to your heart."

Jace rolled his eyes. What a Trick thing to say. What did that even mean? "My point is: getting together with her... I want it so bad, but I don't know how to make it happen."

"Try being yourself."

"That was my thought too. When the op wraps up tomorrow, she'll see me in a new light."

"No," Trick said in exasperation, his expression like Jace was as dumb as a rock. "Not you being the hero. I mean let her see what's underneath."

There *was* nothing underneath. Heroes solved crimes, arrested bad guys, and got the girl. It didn't matter. This was going nowhere, and he wasn't navel-gazing any further.

Jace spun toward the lawn and whistled at Kevin. "Yo. I want you sitting far away from my guest this afternoon."

"If I hadn't chatted her up last month, you never woulda gotten to know her," Kevin called back.

Well, not the softer side that stole his concentration. "Doesn't make much sense, Kev, given she's my boss."

His brother just smirked. "You're welcome just the same."

33

Heidi collected her purse, locking down any hint of relief to be leaving the Quinns. Overall they'd been fun and welcoming, but the insights she'd gained into their family dynamics had pushed a lot of her own childhood buttons.

Connor Quinn, the inflexible father, was strict enough to define as abusive, but his body language contrasted sharply from that "man's man" persona. Inside, he was suffering from chronic worry over each of his sons' success and wellbeing. The frequency of the limbic signals differed in relation to which son he was berating. While the dichotomy didn't excuse his outward behavior, it was hard not to compare to her upbringing.

Her foster father hadn't displayed underlying love for the kids, period. Collecting monthly state checks per kid had been his side business, and when one child returned to their birth parents, another child would be moved in almost immediately. He'd left the day-to-day care of bringing up seven children to his wife.

That overwhelming strain and martyred unhappiness had sent Heidi's foster mom into an early grave, forcing

Heidi, as the eldest daughter, into the sacrificial role at thirteen. The messes, the tears, the fights, the industrial-sized meals and chronic dirty laundry piles... Ugh. The only way she'd escaped that hated life was enrolling in the Army the day after high school graduation.

The difference here was that Olivia Quinn embraced her traditional roles as wife to a fire battalion chief, mother to five strapping boys, cook, housekeeper, and peacemaker, when Connor went too far. That she delighted in this hectic life also went a long way to explaining Jace's misogyny. Oh, she was loved and doted on by each family member, and the youngest son, Sean, seemed to be her designated helper, but Connor issued the commandments and gave out the advice. Olivia was relegated to circling his orbit.

That this sweet woman was okay with her role and found joy in cooking an entire Thanksgiving meal while her men relaxed stuck in Heidi's throat, but she sincerely meant the effusive compliments she paid Olivia for her gracious hospitality.

"It was *very* special meeting you," Olivia said back, with such a pointed look in her eyes that Jace shifted uneasily beside them. Heidi flashed back to Sean's remark that Jace had never brought a woman home. Obviously, his mom was reading too much into this pity invite too.

Heidi turned to Gage, who so reminded her of Dave, in this reiteration of her childhood. He hovered several feet from where they all stood, hands shoved deep in his pockets. His body language resembled a small boy's, torn between the aloofness of not caring to join in the good-byes and the vulnerable longing plainly evident in his eyes. How could anyone miss reading this? How had this big, brawling family overlooked someone this insecure? She'd specifically sat next to him and devoted much of the meal to shoring up his broken self-esteem and soothing the bewilderment at reentering a society that rewarded self instead of brotherhood.

Heidi walked over to him now. "I hope to see you tomorrow," she said gently, shaking his hand. "I think you'll find this is right up your alley."

Gage dropped his gaze. "Thanks. I'll report to reception at eight thirty."

Jace walked her out the front door, and she stood on the stoop, face lifted to the sunset. Thank God for her perfect single life where no one relied on her to take on those female roles of caregiving.

"What was that about?" he asked, closing the door behind them.

She swung around, cocking her head. "What?"

"What you arranged with Gage."

"Oh." She shrugged, walking down the steps. "As luck would have it, your field office scheduled a CAP tomorrow. I checked between dinner and dessert, when you were all out tossing the football."

He followed her down the steps, shaking his head. "Too many acronyms. What the hell is CAP?"

"Community awareness presentation." They walked companionably down the path. "It's like a citizens academy, only instead of a six-week program, it's a day-long course."

His brows rose to comical heights. "Gage? In the FBI?"

"I'd be happy to sponsor him for ATF. He just needs to find buddies on the right side of the law." She pulled her coat tighter against a swirling burst of wind. Damp leaves skittered past her ankles. Oh, for the freedom and warmth of her pantsuits. "The CAP will keep him busy all day, and after the session I'll ask Alma to engage him somehow while the Race is at Johnny's."

"That could work." Jace nodded thoughtfully, then

smiled down at her. "Actually, that's brilliant." Admiration shone from his ocean-blue eyes, and her throat thickened. It was rare to hear a simple, heartfelt compliment from a colleague. No brown-nosing, no condescension, no "but" following afterward.

"Thanks." It was the only word she could squeeze out.

"Let me drive you home." He waved at the mammoth black Escalade in the driveway.

"Wow. Was it worth all the time you spent backtracking to go get your own car today?"

"Hell yeah. Look at this baby." He clicked the remote, and the alarmed chirped. "I've sure missed her on this assignment."

Yep. All dominant male on the outside, hiding those raging insecurities. Just like his dad. This insight had been so helpful.

She pulled up abruptly. *Wait.* His niece had interrupted them earlier. "Do you still need to unload at a hot wash?"

"What?" His eyebrows rose. "Where did that come from?"

"You asked for it last night and mentioned it again when I first arrived. I apologize for not getting with you."

"Garcia gave you a directive. The op takes priority, as it should."

But should it? She'd chosen the Wastewater sting over Evan's progressively troubled body language. Bought into his reluctance to talk about it as a sign that he wanted to keep his head in the game and sort out his feelings later. "Let's go somewhere and talk, Jace."

"Nah. I'm over it." His clipped tone and lack of eye contact said the opposite. "Sorry I freaked out in the van. My head was in a weird place. What you've done with Gage today"—he waved a hand back at the house—"and making sure he's covered tomorrow... That was my only worry."

What a load of bullshit. "Then you won't mind spending half an hour hot-washing it." She used her sharp supervisor tone, and he stiffened. But damn all if he was going to weasel out of an identical scenario as her final days with Evan. On the precipice of a takedown, she didn't need another stressed-out agent shutting down and acting all macho. This time she was listening to instinct. "I need you to be mentally ready for tomorrow, Jace, so even if the feelings have passed, we're talking through them."

He looked down the street, jaw tight, lips drawn in a tight line. "Sure." His heavy exhale misted in the waning light. "But I can't face going back to the bu-house yet. Can we talk at my condo?"

"Oh...um..." Nope. She was willing to do anything for his mental wellbeing—except that, and he had only himself to blame. All afternoon he'd been the perfect gentleman: attentive, funny, thoughtful. Every laugh, every glance her way had fed the Flirt to the point that now Heidi was in a terribly weakened state just offering to be alone with him, period. If she went to his private space, saw how he really lived, the music he listened to, even the color of his bedspread, her professional role would crumble. The sad fact was she didn't want to hear Jace unload as much as she wanted to see him naked. She was falling hard, and at the worst possible time. At least the bu-house was a stark reminder that she was his boss. But how to admit all that?

Like a message from above, her phone dinged. She glanced at the text and groaned. "Garcia," she said with a heavy sigh. "Wants to know if I can meet." Despite all the hours spent at headquarters earlier, he was ordering her back for more strategic coordination. What should she do? The final preparation to take down three terrorist cells and their commander versus the mental health of her UCA. She hit the reply key. "I'll tell him I'll be a while."

"Heidi." Jace laid a hand on her arm. "I promise I'm okay. Go."

She blew out a breath, studying him unabashedly. Candid eyes stared back. His loose stance was equal parts motionless and confident. "Okay," she said reluctantly, and sent Garcia a thumbs-up icon.

"Get in. I'll drive. I've got nothing else going on."

"Thanks," she managed. "Headquarters."

He opened her door—of course he would—and seconds later they were buckled in and peeling off. His comforting clean air and dryer softener scents tingled her nostrils.

"Did we find out where Sheer is staying?" he asked.

"Yep." Heidi stuck her icy hands near the heating vent. "Took some ever-loving skill. That man must have a military or law enforcement background. He expected surveillance and dry-cleaned like a pro."

Jace's head swiveled to her. "He *expected* surveillance?"

"I think it's his MO. Evidently, he did it exiting O'Hare yesterday as well. Once our crew identified his rental, I had staff go back and track it from the airport on CCTV. He pulled all the tricks. He's overly cautious to the point of paranoid. After leaving Nash's last night, it took all six SSG teams over an hour to fool him into thinking he was safe enough to go back to his place. They tracked him to a single-family unit in Berwyn. We've monitored the structure all day. He hasn't left once."

"Good. Hope he ate canned food for Thanksgiving. What's the alias he's using?"

"Edwin Carmichael the third." She settled against the headrest. "It's essential that he joins you guys at the restaurant. We have nothing on him to arrest or detain. Zero to tie him to MOSQMO. What a flying failure it would be to watch him legally skip back out of the country."

"I'll get you the evidence."

She studied his strong profile and self-assured expression in the dusk. Even the way he drove this tank, one-handed and relaxed, exuded pure masculine power. The Flirt shivered.

"Maybe the excitement of blowing up another building will make him wax nostalgic for Mosque Mohammed," Jace said. "He's a psychopath, but he's ego-driven."

"Are you nervous?"

He glanced over with a grin. "Are we starting the hot wash?"

She smiled back, huddling deeper in her coat like a squirmy teenager. "Nope. I'm gonna come up with epic questions for the next one. Make sure you have your tissues handy."

His laugh was deep and carefree. He, too, had not returned to his hardheaded FBI agent-associate self. "I'm not nervous, Heidi. I live for this shit. I can run a multi-agency takedown blindfolded. It's the acting and racial slurs I'll never get used to."

His undercover persona was a far sight better than that first meeting with Travis, the recruiter. "You've done an excellent job moving this op forward," she said sincerely. "Look what you accomplished in less than six weeks."

"What *we* accomplished." He peered over, all traces of a smile gone. "I hope you end up with a commendation for all the brainpower that went on behind the scenes."

She shrugged. "I don't care about badges or commendations or letters for my file as much as I want an ASAC promotion. Even if I have to move from D.C."

"Have you ever put your name up for consideration?"

Heidi cut her gaze to the side window. "Yes." She let the answer lie there as resentment bubbled up all over again. Too many times associates with far less skill and experience had leapfrogged her. All men. All buddies with the higher-ups. She'd learned long ago that pointing out the discrimination was detrimental to career mobility. Grumbling affected choice assignments. Even a caustic word aloud, like right now, for instance, only made her sound like a hysterical shrew. So few male colleagues could commiserate with the frustration of chronic gender bias. Their imaginations didn't stretch that far.

"You know, we're a lot alike, you and I," Jace said after a prolonged silence.

She swept the seething thoughts aside and turned to him. This would be rich. "How so?"

He rounded the final corner onto Roosevelt Road. The lighted FBI headquarters loomed majestically a block down. "Our careers are everything," he said. "Relationships run a distant second. We're both stuck in what we consider a federal position much too low for our expertise." He jerked a thumb at himself. "Me because I'm still earning a college degree, and you because of boobs."

His perception had grown a lot these past weeks. She barely had time to wipe the astonishment from her face when he pulled to the curb, shifted into park, and looked over. "If I don't get a chance to say it tomorrow night, I appreciate your looking beyond my stupid title and picking me for this assignment. No one else would have bucked the system like that."

A sliver of guilt prickled her skin at her original ulterior motive in selecting him, but he didn't need to know that. "You've done an exceptional job with little training."

"Yeah, well." He chuckled. "I don't think undercover work is in my future, but your belief in me means a lot."

She owed him a hot wash. She would never forgive herself ignoring him for Garcia's meeting. "I don't know how long I'll be here, but if it isn't too late, I'm going to insist on that hot wash."

His face in the dashboard light looked grim. A long moment went by. "All right," he said. "Come anytime. I doubt I'll get much sleep tonight. But I'm sick of that bu-house and what it represents. For one night, I'd like to stop being a racist and lie in my own bed."

Lie in my own bed. Oh, God. "If I conduct a hot wash at your place, Jace, I'll end up jumping your bones," she blurted.

Oh. The. *Horror.*

Jace shrugged loosely. "Fine by me."

She gaped at him. "That's your sole reaction?"

"I made my thoughts clear two nights ago." He spread his palms. "We've been like heat-seeking missiles for weeks now. Giving in might actually take some of the pressure off us."

"Or bury us."

"Not everything has to end in catastrophe, Heidi."

She groaned a sigh. So smoking hot, but so naive. "It'll hurt both our careers." *Mine more than yours.* "It'll be detrimental to the op. You were right. Relationships come second for both of us, and we have to remember that."

Leather creaked as he shifted to face her. "One thing we learn as SEALs is to live in the moment, because chances are high it could be our last." He stretched his arm out along the back of her seat, trailing his thumb in a gentle path along her neck. Her nipples hardened to pinpoints, and she shivered in her thick coat. "If anything goes wrong at Johnny's," he said softly, "at least we'll have had tonight."

"And if the takedown is a massive success?" The pariahs loved watching those at the top free-fall.

"Hell, if we're victorious, you'll be dining with the governor, and Webb will turn a blind eye to anything we do. We'll get away with this."

She checked the impulse to correct him. *He'd* get away with it. She'd be tagged for reverse discrimination, a female having a fling with a male under her direct supervision, not to mention accusations of favoritism. Who chose an agent associate with no undercover experience and no right to the assignment? The media's annihilation would harm the snail-paced forward momentum for women in law enforcement. No. The risk was all hers. She couldn't agree to this.

"I'll text you when I'm through," her mouth said, overriding her brain.

Even in the gloom, the look he threw her sparked every nerve. "I'll text you my address."

Heidi stumbled out on legs as wobbly as jelly. Thank God she had a few hours to talk herself out of this, to shore up her ironclad role of supervisor again. If she were heading for his condo now, she'd ignore that whole list of precautions just for one night with him, no holds barred.

34

"What worries you most about tomorrow?"

"That it'll be more of the same," Jace said, airing the underlying misgiving he'd wanted to get off his chest last night. "I'm not a superstitious guy, but this MOSQMO task force has been cursed from the get-go. So much has gone wrong. Gage showing up on Nash's doorstep is just the latest disaster, but not the last. I've got a real bad feeling about this takedown."

Heidi put down the iPad and blew out a breath—clearly a bad sign. Instinctively, he grabbed his beer and swallowed a gulp.

"I agree Gage was a wild card last night," she said, "but the situation is now contained. And as for bad luck or being cursed..." She grimaced. "It was neither. MOSQMO had a traitor funneling information to Thomas Bradley."

He almost choked on his second sip of beer. "Come again?"

"Sergeant Bill Fontana called to warn Bradley a few hours after Case Agent Hennessey ordered Bradley's arrest warrant."

This was crazy! "What? Why? How did you even find that out?"

She filled him in on the call made from Hennessey's office, the long searches through building security and employee files, and how she'd revealed Race members' names to a smaller and smaller core team until the Marion Pen connection. "The point is," she ended, spreading her palms, "the leak is contained, Webb and the police commissioner are dealing with Bill, and this op is back on track."

"Is that why you kept my op a secret?"

"Yes. And why I wouldn't let you communicate with anyone on your team."

He recollected the unauthorized call he'd made to Alma Reyes about Wastewater and a couple of shoot-the-shit conversations with Hennessey out on paternity leave. Shit. He could potentially have done some serious damage. "Why didn't you tell me before tonight?"

"You didn't need one more burden."

"But maybe I could've helped in some way."

She shook her head. "You're dealing with enough. The only reason I told you is because MOSQMO isn't cursed. The problem is solved. So in that light, what *now* worries you most about tomorrow?"

Jace scraped a hand through his hair, trying to bury the shocking news and sort his thoughts. He'd already gone through all possible contingencies for the take-down, same as before any SEAL op, and formulated acceptable responses for each. The one area still preying on his mind was the authenticity of his goddamn acting.

He looked over at Heidi, patiently waiting on his leather sofa, fingers poised over her iPad. How strange to see her in his home. "I'm worried I'll slip up in a way the defense can use against me. What if I say something that lets these motherfuckers off?"

"It'll keep you on your toes," she murmured, typing away. "That's a healthy anxiety to have."

Anxiety! His whole being repelled that word. It implied vulnerability, helplessness, weakness. "I'm not anxious," he said shortly. "I'm saying it's the only aspect of the sting I can't predict."

She nodded absently, finished her note, and raised her head. "You can be a hero and still have angst, you know."

On a philosophical level, she was right, but when it came to *him*, to *his* psyche, it was unacceptable. He glanced at her empty glass. "You want a refill?"

"Sure." The twinkle in her eyes called his bluff, as usual.

Jace grabbed the glass and sauntered into the kitchen for a reprieve. A few weeks ago he'd never have predicted he'd be spilling his guts so openly, and yet Heidi's straightforward, nonjudgmental approach eased the awkwardness. And accessing those airtight emotional vaults around her was becoming a pain-free endeavor.

He refilled the ice and filtered tap water and returned, slowing as he drew closer. She'd switched to typing furiously on her phone, head bowed, strands of black hair curling against her cheek. The stilettos she'd kicked off with a moan as soon as she entered lay on their sides, splashes of royal blue dotting his tan carpet.

After her smoking-hot admission that she wanted to jump his bones, he'd wandered his condo, distracted and horny as a teenager, waiting for her to finish with Garcia. All those hours of anticipation had made him answer her knock rock-hard and ready, but she'd marched past, shrouded in that prickly supervisor role: tone short, mind multitasking, fingers texting Garcia. And here she was again, given a thirty-second break, refocused on the op.

Jace plopped the glass on the coaster and reached

over to still her fingers. The intense concentration on her face morphed to startled confusion as she glanced up. "It's midnight," he said. "Give it a rest."

"I'm just jotting a couple of thoughts in my list app."

"Or," he said lightly, "you're avoiding my turn at a hot-wash question."

She rolled her eyes, but a faint grin appeared. "This is torture."

"Tell me about it." He sat next to her, gently easing the phone from her grip and turning it face down on the cocktail table. He stroked his chin, like he was thinking long and hard about his question, when actually it had been the only thing circumnavigating his mind since she'd hurried into headquarters. "Do you prefer the bottom or the top?"

"Oh, Jace." The words came out in an admonishing groan.

He raised the hand he held and kissed each knuckle, then exposed the soft underbelly of her wrist, lingering over the satiny skin and fluttery pulse with the softest of kisses. Her sigh was barely audible over the whooshing of his own heartbeat.

Her fingers curled through his hair and stroked down his right cheek. "Jace," she began in a we-can't-do-this tone, and suddenly he couldn't bear to hear the rest.

"I want you," he said roughly. "I know everything about us and the timing and the stakes are shit, but I want you. In my bed. Now."

She closed her eyes, inhaling deeply, like in prayer. *Please, God*, he joined in, *let me have read her right*. When she opened her eyes, the naked hunger there jolted him erect. That insanely sexy woman from the wedding was back.

"No," she said on her exhale, stalling his heart. "No bed. Let's do it right here. And I want it dirty."

Lust coursed through him so violently that he gritted his teeth. *Holy Christ... Dirty. Thank you, Lord.* He motioned to the window. "Curtains don't work. The neighbors can see in."

She grinned like he'd just told a joke. "Then turn off the light."

Duh. "See what you do to me? No more blood flow to my brain."

"Could you stop talking and fuck me?"

Impossibly, his cock swelled hard as iron, straining painfully against the zipper. "That's one order I've got no problem following."

HEIDI'S HEART thumped an extra beat at the quiet snick of a drawer, and then Jace was back, tossing a square on the cocktail table. The cushion dipped as he sat next to her, his expression intense, like a coiled predator. "Are you comfortable?" he asked. "The heater makes it hot in here sometimes."

"Oh, it's not the heater," she said with a wry grin.

His gaze roamed her face, like he was planning his strategy of kisses. "You're one hell of a sexy woman," he murmured. "I've wanted to do this since I slipped that garter up your thigh." He reached behind her and snapped off the lamp. The glow still emanating from the kitchen highlighted the hot promise in his eyes.

A wave of need broke through the final wisps of warning, and Heidi surrendered her reason. She tilted her head, and he took her mouth with irresistible authority, meshing soft lips to hers and sweeping out a tongue that tasted of beer. His body felt like she was embracing a furnace.

He threaded fingers through her hair, anchoring her

at an angle that gave him fuller access. Oh yes, this man could do dirty. There was nothing gentle or gentlemanly in the erotic thrusting and curling of his tongue. She almost moaned at the pleasurable assault. If he did this to her mouth, what could he do to the rest of her?

The force of the kiss grew, bowing her into a back-bend along the plush leather arm, and she clung to the roped biceps for balance. No, she was too old for this kind of contortion. Uncurling her legs, she trailed her palms to his broad chest and gently pushed. He broke the kiss and looked down at her in groggy confusion. "I'm not a gymnast," she said apologetically.

"Oh." He shifted to unpin her. "Sorry."

She pressed with more authority until he lay stretched out, then plastered herself atop rippling muscle and a thick, hard erection. An insistent quiver grew in her belly.

She kissed him, teasingly soft, languorously slow, nipping his bottom lip and darting her tongue here and there until his gruff growl vibrated through her. "Kiss me harder, Heidi. This isn't even close to dirty."

She sank everything into the next kiss, exploring his mouth in deep, erotic sweeps. His palms skated up the backs of her thighs, snagging her skirt in the process until it bunched at her hips. He cupped her ass and held her in place while his hips moved in gentle circles. "Do you like it this way?" he asked in lazy rasp. "Or like this?" His pelvis rocked rhythmically in that primal way. She instinctively widened her thighs to straddle him, rubbing herself along his rigid shaft.

"Oh yes," she whispered. "Right there."

He grinned up at her, his heavy-lidded eyes a hypnotic blue. One palm trailed to her lower back, the other to the narrowest part of her panties. He slipped two fingers under the elastic, curling his knuckles to stroke and probe until she arced up at the sizzling sparks, hissing an inhale through clenched teeth. Every sensation seemed heightened after so long.

She found his lips again and fumbled with his shirt buttons, rewarded inch by warm inch with smooth, hard flesh. It had been so long since that first day she'd inspected his racist tattoos that uncovering them again gave her a seismic jolt. "I'd forgotten you had these," she murmured, swiping a thumb down the ink like she could erase it.

His fingers stilled as he glanced down at the symbols. "I've already had to go back and get them darkened."

"Has anyone ever noticed?"

"Well, the Race doesn't strip down and compare torsos. And it is in the teens outside, so I haven't taken my shirt off outdoors lately, but seeing these in the mirror every day helps reinforce my role, so I'm glad I did it."

"I'm glad you'll never have to go back and get them darkened again."

She lowered her head and kissed the trim beard along his jaw, tonguing his neck, tasting salt and damp skin on her way to the hollow where his heartbeat pulsed. His stroking fingers were kindling a primitive desire as they rubbed rhythmically over her. "Oh, man, you're ready," he said, and thrust both digits inside. Heidi's breath caught at the glorious fullness and gliding friction. His other hand swept up her blouse and pinched her bra clasp open, stroking her back.

Her hips matched his cadence, her breath quickening. "Like that," she gasped straining toward the pinnacle.

"Not yet." His low rumble seemed to come from far away as she swirled near the galaxy.

"I'm almost there."

He withdrew his fingers and gripped her hips. "I want us to get there together."

Her whole being throbbed to have him inside her. She couldn't help the exasperated sigh and swung off him, struggling out of her clothes. "Strip," she ordered him. Tomorrow she'd worry about her lack of dignity and inability to play coy or be a vixen.

Jace laughed in a low rumble and grasped her wrist, pulling her down beside him. "We've toyed with each other so many weeks, we ought to make this more than a quickie."

"Sorry, pal. I'm horny."

"I'm asking for five minutes of foreplay," he said with mock indignity. He crunched into a half sit-up and leaned on an elbow, brushing strands of flyaway hair off her cheeks. "I'm not just a staff for your pleasure."

She chuckled at their switched roles, which helped her enflamed state subside. "That's the dumbest thing I've ever heard."

"It was in a porn about a woman being taken by aliens."

She shivered. Could be disgust. Could be the thought of being taken by anything at this point. "If you knew how long it's been for me," she said by way of explanation, "you'd button your lip and perform."

As he threw back his head and laughed, Adam's apple bobbing in that strong neck, she studied the whole magnificent length of him. His shirt flaps were spread on either side of his sculpted torso that tapered to rigid abs, and a half-open fly. His concealed cock strained against the V of white underwear.

She reached for his zipper, and he fell back again, adjusting his hips with a soft grunt as she eased the fabric down. He cupped her naked breast and thumbed a taut nipple, sending a shiver down to her toes.

"Has it been five minutes yet?" she pleaded, shucking his briefs. His cock sprang free, sleek and thick, and she reached for it instinctively. The first stroke along the pulsing shaft triggered a sharp inhale from him. She bent down and suckled the satiny steel, reveling in his hiss of pleasure. The salty taste of him was wildly erotic. She moaned softly, accepting more of him into her mouth.

He uttered her name, holding her head gently as he rocked his hips to meet her. "Enough," he growled after a minute. "I'm too close."

Heidi took her time releasing him in a slow pull of her lips, and he wriggled and gasped. When she sat up, he lay still, eyes squeezed shut, panting shallow breaths. "I almost didn't make it."

She patted his thigh. "Up and at me, soldier." Climbing past him, she crawled to the other end of the sofa, draping over the arm, ass high in the air. "Take me like this."

"Oh, sweet Jesus," he muttered. "I can't get enough of you."

There was a tremor in his voice, and she grinned to herself. Younger women might have tighter bodies, but nothing beat the oversexed hormonal drive of the middle-aged. Seconds later the foil wrapper tore, then once again the cushion gave way to his weight. Her toes curled in anticipation as he knelt behind her.

A callused hand stroked up her back, and the other fondled her breast. The length of his cock rested like a sweet promise between her cheeks. Already impatient, she swirled her hips in a circle. "Dirty," she reminded him in a strained voice. "We can do all that other stuff the next time."

His palm skated down her back, and he paused, hand on his dick, and prodded her entrance. "Long and deep or fast and violent, ma'am?"

She almost giggled at the cowboy drawl. "Just take me, Jake. We'll figure it out."

A breath of a second passed before he thrust partially inside. She writhed at the sensation, her throbbing inner muscles stretching to welcome the invasion. His hands skimmed up to anchor her hips, then he eased in fully, and Heidi dropped her forehead on the sofa arm, gasping in haggard relief. "Yes," she whispered, and her brain added, *Finally!*

With slow, piston-like strokes, he glided in and out of her, his hot, labored breaths fanning her neck. One hand curved around her shoulder, holding her steady. The other snaked under her hip, toying with the juncture they created, finding her nub with ease. Desire, like molten silver, pulsed through her. Her heart thudded so hard that she felt it in her throat.

"Harder?" he rasped.

"Yes."

Heidi gripped the sofa arm as he plunged in with velvet violence. Flesh slapped rhythmically, and his intermittent grunting sounded like excruciating pleasure. The fingertip circling her created its own friction, sparking tingles that quickly grew to a bonfire.

"Yes, Jace," she called out raggedly, arching her spine and thrusting her bottom to feel him up to her hilt.

"Wait," he gasped, beginning to slow. "A light went on next door. They can see right over the fence from up there."

The vision of a stranger watching her kneeling on a sofa being taken from behind sent her into a frenzy. "Fuck me harder," she pleaded. "Oh please, Jace. I'm coming."

His powerful thrusting returned. The hand cupping her shoulder slid down her waist, past her hips, and an instant later she felt his thumb press her sphincter. The shock of that, the blitzing image of a peeping neighbor, and Jace's relentless fingers rolling her swollen nub collided. Her orgasm exploded in a stream of shooting stars and trembling spams. She bucked wildly, convulsing and crying out under his driving thrusts.

His momentum intensified, burying his cock even deeper inside her, then abruptly he stilled. A guttural groan ripped from him as he clutched her hips, holding her motionless as he emptied himself in shuddering waves. Seconds later, he collapsed heavily along her backside, his ragged pants and hot, damp skin sending a delicious shiver through her.

"God," he rasped, "I could get very used to this side of you."

She caught her breath after several gulps. "I call her the Flirt. I rarely allow her free rein."

"Why the hell not?"

Oh, the havoc she'd create. "I have a hard enough time commanding respect without her popping up and sabotaging my image."

Jace kissed her neck tenderly. "She's an amazing extension of you." He wound his arms around her in a bear hug. "If only I'd known to ask that hot-wash question from day one."

They shared a quiet, intimate laugh, then he knelt upright, and she, still glued to his torso, was hauled up too.

Yards away the neighbor's light still blazed, and reality rebounded like a slap. Heidi swiveled from the window, crossing her arms over her breasts.

"Oh, jeez, sorry." Jace disappeared into his bedroom and swiftly returned in boxers, holding a t-shirt. "I'll fix that valance in the morning."

"Please tell me you don't know those neighbors," she mumbled, shrugging into the oversized shirt that smelled of clean fabric softener—a scent she was growing to love.

"Nope. Between work and night school, I don't know anyone around here."

Heidi nodded mutely, her cheeks flaming. The words *work* and *night school* were twin gongs, knocking out her afterglow. What had she been thinking? She had to supervise him mere hours from now, in a sting that would make or break their careers—

"Hey," he said sinking beside her. When she didn't face him, he tilted her chin with a finger. "What kind of overthinking is going on in there?"

She managed a smile, gently disengaging his grasp to tug the damp, sticky hair back behind her ears. How could she make a fast, dignified escape? "I need to get back to the off—"

"No," he interrupted, the word holding all the authority of that over-controlling side of him. "You don't have this kind of epic sex and then go review files and answer emails."

The idea held little appeal, but the point was that she wanted to get dressed and leave.

"Look," he said, cupping her cheek, "why don't you stay the night?"

Because I'm your supervisor. Because we'd be committing professional suicide. Because I barely sleep more than three hours now. "Jace, let's not make this more than it—"

He stopped her with a luscious, devouring kiss that emptied her mind. Oh, yeah. This was why she'd succumbed. His mouth was magical that way. The Flirt clawed to the forefront again and sharpened her talons.

"Stay," he murmured when they came up for air.

"Okay," she whispered. "But I'm setting an alarm for three. I gotta get to headquarters early."

"I'll drive you."

She rested a hand on his arm. "Sleep. You'll need it."

"Nah. Might as well go back to the house." He pulled

her to her feet. "Until then, we grab a bath, and then I'm gonna stretch you out on my bed for all the rest of that foreplay stuff you threw out the window."

Heidi smacked the same arm. "I was prioritizing."

He snickered, planting a kiss on her temple. "I love a woman who goes after what she wants."

"Is that how you're spinning it?"

"Of course." He rose and pulled her up. "How would you describe it?"

"That there's no dignity in a woman begging for sex."

"No kidding?" he said, straight-faced. "That was my favorite part."

35

"Your brother didn't show," Heidi said shrilly. "And he's not responding to calls or texts."

Jace checked the time. Eight thirty. He slammed his mug on the bu-house's cheap Formica. He could have predicted this. Should have. But the rosy glow on her face at "healing" Gage and the gracious invite to CAP had been the hope his entire family craved. Jace had had to force himself not to dump on the moment by projecting all the shitty ways his brother would screw up this lifeline. "Ten to one he found someplace open and went drinking."

"Well, he's now the wild card in our takedown." The piercing voice was chalk on a blackboard. Goosebumps sprouted down his arms. "We've got to find him and contain him before you meet the Race."

He shuffled through his brothers' schedules. Sean was off for the long weekend, and besides, he and Gage were oil and water together. Trick was on duty. "I'll call Kevin." Roust him out of some woman's bed... "We'll find him, Heidi. Focus on your takedown strategy."

He hung up, knowing she wouldn't. She micromanaged every aspect of this broad investigation, like a one-trick pony. Like she had nothing else to live for. Like they hadn't had blazing-hot sex until the three o'clock alarm went off. That was only four hours ago, and already her soft, sexy self was MIA. If anyone needed a hot wash, it was Heidi over her goddamn career fixation.

In the bedroom his designated Race phone dinged a text, and he went to retrieve it.

Sheer. *Change of plans, men. Meet in the alley of Euclid and 25th at eight tonight.*

"What the fuck?" Jace pulled up the attached map link. Instead of meeting inside the Loop, the location was on the west side, probably close to Sheer's safe house. That far meant the Pakistani restaurant was out.

The phone dinged again. *Nash will bring additional supplies.*

Jace read the sentence a second time because his brain couldn't process the extent of the catastrophes. One by one the phone dinged confirmation from the other cell members, and he tossed in a thumbs-up icon before stumbling back to his personal phone in the kitchen. "We're fucked," he said the second Heidi answered.

"I'm in a meet—"

"Get out of it. Sheer not only changed the venue, he made it bigger. Ken Nash is bringing more C-4."

"Hold on." After a fumbling, scratching sound, Heidi was back. "You're on speaker, Jace. SAC Webb and ASAC Garcia are here with me. Do you remind repeating that?"

Jace went over the text messages he'd just received and repeated the odd exchange between Chris and Craig about Sheer changing plans at the last minute. "This has to be his MO," he concluded, his pulse pumping way too hard for the one coffee he'd had. "He scrambles the project and has another plan coordinated and in place at the last second."

"That's awfully risky," Garcia said. "There's no chance to check out the new target's security or observe what kind of police presence is in the vicinity."

Jace paced the small kitchen. "I'll bet he's had it checked out by other cells. I'll bet this alternate op was being planned while he was in Russia. Think about it—his tactic to avoid detection is farming out parts of a mission to all the small armies who act out their task independently, with no knowledge of the others. And at the last second, this master puppeteer sutures all the elements together."

"You're saying there could be more than you nine tonight?" Webb asked in a wary voice.

"Without a doubt, sir."

"We're going to need surveillance for several blocks around that alleyway ASAP." Heidi's voice sounded further away, like she'd turned from the phone to speak to the others. "But if we don't know the target, there's no way to embed SWAT in advance. They'll have to stand by on full alert."

"I didn't give Sheer enough credit," Garcia said. "This bait-and-switch shows a high degree of experience in strategic warfare. Very cunning."

"We'll redirect our troops on this end, Jace," Heidi said, one hundred percent in her forceful case agent role. "Keep us updated."

"Will do." Jace hung up and rummaged through the kitchen drawer that held basic tools. He grabbed a flat-head screwdriver and wooden mallet. Opening the front door, he positioned the screwdriver in the lock, and with two sharp taps, the handle dangled uselessly. He dug out the Race cell phone and dialed Craig, who answered in a low, muffled way.

"Hey, man," Jace said. "Sorry to bother you this early, but someone tried to break into my house while I was out renting the car for tonight. The knob's literally hanging by a screw. Any chance you can help?"

"Yeah, sure. I'll be over in fifteen."

Jace switched phones and spent the time leaving voice and text messages for Gage, then calling Kevin and ordering him to track down their wayward brother. "He's in a bad place," Jace said. "He probably got in a fight with Pop after we left and has gone someplace to lick his wounds. You've gotta find him."

"Where do I start? The bars aren't open this early, and I don't know of any high school friends he hangs with anymore."

"I don't know, Kev. His phone is going straight to voicemail, so it's either off or dead."

Kevin sighed. "Okay. I'm on it. But you owe me."

"Sure. If you find him, keep him occupied and leave me a message where you guys are. I've got an important meeting, so I'm turning off the phone."

Jace hung up, powered down the phone, and hid it in his bedside drawer. The last thing he needed was for both to be in his pockets, ringing or dinging while Craig was here. Next he donned the ball cap and watch, making sure the devices were on and worked, just in case the master surveillance switch didn't pick up words spoken at the door.

When Craig knocked, the flimsy lock released and the door swung open. Jace had strategically positioned himself at the kitchen counter sipping coffee. "Come on in," he called.

"Shit." Craig fiddled with the dangling doorknob. "They did a number. Did they get anything?"

"Nope." Jace glanced around his sparse house as he walked over. "Not much to get. Thankfully, I had the backpack with tonight's supplies with me."

Craig frowned as he placed his toolbox beside the open door. "You rented a car?"

"Under an alias. And I wore this ball cap low. The woman at the counter will never be able to identify me. Besides"—he shrugged—"turns out renting was a good call, now that Sheer changed locations. Wanna ride to Berwyn?"

After a short pause, Craig nodded. "Thanks. You never know what security cameras will track us to the final target now, and I don't want my company pickup in that convoy." He flipped open his toolbox, and Jace offered him coffee. "Naw, this should take less than ten minutes."

Jace leaned a shoulder against the wall, adopting a casual expression despite his churning mind. This was his last chance to get anything out of Craig. Somehow he had to pose questions to get the locksmith to incriminate himself, Chris, and potentially Sheer in the Mosque Mohammed bombing. It would be six months ago next week, and already the media was gunning for heads, demanding accountability, and gleefully alerting the public of the two planned march locations.

"Switching the target the day of is pretty impulsive."

Craig let out a short laugh as he stuck the screwdriver into the remaining screw head. "That's totally Sheer's style. It's why he looked so bored at Nash's."

"So you and Chris already knew we were wasting our time."

Craig's smile embodied smug arrogance, an expression so familiar that it led to a flicker of discomfort. This op was awakening some ugly insights into Jace's own conceited reactions and his go-to SEAL manner of superiority. Jace shut the thought down and plunked the mug on the console.

"Have you met him in person before?"

Craig yanked the bent doorknob out in two pieces. "Yeah. A couple of times." Already his tone was reluctant, his face closing down.

Jace scratched his beard absently. "The fact that he wants Nash to bring supplies tonight means it a much bigger job than we anticipated."

"Also vintage Sheer." Craig lowered his head, digging around in his toolbox.

Jace waited him out. To counter with another question this fast was too risky. He'd do what Heidi did in the damn hot washes and stay silent. Most humans couldn't stand the gap and filled it with words. What an exceedingly hard strategy. His jaw began to prickle from the rhythmic scratching. He shoved his hand in his pocket. *Answer, damn it!* Maybe this strategy wouldn't work on an introvert like Craig—he was a lot like Sean, who basked in stillness.

"We had plans to take out a nigger center over at UIC," Craig said out of the blue. "Kind of like this toe-rag restaurant. We weren't aiming high, chose a Sunday when it was closed. Chose it for the message, you know." Craig sat back, studying the screwdriver in his hand. "Sheer came to town the day before. Next thing you know, same thing. We were given different marching orders: rent a truck, meet up with Sheer and another Race cell, who were all loaded down with their own materials.

"Sheer led us to a far bigger place, completely crowded, and had every detail of this new plan figured out." Craig looked up, respect shining from those killer eyes. "We were just following directives, you know? But his *vision*, man. It was a thing of glory."

Jace managed a nod. Even with Chaz's warnings ringing in his ears, he had to push it. "That mosque over on Wabash."

Craig shrugged noncommittally, so Jace kept going. "I remember seeing the devastation on TV that night and thinking, 'Shit, I wish I'd been a part of that.' It was epic. A couple more missions that size, and we'd finally start the revolution we only sit around talking about. You guys are fucking rock stars in our world."

"Right?"

Jace blinked down at the man's grin. What? His heart drummed against his ribcage. "I can't understand why Sheer isn't crowing like a rooster. The Race should totally claim credit. Think what it would do for recruitment."

Craig shook his head as he broke open the packaging for a new doorknob kit in nickel finish. "He's too cautious. So many groups have been brought down by letting anyone and everyone in. You open yourself up to the seriously deranged or guys who aren't that serious. Besides, Sheer figured if he took public credit, he'd be handing law enforcement a clear-cut case. He ain't helping those fucks out. Based on the papers, the FBI has bungled the search a million ways from Sunday and still have no clue who's behind it."

He fit the parts in either side of the door and picked up his screwdriver again. "The point is, he sees miles beyond the rest of us. Like he sits around thinking through all the angles and each one's cause and effect. Keep quiet or take credit? Choose a small, safe venue like we did, or take out hundreds so the public reels in the void of not knowing who did it and why. Suffers the anticipation of the next strike." Craig nodded to himself. "There's great fear when sheeple don't know who the enemy is, you know? He's a brilliant man, Sheer."

Jace reached for spontaneous-sounding enthusiasm. "So you're saying tonight we're probably targeting a populated place?"

"I can guarantee it." Craig's face was alight with joy as

he finished the repairs. "It'll be a place cherished by some minority, and if I know Sheer, the damage will be a hell of a lot bigger than June."

Jace's breath grew shallow. "With Nash bringing more C-4, it'll definitely be bigger than the mosque."

Craig stood up. "I wouldn't put it past Sheer to have a couple more cells bringin' their own inventory too. Shit, I get hard just thinking about tonight."

Jace nodded to the door. "What do I owe you?"

"Nothin'. I appreciate the ride tonight." Craig gave his exact address and picked up his toolbox. "Tonight's gonna be epic. Just stay loose and flexible and listen to every order." They shook hands, and Craig opened and closed the door a couple of times. He nodded his approval.

"Pick you up at seven thirty," Jace said. "Thanks again."

He shut the door and peered out the peephole until Craig disappeared to the left. This op was officially beyond any nightmare mission in his experience. He went to call Heidi. He sure as shit hoped she'd know what to do.

36

T he jam-packed conference room was in utter chaos. Team members, even those who'd requested the day after Thanksgiving off, were milling about. Top commanders with SWAT, HAZMAT, the CFD, CPD, Illinois State Police, Illinois Bomb Squad, and, of course, ATF and FBI looked serious and official as they glad-handed each other. An undercurrent of excitement hummed through the drone of conversation. Heather had someone higher up in the DOJ on a conference line, and scores more agents and analysts were scrambling around handing over files, typing on laptops, or jabbering on cell phones as they got up to speed.

Webb sat at the head of the long table, grimly thumbing through the pinging texts that kept lighting his phone screen. To his left, Heidi sat stiffly, absorbing the sights and sounds, the determination, tension, and undercurrent of elation. The time of death on her management of this op had been one minute after Sheer's bait-and-switch text to Jace. The target would be a populated area; the additional explosives would be live. Webb had instantly taken command. She'd predicted this boys'-club power play in her interview and was heartily sick and tired of being right. Of being shuttled into a minor role at the most crucial moment.

She should be glad that Sheer's bait-and-switch was no longer her responsibility. Law enforcement figuring out anything in advance to station troops and support at the target, evacuate potential victims and the periphery, and contain an explosion was nearly impossible. The pending failure would be epic. The blame would not reflect solely on her now. And yet her jaw muscles ached from her clenched teeth, and her stiff neck had triggered a headache.

"May I have everyone's attention?" Webb said, and the room instantly silenced. "Have a seat, people." He held up his phone. "Phones on vibrate only, please. We have a lot to get through."

The officials hastily grabbed chairs, and the pecking order around the table was quickly established. Head honchos in comfortable leather conference chairs; the aides and underlings in the outer ring of hard plastic seats.

Webb turned to her. "Why don't you update the enhanced team on where we are?"

Heidi stood, licking her lips as she scanned the hastily typed notes on her cell phone. She began with a brief description of the Race and Calvin Sheer, the initial plan to plant Jace undercover to gain insight into the Mosque Mohammed bombing, which led to the original Pakistani target for this evening. After pausing for a deep breath, she then explained how Sheer had not only blown that plan to smithereens but had chosen a new target, new meeting place, and an unknown amount of additional C-4.

"So we are talking about live explosives now, which, on its own, is of grave concern. Adding to that, according to a Race member we now know was part of the mosque bombing, Sheer is known to choose a highly populated area instead of an empty structure."

She paused when the room erupted in concerned murmurs.

Webb held up a hand. "At this point," he said solemnly, "all we know for sure is the target is a minority group, and when the cell members meet at a location in Berwyn tonight, they'll receive final instructions." He nodded his thanks, and Heidi sat down, teeth clamping back together.

"Our task today is to draw up new operational plans for every contingency." Webb perched half-moon readers on his nose and looked at the scattered paperwork in front of him. "We're looking for ideas on how surveillance will work, we need tons more SSG units on the road working multiple angles of surveillance, new communication strategies, security enhancements and"—his gaze swept down the table and landed on the SWAT commander—"tactical strategy. All without knowing the new target location."

He rummaged through the papers and pulled out a sheet. "I want to know what events, programs, educational classes, or art presentations are being held around the city tonight, especially if it's celebrating minorities or hosted by a cultural group." Several analysts got up and left the room.

Heidi's phone buzzed, and she clutched it in her lap before looking at the screen. Chaz was ringing her back. She mutely nodded to the SAC and pushed her chair back, scurrying out into the hall too, breathlessly answering, "Hello."

"Got your message. Can't believe it all went so FUBAR."

At the sound of his deep, confident voice, a sliver of tension eased. "I wish you were still here."

"In Miami," he said with a chuckle. "About to start an easy Group Two that should wrap by year's end. And the weather's sure better."

"Any way you can fly up for a quick twenty-four hours?"

"Sorry, Heidi. I'm mired in strategy meetings."

"But..." She paced down the hall with mounting helplessness. "What did you do when an op took a sudden left turn like this?"

"The shit you described in your voicemail is beyond even my wheelhouse," he said. "But there were times I'd be at a meet and the perp would get paranoid and demand another venue we hadn't counted on. You need to keep the backup support spread out and flexible. All options stay on the table; every department is ready to roll. And Jace needs to keep a level head and stay in character, no matter what."

She kneaded the throbbing in her left temple. "Any way you can call him and walk him through some scenarios?" It was asking a lot. They'd never gotten along. "Strictly as a favor to me?"

He laughed. "You make it sound like Jace Quinn won't be eager to accept advice and recommendations from me, Case Agent Hall."

"You know what I—"

"I know." The words were warm and sympathetic. "I'll call. It's up to him if he chooses to listen this time."

She exhaled audibly. Her legs were so quivery that she propped herself against the wall. "I owe you."

"Did you two ever get together?" His tone was more curious than nosy.

She pictured Jace in the moonlight of his bedroom,

smiling down at her spread-eagled form. He was facing such danger now.

"I wouldn't answer me either," Chaz said, reading the silence. "Don't worry, you'll get your chance. I'll make sure he's prepared. Go concentrate on your end."

She nodded, fighting the thickening in her throat. "Thanks," she managed. "I'll tell him you'll call."

"Naw. Let him think I'm calling out of the blue. You know how he hates taking orders from you. Maybe if this isn't an authorized conversation, he'll be more willing to listen."

"I'm up for anything," she admitted. "I've never been so scared going into a takedown." Because there was no takedown. They had no strategy.

"The whole thing sounds like a setup to me."

Heidi signed off and smiled absently at personnel who passed. She glanced at the closed conference room door. At the meeting she should be heading. She glanced down at her phone, so it looked like she wasn't loitering or dragging her feet getting back in there.

When Chaz had mentioned a setup, something inside her had struck like a gong of doom. Was there more to Sheer's change of plans than even Jace or Craig knew?

JACE PULLED in the bu-house garage with the newly rented car. One more impulsive lie he'd been lucky not to get caught in. All Craig would've had to do was ask to see the bricks of C-4 Jace had claimed were already in the trunk. He shook his head as he cut the engine. This undercover work was giving him an ulcer. Maybe it took a certain type of person to lie so blithely and stay ahead of it all. He'd finally found a high-octane career that wasn't for him.

Letting himself into the kitchen, he tossed his keys on the counter just as the phone in his right pocket buzzed. His personal one. It had been Chaz's suggestion, putting the personal phone for FBI business on that side—for the right side of the law—and his bu-phone for UC work in the left. He dug out the personal phone. "Speak of the devil," he muttered to the caller ID before answering.

"Heidi tells me you've got a quagmire on your hands," Chaz said.

"It's fucked up for sure."

"You up for a quick conversation? I'm between meetings."

"Man, I was just thinking how much I wasn't cut out for undercover work, and then you mention meetings." Jace chuckled. "I'll do this 'til the cows come home if it means missing those bureaucratic snooze-fests."

"I'd kill to be where you are now. So what's up?"

"I've got taped evidence that Chris and Craig helped Thomas Bradley blow the mosque, and that it was Sheer's plan. Evidently he scraps whatever ideas his members come up with and implements new venues packed with humans and a whole lot more combustibles."

"Heidi said you won't find out the target until tonight."

"That's right. I'd appreciate any advice."

"Hmm. Let's be quiet and enjoy that last sentence, shall we?"

Jace joined in the companionable chuckle. It took Chaz leaving to realize how crucial his advice had been. And appreciate his generosity in sharing his own mistakes on ops as cautionary tales.

"First, know your team is behind you," Chaz said. "They'll amass a whole lot more manpower than they'd planned and blanket everyone across the city to react with lightning speed when Sheer gives you final coordinates, okay? So don't worry about your six—they've got you."

Jace inhaled. "Check."

"You still implement your emergency word and signal?"

"Yeah. The word is now 'torque,' or if I take off my coat and throw it on the ground, the cavalry comes running."

"Good. So tonight, when you get to the rendezvous place with the rest of the Race brothers, keep your head in the game. You're a white supremacist who's about to see his dreams come true. Every lie out of your mouth has to be convincing. Every expression on your face has to mirror their joy. No wincing, no hesitating, no balking. If Sheer orders you to plant bombs in a little Black nursery school, you whoop and holler, got it?"

Jace hesitated. *Little Black nursery school.* The stark reality of what he faced shuddered through him. More than half the C-4 was live. What if backup didn't get there in time? What if he, a lone FBI agent, became responsible for the kind of mass destruction Chicago had seen in June?

Jace wiped the perspiration on his forehead. He couldn't go through with this tonight. There were too many variables. Should he tell Chaz? If anyone could connect to cold feet and second-guessing, it was him. "Ever feel like you can't go through with it?"

"Yeah." Chaz barked out a short laugh. "I can confidently say I feel that before every takedown. All your months of hard work, all the insane hours will rest on this final performance."

"But how do you get past the doubts?"

"You remind yourself this is the only way to bring these monsters down. If there'd been an easier, more cost-effective method, the agency would have done it.

This is the last time you have to be one of them, so tonight's for all the money. Let Jason McGowan take over your brain and be in your heart. No way can you get through this keeping the real you compartmentalized somewhere. Once the op is over, you'll have the luxury of letting go of whatever sick shit you said and did, but *every* moment tonight, you bury Jace Quinn. He will kill you. You hear?"

Jace contemplated the floor. He was so unprepared. "I'm envious of you, man. I wish I could snap my fingers and have your expertise."

"You're better than you know. I think that's why we knocked heads so much. Your instincts are there, and you have a hell of a lot more balls than I did on my first UCO. Take the Race down tonight, Jace. Annihilate them off the fucking face of this earth. I say this as an FBI agent, a Black man, and a compassionate human being. Make me proud."

Jace hung up, less than convinced. He'd better get his head in the game, though. These jitters wouldn't fly in the presence of someone as astute as Sheer. He scrolled through his phone and called Kevin. "Any word?"

"No one's seen him or heard from him. His voicemail is now full."

Jace squeezed the bridge of his nose. "Keep at it. We've gotta find him."

"Why is this such a big deal?"

"It's classified. I can only tell you he's in grave danger if we don't find him by eight tonight."

37

"Welcome, all," Sheer exclaimed, wide arms encompassing the fourteen men standing in the empty toolshed. "Tonight we make history."

His followers clapped, and one new guy whistled shrilly. Most stamped in place in the unheated structure. Jace jammed his fists back into his jacket pockets. Inside the thermal warmth, his drenched shirt stuck to his back as adrenalin pumped through him. He kept darting his gaze to the door, expecting Gage to saunter in. With Jace's personal cell phone at home, he was out of the loop on what was or was not happening with his brother.

"Our target tonight," Sheer went on in the murky light of lanterns and flashlights, "is the most diverse neighborhood in Chicago, Albany Park."

Well, shit, if that wasn't right next door to where the bu-house was. Jace exchanged raised eyebrows with Craig, then redirected his attention. Sheer fanned out five letter-sized envelopes and held them over his head. "Each cell leader will retrieve one of these. Inside you'll find instructions on which structure you've been assigned.

Could be a residence owned by wetbacks holding a quinceañera tonight, or the community center holding a cultural meet-and-greet for those goddamn towelheads, or a popular restaurant in Koreatown. Or it could be none of those." He smiled broadly, waving the envelopes. "Race cells operate independently."

Jace swallowed hard. Hopefully, the task force was out in the dark Berwyn neighborhoods attaching GPS trackers to the vehicles these men had come in. Chaz's words resonated again. The team had his back; he just had to concentrate on his role. "Go grab an envelope, Nate," he called. "Let's get this shit started."

Sheer held up a hand. "Each cell has a member who's familiar with C-4," he went on. "Each of these detailed instructions indicates how many bricks you'll need, the structure's layout, and the recommended places to place the bricks for obliteration." He flipped his arm over and looked at his watch. "We synchronize to blow the structures one hour from now. My watch shows eight oh-seven."

Everyone adjusted their watches, then the leaders surged forward amid excited murmurs. "Once you have a chance to study your instructions," Sheer said over the noise, "go to either Jason, the one in the green ball cap, or Ken, over there in the blue-and-black striped shirt. Let them know your inventory requirements, collect what you need, then head on out."

Something slammed against the shed door, and several men jumped. Was the task force moving in? The door burst open and Gage staggered inside, obscenities flying. Jace's heart stalled out.

"Sorry, everybody. Got lost." The words slurred together.

Sliding a step from the ring of lanterns at Sheer's feet, Jace dipped his cap below his brow and pretended to rummage in his knapsack. He could only see peripherally now. The silence was total and deafening.

"Son, we won't be needing you in your condition." Sheer's voice was ice cold. He turned to Chris, comically frozen in mid-step, clutching his envelope. "Isn't he yours?"

"Yes, sir. Gage Quinn." Chris threw Gage a deadly scowl, not that it was acknowledged or even noticed.

Sheer frowned in Gage's direction again. "You left before the last meeting."

"My mom was sick," Gage said, struggling to stand motionless. "And then she wasn't."

The members looked at each other, eyebrows knotted in confusion. Sheer's face shut completely down. "Get him outta here."

Chris and Craig stepped to either side of Gage. "Come on," Chris muttered as they hauled him toward the door. "You don't belong with us."

"Wait—" Gage craned his head and looked around, eyes wild and glassy as he tried to find a friendly face. Jace stayed motionless, head lowered, his breath suspended halfway through an exhale. Every molecule screamed in panic. "Wait," Gage said again. "I wanna help."

The trio disappeared, the door clattered shut, and Jace shuddered the exhale. Within seconds, the cell leaders were lining up behind him or Nash with their explosives requests. Jace handed out bricks, his attention raggedly split between tracking which cells were receiving the live supplies from Ken and envisioning what could possibly be happening to Gage. Were Chris and Craig pouring him into a cab or offing him and dumping the body in an alley? Christ, what should he do? This was a nightmare!

His brain frantically commanded him to draw the

Glock 43 in his boot holster, contain the scene, and recall Chris and Craig. But the magazine only held six bullets. Maybe he should take off his coat and throw it in front of the pin-sized camera in his cap to signal backup.

He opted for neither. Two Race members were escorting a drunk man out of the meeting—he was reading too much into this. He couldn't compromise the takedown.

Compartmentalizing the raw fear, he handed out the bricks with a surprisingly steady hand. He kept forgetting about the FBI backup. Kept shouldering all the responsibility for life turning out right.

Heidi was listening in, so she'd have heard Gage arrive and be escorted out. She would intervene. He had to trust her and concentrate on his role. Already he was slipping. If anyone was paying attention, it would look strange that he hadn't been curious enough to ask Nate what their mission was.

Chris stomped back in, still scowling, and headed straight to Ken for his C-4. Three bricks were handed over, along with what sounded like murmured words of commiseration from one leader to another for having dead weight on his staff.

"Does everyone have what they need?" Jace asked for the benefit of FBI surveillance. "Chris, you've got Ken's stash, Ken's also working off his, and you"—he looked at a short, squat man whose stiff yellow hair resembled a troll doll Tina had—"did you get yours already?"

"Yeah, I went to him." Troll jerked a head toward Nash too, before walking back to his two cell members in the far corner. Jace kept his head level, the camera pointed right at him. Hopefully the team had full visual on his odd looks. Hopefully they'd concentrate on the three cells who'd just confirmed they had live explosives.

"Any questions?" Sheer said. "No? Let's move out."

The men trooped to the door. They each shook Sheer's hand as he uttered parting words of encouragement. Jace acknowledged Nate's chin jerk in the direction of the exit but didn't fall in line behind his leader. Instead, he stooped to retie the lace on his boot, delaying the task so he'd be the last one out. Craig had never shown back up. Chris was already outside. What was happening to Gage?

Jace shuffled forward and got in the back of the dwindling line behind the troll. His compartmentalizing was slipping. He could barely hang on to his role in the surging panic. Everything was fucked up.

All too soon, Sheer's grinning mug was inches away. "Epic night, McGowan. Are you ready?"

"Living for nine oh-eight." Jace glanced at the time on his watch and smirked. "I like how big you think."

"This is nothing. Do a chain of explosions like this a thousand more nights and we'll topple civilized society. The sheeple won't trust the government to protect them, and that's when we march right in as saviors."

Jace nodded and waved a hand for Sheer to exit first. Instead, Sheer extinguished the last lantern, plunging them into darkness. "Why don't you ride with me?"

A red alert buzzed in Jace's ears. *Never get in the suspect's vehicle.* "Thanks, but I brought my rental," he said casually. "Drove Craig over."

"Craig will obviously go with Chris now." Sheer's tone was a little sharper. In the distance, men walked in murmuring clusters, flashlights swinging. "No need to take your car. You're coming with me."

The buzzing got louder. Something was definitely not right. "You're joining our cell?" It would've sounded a hell of a lot better if he'd identified the mission. "You're joining us at the cultural center exhibition?" Or "For the quinceañera?" But he didn't know his mission—and if Sheer asked him now, he was fucked.

The sound of a hammer cocking stopped him cold. "Remove the watch," Sheer ordered. "Now."

How did he *know*? Cold beads of sweat trickled down Jace's temple. Here he'd thought he was fucked before. *Shout the emergency word.* But if he did, it would be all over. The task force would sweep in and capture the cells before the attempted terror acts could be set. The op would be aborted because he'd chickened out.

No. Jace wrenched off the wristwatch, and Sheer spiked it on the ground, stomped it to smithereens, and chucked it over a nearby fence. In seconds, his ball cap was wrenched off and whipped in that direction too. "You got any other surveillance on you?"

"What?"

"Every leader likes enthusiasm," Sheer said with disgust, jamming the gun in Jace's forehead, "but you are off the charts. All those questions? All the offers to help? Where's your gun?"

"I don't know what you're talking about." Jace's vision was adjusting. He could make out Sheer's cold expression and glittering eyes. The roar of a pickup came from a few blocks down. The last of the vehicles was departing. Besides the loud thumping of his heart, the only other sound was the unholy screech of a cat somewhere nearby.

"Gun. Now."

Jace slowly crouched and reached into his boot. Maybe he could spring forward, tackle Sheer in the solar plexus. His complicity was on tape. Why not take him out?

The gun pressed harder. "Think twice. I've still got your brother."

A fresh surge of panic pumped through him. The

sweat was almost blinding. How did Sheer know Gage was his brother? The answers would come, but for right now, Jace withdrew his Glock from the custom ankle holster and handed it over. Sheer shoved it in his pocket.

"Cell phone."

Jace complied. The bu-phone went over the fence, clunking against something wooden.

"Put your hands up slowly, turn around, and move." They walked several yards down the dark, narrow alley in silence. "Left here."

Jace complied, slipping through a missing board in a fence. Crossing a grassy yard, Sheer directed him left again through another fence. Why not make a last-ditch effort to maintain his character? Chaz would have.

"We could have set off the biggest chain of explosions in U.S. history, and you're letting your paranoid delusions ruin everything." But already Jace's survival instincts were taking over. If Sheer knew Gage was his brother, then he knew Jason McGowan was a fraud. The op was over; no one was listening in anyway. The emergency word and gesture to indicate he was in severe danger were useless.

"Take a right." They stepped through a narrow opening in a hedge, out onto a driveway. Gravel crunched as Sheer pointed left. "There." A dark sedan was parked deep in the shadows. "Keys are in the ignition. You're driving."

Once they both climbed in, he tossed Jace a cell phone. "Call your people off."

"Calvin—"

"Now. We've got your brother. We've got you. Your tracking and recording devices are gone. We've zigzagged through neighborhood yards that can't possibly be under surveillance. Even SSGs in infrared goggles won't have tracked us."

SSGs? This guy did have an LEO background. "What branch of law enforcement?"

"Shut the fuck up."

Jace complied and placed the call. Heidi answered on the first ring. "Ja—"

"They've got Gage. Call everyone off." She was all about the job, no matter the tough calls. She'd never jeopardize an entire op and endanger all those lives by calling it quits, but his voice had the realistic ring of a frantic brother, so hopefully it would fool Sheer.

"Where are—"

Sheer grabbed the phone and shut it off. "Reverse out of here and take a left. Keep the lights off and your eyes peeled." He pressed the Glock into Jace's right temple. "You so much as hit a speed bump, and I'll squeeze this trigger."

38

"Where the fuck is he?" Heidi shrieked into the walkie-talkie. The air in the crowded van was thick and humid, the bodies of her support staff too close. She had a civilian hostage and now an agent was missing. How had this gotten so out of control?

One by one, each of the remaining SSGs encompassing the block around the shed checked in. Sheer and Jace had somehow disappeared into the night. Heidi enlarged the GPS map on the monitor, scanning the interconnected alleys of Berwyn, a maze that left dozens of ways to travel through the tiny town without taking main streets. Sheer had chosen his meeting place well. And because there were now more cells than expected, she was left with few remaining SSG units. No way could they cover all of these escape routes.

Her walkie-talkie crackled to life. "Unit fifteen, checking in."

"Go, fifteen."

"The Camaro containing the hostage just entered the Eisenhower Expressway, heading southbound."

She glanced at the moving dots on the monitor showing both vehicles. "Copy," she said. "Authorizing a PIT maneuver at your discretion."

"Copy."

The tactical ramming maneuver would be the fastest, most effective way to contain the scene, and the shock of spinning the Camaro in a one-eighty would hopefully give the agents the upper hand in exiting their vehicle and leveling weapons. She lowered the walkie-talkie, glancing around at the solemn faces. Alma mutely held out a bottle of water, but Heidi shook her head. Her stomach was a ball of knots.

"Unit three to unit one."

Heidi raised the device to her lips again. "Go, three."

"An unidentified sedan just exited the alley half a mile from the shed with headlights doused. Driver and passenger look to be male. Trying to get a better visual. Check that, headlights are on now that they pulled onto a main street."

Hope surged through her. "Copy, unit three. Extinguish your lights if need be and follow. Unit four, be ready to leapfrog unit three. Unit seven, maintain your surveillance of any other exits in the area until we have confirmation that Jace is in that vehicle."

A chorus of "copy" followed, and Heidi grabbed the secure open line that connected her to the command center. "Case Agent Hall reporting to SAC Webb."

"Webb here."

Heidi gripped the receiver and brought Webb up to date. "Jace's cover is blown. Request permission to wrap up the five targets immediately, arrest the Race members, and concentrate on rescuing the Quinn brothers."

"I'll put ASAC Garcia in charge of rounding up the Race members. You concentrate on finding Jace and the brother."

"Copy." Heidi sat back, her exhale streaming a seedling of relief at the help. There were way too many moving parts to this op. "Adam, can you pinpoint the cell number in that vehicle?" She pointed to the dot believed to be Sheer and Jace.

"Sure can, ma'am." The young techie from the IT forensic lab who'd helped her with the mosque tapes swiveled in his seat and grabbed a keyboard. He began typing code with lightning speed.

Heidi turned to the next problem. If Craig had taken Gage hostage in Chris's Camaro, then how had Chris exited Berwyn? Where was he now? He was the lone wolf of that cell, with orders and live explosives. She ran through the list of SSG assignments. Unit thirteen had been assigned to Chris and Craig's cell. "Unit one to unit thirteen."

"Thirteen here."

"What's your status?"

"A rideshare just dropped our suspect off at the library on West Foster Avenue. Place is lit and well populated. ASAC has ordered us to detain."

"Copy." Another breath of relief. Chris was taken care of.

"Ma'am?"

Heidi spun around in her seat. "Whatcha got, Adam?"

He pointed to a series of code onscreen. "Based on triangulating the cell towers along the route they've been driving, this is the phone number in that car."

Heidi leaned forward and peered at the number. It was the one Jace had just called her with. She raised both the walkie-talkie and her open line to Webb. "This is unit one to SAC Webb and units three, four, and seven. Confirming Agent Associate Jace Quinn and our prime suspect, Calvin Sheer, are in the vehicle you're following."

"Good work, Heidi," Webb said in her ear, followed by

muffled orders on his end. The three SSG units all copied.

"Stand by for orders." She waited on the line for Webb to finish his own communication.

Within seconds, he was back. "We're going to surround the vehicle, Heidi."

Fear gripped her throat. "Sir, Sheer must have a gun on him." No way would Jace have willingly gotten into that car.

"We're taking that probability into consideration. We'll follow their route and position SWAT and CPD at an intersection to surround and take down when they're stopped at a red light."

"Copy." Heidi relayed the orders to her SSGs and turned to Alma in the driver's seat. "Follow Jace. Adam, lock your wheels."

He rolled his swivel chair back beside her, and they both locked into the grooves in the van floor. The second the double click of seatbelts sounded, the van lurched forward.

"Let's hope we're not too late," Adam said, which of course they were all thinking, but was the last thing a street agent would've said aloud.

Heidi closed her eyes at the cursed luck, the very luck she'd assured Jace he wouldn't face. Her heart squeezed at the danger he was in. She'd never felt this way about anyone before. All those hot-wash evenings had revealed the real him, not the hero he showed the world, and that was the guy she'd fallen for. There'd been so many chances to be honest about her feelings, but when it was his turn to ask a question, she'd chosen to stay locked in that professional supervisory role and worry about the cost to her career. Heidi sent up a prayer for Jace to keep a cool, calculated head until SWAT arrived. She had so much left to say.

SHEER AWKWARDLY TOGGLED the passenger-side mirror with his left hand again, peering at headlights and shadows behind them. "They're good, I'll give them that," he murmured. The gun resting in his right hand was still aimed at Jace.

During the six minutes he'd been driving, Jace had had ample time to process the situation and focus his thoughts on one solitary goal. At the very next opportunity, he would disarm Sheer. All that was required was a momentary distraction, like someone cutting them off or something disruptive happening on the sidewalks that would pull Sheer's attention even for an instant.

Jace kept his hands loosely on the wheel, at ten and two for the most flexible options, reviewing the sequence again. Identify a distraction, slam on the brakes, throat chop with the blade of his right hand, twist the gun with his left. He breathed evenly, all senses on high alert, heart thrumming steadily. A light, almost immortal calm came over him. He lived for this shit. It was happening. This op was almost over. He could taste the cold beer he'd drink in celebration.

"You've been trained by the U.S. military," he remarked in a casual voice. "Everything about you has the stamp of our elite tactics."

Sheer's gaze never veered from tracking movement along the one-story mom-and-pop shops on North Pulaski—he'd observe, discard, and push on. "Force Recon," he finally said, pride threading his voice. He had a right to that. Force Reconnaissance was the Marine equivalent of a Navy SEAL, among the toughest of all the military branches.

Jace's confident euphoria disappeared. Sheer was operating from the same highly trained, multi-focused approach. All senses at the ready, all options of offensive or defensive action on the table. SEAL versus Marine. Who'd win in thirty or forty seconds?

Jace slowed for a yellow light. Sheer steadied the Glock. Jace didn't spare him a glance as he braked.

Staring straight ahead, he asked, "So what made you turn your back on serving your country and safeguarding the rights of its citizens?" Gage was seeking this tight-knit brotherhood because of his failure to acclimate back into society. Sheer bore none of those signs.

"The Race is the only true resistance movement against a government that's grossly overstepped its authority."

"You're resisting the Deep State by slaughtering innocent citizens? That sounds like a disconnect to me."

"Collateral damage." Sheer flicked him a dismissive glance. "Sleepwalkers beyond redemption."

"How'd you know I was FBI? Or that Gage was my brother?"

Sheer snorted. "I vet all my candidates thoroughly. You—I gotta say—had me fooled, but your brother's got family photos posted all over his social media pages, and since I'd just finished scrutinizing your background, I identified you immediately. Unfortunately, I was already in the States."

"Why not take the first plane back to Moscow, then?"

"What's the fun in that?" Sheer chuckled. "Having the feds on my ass just makes the game more interesting. Who has the higher capacity for intelligence and strategy? I'm betting on me."

What an arrogant motherfucker. The light turned green, and Jace eased on the gas. "Why compromise five cells of your men?"

"You'd already ID'd Ken, my greatest asset. I might as

well go through with my plans and use his supply of C-4 to my advantage while it's still available."

Actually, he was insane to go up against the sophisticated manpower and technological capabilities hunting them. "Every law enforcement agency in Chicago is blanketing the city right now. You're doomed to fail, Sheer."

Sheer shrugged, resuming his scrutiny of the pedestrians. "What are the odds they're going to find and secure all five cells and five individual targets? Which of my men are carrying live explosives? On top of that, your agencies will spread themselves thinner looking for you and your brother." He turned, cocking his head. "Get my point? I even allowed your ball cap to film it in the name of good sportsmanship—that's how much confidence I have in their failure. Your government agencies have grown too large and encumbered to swivel in fluid situations like this one, so why not attack them in their Achilles heel?"

He waved the gun dismissively. "You may capture the few soldiers you ID'd before I was onto you, so but I brought in unidentified others who are now holding top-secret instructions to annihilate unknown targets. Your side hasn't had time to react, and even if they did, it doesn't factor in their thumb-up-their-butt approach, which is the bureaucratic need to do research and hold meetings and formulate a response plan before any action is taken."

Jace winced. He'd mirrored those same opinions last spring when spontaneous action was required on multiple fronts, but Margo had dragged out decision-making in favor of more research and long strategy meetings.

Heidi was different, though. Sheer had met his match. Jace recollected Chaz's advice to let the task force do their jobs and cover his back. "What are your plans for Gage? He's had nothing to do with any of this."

Instead of responding, Sheer craned his neck, frowning at something behind them. "Shit," he muttered, reaching to adjust the mirror with his left hand again. The element of distraction Jace had been searching for.

Now! He simultaneously stomped the brakes and slammed a backhand into Sheer's throat just as the gun exploded in the close compartment. A razor-sharp blow lanced through Jace's left shoulder. Someone cried out— it had to be him, because he'd crushed Sheer's windpipe. Jace clamped his hand on top of Sheer's right fist, suppressing the weapon. The muzzle was pointed toward the passenger-side floor between his legs.

Unable to articulate, Sheer gargled something unintelligible, then growled furiously and spat a wad of warm saliva on their clasped hands. Instantly Jace's grip grew slippery. Containing Sheer with his left arm was impossible; the radiating pain left him immobile. Sheer reached with his other hand and easily wrenched the Glock free.

"SWAT!" multiple voices shouted. "Hands in the air." The night lit up with blinding white lights and swirling red and blue. The car was surrounded by men in black gear pointing AR15s and MP5s at Sheer's torso.

"Surrender," Jace said, his voice a haggard growl. "You so much as twitch a muscle and they'll shoot. You know that."

Gasping laborious breaths, Sheer slowly turned his gaze from the barrels of the assault rifles to Jace. Humor lit his eyes. Hate. Defeat. Jace opened his mouth to utter a sharper warning when Sheer raised the gun.

Glass exploded in flying shards as bullets ripped into the rocking sedan. Jace ducked to the left, eyes squeezed shut, but it was already over. Pungent odors of gunpowder and blood filled his lungs.

"Quinn!" someone shouted. "Quinn, you okay?"

Jace straightened slowly, nodding at no one. In the distance, Heidi screamed his name. Then much closer. He looked out his window, the burning in his shoulder making time pass in slow motion. She was hammering against the door. Jace reached with his right hand and pressed the unlock button. She swung the door wide.

"Medic!" she screamed. "Oh God, are you okay?" She fumbled with his seatbelt, almost falling on him in her haste. "You dumbass. You knew not to get in the car. Why didn't you call the op?"

The other door creaked open. One of the SWAT members held two fingers to Sheer's nonexistent pulse. "You did good," the man said to Jace, with a grin. "Although we had a fully organized takedown approach at that next light."

"Gage," Jace gasped to Heidi.

"He's fine."

"The other cells...three have live—"

"We know, Jace. They've all been captured. The op was a blazing success. We need to take care of you now."

"I've never been shot before." His voice wavered and tunnel vision started. Maybe it was the adrenalin dump. "I'm okay." Except for searing pain and the overwhelming urge to throw up at the sight of the bloodied, bullet-ridden body. It was beside him, and he was stuck here. "Get me outta here, Heidi. You gotta get me out."

"Ma'am." An EMT behind Heidi clasped her bicep, gently pulling her from Jace's side.

"Get me outta here," he said to the tech. One of Sheer's eyes was dangling... Oh shit, he was gonna hurl.

"I'll meet you at the hospital, okay?" she said quickly, the look in her eyes urgent, like she had so much else to say. Instead she repeated the inane phrase. The EMT bent over Jace.

"I'm not Evan," he gasped over the man's shoulder. "I'm not gonna die."

"You better not," she called back. Her lips quivered. "I have some serious critiques about your handling of this op."

"Women," the EMT quipped. "Always bitching about something, am I right?"

"Shut up." Jace gulped weakly. "She's got more guts and courage than either of us."

The guy snorted. Jace spewed all over him.

39

"It's probably booby-trapped," Adam said, scrutinizing the laptop on Sheer's kitchen counter. "Pressing any key or double-clicking one of these icons could release a virus, destroying whatever's on here."

"Then don't press anything." Heidi opened another drawer. Only utensils. "Unplug it and send it to computer forensics." She felt around the back of the drawer, then slammed it and opened the next.

"Unplugging might trigger a wipe too." Adam nodded to the cord stretching to the wall.

"All right." Heidi let out an exasperated breath. Accessing the information was crucial. Sheer would definitely have a database of names, numbers, and cell groupings for them to work off. Hopefully, prior criminal activity linked to specific cells too. "Call computer forensics and get someone down here."

He took out his phone and wandered into the living room as Alma came out of the bedroom. "Nothing of substance in there."

"Same for the kitchen." Heidi blew out a breath,

hands on hips, looking around the small space. "Why don't you guys call it a night? I'll wait for the computer tech."

"Let's just bring it with us."

"Adam says even touching it could trigger a wipe. You both go; I'll catch a rideshare." With them gone, she wouldn't have to cover up her gnawing worry for Jace. It had been over an hour since she'd watched the ambulance roar away, lights and sirens screaming. How was he?

Adam got off his phone. "They're sending someone stat."

"Great. You guys did exceptional work. Alma, I'll see you at tomorrow's eight o'clock, right?"

"Yep."

"Adam, have a great weekend." The two said goodnight and left her to babysit the laptop in silence. Heidi plopped on the sofa and called the hospital, using her title and both agencies to try to get around the HIPAA regulations. Finally, a nurse took pity on her and said Jace was out of surgery and resting comfortably. Heidi hung up and fell against the cushion, allowing the first glimmer of relief to seep through the stress.

Except for Sheer's death and Jace's injury, the aftermath of the op was a huge success. The stash of live explosives had been accounted for and contained. Thirteen cell members were being processed downtown, although Ken Nash's lawyer was moving heaven and earth to immediately bond his client out. Gage was safe and sobering up at headquarters. Best of all, not one Chicago citizen had been harmed by the Race. Second best of all, Heidi had received tons of congratulatory wellwishes from prominent ATF, FBI, and CPD personnel.

Since there was nothing she could do for Jace, she answered some texts, sent directives in others, and then scanned her email. Evan Cartwright's family had accepted an undisclosed sum through mediators, and the civil case had been dropped. A judge had finally signed the warrant to access the fuel inventory of Ken Nash's Formula One team. Bill Fontana had fully confessed to his commander about tipping off Bradley. Satellite media vans were parked along Roosevelt waiting for SAC Webb's statement. Heidi had chosen to search Sheer's safe house instead of standing among the line of good old boys mugging for cameras. Limelight credit made her squeamish.

Heidi brought up her list app and jotted notes for tomorrow's meeting, so focused that she jumped at the sharp rap on the door. Crossing to the foyer, she peered through the peephole. A shiny gold FBI badge was pressed up to the lens, blocking any other view. She opened the door and smiled up at the very good-looking, vaguely familiar man. "Thanks for coming so quickly." Funny, she didn't know anyone from computer forensics. "I'm Case Agent Heidi Hall."

"Nice to finally meet you," the man said, striding in. "Mark Hennessey."

Heidi froze, hand still on the doorknob. A critical mistake. By the time warning bells sounded, Mark had drawn his Glock 19. "Shut it, lock it, then hand over your weapon. Slowly, butt first."

She complied almost in slow motion. Shock made it seem like an out-of-body experience—like she was watching the scene dispassionately, thinking stupid thoughts like he looked ten years older than his wedding photo, and for a colleague threatening her life, he came off pretty cool and collected. And rested, for a new father. "What...what are you doing?" she sputtered, staring at the barrel pointing at her heart. Her exhausted brain wasn't connecting the dots. Somehow he knew this was

Sheer's safe house, and he was presently threatening her life. But why? "Sheer is dead."

"Yeah, I've been listening to the scanner."

"But we didn't give out this address." And then it dawned. Her heart iced over at the stunning revelation. *Shit.* "Your name is on that laptop."

He didn't respond. Didn't emit a single limbic signal to guide her. She had to keep him here in the foyer, with his back to the kitchen, for as long as possible. Maybe when the tech arrived the knock would distract him long enough that she could somehow disarm him. "You must have known Bill was betraying the team," she said, blathering her suspicions loudly as her mind churned out survival options. "You told me you were too busy planning Bradley's arrest to investigate your office being broken into, but you weren't planning to follow up finding the traitor, were you? You *wanted* Bradley to be...what? Warned off? Killed?"

Hennessey simultaneously shifted his weight and broke eye contact. Finally. Key body signals indicating discomfort. Somehow she'd struck a nerve. So, if he'd wanted Bradley out of the picture, that meant... "You knew he'd hadn't committed suicide. And you wouldn't have opened a murder inquiry after forensics came back with that undetermined finding, right? What you hadn't counted on was your wife's accident taking you off the investigation so soon."

Hennessey shrugged, but shifted more. "I saw the extent of the decomp. I knew there wouldn't be much for the ME to work with. What I wasn't expecting was for Bradley to fuck things up by being left-handed."

A chill shuddered through her at his tone. "*You* killed him?"

A moment went by, filled with him frowning, deep in thought, debating something. "Sheer was pathological about operating under the radar," he finally said, "so once irrefutable evidence linked Bradley to the rental truck, he became a liability. When you decided to open a cause-of-death inquiry, I pushed you to choose Fontana to lead it. That was the only way to ensure the inquiry went nowhere."

Heidi massaged her temples. This was all too much. "So you, the case agent heading the MOSQMO investigation, were actually in on the bombing."

"I had nothing to do with June second. My role was more of a crime scene cleaner. I made sure any evidence or witness interviews that even remotely pointed to the Race disappeared. Then I effusively encouraged my team to run in circles."

But solving major cases was the only way to get promoted. "Again"—Heidi spread her hands—"why sabotage your career to cover for Sheer? Who is he to you?"

"None of your business."

"Somebody important." She shook her head. "There's no way you'd ditch your sworn duty unless it was a close family member or something."

For a fraction of a second, his eyes shifted. "Doesn't matter now, does it?" he said casually, waving his pistol twice in the direction of the kitchen. "Sheer's dead and you won't be around too much longer either. Let's go."

She slunk by him, heading toward the open laptop on the counter as slowly as possible. How could she control this situation?

"What was your end game, anyway?" she asked over her shoulder. "You had a baby on the way. The investigation would be led by someone else eventually."

"I was banking on two things. Poor team morale after so many months without viable headway, and that the new case agent wouldn't waste time allocating resources to review old, dead leads."

Wait. She spun around. "You headed the confidential informant team with Jace. That t-shirt slogan was one of the clues you buried."

"Until you pulled him in and reviewed his files." He waved the Glock again, and she crossed the remaining feet into the kitchen. She was out of time.

Spinning to face him again, she leaned back against the counter, blocking the laptop. "Computer forensics is due any minute."

"I anticipated you'd call them," he said with a nod. "When I saw Alma and Adam leave, I called the tech lab to override your request. Hand over the laptop, Heidi."

She gulped. There was no one riding in to save the day.

No one? Where the hell had that come from? She had her wits, her talent at reading body language, and years of self-defense training. Her entire career had been spent proving she was as good as, if not better than, a man at anything she put her mind to. Where was her ingenuity?

"I can't let you do this," she said, peripherally assessing her options. The butcher block of knives was three feet to her left. Too far. The frying pan on the stove was within reach, but too small. Maybe if wielded with enough force, though, it could stun him long enough to secure his weapon.

He stepped toward her. "Fine, I'll get it myself."

"Wait." She needed to create a nanosecond of distraction. His most striking visceral reaction had been the eye blocking when she mentioned family. "Sheer had at least five aliases, so I'll bet you knew him by another name. A name I could connect with your past. Like your brother." A faint grin appeared. Way off base. "Or cousin. Or maybe he's had a run-in with the law before, and you've covered for him." No change. Her heart raced in her growing panic. "You definitely have something connecting you. Or someone."

The grin disappeared. *Bingo.* A third person was involved. Who was the third person that Hennessey would protect at the expense of his career and freedom? A revelation sparked. Heidi had nothing to lose. "Sheer's your brother-in-law, isn't he?"

His eyes shifted left. Heidi swung her arm in an arc, snatching the pan and continuing the momentum toward his face just as his eyes shifted back. The metal connected to his right temple with a ghastly gong, followed by a howl of pain as his head snapped and his body reeled off balance. She grabbed his wrist, simultaneously twisting and slamming it against the counter's sharp corner. The Glock clattered across the Formica. She pivoted, clutched his shirt, and kneed him in the groin.

Hennessey dropped in a convulsive heap, retching and heaving animalistic groans. She grabbed the pistol, then stooped over him to retrieve hers.

It was over. She was safe. The laptop was secure.

Bracing herself heavily against the counter, she gulped shuddering breaths. She'd done it. Relied on her ingenuity. Proved her worth against a much larger, physically stronger opponent for real, instead of in controlled training sessions. This was the closest she'd ever come to dying in the line of duty, and a sudden revelation struck her immobile.

Maybe part of lamenting the double standards all these years had been directed at herself. Her self-worth had been formed by keeping eight family members alive, and she'd always struggled to overcome that persona. Working so much overtime, putting in a hundred and ten percent and not setting realistic boundaries hadn't just been about proving herself to the good old boys' club.

She'd been trying to convince herself she could amount to a kickass agent fighting for good.

Tears blinded her eyes. She'd lived up to her vision. She'd be okay. And suddenly this be-all, end-all career wasn't as important as checking up on Jace. Share what he'd come to mean to her. This man she loved so badly she chewed off her nails each time he encountered danger. What had taken her so long to figure her own emotions out?

Regaining her composure, Heidi stooped and checked on Hennessey, who remained incapacitated with pain. Her body shakes had dwindled enough to be able to dig out her cell phone and call for backup. When several squad cars arrived minutes later, she watched the arrest in exhausted silence. It had been a long and shocking day, but before she could enjoy any shuteye, she had to own up to Jace.

40

"When do you get off shift?" Kevin's ultra-smooth voice cut through the thick gray nothingness. Jace opened groggy eyes, immediately squinting at the harsh light. To his left, a pretty blond nurse stood in front of a laptop on a wheely desk. His smiling brother lounged against the opposite wall. On a green vinyl recliner in the far corner, Sean, looking cranky and sleepy, watched the exchange like he was suffering through a monster truck rally.

"I'm dying here," Jace croaked from parched lips, "and you're trying to score with the nurse?"

She immediately swung his way, smiling brightly. "There's our hero. Hi, Agent Quinn, I'm Jessica Pickering, your third shift nurse. How are you feeling?"

The familiar hot-wash question jolted him alert. Oh yeah, he'd been shot. His left shoulder felt tight and heavy, like a boulder pressed it into the mattress. An IV bag hung from a pole on the right side of the bed. The clock across the room showed one thirty. "Where am I?"

"Methodist, sir."

He eyed Kevin. "Is Heidi here?"

"Haven't seen her." He shrugged loosely. "Mom and Dad were, but once you got out of surgery they went down to the station to see what they could do for Gage. Called us to come sit with you."

Thank God Gage was okay, even though he was in for a world of shit. Heidi was probably down there as well, interviewing Race members. Damn it! Being in on the arrest process and seeing those assholes' faces as they were perp-walked past had been a great motivator. Instead he was lying here, wearing this open-backed gown. He attempted to sit up, and pain knifed through him. "Oh shit," he groaned.

"Oh, no moving, sir." Jessica gently pressed him back on the mattress. "You'll tear your stitches." She bent over him, prodding areas close to his wound, and he tightened every torso muscle in an effort to hold back the scream.

"I'm fine," he said between clenched teeth. Luckily, his brothers were distracted—Kevin was ogling Jessica's cleavage and Sean was shaking his head and rolling his eyes, probably at everyone. Basically, by Quinn standards, all was normal. "You guys don't need to stay."

Sean stood at once and snatched his jacket.

"Bro." Kevin dragged his gaze reluctantly back to Jace. "You're all over the news. The city is celebrating the FBI agent who stopped a terrorist attack. We want to be here for you."

Thankfully, Jessica straightened and snapped off her gloves. Jace almost groaned in relief. "Then do something useful." His voice came out like a croak. "I've gotta get a hold of Heidi."

"There are a couple of agents in the waiting area," Sean said from the doorway. "I recognized them when we got off the elevator."

"Go get 'em."

"Only two visitors at a time," Jessica said, throwing

Kevin a fathomless look. His matinee-idol smile flashed full throttle.

"I'll go hang at the nurses' station, then."

"Guess I'll get the agents," Sean grumbled. "Goodnight."

The three trooped out, and Jace allowed himself a long hiss of pain. Shit, getting shot was for the birds.

Minutes later, the door opened. Josh and Manny came in. "You doin' okay?" Manny asked.

"Flesh wound." Both of their faces looked pale, their expressions stricken. "Wait. What happened?"

"It's Mark, man." Manny shuffled his feet and stuck his hands in his pockets. "Turns out he was helping Sheer all along."

"Played us all for stooges," Josh muttered, barely audible over the buzzing beginning in Jace's ears.

"Mark *Hennessey*?" Jace blinked rapidly. Was he still in surgery and this was some kind of weird, anesthesia-induced nightmare? Bill Fontana was the leak.

Josh nodded. "Heidi's the one that figured it out. She was in Sheer's safe house guarding his laptop when Mark came and held her at gunpoint. Hey—" He rushed forward as Jace growled his way into a sitting position. "Lie down."

"I gotta go." Of course she was in danger. He hadn't been there, and as usual, people got hurt. Jace slid his legs off the bed, ignoring the stabbing pain. His brain began blinking red-alert signals that passing out was imminent.

"She's okay, Jace," Manny said, waving him back. "Mark's in custody."

"I don't believe it." Heidi overpowering Mark? "Call the nurse. I need this IV out."

Manny moved in as Jace teetered by the edge of the

bed. "You're in no shape to do anything. The crisis is over. She took that motherfucker down."

None of this made sense. Mark was a great friend. He was the laid-back, fun supervisor who'd boosted morale and propped them back up again and again to search for more leads.

"Get your ass back in bed this instant, Agent Associate Quinn," a familiar voice barked. Jace's heart thrummed as he peered unsteadily over his shoulder. An outraged-looking Heidi stood in the open doorway. "There will be no heroics from you tonight."

Jace eased out a pained breath, catching Josh's head jerk. "She can see your ass," the agent mouthed, pointing to the gown.

The cool air on Jace's backside registered the same moment as the burn in his face. "Christ." He collapsed onto the mattress, gritting his teeth at the fresh waves of intense pain.

"Gentlemen, I'll see you at eight tomorrow. Great work tonight. You've both earned your rest." Heidi stepped aside, still palming the open door. The agents murmured their goodnights and exited swiftly, shoulders bowed.

"Well." She sauntered to the foot of the bed. "You look a little worse for wear."

"They said Mark is with the Race?"

She shook her head. "He isn't a member."

Jace sank into the pillow, partly in relief, partly because those thirty seconds on his feet had wiped the hell out of him. "Then what the fuck happened tonight?"

"Mark is married to Sheer's sister—"

"Julie?"

"—and he hindered the task force's progress from the moment he realized the mosque explosion could be tied to Sheer."

"But..." Jace frowned at the wall behind her. This was even crazier. "He's my friend." Jace's few unauthorized calls to shoot the shit with Mark came roaring back. He'd told Mark about the secret undercover op, why wouldn't he? Mark had been his supervisor. Had a vested interest in the case. Oh shit! No wonder Sheer knew who he was and what kind of surveillance gear he wore. Jace clenched his jaw as the full scope of Mark's betrayal wedged in his gut like a jagged rock. "The fucker almost got me killed tonight."

"He'll be going away for a long time."

He jerked his head at the door. "They said he pulled his gun on you."

She stepped forward, fiddling with his blanket like she didn't know whether to tug it up or smooth it over his waist. "He did. I was able to disarm him and call for backup."

He reached out and stilled her fingers. "I should have—"

"Enough." She squeezed his hand and smiled, weariness etching her features. "No more shoulds. No more heroics. I'm living proof you don't have to shoulder all the responsibility all the time. Now get some rest."

"I couldn't stop thinking about you," he blurted. "In the car with Sheer... I couldn't stop thinking about us." His brain caught up with his mouth. *Shit.* What the hell was this gooey blathering? His instinct was to add a joke or excuse the babbling on pain meds, but he owed her. They'd both been close to death tonight, and holding back his thoughts or compartmentalizing emotions wouldn't wash here. He loved her. He wasn't ready to say that, but at least he could be honest.

"I want this to work, Heidi. I know we've got an uphill battle. I know dating me will get you in trouble. Somehow, though"—he squeezed her fingers—"we need to find a workaround. Life is too short to follow the regs."

Once again he halted as insecurities piled up. Shouldn't she have said something by now? Agreed? Smiled? She'd spent the whole time frozen, staring at their joined hands, mouth pressed into a grim line. That wasn't good. "Talk to me."

She exhaled softly, letting another moment pass. "I've dated law enforcement guys my entire adult life," she finally said without lifting her eyes. "We start out as respectful equals, but it never stays that way once things get serious." She licked her lips and huffed out another breath. "Men begin expecting me to change. I slowly get relegated into the role of playing house. Cooking and caring for them like a substitute mom. And then...well, my affection goes south pretty fast."

She finally made eye contact, and the sorrow there stole his breath. "I told you before I'm not good girlfriend material. I'd hate for us to go to all these lengths and defy the rules just for it not to work out."

"So your career still comes first. You're not even going to try?" His voice cracked on the last word. He eased his hand from hers.

Heidi flinched like he'd slapped her and stared at the floor like she was gathering her thoughts. "You've been through a lot tonight, Jace. Things will look clearer in the morning."

It was such a trite blowoff that words failed him. He wasn't playing this game. "Well, thanks for checking up on me, Case Agent Hall."

———

HEIDI EASED the door closed and stood stock-still, fists clenched. Around her, the steady beeps of machines down the corridor and quiet murmurs of two nurses at the circular station were white noise to her screaming thoughts.

After all those nights of prying into Jace's emotions, his spontaneous honesty in there had knocked her flat. The watershed moment earlier, about the stupidity of prioritizing her career over her love, had vanished the moment he began speaking. Instead, she'd reacted with the same old fear. Visualized plodding down the same old path as her usual relationships. This was Jace. Nothing about him was usual. Seriously. She was a gutless wonder.

Bracing herself, she pushed through his door again. He was drinking water through a straw, and his eyes turned wide and wary, like she was coming back to deliver another blow. "I'm a coward," she blurted. "And I'm wrong."

He swallowed the liquid and slowly placed the cup on his tray table, watching it instead of her. "Well," he said in an even voice. "How do you feel about that?"

Instantly she caught the mimicked hot-wash question and the crinkling in the corners of his eyes. "Oh, Jace." She rushed to his bedside and grabbed his hand. "I don't want my career to rule my life anymore. Yes. Yes, I'd like to give *us* a try." She bent and kissed his cheek, his forehead, and finally his lips. "But I can't promise you anything because—"

"You're a bad girlfriend. Yeah. I got the memo." He grinned up at her, squeezing her fingers. "I haven't seen you fail at anything yet, Heidi. I have faith we can work. Hell, after all the time we've spent together, we're kinda halfway there."

"We have a long way to go getting this case ready for trial. It means we remain professional during work hours."

"Agreed."

"And I'm still your boss. You follow all my orders."

"Naturally."

"And I'm going to insist we still do the hot-wash questions. The fallout will still be hard on you."

He rolled his eyes and twisted his mouth, like he was contemplating refusing.

"Seriously, Jace? This is the hill you're willing to die on?"

"All right," he finally said. "Hot washes every night. Only on the condition that you start answering mine."

"Deal." She leaned in and kissed him.

EPILOGUE

Even in the backstage gloom, Heidi's panic was plainly evident. Her rigid shoulders were hitched to her ears; her profile was ashen. Jace reached for her hand—yep, cold, clammy, and trembling—and gave it a squeeze. She didn't even notice. That was another tell. To her, public handholding was way too much PDA.

Several yards away on the blindingly bright stage, SAC Webb was winding up the climax of his story about Calvin Sheer's capture. The missing details would be his birth name, Gregory Wilson, older brother to Julie Wilson Hennessey, and that Sheer had been Mark Hennessey's college roommate, who'd introduced him to Julie. The FBI protected their own, even if that agent had been fired months ago and was facing federal charges for first-degree murder and multiple counts of obstruction of justice.

"It's taken crucial know-how from our cyber-forensics team to uncover a cache of names matching crimes all around the Western world," Webb said, "but as I speak, arrests are taking place, and the demise of this global white supremacist group is imminent." He paused for hearty applause and whistles.

"And so," he continued, "nearing the first anniversary of Chicago's bloodiest terror attack, it is with great pleasure I award the Federal Bureau of Investigation's Shield of Bravery to two MOSQMO task force members who clearly went above and beyond by exhibiting diligence, dedication, and courage in the line of duty.

"Help me welcome Assistant Special Agent in Charge Heidi Hall from the Bureau of Alcohol, Tobacco, Firearms and Explosives, and Special Agent Jason Quinn with Chicago's office of the FBI."

Thunderous clapping erupted on the other side of the bunched curtain. Jace turned again to Heidi, who gulped hard, eyes wide with terror. Who knew that receiving accolades and distinguished medals in front of hundreds was what truly scared her?

"Let's do this," he called over the applause, and pulled her onstage.

The second they stepped into the glaring spotlight, she wrenched her hand free. Jace didn't blame her. Although their relationship was universally accepted, now that the actual investigation had turned to processing mounds of evidence for Heather, he'd witnessed the starkly different reactions around headquarters. She often got the critical side-eye, while he got a clap on the back for "bagging the supe." How had he never clued in before? How could he shield Heidi from the bullshit? Confronting overt bias had changed a few minds and altered behavior, but he was on the warpath to educate others.

They halted near the podium and faced the sea of smiling faces. His family was in the front row. Maybe that was her foster brother, Dave over on the far right. It was hard to be sure, given the blinding lights.

SAC Webb, looking formidably officious, pinned their badges and shook their hands, followed by ASAC Garcia, eyes twinkling, presenting the heavy-framed plaques of commendation.

Heidi thanked both softly and nodded to the clapping audience. Perspiration sheened her face, and her smile was the definition of tortured strain. Flashes went off, blinding Jace further. He waved to the well-wishers, then nudged Heidi to cross the last half of stage. If he didn't get her out of here, she'd do something she'd never forgive herself for, like fainting, crying, or tossing her cookies. She'd worked so hard to have her brilliance and tough-ness acknowledged—it was a shame she couldn't enjoy the tributes.

Once they were back in the dark alcove, Heidi shuddered a breath.

"You okay?"

Her laugh was stilted, but the color was already returning. "Two down, one to go."

Last month CPD had awarded them their own special commendation, and later this summer, ATF in D.C. also planned to commemorate their actions. "Just think," he said, "you'll be a pro by then."

He kept the kiss quick because stagehands and individuals wearing headsets milled about on this side. He peered out the heavy curtain. People were beating their way to the exit, where a bar and buffet had been set up in the large foyer. "Crowd is starting to leave," he said, turning back. "Let's go grab a drink."

"A stiff one." She blotted her face with a tissue, fanning herself with her other hand.

"Come on, you look beautiful."

"Eyes up here, Buster."

Within minutes they were in the great hall, surrounded by well-wishers, who were shouting their congrats above the reverberating cacophony. Slowly inching their way toward the bar, they shook hands, profusely thanked people for each compliment, and posed for media pictures with their medals.

Someone tapped Jace on the shoulder, and he winced. Even though the bullet hole had long since healed, once in a while, especially in a formfitting suit coat, the wound still ached. He swung around.

Trick held out two flutes of champagne, sporting a sympathetic grin at the pandemonium surrounding them. He jerked his head left. "We carved out a mini compound over by the window," he hollered.

Jace nodded, handing Heidi a flute, then posed with her as the photographer for the *Tribune* raised his camera. Jace grinned easily as the flash went off.

Heidi was pulled into an impromptu interview with the *Tribune* reporter about her recent promotion to ASAC and her eventual move back to the D.C. office, once the federal trials for each Race member concluded.

Jace stood beside her, smiling at the respect she was receiving and her joy at reaching this promotion, even though it was a further speed bump in their relationship. The higher-ups in the Chicago office were already grooming *him* for an ASAC role too, now that he'd earned his degree and his golden-boy rep as a results-driven street agent was solidly intact.

What had taken Heidi over twenty years to achieve, he'd earn in a little over five. Sure, he could tout the extended years of leadership experience in the SEALs and discount their nine-year age difference. But bottom line, the gender discrimination was there if anyone took the time to look. Jace wasn't an idiot, even if it had taken him a while to catch on. He'd gladly accept the raise and responsibility, and Heidi would have the grace and dignity to be delighted for him. But as ASAC, a position that included hiring and promoting, he'd pay close attention to merits over gender.

Eventually they shuffled through the throng to the tall bar table covered in a long white cloth, where the Quinns and Dave were clustered. Jace shook Dave's hand and greeted him with sincere affection. He and Heidi didn't see her brother often, but when they were together, she was sharply protective of the extremely shy man. Dave coming out tonight and sitting in an overcrowded, loud ballroom to witness his sister's success must have taken great courage.

Mom kissed Heidi's cheek and gushed over her sleek black dress. "How many more months until you return to D.C.?" she asked fretfully, right on cue. Mom probably had a calendar she was marking off—she knew the answer.

"I'm here until the very last case has been tried in federal court, Olivia," Heidi said with her usual patience. "At least another year."

The unspoken question Mom never raised but was clearly at the forefront of her mind was: would Jace transfer to the FBI's D.C. branch then too? The answer, if either woman had bothered to ask, was hell yes, even if it meant transferring to a different agency.

Neither suspected he'd already shopped for a ring and planned to propose to Heidi as soon as he gathered the guts. And that whole remove-the-garter part of their reception would be talked about for years—he'd make sure of it.

Sean sidled over. "Congrats on being a hero yet again." He said it without malice, but Jace smirked in brotherly arrogance anyway.

"What's new with you?"

"Not much with me, but Gretch got accepted into the FBI. She's off to Quantico next month."

"No kidding?" Jace shook his head. "God help us all." Actually, Sean's girlfriend would make a killer agent. Probably even excel at undercover work. It took a lot of self-confidence and more than a healthy ego to pull off that role, and Gretch had an abundance of both.

"Son." Pop shook his hand.

"How's Gage doing?" Jace asked quietly.

"The rehab center requested we join him in family counseling." Pop blanched and swigged some champagne. To have tried so hard to mold five overly active boys into upstanding men and now have some professional imply he'd messed up had to be hard.

"I'd be happy to participate," Jace said automatically, then inwardly flinched. Hot washes never got easier, and now this? Although therapy would probably do his family good.

"The good thing," Pop continued, "is the AUSA you're working with—"

"Heather."

"Yes, she's making his successful completion of rehab a condition of whether to seek prosecution."

Heather had nothing on Gage—the guy had left both scenes before any conspiracy to commit crimes occurred —but keeping him on the hook had scared Gage right into rehab.

"I'll make sure he stays committed, Pop, and that she fulfills her promise." He caught Heidi's wrinkling brow as she overheard him. *Uh-oh.* Something he'd said would be hot-washed later...

Pop patted his good shoulder. "I knew you would."

"Where's Kevin?"

"Out," Mom said, and pursed her lips like she'd bitten down on a lemon wedge. Trick cocked a knowing eyebrow at him, and Jace nodded back. To Kevin, a date preempted any family gathering. This time it was Mom who had her sights on a wayward son, and that was not the parent any of the brothers wanted to piss off. It suddenly struck him that between Mom, Heidi, Gretch, and Zamira, he was surrounded by some pretty badass women who could never fit in those categories he used to use. It had taken awhile to recognize inner strength was so much more powerful than brawn.

MANY HOURS LATER, Heidi lay sated in Jace's arms, recollecting her terror at the accolades with self-effacing humor. There were many things he was still learning about this complex, dynamic lover—the foremost being her hatred of gender role expectations, although she was struggling to overcome that in micro-increments. She preferred the gun range to laundry, takeout to cooking, and task force paperwork to snuggling. All different than anything he was used to, but so worth the adjustment.

Professionally she saw minutiae he couldn't yet begin to recognize, but he'd come to rely on her insight. Therefore, the glare she'd thrown him tonight at the reception needed clarification. He leaned on an elbow, trailing a thumb down the curve of her slim neck. "Why'd you give me that look when I agreed to help Gage?"

"Because you're still allowing yourself to get sucked into the role of savior to your brothers and their never-ending problems."

He shrugged. "That's who I am, Heidi. It's better than my other options. Trick is the placater, Kevin is the charmer, Gage needs gobs of attention and acts like the youngest, Sean, who *is* the youngest, acts like an isolated only child..."

"Exactly. They all act like themselves. Being the hero all the time seems like unfair pressure on you."

"Well, I'm not the hero all the time." Jace slipped the sheet down, enjoying the soft, luscious view. "But you have to admit, I excel at it most of the time."

Heidi rolled her eyes, smiling. "That's not my point. If you're running around saving others, who's there to save you?"

He reached for her, considering. "I sure as hell hope it's you." He kissed her thoroughly, languidly, reveling in her soft moans. Long minutes later, he broke the kiss, smoothing her hair along the pillow. The diamond ring was burning a hole in his bureau drawer, and this was a perfect segue. "I have something very special planned before round two."

"Go for it," she said, eyes lighting in anticipation. "Wow me."

ACKNOWLEDGMENTS

To get a feel for the danger and isolation my undercover agent would face, I read a stack of memoirs by retired FBI agents, and highly recommend them if you're interesting in mesmerizing, real-world details of undercover careers, white supremacy, reading body language, conducting terrorist investigations, and the dangers these brave agents face every day. I've listed the memoirs in the FAQ section of my website.

In fleshing out this novel, I'd also like to thank the following people:

To developmental editor Anya Kagan of Touchstone Editing, for your unflinching courage to read my rough drafts and mold that dreck into concise intrigue while sprinkling in gentle grammatical lessons I'll never pay attention to and propping me up with a whole lot of cyber hugs. You are astoundingly gifted, and I'm always aware of how lucky I am to work with you.

To Heidi Horne Gerson, for the enthusiastic emails after my last release. At a moment I was crippled with insecurity about my writing and fearful about the reception that story would face, your words and encouragement meant more to me than I can ever express. I hope you enjoy my kickass heroine, Heidi!

To retired ATF Senior Special Agent Cynthia Beebe, for your time answering my broad plot questions and generously giving me an ARC of your fantastic memoir, *Boots in the Ashes*. I learned so much about your courageous career and greatly admire your grace under pressure. That being said, you'll find I made a lot of stuff up.

To Christa Holland, of Paper and Sage, for once again designing a captivating cover for this final book in the *Damaged Heroes* series.

To copy editor Arran McNicol of Editing720, for catching all the errors and pointing them out so hilariously. I'll thank you here, while you're editing this page, so you don't have to buy the actual romance.

To longtime friend, Cheri Jetton, for your proofreading skills. (Readers, if anyone finds a mistake, please contact her. I'm absolving myself of all responsibility.)

To John Stanton, for reading my action scenes and changing the sissy words into alpha-speak.

To Donnell Bell, for contacting her LEO friends like Pat Howley, who answered a crucial FBI UCA question that would make or break this story.

To Anne Peck, for brainstorming incredible risks inherent in an FBI/ATF, in-love-with-your-boss romance.

And finally, most importantly, to Scott, for your never-ending patience and support in this last rollercoaster ride. I'm beginning to think golfing may be an easier pastime for me.

ABOUT THE AUTHOR

ROMANTIC SUSPENSE THAT KEEPS YOU UP ALL NIGHT

Sarah Andre is a RITA® finalist, which is Romance Writers of America highest award of distinction. She lives in serene Southwest FL with her husband and two naughty Pomeranians. When she's not writing, Sarah is either reading or coloring. Yes, you read that right. She's all over those coloring books for adults.

For more information please visit:
www.SarahAndre.com

facebook.com/SarahAndreNovels

twitter.com/SarahRSWriter

goodreads.com/Sarah_Andre

bookbub.com/authors/sarah-andre

ALSO BY SARAH ANDRE

Locked, Loaded and Lying

THE DAMAGED HEROES SERIES:

Tall, Dark and Damaged

Capturing the Queen

A Savage Trick

Incendiary Attraction

Made in the USA
Columbia, SC
26 November 2022